MAY 1 3

Prodigy

A LEGEND NOVEL

Prodigy

Marie Lu

THORNDIKE PRESS
A part of Gale, Cengage Learning

GALE
CENGAGE Learning

Detroit • New York • San Francisco • New Haven, Conn • Waterville, Maine • London

GALE
CENGAGE Learning®

Recommended for Young Adult Readers.
Copyright © 2012 by Xiwei Lu.
Map illustration by Peter Bollinger.
Thorndike Press, a part of Gale, Cengage Learning.

Thorndike Press® Large Print The Literacy Bridge.
The text of this Large Print edition is unabridged.
Other aspects of the book may vary from the original edition.
Set in 16 pt. Plantin.

LIBRARY OF CONGRESS CATALOGING-IN-PUBLICATION DATA

Lu, Marie, 1984-
    Prodigy : a Legend novel / by Marie Lu. — Large print edition.
    pages cm
    "Thorndike Press Large Print The Literacy Bridge."
    Originally published in New York by G. P. Putnam's Sons, 2012.
    Summary: June and Day make their way to Las Vegas where they join the
rebel Patriot group and become involved in an assassination plot against
the Elector in hopes of saving the Republic.
    ISBN 978-1-4104-5512-3 (hardcover) — ISBN 1-4104-5512-2 (hardcover)
    1. Large type books. [1. Fugitives from justice—Fiction. 2. Criminals—Fiction.
3. Soldiers—Fiction. 4. War—Fiction. 5. Government, Resistance to—Fiction.
6. Assassination—Fiction. 7. Science fiction. 8. Large type books.] I. Title.
PZ7.L96768Pro 2013
[Fic]—dc23   2012043187

Published in 2013 by arrangement with G. P. Putnam's Sons, a division
of Penguin Young Readers Group, a member of Penguin Group (USA)
Inc.

Printed in Mexico
2 3 4 5 6 7 17 16 15 14 13

To Primo Gallanosa, for being my light

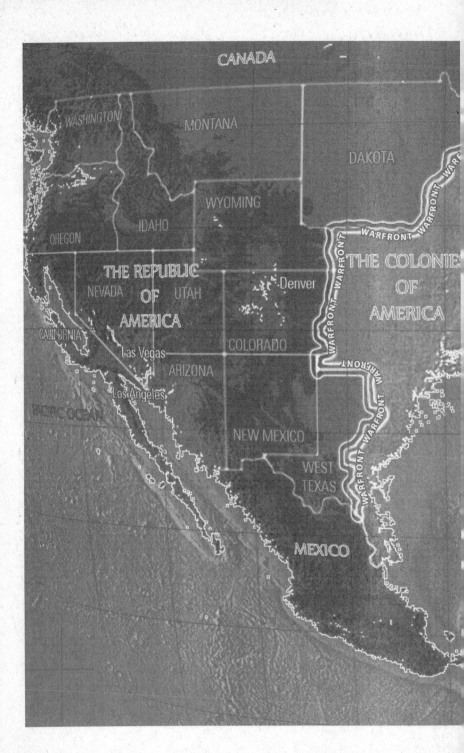

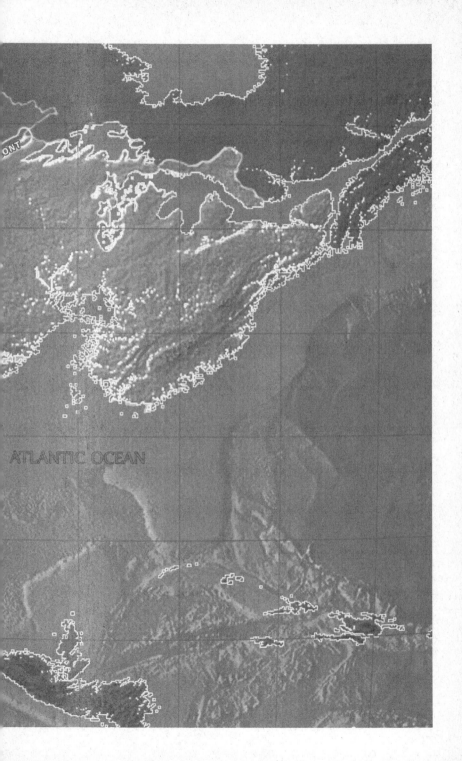

■ ■ ■ ■

LAS VEGAS, NEVADA
REPUBLIC OF
AMERICA
POPULATION:
7,427,431

■ ■ ■ ■

JUNE

Jan. 4. 1932 Hours.
Ocean Standard Time.
Thirty-five days after Metias's death.

Day jolts awake beside me. His brow is covered with sweat, and his cheeks are wet with tears. He's breathing heavily.

I lean over him and brush a wet strand of hair out of his face. The scrape on my shoulder has scabbed over already, but my movement makes it throb again. Day sits up, rubs a hand wearily across his eyes, and glances around our swaying railcar as if searching for something. He looks first at the stacks of crates in one dark corner, then at the burlap lining the floor and the little sack of food and water sitting between us. It takes him a minute to reorient himself, to remember that we're hitching a ride on a train bound for Vegas. A few seconds pass before he releases his rigid posture and lets himself sag back against the wall.

11

I gently tap his hand. "Are you okay?" That's become my constant question.

Day shrugs. "Yeah," he mutters. "Nightmare."

Nine days have passed since we broke out of Batalla Hall and escaped Los Angeles. Since then, Day has had nightmares every time he's closed his eyes. When we first got away and were able to catch a few hours of rest in an abandoned train yard, Day bolted awake screaming. We were lucky no soldiers or street police heard him. After that, I developed the habit of stroking his hair right after he falls asleep, of kissing his cheeks and forehead and eyelids. He still wakes up gasping with tears, his eyes hunting frantically for all the things he's lost. But at least he does this silently.

Sometimes, when Day is quiet like this, I wonder how well he's hanging on to his sanity. The thought scares me. I can't afford to lose him. I keep telling myself it's for practical reasons: we'd have little chance of surviving alone at this point, and his skills complement mine. Besides . . . I have no one left to protect. I've had my share of tears too, although I always wait until he's asleep to cry. I cried for Ollie last night. I feel a little silly crying for my dog when the Republic killed our families, but I can't help myself. Metias was the one who'd brought him home, a white ball of giant paws and floppy ears and warm brown eyes, the sweetest, clumsiest creature I'd ever seen. Ollie was my boy, and I'd left him behind.

"What'd you dream?" I whisper to Day.

"Nothing memorable." Day shifts, then winces as he accidentally scrapes his wounded leg against the floor. His body tenses up from the pain, and I can tell how stiff his arms are beneath his shirt, knots of lean muscle earned from the streets. A labored breath escapes his lips. *The way he'd pushed me against that alley wall, the hunger in his first kiss.* I stop focusing on his mouth and shake off the memory, embarrassed.

He nods toward the railcar doors. "Where are we now? We should be getting close, right?"

I get up, glad for the distraction, and brace myself against the rocking wall as I peer out the railcar's tiny window. The landscape hasn't changed much — endless rows of apartment towers and factories, chimneys and old arching highways, all washed into blues and grayish purples by the afternoon rain. We're still passing through slum sectors. They look almost identical to the slums in Los Angeles. Off in the distance, an enormous dam stretches halfway across my

13

line of vision. I wait until a JumboTron flashes by, then squint to see the small letters on the bottom corner of the screen. "Boulder City, Nevada," I say. "Really close now. The train will probably stop here for a while, but afterward it shouldn't take more than thirty-five minutes to arrive in Vegas."

Day nods. He leans over, unties our food sack, and searches for something to eat. "Good. Sooner we get there, sooner we'll find the Patriots."

He seems distant. Sometimes Day tells me what his nightmares are about — failing his Trial or losing Tess on the streets or running away from plague patrols. Nightmares about being the Republic's most wanted criminal. Other times, when he's like this and keeps his dreams to himself, I know they must be about his family — his mother's death, or John's. Maybe it's better that he doesn't tell me about those. I have enough of my own dreams to haunt me, and I'm not sure I have the courage to know about his.

"You're really set on finding the Patriots, aren't you?" I say as Day pulls out a stale hunk of fried dough from the food sack. This isn't the first time I've questioned his insistence on coming to Vegas, and I'm careful about the way I approach the topic. The

14

last thing I want Day to think is that I don't care about Tess, or that I'm afraid to meet up with the Republic's notorious rebel group. "Tess went with them willingly. Are we putting her in danger by trying to get her back?"

Day doesn't answer right away. He tears the fried dough in half and offers me a piece. "Take some, yeah? You haven't eaten in a while."

I hold a hand up politely. "No, thanks," I reply. "I don't like fried dough."

Instantly I wish I could stuff the words back in my mouth. Day lowers his eyes and puts the second half back into the food sack, then quietly starts eating his share. What a stupid, stupid thing for me to say. *I don't like fried dough.* I can practically hear what's going through his head.

Poor little rich girl, with her posh manners. She can afford to dislike *food.* I scold myself in silence, then make a mental note to tread more carefully next time.

After a few mouthfuls, Day finally responds, "I'm not just going to leave Tess behind without knowing she's okay."

Of course he wouldn't. Day would never leave anyone he cares about behind, especially not the orphan girl he's grown up with on the streets. I understand the potential

15

value of meeting the Patriots too — after all, those rebels *had* helped Day and me escape Los Angeles. They're large and well organized. Maybe they have information about what the Republic is doing with Day's little brother, Eden. Maybe they can even help heal Day's festering leg wound — ever since that fateful morning when Commander Jameson shot him in the leg and arrested him, his wound has been on a roller coaster of getting better and then worse. Now his left leg is a mass of broken, bleeding flesh. He needs medical attention.

Still, we have one problem.

"The Patriots won't help us without some sort of payment," I say. "What can we give them?" For emphasis, I reach into my pockets and dig out our meager stash of money. Four thousand Notes. All I had on me before we made a run for it. I can't believe how much I miss the luxury of my old life. There are *millions* of Notes under my family name, Notes that I'll never be able to access again.

Day polishes off the dough and considers my words with his lips pressed together. "Yeah, I know," he says, running a hand through his tangled blond hair. "But what do you suggest we do? Who else can we go to?"

I shake my head helplessly. Day is right about that — as little as I'd like to see the Patriots again, our choices are pretty limited. Back when the Patriots had first helped us escape from Batalla Hall, when Day was still unconscious and I was wounded in the shoulder, I'd asked the Patriots to let us go with them to Vegas. I'd hoped they would continue to help us.

They'd refused.

"You paid us to get Day out of his execution. You *didn't* pay us to carry your wounded asses all the way to Vegas," Kaede had said to me. "Republic soldiers are hot on your trail, for crying out loud. We're not a full-service soup kitchen. I'm not risking my neck for you two again unless there's money involved."

Up until that point, I'd almost believed that the Patriots cared about us. But Kaede's words had brought me back to reality. They'd helped us because I'd paid Kaede 200,000 Republic Notes, the money I'd received as a reward for Day's capture. Even then, it had taken some persuasion before she sent her Patriot comrades in to help us.

Allowing Day to see Tess. Helping Day fix his bad leg. Giving us info about the whereabouts of Day's brother. All these things

17

will require bribes. If only I'd had the chance to grab more money before we left.

"Vegas is the worst possible city for us to wander into by ourselves," I say to Day as I gingerly rub my healing shoulder. "And the Patriots might not even give us an audience. I'm just trying to make sure we think this through."

"June, I know you're not used to thinking of the Patriots as allies," Day replies. "You were trained to hate them. But they *are* a potential ally. I trust them more than I trust the Republic. Don't you?"

I don't know if he means for his words to sound insulting. Day has missed the point I'm trying to make: that the Patriots probably won't help us and then we'll be stuck in a military city. But Day thinks I'm hesitating because I don't trust the Patriots. That, deep down, I'm still June Iparis, the Republic's most celebrated prodigy . . . that I'm still loyal to this country. *Well, is that true?* I'm a criminal now, and I'll never be able to go back to the comforts of my old life. The thought leaves a sick, empty feeling in my stomach, as if I miss being the Republic's darling. Maybe I do.

If I'm not the Republic's darling anymore, then who am I?

"Okay. We'll try to find the Patriots," I say.

It's clear that I won't be able to coax him into doing anything else.

Day nods. "Thanks," he whispers. The hint of a smile appears on his lovely face, pulling me in with its irresistible warmth, but he doesn't try to hug me. He doesn't reach for my hand. He doesn't scoot closer to let our shoulders touch, he doesn't stroke my hair, he doesn't whisper reassuringly into my ear or rest his head against mine. I hadn't realized how much I've grown to crave these little gestures. Somehow, in this moment, we feel very separate.

Maybe his nightmare had been about me.

It happens right after we reach the main strip of Las Vegas. The announcement.

First of all, if there's one place in Vegas that we shouldn't be, it's the main strip. JumboTrons (six packed into each block) line both sides of the city's busiest street, their screens playing an endless stream of news. Blinding clusters of searchlights sweep obsessively along the walls. The buildings here must be twice as large as the ones in Los Angeles. The downtown is dominated by towering skyscrapers and enormous pyramid-shaped landing docks (eight of them, square bases, equilateral triangle sides) with bright lights beaming

19

from their tips. The desert air reeks of smoke and feels painfully dry; no thirst-quenching hurricanes here, no waterfronts or lakes. Troops make their way up and down the street (in oblong square formations, typical of Vegas), dressed in the black, navy-striped uniforms of soldiers rotating out to and back from the warfront. Farther out, past this main street of skyscrapers, are rows of fighter jets, all rolling into position on a wide strip of airfield. Airships glide overhead.

This is a military city, a world of soldiers.

The sun has just set when Day and I make our way out onto the main strip and head toward the other end of the street. Day leans heavily on my shoulder as we try to blend in with the crowds, his breath shallow and his face drawn with pain. I try my best to support him without looking out of place, but his weight makes me walk in an unbalanced line, as if I'd had too much to drink. "How are we doing?" he murmurs into my ear, his lips hot against my skin. I'm not sure if he's half-delirious from the pain or if it's my outfit, but I can't say I mind his blatant flirtation tonight. It's a nice change from our awkward train ride. He's careful to keep his head down, his eyes hidden under long lashes and tilted away from the soldiers bustling back and forth along the sidewalks. He shifts uncomfortably in his military jacket and pants. A black soldier's cap hides his white-blond hair and blocks a good portion of his face.

"Well enough," I reply. "Remember, you're drunk. And happy. You're supposed to be lusting over your escort. Try smiling a little more."

Day plasters a giant artificial smile on his face. As charming as ever. "Aw, come on, sweetheart. I thought I was doing a pretty good job. I got my arm around the prettiest escort on this block — how could I *not* be lusting over you? Don't I *look* like I'm lusting? This is me, lusting." His lashes flutter at me.

He looks so ridiculous that I can't help laughing. Another passerby glances at me. "*Much* better." I shiver when he nudges his face into the hollow of my neck. *Stay in character. Concentrate.* The gold trinkets lining my waist and ankles jingle as we walk. "How's your leg?"

Day pulls away a little. "Was doing fine until you brought it up," he whispers, then winces as he trips over a crack in the sidewalk. I tighten my grip around him. "I'll make it to our next rest stop."

"Remember, two fingers against your

brow if you need to stop."

"Yeah, yeah. I'll let you know if I'm in trouble."

Another pair of soldiers pushes past us with their own escorts, grinning girls decked out in sparkling eye shadow and elegantly painted face tattoos, their bodies covered thinly by dancer costumes and fake red feathers. One of the soldiers catches sight of me, laughs, and widens his glazed eyes.

"What club you from, gorgeous?" he slurs. "Don't remember your face around here." His hand goes for my exposed waist, hungering for skin. Before he can reach me, Day's arm whips out and shoves the soldier roughly away.

"Don't touch her." Day grins and winks at the soldier, keeping up his carefree demeanor, but the warning in his eyes and voice makes the other man back off. He blinks at both of us, mumbles something under his breath, and staggers away with his friends.

I try to imitate the way those escorts giggle, then give my hair a toss. "Next time, just go with it," I hiss in Day's ear even as I kiss him on the cheek, as if he were the best customer ever. "Last thing we need is a fight."

"What?" Day shrugs and returns to his

22

painful walk. "It'd be a pretty pathetic fight. He could barely stand."

I shake my head and decide not to point out the irony.

A third group of soldiers stumbles past us in a loud, drunken daze. (Seven cadets, two lieutenants, gold armbands with Dakota insignias, which means they just arrived here from the north and haven't yet exchanged their armbands for new ones with their warfront battalions.) They have their arms wrapped around escorts from the Bellagio clubs — glittering girls with scarlet chokers and *B* arm tattoos. These soldiers are probably stationed in the barracks above the clubs.

I check my own costume again. Stolen from the dressing rooms of the Sun Palace. On the surface, I seem like any other escort. Gold chains and trinkets around my waist and ankles. Feathers and gold ribbons pinned into my scarlet (spray-painted), braided hair. Smoky eye shadow coated with glitter. A ferocious phoenix tattoo painted across my upper cheek and eyelid. Red silks leave my arms and waist exposed, and dark laces line my boots.

But there's one thing on my costume that the other girls don't wear.

A chain of thirteen little glittering mirrors. They're partially hidden amongst the other ornaments wrapped around my ankle, and from a distance it would seem like another decoration. Completely forgettable. But every now and then, when streetlights catch it, it becomes a row of brilliant, sparkling lights. Thirteen, the Patriots' unofficial number. This is our signal to them. They must be watching the main Vegas strip all the time, so I know they'll at least notice a row of flashing lights on me. And when they do, they'll recognize us as the same pair they helped rescue in Los Angeles.

The JumboTrons lining the street crackle for a second. The pledge should start again any minute now. Unlike Los Angeles, Vegas runs the national pledge five times a day — all the JumboTrons will pause in whatever ads or news they're showing, replace them with enormous images of the Elector Primo, and then play the following on the city's speaker system: *I pledge allegiance to the flag of the great Republic of America, to our Elector Primo, to our glorious states, to unity against the Colonies, to our impending victory!*

Not long ago, I used to recite that pledge every morning and afternoon with the same enthusiasm as anyone else, determined to keep the east coast Colonies from taking control of our precious west coast land. That was before I knew about the Republic's role in my family's deaths. I'm not sure what I think now. Let the Colonies win?

The JumboTrons start broadcasting a newsreel. Weekly recap. Day and I watch the headlines zip by on the screens:

REPUBLIC TRIUMPHANTLY TAKES OVER MILES OF COLONIES' LAND IN BATTLE FOR AMARILLO, EAST TEXAS

FLOOD WARNING CANCELLED FOR SACRAMENTO, CALIFORNIA

ELECTOR VISITS TROOPS ON NORTHERN WARFRONT, BOOSTS MORALE

Most of them are fairly uninteresting — the usual headlines coming in from the warfront, updates on weather and laws, quarantine notices for Vegas.

Then Day taps my shoulder and gestures at one of the screens.

QUARANTINE IN LOS ANGELES EXTENDED TO EMERALD, OPAL SECTORS

"Gem sectors?" Day whispers. My eyes are still fixed on the screen, even though the headline has passed. "Don't rich folks live there?"

I'm not sure what to say in return because I'm still trying to process the information myself. Emerald and Opal sectors . . . Is this a mistake? Or have the plagues in LA gotten serious enough to be broadcast on *Vegas* JumboTrons? I've never, *ever* seen quarantines extended into the upper-class sectors. Emerald sector borders Ruby — does that mean my home sector is going to be quarantined too? What about our vaccinations? Aren't they supposed to prevent things like this? I think back on Metias's journal entries. *One of these days,* he'd said, *there will be a virus unleashed that none of us will be able to stop.* I remember the things Metias had unveiled, the underground factories, the rampant diseases . . . the systematic plagues. A shiver runs through me. Los Angeles will quell it, I tell myself. The plague will die down, just like it always does.

More headlines sweep by. A familiar one is about Day's execution. It plays the clip of the firing squad yard where Day's brother John took the bullets meant for Day, then fell facedown on the ground. Day turns his eyes to the pavement.

Another headline is newer. It says this:

26

MISSING
SS NO: 2001963034

JUNE IPARIS
AGENT, LOS ANGELES CITY PATROL
AGE/GENDER: 15, FEMALE
HEIGHT: 5'4"
HAIR: BROWN
EYES: BROWN
LAST SEEN NEAR BATALLA HALL, LOS
ANGELES, CA
350,000 REPUBLIC NOTES REWARD
IF SEEN, REPORT IMMEDIATELY TO
YOUR LOCAL OFFICIAL

That's what the Republic wants their people to think. That I'm missing, that they hope to bring me back safe and sound. What they *don't* say is that they probably want me dead. I helped the country's most notorious criminal escape his execution, aided the rebel Patriots in a staged uprising against a military headquarters, and turned my back on the Republic.

But they wouldn't want that information going public, so they hunt for me quietly. The missing report shows the photo from my military ID — a face-forward, unsmiling shot of me, barefaced but for a touch of gloss, dark hair tied back in a high ponytail, a gold Republic seal gleaming against the black of my coat. I'm grateful that the phoenix tattoo hides half of my face right now.

We make it to the middle of the main strip before the speakers crackle again for the pledge. Day and I stop walking. Day stumbles again and almost falls, but I manage to catch him fast enough to keep him upright. People on the street look up to the JumboTrons (except for a handful of soldiers who line the edges of each intersection in order to ensure everyone's participation). The screens flicker. Their images vanish into blackness, and are then replaced by high-definition portraits of the Elector Primo.

I pledge allegiance —

It's almost comforting to repeat these words with everyone else on the streets, at least until I remind myself of all that's changed. I think back to the evening when I'd first captured Day, when the Elector and his son came to personally congratulate me for putting a notorious criminal behind bars. I recall how the Elector had looked in person. The portraits on the JumboTrons show the same green eyes, strong jaw, and curled locks of dark hair . . . but they leave out the coldness in his expression and the sickly color of his skin. His portraits make him seem fatherly, with healthy pink cheeks. Not how I remember him.

— *to the flag of the great Republic of America* —

Suddenly the broadcast pauses. There's silence on the streets, then a chorus of confused whispers. I frown. Unusual. I've *never* seen the pledge interrupted, not even once. And the JumboTron system is hooked up so one screen's outage shouldn't affect the rest.

Day looks up to the stalled screens while my eyes dart to the soldiers lining the street. "Freak accident?" he says. His labored breathing worries me. *Hang on just a little longer. We can't stop here.*

I shake my head. "No. Look at the troops." I nod subtly in their direction. "They've changed their stances. Their rifles aren't slung over their shoulders anymore — they're holding them now. They're bracing themselves for a reaction from the crowd."

Day shakes his head slowly. He looks unsettlingly pale. "Something's happened."

The Elector's portrait vanishes from the JumboTrons and is immediately replaced with a new series of images. They show a man who is the spitting image of the Elector — only much younger, barely in his twenties, with the same green eyes and dark, wavy hair. In a flash I recall the touch of excitement I'd felt when I first met him at the celebratory ball. This is Anden Stavropoulos, the son of the Elector Primo.

Day's right. Something big has happened. *The Republic's Elector has died.*

A new, upbeat voice takes over the speakers. "Before continuing our pledge, we must instruct all soldiers and civilians to replace the Elector portraits in your homes. You may pick up a new portrait from your local police headquarters. Inspections to ensure your cooperation will commence in two weeks."

The voice announces the supposed results of a nationwide election. But there's not a single mention of the Elector's death. Or of his son's promotion.

The Republic has simply moved on to the next Elector without skipping a beat, as if Anden were the same person as his father. My head swims — I try to remember what I'd learned in school about choosing a new Elector. The Elector always picked the successor, and a national election would confirm it. It's no surprise that Anden is next in line — but our Elector had been in power for decades, long before I was born. Now he's gone. Our world has shifted in a matter

30

of seconds.

Like me and Day, everyone on the street understands what the appropriate thing to do is: As if on cue, we all bow to the JumboTron portraits and recite the rest of the pledge that has reappeared on the screens. *"— to our Elector Primo, to our glorious states, to unity against the Colonies, to our impending victory!"* We repeat this over and over for as long as the words stay on the screen, no one daring to stop. I glance at the soldiers lining the streets. Their hands have tightened on their rifles. Finally, after what seems like hours, the words disappear and the JumboTrons return to their usual news rolls. We all begin walking again, as if nothing had happened.

Then Day stumbles. This time I feel him tremble, and my heart clenches. "Stay with me," I whisper. To my surprise I almost say, *Stay with me, Metias.* I try to hold him up, but he slips.

"I'm sorry," he murmurs back. His face is shiny with sweat, his eyes shut tightly in pain. He holds two fingers to his brow. *Stop.* He can't make it.

I look wildly around us. Too many soldiers — we still have a lot of ground to cover. "No, you have to," I say firmly. "*Stay* with me. You can make it."

But it's no use this time. Before I can catch him, he falls onto his hands and collapses to the ground.

DAY

The Elector Primo is dead.

This whole display seems pretty anticlimactic, doesn't it? You'd think the Elector's death would be accompanied by a goddy funeral march of some sort, panic in the streets, national mourning, marching soldiers firing off salutes into the sky. An enormous banquet, flags flying low, white banners hanging over every building. Something cracked like that. But I haven't lived long enough to see an Elector die. Outside of the promotion of the late Elector's desired successor and some fake national election for show, I wouldn't know how it goes.

I guess the Republic just pretends it never happened and skips right ahead to the next Elector. Now I remember reading about this in one of my grade school classes. *When the time comes for a new Elector Primo, the country must remind the people to focus on the positive. Mourning brings weakness and chaos. Moving forward is the only way.* Yeah. The government's *that* scared of showing uncertainty to their civilians.

But I only have a second to dwell on this.

We've barely finished the new pledge when a rush of pain hits my leg. Before I can stop myself, I double over and collapse down onto my good knee. A couple of soldiers turn their heads in our direction. I laugh as loud as I can, pretending the tears in my eyes are from amusement. June plays along, but I can see the fear on her face. "Come on," she whispers frantically. One of her slender arms wraps around my waist, and I try to take the hand she offers me. All around the sidewalk, people are noticing us for the first time. "You have to get up. *Come on.*"

It takes all my strength to keep a smile on my face. *Focus on June.* I try to stand — then fall again. Damn. The pain is too much. White light stabs at the back of my eyes. *Breathe,* I tell myself. *You can't faint in the middle of the Vegas strip.*

"What's the matter, soldier?"

A young, hazel-eyed corporal is standing in front of us with his arms crossed. I can tell he's kind of in a hurry, but apparently it's not urgent enough to keep him from checking on us. He raises an eyebrow at me. "Are you all right? You're pale as porcelain, kid."

Run. I feel an urge to scream at June. *Get out of here — there's still time.* But she saves me from speaking. "You'll have to forgive him, sir," she says. "I've never seen a Bellagio patron drink so much in one sitting." She shakes her head regretfully and waves him back with one hand. "You might want to step away," she continues. "I think he needs to throw up." I find myself amazed — yet again — at how smoothly she can become another person. The same way she fooled me on the streets of Lake.

The corporal gives her an ambivalent frown before turning back to me. His eyes focus on my injured leg. Even though it's hidden under a thick layer of pants, he studies it. "I'm not sure your escort knows what she's talking about. Seems like you could use a trip to the hospital." He raises a hand to wave down a passing medic truck.

I shake my head. "No, thank you, sir," I manage to say with a weak laugh. "This darling's telling me too many jokes. Gotta catch my breath is all — then gotta go sleep it off. We're —"

But he's not paying attention to what I'm saying. I curse silently. If we go to the hospital, they'll fingerprint us, and then they'll know exactly who we are — the Republic's two most wanted fugitives. I don't dare glance at June,

35

but I know she's trying to find a way out too.

Then someone pokes her head out from behind the corporal.

She's a girl both June and I recognize right away, although I've never seen her in a freshly polished Republic uniform before. A pair of pilot goggles hangs around her neck. She walks around the corporal and stands in front of me, smiling indulgently. "Hey!" she says. "I *thought* that was you — I saw you stumbling around like a madman all the way down the street!"

The corporal watches as she drags me to my feet and claps me hard on the back. I wince, but give her a grin that says I've known her all my life. "Missed you," I decide to say.

The corporal gestures impatiently at the new girl. "You know him?"

The girl flips her black, bobbed hair and gives him the most flirtatious grin I've ever seen in my life. "*Know* him, sir? We were in the same squadron our first year." She winks at me. "Seems like he's been up to no good in the clubs again."

The corporal snorts in disinterest and rolls his eyes. "Air force kids, eh? Well, make sure he doesn't cause another public scene. I've half a mind to call your commander." Then he seems to remember what he'd been rushing to do and hurries away.

I exhale. Could we have pulled *any* closer of a call?

After he leaves, the girl smiles winsomely at me. Even under a sleeve, I can tell that one of her arms is in a cast. "My barracks are close by," she suggests. Her voice has an edge to it that tells me she's not happy to see us. "How about you rest there for a while? You can even bring your new plaything." The girl nods at June as she says this.

Kaede. She hasn't changed a bit since the afternoon I met her, when I thought she was just a bartender with a vine tattoo. Back before I knew she was a Patriot.

"Lead the way," I reply.

Kaede helps June guide me down another block. She stops us at the elaborately carved front doors of Venezia, a high-rise set of barracks, then ushers us past a bored entrance guard and through the building's main hall. The ceiling is high enough to make me dizzy, and I catch glimpses of Republic flags and Elector portraits hanging between each stone pillar that lines the walls. Guards are already rushing to replace the portraits with updated ones. Kaede guides us along while blabbing a nonstop stream of random small talk. Her black hair's even shorter now, cut straight and even with her chin, and her smooth-lidded eyes are smudged with deep navy eye

37

shadow. I never noticed that she and I are pretty much the same height. Soldiers swarm back and forth, and I keep expecting one of them to recognize me from my wanted ads and sound the alarm. They'll notice June behind her disguise. Or realize that Kaede isn't a real soldier. Then they'll all be on top of us, and we won't even have a chance.

But no one questions us, and my limp actually helps us blend in here; I can see several other soldiers with arm and leg casts. Kaede guides us onto the elevators — I've never ridden one, because I've never been in a building with full electricity. We get off on the eighth floor. Fewer soldiers are up here. In fact, we pass through a completely empty section of hallway.

Here, she finally drops her perky façade. "You two look about as good as gutter rats," Kaede mutters as she taps softly against one of the doors. "That leg still buggin' you, yeah? You're pretty stubborn if you came all the way out here to find us." She sneers at June. "Those goddy obnoxious lights strung on your dress nearly blinded me."

June exchanges a glance with me. I know exactly what she's thinking. *How in the world can a group of criminals be living in one of Vegas's largest military barracks?*

Something clicks behind the door. Kaede

throws it open, then walks in with her arms outstretched. "Welcome to our humble home," she declares with a grand sweep of her hands. "At least for the next few days. Not too shabby, yeah?"

I don't know what I expected to see. A group of teens, maybe, or some low-budget operation.

Instead we enter a room where only two other people are waiting for us. I look around in surprise. I've never been inside a real Republic barrack before, but this one must be reserved for officers — there's no way they'd use this to house regular soldiers. First off, it's not a long room with rows of bunk beds. It could be an upscale apartment for one or two officials. There are electric lights on the ceiling and in the lamps. Marble tiles of silver and cream cover the floor, the walls are painted in alternating shades of off-white and a deep wine color, and the couches and tables have thick red rugs cushioning their legs. A small monitor sits flush against one of the walls, mutely showing the same newsreel that's playing on the JumboTrons outside.

I let out a low whistle. "Not shabby at all." I smile, but it fades away when I glance over at June. Her face is tense beneath her phoenix tattoo. Even though her eyes stay neutral, she's definitely unhappy and not as impressed as I am. Well, why should she be? I bet her own apartment had been just as nice as this. Her eyes wander around the room in an organized sweep, noticing things that I'd probably never see. Sharp and calculating like any good Republic soldier. One of her hands lingers near her waist, where she keeps a pair of knives.

An instant later, my attention turns to a girl standing behind the center couch. She locks her eyes onto mine and squints as if to make sure she's really seeing me. Her mouth opens in shock, small pink lips formed into an O. Her hair is too short to braid now — it drapes to the middle of her neck in a messy bob. *Wait a sec.* My heart skips a beat. I hadn't recognized her because of that hair.

Tess.

"You're here!" she exclaims. Before I can reply, Tess runs over to me and throws her arms around my neck. I hobble backward, struggling to keep my balance. "It's really you — I can't believe it, you're here! You're okay!"

I can't think straight. For a second, I can't even feel the pain in my leg. All I can do is wrap my arms tight around Tess's waist, bury my head in her shoulder, and close my eyes. The weight on my mind lifts and leaves me weak with relief. I take a deep breath, taking comfort in her warmth and the sweet scent of her hair. I'd seen her every single day since I was twelve years old — but after only a few weeks apart, I can suddenly see that she's not that ten-year-old kid I'd met in a back alley. She seems different. Older. I feel something stir in my chest.

"Glad to see you, cousin," I whisper. "You look good."

Tess just squeezes me tighter. I realize that she's holding her breath; she's trying hard not to cry.

Kaede is the one who interrupts the moment. "Enough," she says. "This isn't the damn opera." We break apart to laugh awkwardly at each other, and Tess wipes her eyes with the back of a hand. She exchanges an uncomfortable smile with June. Finally, she turns away and hurries back to where another person, a man, is waiting.

Kaede opens her mouth to say something else, but the man stops her with a gloved hand. This surprises me. Judging from how bossy she is, I would've assumed that Kaede's in charge of the group. Can't imagine this girl taking orders from anyone. But now she just purses her lips and flops onto the couch as the man rises to address us. He's tall, probably in his early forties, and built with a bit of strength in his shoulders. His skin is light brown and his curly hair is pulled back into a short, frizzy tail. A pair of thin, black-rimmed glasses rest on his nose.

"So. You must be the one we've all heard so much about," he says. "Pleased to meet you, Day."

I wish I could do better than standing hunched over with pain. "Likewise. Thank you for seeing us."

"Please forgive us for not escorting you both to Vegas ourselves," he says apologetically, adjusting his glasses. "It seems cold, but I don't like risking my rebels needlessly." His eyes swivel to June. "And I'm guessing you're the Republic's prodigy."

June inclines her head in a gesture that oozes high class.

"Your escort costume is so convincing, though. Let's just conduct a quick test to prove your identity. Please close your eyes."

June hesitates for a second, then obliges.

The man waves a hand toward the front of the room. "Now hit the target on the wall with one of your knives."

I blink, then study the walls. Target? I hadn't even noticed that a dartboard with a three-ring target is on one of the walls near the door we came through. But June doesn't miss a beat. She flips out a knife from her waist, turns, and throws it straight toward the dart-board without opening her eyes.

It slams deep into the board, just a few inches shy of the bull's-eye.

The man claps his hands. Even Kaede utters a grunt of approval, followed by a roll of her eyes. "Oh, for chrissake," I hear her mutter. June turns back to us and waits for the man's response. I'm stunned into silence. Never in my life have I seen anyone handle a blade like that. And even though I've seen plenty of amazing things from June, this is the first time I've witnessed her using a weapon. The sight sends both a thrill and a shiver through me, bringing memories that I've forced into a closet in my mind, thoughts I need to keep buried if I want to stay focused, keep going.

"Pleased to meet you, Ms. Iparis," the man says, tucking his hands behind his back. "Now, tell me. What brings you here?"

June nods at me, so I speak up instead. "We need your help," I say. "Please. I came for Tess, but I'm also trying to find my brother Eden. I don't know what the Republic's using him for or where they're keeping him. We figured you were the only people outside the military who might be able to get information. And finally, it seems like my leg needs to be operated on." I suck in my breath as another spasm of agony sears my wound. The man glances down at the leg; his eyebrows furrow in concern.

"That's quite a list," he says. "You should sit. You seem a bit unsteady on your feet." He waits patiently for me to move, but when I don't budge, he clears his throat. "Well, you've introduced yourselves — it's only fair for me to do the same. My name is Razor, and I currently head the Patriots. I've been leading the organization for quite a few years, longer than you've been causing trouble on the streets of Lake. You want our help, Day, but I seem to remember your declining our invitations to join us. Several times."

He turns to tinted windows that face the pyramid-shaped landing docks lining the strip. The view from here is amazing. Airships glide back and forth in the night sky, covered in lights, several of them docking right over the pyramids' tops like puzzle pieces. Occasionally we see formations of fighter jets, black eaglelike shapes, taking off from and landing on the airship decks. It's a never-ending stream of activity. My eyes dart from building to building; the pyramid docks in particular would be the easiest to run, with grooves cut into each side and steplike ridges lining their edges.

I realize that Razor is waiting again for me to respond. "I wasn't entirely comfortable with your organization's body count," I offer.

44

"But now apparently you are," Razor says. His words are scolding, but his tone is sympathetic as he puts his palms together and presses the fingertips to his lips. "Because you need us. Correct?"

Well, I can't argue with that. "I'm sorry," I say. "We're running out of options. But believe me, I'll understand if you turn us away. Just don't turn us in to the Republic, please." I force a smile.

He chuckles at my sarcasm. I focus on the crooked bump of his nose and wonder if he'd broken it before. "At first, I was tempted to let you both wander Vegas until you were caught," he continues. His voice has the smoothness of an aristocrat, cultured and charismatic. "I'll be blunt with you. Your skills are not as valuable to me as they used to be, Day. Over the years, we've recruited other Runners — and now, with all due respect, adding another one to our team isn't a priority. Your friend already knows" — he pauses to nod at June — "that the Patriots are not a charity. You're asking us for a great deal of help. What will you give us in return? You can't be carrying much money."

June gives me a pointed look. She may have warned me about this on our train ride, but I can't give up now. If the Patriots turn us down, we'll really be on our own. "We don't have a lot of money," I admit. "I'm not going to speak for June, but if there is *anything* I can do in exchange for your help, just say the word."

Razor crosses his arms, then walks to the apartment's bar, an elaborate granite counter embedded into the wall and shelving dozens of glass bottles of all shapes and sizes. He takes his time pouring a drink; we wait. When he finishes preparing it, he takes the glass in one hand and wanders back to us. "There *is* something you can offer," he starts. "Fortunately, you've arrived on a very interesting night." He takes a sip of the drink and sits down on the couch. "As you probably learned while down on the street, the former Elector Primo died today — something many in the Republic's elite circles have seen coming. At any rate, his son, Anden, is now the Republic's new Elector. Practically a boy, and *greatly* disliked by his father's Senators." He leans forward, saying each word carefully and with weight. "Rarely has the Republic been as vulnerable as it is now. There will never be a better time to spark a revolution. Your physical skills might be expendable to us, but there are two things you can give us that our other Runners can't. One: your fame, your status as the people's champion. And two" — he points his drink at June — "your lovely friend."

I stiffen at that, but Razor's eyes are warm as honey and I find myself waiting to hear the rest of his proposal.

"I'd be happy to take you in, and you'll both be well cared for. Day, we can get you an excellent doctor, and pay for an operation that'll make your leg better than new. I don't know the whereabouts of your brother, but we can help you find him, and eventually, we can help you both escape into the Colonies if that's what you want. In return, we'd ask for your help with a new project. No questions asked. But you'll both need to pledge your allegiance to the Patriots before I'll reveal any details about what you'll be doing. These are my terms. What do you think?"

June looks from me to Razor. Then she lifts her chin higher. "I'm in. I'll pledge allegiance to the Patriots."

There's a slight falter in her words, like she knows she's truly turned her back on the Republic. I swallow hard. I hadn't expected her to agree so quickly — I'd thought she would need some persuading before she committed herself to a group that she so obviously hated just a few weeks ago. The fact that she said yes tugs at my heart. If June is giving herself to the Patriots, then she must realize that we have no better choice. And she's doing this for my sake. I raise my own voice.

47

"Me too."

Razor smiles, rises from the couch, and holds up his drink as if to toast us. Then he sets it down on the coffee table and comes over to give each of us a firm handshake. "It's official, then. You're going to help us assassinate the new Elector Primo."

JUNE

I don't trust Razor.

I don't trust him because I don't understand how he can afford to hide out in such nice quarters. An officer's quarters, in *Vegas* of all places. These rugs are each worth at least 29,000 Notes, made from some sort of expensive synthetic fur. Ten electric lights in one room — all switched on. His uniform is spotless and new. He even has a customized gun hanging on his belt. Stainless steel, probably lightweight, hand embellished. My brother used to have guns like that. Eighteen thousand Notes and up for a single one. What's more, Razor's gun must be hacked. No way the Republic is tracking those for fingerprints or locations. Where did the Patriots get the money and skills to hack such advanced equipment?

This all leads me to two theories:

One — Razor must be some sort of commander in the Republic, a double-crossing officer. How else can he stay in this barrack apartment without being detected?

Two — the Patriots are being funded by someone with deep pockets. The Colonies? Possibly.

In spite of all my suspicions and guesses, Razor's offer is still as good as we're going to get. We have no money to buy help on the black market, and without help, we have no chance of finding Eden *or* making it to the Colonies. Also, I'm not even sure we *could* have turned down Razor's offer. He certainly hasn't threatened us in any way, but I doubt he'd just let us walk back out onto the streets, either.

Out of the corner of my eye, I see Day waiting for my response to Razor's statement. All I need to see are the paleness of his lips and the pain laced across his face, just a few of the dozen signs of his fading strength. At this point, I think his life depends on our deal with Razor.

"Assassinating the new Elector," I say. "Done." My words sound foreign and distant. For a moment, I think back on meeting Anden and his late father at the ball celebrating Day's capture. The thought of killing Anden makes my stomach churn. *He's the Republic's* Elector *now.* After everything that's happened to my family, I should be happy for the opportunity to kill him. But I'm not, and it confuses me.

If Razor notices my hesitation, he doesn't show it. Instead, he nods approvingly. "I'll put out an urgent call for a Medic. They probably won't be able to come until midnight — that's when the shifts change. It's the fastest we can be on such a tight schedule. Meanwhile, let's get you two out of those disguises and into something more presentable." He glances over at Kaede. She's leaning against the couch with hunched shoulders and an irritated scowl, chewing absently on a lock of her hair. "Show them to the shower and give them a pair of fresh uniforms. Afterward, we'll have a late supper, and we can talk more about our plan." He spreads his arms wide. "Welcome to the Patriots, my young friends. We're glad to have you."

And just like that, we're officially bound to them. Maybe it's not such a bad thing, either — maybe I never should've argued with Day about this in the first place. Kaede motions for us to follow her into an adjoining hall in the apartment and guides us to a spacious bathroom, complete with marble tiles and porcelain sinks, mirror and toilet, bathtub and shower with frosted glass walls. I can't help admiring it all. This is wealth beyond even what I had in my Ruby sector apartment.

"Don't be all night about it," she says. "Take turns — or get cozy and shower together, if that's faster. Just be back out there in a half hour." Kaede grins at me (although the smile doesn't touch her eyes), then gives Day a thumbs-up as he leans heavily on my shoulder. She turns away and disappears back down the hall before I can reply. I don't think she's forgiven me entirely for breaking her arm.

Day slouches the instant Kaede's gone. "Can you help me sit down?" he whispers.

I put the toilet cover down and ease him gently onto it. He stretches out his good leg, then tenses his jaw as he tries to straighten out the injured one. A moan escapes his lips. "I've gotta admit," he mutters, "I've had better days."

"At least Tess is safe," I reply.

This eases some of the pain in his eyes. "Yes," he echoes, sighing deeply. "At least Tess is safe." I feel an unexpected twinge of guilt. Tess's face had looked so sweet, so wholly *good*. And the two of them were separated because of *me*.

Am *I* good? I don't really know.

I help Day take off his jacket and cap. His long hair drapes in strings across my arms.

"Let me see that leg." I kneel, then pull a knife from my belt. I slice the fabric of his pant leg up to the middle of his thigh. His leg muscles are lean and tense, and my hands tremble as they brush up along his skin. Gingerly, I pull the fabric apart to expose his bandaged wound. We both suck in our breath. The cloth has a massive circle of dark, wet blood, and underneath it, the wound is oozing and swelling. "That Medic better get here soon," I say. "Are you sure you can shower on your own?"

Day jerks his eyes away, and his cheeks turn red. "Of course I can."

I raise an eyebrow at him. "You can't even stand."

"Fine." He hesitates, then blushes. "I guess I could use some help."

I swallow. "Well. A bath instead, then. Let's do what we have to do."

I start filling up the bathtub with warm water. Then, I take the knife and slowly cut through the blood-soaked bandages wrapped around Day's wound. We sit there in silence, neither of us meeting the other's eyes. The wound itself is as bad as ever, a fist-size mass of pulped flesh that Day avoids looking at.

"You don't have to do this," he mutters, rolling his shoulders in an attempt to relax.

"Right." I give him a wry smile. "I'll just wait outside the bathroom door and come help after you slip and knock yourself out."

"No," Day replies. "I mean, you don't have to join the Patriots."

My smile dies. "Well, we don't have much of a choice, do we? Razor wants both of us on board, or he's not going to help us at all."

Day's hand touches my arm for a second, stopping me in the middle of untying his boots. "What do you think of their plan?"

"Assassinating the new Elector?" I turn away, concentrating on unlacing, then loosening each of his boots as carefully as I can. It's a question I haven't figured out yet, so I deflect it. "Well, what do you think? I mean, you go out of your way to avoid hurting people. This must be kind of a shock."

I'm startled when Day just shrugs. "There's a time and place for everything." His voice is cold, harsher than usual. "I never saw the point of killing Republic soldiers. I mean, I hate them, but they're not the *source*. They just obey their superiors. The Elector, though? I don't know. Getting rid of the person in charge of this whole goddy system seems like a small price to pay for starting a revolution. Don't you think?"

I can't help feeling some admiration for Day's attitude. What he says makes perfect sense. Still, I wonder if he would've said the same thing a few weeks ago, before everything that had happened to his family. I don't dare mention the time I'd been introduced to Anden at the celebratory ball. It's harder to reconcile yourself to killing someone who you've actually met — and admired — in person. "Well, like I said. We don't have a choice."

Day's lips tighten. He knows I'm not telling him what I really think. "It must be hard for you to turn your back on your Elector," he says. His hands stay slack beside him.

I keep my head down and start pulling off his boots.

While I put his boots aside, Day shrugs out of his jacket and starts unbuttoning his vest. It reminds me of when I'd first met him back on the streets of Lake. Back then, he would take off his vest every night and give it to Tess to use as a pillow. That was the most I'd ever seen Day undress. Now he unbuttons his collar shirt, exposing the rest of his throat and a sliver of his chest. I see the pendant looped around his neck, the United States quarter dollar covered with smooth metal on both sides. In the quiet dark of the railcar, he'd told me about his father's bringing it back from the warfront. He pauses when he finishes undoing the last button, then closes his eyes. I can see the pain slashed across his face, and the sight tears at me. The Republic's most wanted criminal is just a boy, sitting before me, suddenly vulnerable, laying all his weaknesses out for me to see.

I straighten and reach up to his shirt. My hands touch the skin of his shoulders. I try to keep my breathing even, my mind sharp and calculated. But as I help him pull off the shirt and reveal his bare arms and chest, I can feel the corners of my logic growing fuzzy. Day is fit and lean under his clothes, his skin surprisingly smooth except for an occasional scar (he has four faint ones on his chest and waist, another one that's a thin diagonal line running from left collarbone to right hip bone, and a healing scab on his arm). He holds me with his gaze. It's hard to describe Day to those who have never seen him before — exotic, unique, overwhelming. He's very close now, close enough for me to see the tiny rippled imperfection in the ocean of his left eye. His breaths come out hot and shallow. Heat rises on my cheeks, but I don't want to turn away.

"We're in this together, right?" he whispers. "You and me? You *want* to be here, yeah?"

There's guilt in his questions. "Yes," I reply. "I *chose* this."

Day pulls me close enough for our noses to touch. "I love you."

My heart flips in excitement at the desire in his voice — but at the same time, the technical part of my brain instantly flares up. *Highly improbable,* it scoffs. *A month ago, he didn't even know I existed.* So I blurt out, "No, you don't. Not yet."

Day furrows his eyebrows, as if I'd hurt him. "I mean it," he says against my lips.

I'm helpless against the ache in his voice. But still. *They're just the words of a boy in the heat of the moment.* I try to force myself to say the same back to him, but the words freeze on my tongue. How can he be so sure of this? *I* certainly don't understand all these strange new feelings inside me — am I here because I love him, or because I *owe* him?

Day doesn't wait for my answer. One of his hands trails around my waist and then flattens against my back, pulling me closer so that I'm seated on his good leg. A gasp escapes me. Then he presses his lips against mine, and my mouth parts. His other hand reaches up to touch my face and neck; his fingers are at once coarse and refined. Day slowly moves his lips away to kiss the side of my mouth, then my cheek, then the line of my jaw. My chest is now solidly against his, and my thigh brushes against the soft ridge of his hip bone. I close my eyes. My thoughts feel muffled and distant, hidden behind a shimmery haze of warmth. An undercurrent of practical details in my mind struggles up to the surface.

"Kaede's been gone for eight minutes," I breathe through Day's kisses. "They expect us back out there in twenty-two."

Day twines his hand through my hair and gently pulls my head back, exposing my neck. "Let them wait," he murmurs. I feel his lips work softly along the skin of my throat, each kiss rougher than the last, more impatient, more urgent, hungrier. His lips come back up to my mouth, and I can feel the remnants of any self-control slipping away from him, replaced with something instinctive and savage. *I love you,* his lips are trying to convince me. They're making me so weak that I'm on the verge of collapsing to the floor. I've kissed a few boys in the past . . . but Day makes me feel like I've never been kissed before. Like the world has melted away into something unimportant.

Suddenly he breaks free and groans softly in pain. I see him squeeze his eyes shut, then take a deep, shuddering breath. My heart is pounding furiously against my ribs. The heat fades between us, and my thoughts snap back into place as I remember with a slow, sinking feeling where we are and what we still need to do. I'd forgotten that the water's still running — the tub is almost full. I reach over and twist the faucet back. The tiled floor is cold against my knees. I'm tingling all over.

"Ready?" I say, trying to steady myself. Day nods wordlessly. Moment's over; the brightness in his eyes has dimmed.

I pour some liquid bath gel into the tub and splash the water around until it froths up. Then I get one of the towels hanging in the bathroom and wrap it around Day's waist. Now for the awkward part. He manages to fumble underneath the towel and loosen his pants, and I help him tug them off. The towel covers everything that needs to be covered, but I still avert my eyes.

I help Day — now wearing nothing except for the towel and his pendant — to his feet, and after some struggling, we manage to get his good leg into the tub so I can lower him gently into the water. I'm careful to keep his bad leg high and dry. Day clenches his jaw to keep from crying out in pain. By the time he settles into the bath, his cheeks are moist from tears.

It takes fifteen minutes to scrub him, and all of his hair, clean. When we're finished, I help him stand and close my eyes as he grabs a dry towel to wrap around his waist. The thought of opening my eyes right now and seeing him naked before me sends blood coursing fiercely through my veins. *What* does *a naked boy look like, anyway?* I'm annoyed by how obvious the heat of my blush must be. Then the moment's over; we spend another few minutes struggling to get him out of the tub. When he's finally done and sitting on the toilet seat cover, I walk over to the bathroom door. I hadn't noticed before, but someone had opened the door a crack and dropped off a new pair of soldier uniforms for us. Ground battalion uniforms, with Nevada buttons. It's going to feel weird to be a Republic soldier again. But I bring them inside.

Day gives me a weak smile. "Thanks. Feels good to be clean."

His pain seems to bring back the worst of his memories from the last few weeks, and now all his emotion plays out plainly on his face. His smiles have become half of what they used to be. It's as if most of his happiness had died the night he lost John, and only a tiny slice of it remains — mostly a piece that he saves for Eden and Tess. I secretly hope he saves a part of his joy for me too. "Turn around and change into your clothes," I say. "And wait outside the bathroom for me. I'll be quick."

We get back to the living room seven minutes late. Razor and Kaede are waiting for us. Tess sits alone on a corner of the couch, her legs folded up to her chin, watching us with a guarded expression. An instant later, I smell the aromas of baked chicken and potatoes. My eyes dart to the dining room table where four dishes loaded with food sit neatly, beckoning to us. I try not to react to the smell, but my stomach rumbles.

"Excellent," Razor says, smiling at us. He lets his eyes linger on me. "You two clean up nicely." Then he turns to Day and shakes his head. "We arranged for some food to be brought up, but since you're having surgery within the next few hours, you're going to have to keep your stomach empty. I'm sorry — I know you must be hungry. June, please help yourself."

Day's eyes are also fixed on the food.

"That's just great," he mutters.

I join the others at the table while Day stretches out on the couch and makes himself as comfortable as he can. I'm about to pick up my plate and sit next to him, but Tess beats me to it, seating herself on the edge of the couch so her back touches Day's side. As Razor, Kaede, and I eat in silence at the table, I occasionally steal glances at the couch. Day and Tess talk and laugh with the ease of two people who have known each other for years. I concentrate on my food, the heat of our bathroom encounter still burning on my lips.

I've counted off five minutes in my head when Razor finally takes a sip of his drink and leans back. I watch him closely, still wondering why one of the Patriots' leaders — the head of a group that I'd always associated with savagery — is so polite. "Ms. Iparis," he says. "How much do you know about our new Elector?"

I shake my head. "Not much, I'm afraid." Beside me, Kaede snorts and continues digging into her dinner.

"You've met him before, though," Razor says, revealing what I'd hoped to keep from Day. "That night at the ball, the one held to celebrate Day's capture? He kissed your hand. Correct?" Day pauses in his conversation with Tess. I cringe inwardly.

Razor doesn't seem to notice my discomfort. "Anden Stavropoulos is an interesting young man," he says. "The late Elector loved him a great deal. Now that Anden is Elector, the Senators are uneasy. The people are angry, and they couldn't care less if Anden is different from the last Elector. No matter what speeches Anden gives to please them, all they're going to see is a wealthy man who has no idea how to heal their suffering. They're furious with Anden for letting Day's execution go through, for hunting him down, for not saying a word against his father's policies, for putting a price on finding June . . . the list goes on. The late Elector had an iron grip on the military. Now the people just see a boy king who has the chance to rise up and become another version of his father. These are the weaknesses we want to exploit, and this brings us to the plan we currently have in mind."

"You seem to know a great deal about the young Elector. You also seem to know a great deal about what happened at the celebratory ball," I reply. I can't hold in my suspicion any longer. "I suppose that's because you were also a guest that night. You must be a Republic officer — but without a rank high enough to get you an audience with the Elector." I study the room's rich velvet carpets and granite counters. "These are your *actual* office quarters, aren't they?"

Razor seems a little put off by my criticism of his rank (which, as usual, is a fact that I hadn't meant as an insult), but quickly brushes it off with a laugh. "I can see there'll be no secrets with you. Special girl. Well, my official title is Commander Andrew DeSoto, and I run three of the capital's city patrols. The Patriots gave me my street name. I've been organizing most of their missions for a little over a decade."

Day and Tess are both listening intently now. "You're a Republic officer," Day echoes uncertainly, his eyes glued to Razor. "A commander from the capital. Hm. *Why* are you helping the Patriots?"

Razor nods, resting both of his elbows on the dinner table and pressing his hands together. "I suppose I should start by giving you both some details about how we work. The Patriots have been around for thirty or so years — they started as a loose collection of rebels. Within the last fifteen years, they've banded together in an attempt to organize themselves and their cause."

"Razor's coming changed everything, so I hear," Kaede pipes up. "They'd rotated through leaders all the time, and funding had always been a problem. Razor's connections to the Colonies have been bringing in more money for missions than ever before."

Metias *had* been busier over the last couple of years in dealing with Patriot attacks in Los Angeles, I recall.

Razor nods at Kaede's words. "We're fighting to reunite the Colonies and the Republic, to return the United States to its former glory." His eyes take on a determined gleam. "And we're willing to do whatever it takes to achieve our goal."

The old United States, I think, as Razor continues. Day had mentioned the United States to me during our escape from Los Angeles, although I was still skeptical. Until now. "How does the organization work?" I ask.

"We keep an eye out for people who have the talents and skills we need, and then we try to recruit them," Razor says. "*Usually* we're good at getting people on board, although some people take longer than others." He pauses to tip his glass in Day's direction. "I am considered a Leader in the Patriots — there are only a few of us, working from the inside and architecting the rebels' missions. Kaede here is a Pilot."

Kaede waves a hand around as she continues to inhale her food. "She joined us after she was expelled from an Airship Academy in the Colonies. Day's surgeon is a Medic, and young Tess here is a Medic in training. We also have Fighters, Runners, Scouts, Hackers, Escorts, and so on. I would place you as a Fighter, June, although your abilities seem to cross into several categories. And Day, of course, is the best Runner I've ever seen." Razor smiles a little and finishes his drink. "The two of you should technically be a new category altogether. Celebrities. That's how you're going to be most useful to us, and that's why I didn't throw you both back out on the street."

"So kind of you," Day says. "What's the plan?"

Razor points at me. "Earlier, I asked you how much you knew about our Elector. I heard a few rumors today. They say Anden was quite taken with you at the ball. Someone heard him asking if you could be transferred to a patrol in the capital. There's even a rumor that he wanted you tapped to train as the Senate's next Princeps."

"The next Princeps?" I shake my head automatically, overwhelmed with the idea. "Probably nothing more than a rumor. Even ten years of training wouldn't be enough to prepare me for that." Razor just laughs at my declaration.

"What's a Princeps?" Day speaks up. He sounds annoyed. "Some of us aren't versed in the Republic's hierarchy."

"The leader of the Senate," Razor replies casually, without turning in his direction. "The Elector's shadow. His, or her, partner in command — and sometimes *more*. It frequently turns out that way in the end, after a requisite decade of training. Anden's mother was the last Princeps, after all."

I glance instinctively toward Day. His jaw is tight and he's holding very still, little signs that say that he'd rather not be hearing what the Elector thinks of me or that he might want me as a future *partner*. I clear my throat. "Those rumors are exaggerated," I insist again, just as uncomfortable as Day is with this conversation. "Even if that *were* true, I'd still be one of several Princeps-in-training, and I can guarantee you that their other choices would be experienced Senators. But how are you planning to use that information in your assassination? Do you think I'm going to —"

Kaede breaks through my words with a loud laugh. "You're blushing, Iparis," she says. "Do you like the idea that Anden's crushin' on you?"

"No!" I say, a bit too quickly. Now I feel the heat rising on my face, although I'm pretty sure it's because Kaede is irritating me.

"Don't be so goddy arrogant," she says. "Anden is a handsome guy with a lot of power and a lot of options. It's okay to feel flattered. I'm sure Day understands."

Razor saves me from responding by frowning in disapproval. "Kaede. Please." She makes a pouty face at him and returns to her meal. I glance at the couch. Day is staring up at the ceiling. After a short pause, Razor goes on. "Even now, Anden can't be sure that you did everything against the Republic on *purpose*. For all he knows, you may have been taken hostage when Day escaped. Or forced to join Day against your will. There's enough uncertainty for him to insist that the government list you as a missing person instead of a wanted traitor. My point is this: Anden is interested in you, and that means he can be influenced by what you tell him."

"So you want me to go back to the Republic?" I say. My words seem to echo. From the corner of my eye, I see Tess shift unhappily on the couch. Her mouth quivers with some unspoken phrase.

Razor nods. "Exactly. Originally, I was going to use spies from my own Republic patrols to get close to Anden — but now we have a better alternative. *You.* You tell the Elector that the Patriots are going to try to kill him — but the plan you tell him about will be a decoy. While everyone's distracted with the fake plan, we'll strike with the real one. Our goal is not only to kill Anden, but to turn the country completely against him, so that his regime will be doomed even if our plan fails. That's what you two can do for us. Now, we've heard reports that the new Elector is going to be heading for the warfront within the next couple of weeks, to get updates and progress reports from his colonels. The RS *Dynasty* airship launches toward the warfront early tomorrow afternoon, and all of my squadrons will be on it. Day will join me, Kaede, and Tess on that ride. We'll organize the real assassination, and you'll lead Anden to it." Razor crosses his arms and studies our faces, waiting for our reactions.

Day finally finds his voice and interrupts him. "This is going to be incredibly dangerous for June," he argues as he props himself up straighter on the couch. "How can you be sure she'll even reach the Elector after the military gets her back? How do you know they won't just start torturing information out of her?"

"Trust me, I know how to avoid that," Razor replies. "I haven't forgotten about your brother, either . . . If June can get close enough to the Elector, she may find out where Eden is on her own."

Day's eyes light up at that, and Tess squeezes his shoulder.

"As for you, Day, I've never seen the public rally behind *anyone* the way they have for you. Did you know that streaking your hair red has become a fashion statement overnight?" Razor chuckles and waves a hand at Day's head. "That's power. Right now, you probably have just as much influence as the Elector. Maybe more. If we can find a way to use your fame to work the people up into a frenzy, by the time the assassination happens, Congress will be powerless to stop a revolution."

"And what do you plan to *do* with that revolution?" Day asks.

Razor leans forward, and his face turns determined, even hopeful. "You want to know why I joined the Patriots? For the same reasons *you've* been working against the Republic. The Patriots know how you've suffered — we've all seen the sacrifices you've made for your family, the pain the Republic has caused you. June," Razor says, nodding at me. I cringe; I don't want a reminder of what happened to Metias. "I have seen your suffering too. Your whole family destroyed by the nation you once loved. I've lost count of the number of Patriots who have come from similar circumstances."

Day turns his stare back up at the ceiling at the mention of his family. His eyes stay dry, but when Tess reaches out and grabs his hand, he tightens his fingers around hers.

"The world outside of the Republic isn't perfect, but freedoms and opportunities *do* exist out there, and all we need to do is let that light shine into the Republic itself. Our country is on the brink — all it needs now is a hand to tip it over." He rises halfway off his chair and points at his chest. "*We* can be that hand. With a revolution, the Republic comes crashing down, and together with the Colonies we can take it and rebuild it into something great. It'll be the United States again. People will live freely. Day, your little brother will grow up in a better place. That's worth risking our lives for. That's worth *dying* for. Isn't it?"

I can tell Razor's words are stirring something in Day, coaxing out a gleam in his eyes that takes me aback with its intensity. "Something worth dying for," Day repeats.

71

I should be excited too. But somehow, *still,* the thought of the Republic crashing down sends a pulse of nausea through me. I don't know if it's brainwashing, years of Republic doctrine drilled into my brain. The feeling lingers, though, along with a flood of shame and self-hate.

Everything I am familiar with is gone.

DAY

The medic shows up in a quiet flurry sometime after midnight. She preps me. Razor drags a table from the living room to one of the smaller bedrooms, where boxes of random supplies — food, nails, paper clips, canteens of water, you name it, they got it — are stacked in the corners. She and Kaede lay a sheet of thick plastic under the table. They strap me down to the table with a series of belts. The Medic carefully prepares her metal instruments. My leg lies exposed and bleeding. June stays by my side while they do all this, watching the Medic as if her supervision alone will ensure that the woman makes no mistakes. I wait impatiently. Every moment that passes brings us closer to finding Eden. Razor's words stir me each time I think about them. Dunno — maybe I should've joined the Patriots years ago.

Tess bustles efficiently about the room as the Medic's assistant, putting gloves on her hands after scrubbing up, handing her supplies, watching the process intently when there's nothing for her to do. She manages to avoid June. I can tell by Tess's expression that she's nervous as hell, but she doesn't utter a word about it. The two of us had chatted with each other pretty easily during dinner, when she'd sat on the couch beside me — but something has changed between us. I can't quite put my finger on it. If I didn't know any better, I'd think that Tess was *into* me. But it's such a weird thought, I quickly push it away. *Tess,* who's practically my sister, the little orphan girl from Nima sector?

Except she's *not* just a little orphan girl anymore. Now I can see distinct signs of adulthood on her face: less baby fat, high cheekbones, eyes that don't seem quite as enormous as I remember. I wonder why I never noticed these changes before. It only took a few weeks of separation to become obvious. I must be dense as a goddy brick, yeah?

"Breathe," June says beside me. She sucks in a lungful of air as if to demonstrate how it's done.

I stop puzzling over Tess and realize that I've been holding my breath. "Do you know how long it'll take?" I ask June. She pats my hand soothingly at the tension in my tone, and

I feel a pinch of guilt. If it wasn't for me, she'd still be on her way to the Colonies right now.

"A few hours." June pauses as Razor takes the Medic aside. Money exchanges hands — they shake on it. Tess helps the Medic put on a mask, then gives me a thumbs-up. June turns back to me.

"Why didn't you tell me you'd met the Elector before?" I whisper. "You always talked about him like he was a complete stranger."

"He *is* a complete stranger," June replies. She waits for a while, like she's double-checking her words. "I just didn't see the point in telling you — I don't *know* him, and I don't have any particular feelings toward him."

I think back to our kiss in the bathroom. Then I picture the new Elector's portrait and imagine an older June standing beside him as the future Princeps of the Senate. On the arm of the wealthiest man in the Republic. And what am I, some dirty street con with two Notes in his pocket, thinking I'll actually be able to hang on to this girl after spending a few weeks with her? Besides, have I already forgotten that June once belonged to an elite family — that she was mingling with people like the young Elector at fancy dinner parties and banquets back when I was still hunting for food in Lake's trash bins? And this is the *first* time I've pictured her with upper-class men? I suddenly feel so stupid for telling her that I love her, as if I'd be able to make her love me in return like some common girl from the streets. *She didn't say it back, anyway.*

Why do I even care? It shouldn't hurt this much. Should it? Don't I have more important stuff to worry about?

The Medic walks over to me. June squeezes my hand; I'm reluctant to let go. She *is* from a different world, but she gave it all up for me. Sometimes I take this for granted, and then I wonder how I have the nerve to doubt her, when she's so willing to put herself in danger for my sake. She could easily leave me behind. But she doesn't. *I chose this,* she'd told me.

"Thanks," I say to her. It's all I can manage.

June studies me, then gives me a light kiss on the lips. "It'll all be over before you know it, and then you'll be able to scale buildings and run walls as fast as you ever did." She lingers for a moment, then stands up and nods to the Medic and Tess. Then she's gone.

I close my eyes and take a shuddering breath as the Medic approaches. From this angle, I can't see Tess at all. Well, whatever this'll feel like, it can't be as bad as getting shot in the leg. Right?

The Medic covers my mouth with a damp cloth. I drift away into a long, dark tunnel.

76

Sparks. Memories from some faraway place.

I'm sitting with John at our little living room table, both of us illuminated by the unsteady light of three candles. I'm nine. He's fourteen. The table is as wobbly as it's ever been — one of the legs is rotting away, and every other month or so, we try to extend its life by nailing more slabs of cardboard to it. John has a thick book open before him. His eyebrows are scrunched together in concentration. He reads another line, stumbles on two of the words, then patiently moves on to the next.

"You look really tired," I say. "You should probably go to bed. Mom's going to be mad if she sees you're still up."

"We'll finish this page," John murmurs, only half listening. "Unless *you* need to go to bed."

That makes me sit up straighter. "I'm not tired," I insist.

We both hunch over the pages again, and John reads the next line out loud. " 'In Denver,' " he says slowly, " 'after the . . . completion . . . of the northern Wall, the Elector Primo . . . officially . . . officially . . . ' "

" 'Deemed,' " I say, helping him along.

" 'Deemed . . . it a crime . . .' " John pauses here for a few seconds, then shakes his head and sighs.

" 'Against,' " I say.

John frowns at the page. "Are you sure? Can't be the right word. Okay then. 'Against. Against the state to enter the . . .'" John stops, leans back in his chair, and rubs at his eyes. "You're right, Danny," he whispers. "Maybe I should go to bed."

"What's the matter?"

"The letters keep smearing on the page." John sighs and taps a finger against the paper. "It's making me dizzy."

"Come on. We'll stop after this line." I point to the line where he had paused, then find the word that was giving him trouble. "'Capital,'" I say. "'A crime against the state to enter the capital without first obtaining official military clearance.'"

John smiles a little as I read the sentence to him without a hitch. "You'll do just fine on your Trials," he says when I finish. "You and Eden both. If *I* squeaked by, I know *you'll* pass with flying colors. You've got a good head on your shoulders, kid."

I shrug off his praise. "I'm not *that* excited about high school."

"You should be. At least you'll get a chance to go. And if you do well enough, the Republic might even assign you to a college and put you in the military. That's something to be excited about, right?"

Suddenly there's pounding on our front door.

I jump. John pushes me behind him. "Who is it?" he calls out. The knocking gets louder until I cover my ears to block out the noise. Mom comes out into the living room, holding a sleepy Eden in her arms, and asks us what's going on. John takes a step forward as if to open the door — but before he can, the door swings open and a patrol of armed street police barge in. Standing in front is a girl with a long dark ponytail and a gold glint in her black eyes. Her name is June.

"You're under arrest," she says, "for the assassination of our glorious Elector."

She lifts her gun and shoots John. Then she shoots Mom. I'm screaming at the top of my lungs, screaming so hard that my vocal cords snap. Everything goes black.

A jolt of pain runs through me. Now I'm ten. I'm back in the Los Angeles Central Hospital's lab, locked away with who knows how many others, all strapped to separate gurneys, blinded by fluorescent lights. Doctors with face masks hover over me. I squint up at them. *Why are they keeping me awake?* The lights are so bright — I feel . . . slow, my mind dragging through a sea of haze.

I see the scalpels in their hands. A mess of mumbled words passes between them. Then I feel something cold and metallic against my knee, and the next thing I know, I arch my back and try to shriek. No sound comes out. I want to tell them to stop cutting my knee, but then something pierces the back of my head and pain explodes my thoughts away. My vision tunnels into blinding white.

Then I'm opening my eyes and I'm lying in a dim basement that feels uncomfortably warm. I'm alive by some crazy accident. The pain in my knee makes me want to cry, but I know I have to stay silent. I can see dark shapes around me, most of them laid out on the ground and unmoving, while adults in lab coats walk around, inspecting the bundles on the floor. I wait quietly, lying there with my eyes closed into tiny slits, until those walking leave the chamber. Then I push myself up onto my feet and tear off a pant leg to tie around my bleeding knee. I stumble through the darkness and feel along the walls until I find a door that leads outside, then drag myself into a back alley. I walk out into the light, and this time June is there, composed and unafraid, holding her cool hand out to help me.

"Come on," she whispers, putting her arm around my waist. I hold her close. "We're in this together, right? You and me?" We walk to the road and leave the hospital lab behind.

But the people on the street all have Eden's white-blond curls, each with a scarlet streak of blood cutting through the strands. Every door we pass has a large, spray-painted red *X* with a line drawn through its center. That means everybody here has the plague. A mutant plague. We wander down the streets for what seems like days, through air thick as molasses. I'm searching for my mother's house. Far in the distance, I can see the glistening cities of the Colonies beckoning to me, the promise of a better world and a better life. I'm going to take John and Mom and Eden there, and we'll be free from the clutches of the Republic at last.

Finally, we reach my mother's door, but when I push it open, the living room is empty. My mother isn't there. John is gone. *The soldiers shot him,* I remember abruptly. I glance to my side, but June has vanished, and I'm alone in the doorway. Only Eden's left . . . he's lying in bed. When I get close enough for him to hear me coming, he opens his eyes and holds his hands out to me.

But his eyes aren't blue. They're black, because his irises are bleeding.

I come to slowly, very slowly, out of the darkness. The base of my neck pulses the way it does when I'm recovering from one of my headaches. I know I've been dreaming, but all I remember is a lingering feeling of dread, of something horrible lurking right behind a locked door. A pillow is wedged under my head. A tube pokes out of my arm and runs along the floor. Everything's out of focus. I struggle to sharpen my vision, but all I can see is the edge of a bed and a carpet on the floor and a girl sitting there with her head resting on the bed. At least, I *think* it's a girl. For an instant I think it might be Eden, that somehow the Patriots rescued him and brought him here.

The figure stirs. Now I see that it's Tess.

"Hey," I murmur. The word slurs out of my mouth. "What's up? Where's June?"

Tess grabs my hand and stands up, stumbling over her reply in her rush. "You're awake," she says. "You're — how are you feeling?"

"Slow." I try to touch her face. I'm still not entirely convinced that she's real.

Tess checks behind her at the bedroom door to make sure no one else is there. She holds up a finger to her lips. "Don't worry," she says quietly. "You won't feel slow for long. The Medic seemed pretty happy. Soon you'll be better than new and we can head for the warfront to kill the Elector."

It's jarring to hear the word *kill* come so smoothly out of Tess's mouth. Then, an instant later, I realize that my leg doesn't hurt — not even the smallest bit. I try to prop myself up to see, and Tess pushes the pillows up behind my back so I can sit. I glance down at my leg, almost afraid to look.

Tess sits beside me and unwraps the white bandages that cover the area where the wound was. Under the gauze are smooth plates of steel, a mechanical knee where my bad one used to be, and metal sheets that cover half my upper thigh. I gape at it. The parts where metal meets flesh on my thigh and calf feel molded tightly together, but only small bits of redness and swelling line the edges. My vision swims.

Tess's fingers drum expectantly against my blankets, and she bites her round upper lip. "Well? How does it feel?"

"It feels like . . . nothing. It's not painful at all." I run a tentative finger over the cool metal, trying to get used to the foreign parts embedded in my leg. "She did all this? When can I walk again? Has it really healed *this* quickly?"

Tess puffs up a little with pride. "I helped the Medic. You're not supposed to move around much over the next twelve hours. To let the healing salves settle and do their work." Tess grins and the smile crinkles up her eyes in a familiar way. "It's a standard operation for injured warfront soldiers. Pretty awesome, yeah? You should be able to use it like a regular leg after that, maybe even better. The doctor I helped is really famous from the war-front hospitals, but she also does black-market work on the side, which is lucky. While she was here, she showed me how to reset Kaede's broken arm too, so it'd heal faster."

I wonder how much the Patriots spent on this surgery. I'd seen soldiers with metal parts before, from as little as a steel square on their upper arms to as much as an entire leg replaced with metal. It can't be a cheap operation, and from the appearance of my leg, the doctor used military-grade healing salves. I can already tell how much power my leg will have when I recover — and how much more quickly I'll be able to get around. How much sooner I can find Eden.

"Yeah," I say to Tess. "It's amazing." I crane my neck a little so I can focus on the bedroom door, but this makes me dizzy. My head is pounding up a storm now, and I can hear low voices coming from farther down the hall. "What's everyone doing?"

Tess glances over her shoulder again and then back to me. "They're talking about the first phase of the plan. I'm not in it, so I'm sitting out." She helps me lie back down. Then an awkward pause follows. I still can't get used to how different Tess seems. Tess notices me admiring her, hesitates, and smiles awkwardly.

"When all this is finished," I begin, "I want you to come with me to the Colonies, okay?" Tess breaks into a smile, then smoothes my blankets nervously with one hand as I go on. "If everything goes according to the Patriots' plans, and the Republic really does fall, I don't want us to be caught in the chaos. Eden, June, you, and me. Got it, cousin?"

Tess's burst of enthusiasm wanes. She hesitates. "I don't know, Day," she says, glancing over toward the door again.

"Why? You afraid of the Patriots or something?"

"No . . . they've been good to me so far."

"Then why don't you want to come?" I ask her quietly. I'm starting to feel weak again, and it's hard to keep things from getting foggy. "Back in Lake, we always said that we'd escape to the Colonies together if we got the chance. My father told me that the Colonies must be a place full of —"

"Freedom and opportunities. I know." Tess shakes her head. "It's just that . . ."

"That what?"

One of Tess's hands slides over to tuck inside my own. I picture her as a kid again, back when I first found her rummaging through that garbage bin in Nima sector. Is this really the same girl? Her hands aren't as small as they used to be, although they still fit neatly into mine. She looks up at me. "Day . . . I'm worried about you."

I blink. "What do you mean? The surgery?"

Tess gives me an impatient shake of her head. "No. I'm worried about you because of *June.*"

I breathe deeply, waiting for her to continue, afraid of what she'll say.

Tess's voice changes into something strange, something I don't recognize. "Well . . . if June travels with us . . . I mean, I know how attached you are to her, but just a few weeks ago she was a Republic *soldier.* Don't you see that expression she gets now and then? Like she misses the Republic, or wants to go back or something? What if she tries to sabotage our plan, or turns on you while we're trying to get to the Colonies? The Patriots are already taking precautions —"

"Stop." I'm a little surprised by how loud and irritated I sound. I've never raised my voice to Tess before, and I regret it instantly. I can hear Tess's jealousy in every word she says, the way she spits June's name out like she can't wait to get it over with. "I understand that it's only been a few weeks since everything's happened. Of course she's going to have moments of uncertainty. Right? Still, she's *not* loyal to the Republic anymore, and we're in a

86

dangerous place even if we don't travel with her. Besides, June has skills that none of us have. She broke me out of Batalla Hall, for crying out loud. She can keep us safe."

Tess purses her lips. "Well, how do you feel about what the Patriots are planning for her? What about her relationship with the Elector?"

"What relationship?" I hold up my hands weakly, trying to pretend that it doesn't matter. "It's all part of the game. She doesn't even know him."

Tess shrugs. "She will soon," she whispers. "When she has to get close enough to manipulate him." Her eyes lower again. "I'll *go* with you, Day. I'd go anywhere with you. But I just wanted to remind you about . . . her. Just in case you hadn't thought of things that way."

"Everything will be okay," I manage to say. "Just trust me."

The tension finally passes. Tess's face softens into its familiar sweetness, and my irritation slips away as quickly as it had come. "You've always watched out for me," I say with a smile. "Thanks, cousin."

Tess grins. "Someone has to, yeah?" She gestures at my rolled-up sleeves. "I'm glad the uniform fits you, by the way. It seemed too big when it was folded, but I guess it turned out all right." Without warning, she leans over and gives me a quick kiss on the cheek. She jumps away almost instantly. Her face is bright pink. Tess has kissed me on the cheek before, when she was younger, but this is the first time I've felt something *more* in her gesture. I try to figure out how, in less than a month, Tess left her childhood behind and became an adult. I cough uncomfortably. It's an odd new relationship.

Then she stands up and pulls her hand away. She looks toward the door instead of at me. "Sorry, you should be resting. I'll check on you later. Try to go back to sleep."

That's when I realize that Tess must've been the one to drop off our uniforms in the bathroom. She might've seen me kissing June. I try to think through the fog in my mind, to say something to her before she leaves, but she's already walked out the door and disappeared down the hall.

JUNE

0545 Hours.
Venezia.
Day One as an official member of the Patriots.
I chose not to be in the room during the surgery; Tess, of course, stayed to assist the Medic. The image of Day lying unconscious on the table, face pale and blank, head turned ninety degrees to the ceiling, would remind me a little too much of the night I'd hunched over Metias's dead body in the hospital alley. I prefer not to let the Patriots see my weaknesses. So I stay away, sitting alone on one of the couches in the main room.

I also keep my distance in order to really think about Razor's plan for me:

I'm going to be arrested by Republic soldiers.

I'm going to find a way to get a private audience with the Elector, and then I'm going to gain his trust.

I'm going to tell him about a bogus assassination plot that will lead to a full pardon of all my crimes against the Republic.

Then I'm going to lure him to his *actual* assassination.

That's my role. Thinking about it is one thing; pulling it off is another. I study my hands and wonder whether I'm ready to have blood on them, whether I'm ready to kill someone. What was it Metias had always told me? *"Few people ever kill for the right reasons, June."* But then I remember what Day said in the bathroom. *"Getting rid of the person in charge seems like a small price to pay for starting a revolution. Don't you think so?"*

The Republic took Metias away from me. I think of the Trials, the lies about my parents' deaths. The engineered plagues. From this luxury high-rise I can see Vegas's Trial stadium behind the skyscrapers, gleaming, off in the distance. Few people kill for the right reasons, but if *any* reason is the right one, it must be this. Isn't it?

My hands are trembling slightly. I steady them.

It's quiet in this apartment now. Razor has left again (he stepped out at 0332 in full uniform), and Kaede is dozing on the far end of my couch. If I were to drop a pin on the marble floor in here, the sound would probably hurt my ears. After a while, I turn my attention to the small screen on the wall. It's muted, but I still watch the familiar cycle of news play. Flood warnings, storm warnings. Airship arrival and departure times. Victories against the Colonies along the warfront. Sometimes I wonder whether the Republic makes up those victories too, and whether we're actually winning or losing the war. The headlines roll on. There's even a public announcement warning that any civilian caught with a red streak in his or her hair will be arrested on sight.

The news cycle ends abruptly. I straighten when I see the next bit of footage: The new Elector is about to give his first live speech to the public.

I hesitate, then glance over at Kaede. She seems to be sleeping pretty soundly. I get up, cross the room on light feet, then skim a finger across the monitor to turn up the volume.

The sound is tiny, but enough for me to hear. I watch as Anden (or rather, the Elector Primo) steps gracefully up to the podium. He nods to the usual barrage of government-appointed reporters in front of him. He looks exactly the way I remember him, a younger version of his father, with slender glasses and a regal tilt to his chin, dressed impeccably in a formal, gold-trimmed black uniform with double rows of shining buttons.

"Now is a time of great change. Our resolve is being tested more than ever, and the war with our enemy has reached a climax," he says. He speaks as though his father hadn't died, as if he had always been our Elector Primo. "We have won our last three warfront battles and seized three of the Colonies' southern cities. We are on the brink of victory, and it won't be long before the Republic spans to the edge of the Atlantic Ocean. It is our manifest destiny."

He goes on, reassuring the people of our military's strength and promising later announcements about changes he wants to implement — who knows how much of it is true. I go back to studying his face. His voice is not unlike his father's, but I find myself drawn to the sincerity in it. Twenty years old. Maybe he actually believes everything he's saying, or maybe he just does a great job of hiding his doubts. I wonder how he feels about his father's death, and how he is able, at press conferences like this, to pull himself together enough to play his role. No doubt Congress is eager to manipulate such a young new Elector, to try to run the show behind the scenes and push him around like a chess piece. Based on what Razor said, they must be clashing daily. Anden might be as power-hungry as his father was if he refuses to listen to the Senate at all.

What exactly *are* the differences between Anden and his father? What does Anden think the Republic should be — and for that matter, what do *I* think it should be?

I mute the screen again and walk away. *Don't dwell too deeply on who Anden is.* I can't think about him as if he were a real person — a person I have to kill.

Finally, as the first rays of dawn start spilling into the room, Tess comes out of the bedroom with the news that Day is awake and alert. "He's in good shape," she says to Kaede. "Right now he's sitting up, and he should be able to walk around in a few hours." Then she sees me and her smile fades. "Um. You can see him if you want."

Kaede cracks open an eye, shrugs, and goes back to sleep. I give Tess the friendliest smile I can manage, then take a deep breath and head for the bedroom.

Day is propped up with pillows and covered up to his chest with a thick blanket. He must be tired, but he still winks when he sees me walk in, a gesture that makes my heart skip a beat. His hair spills around him in a shining circle. A few bent paper clips lie in his lap (taken from the supply boxes in the corner — I guess he *did* get up). Apparently he was in the middle of making something out of them. I let out a sigh of relief when I can tell that he's not in any pain. "Hey," I say to him. "Glad to see you're alive."

"Glad to see I'm alive too," he replies. His eyes follow me as I sit down next to him on the bed. "Did I miss anything while I was out?"

"Yeah. You missed listening to Kaede snore on the couch. For someone always ducking the law, that girl sure sleeps soundly."

Day laughs a little. I marvel again at his high spirits, something I haven't seen much of over the last few weeks. My gaze wanders to where the blanket covers his healing leg. "How is it?"

Day scoots the blanket aside. Underneath, there are plates of smooth metal (steel and titanium) where his wound had been. The Medic also replaced his bad knee with an artificial one, and now a good third of his leg is metallic. He reminds me of the soldiers who come back from the warfront, with their synthetic hands and arms and legs, metal where skin used to be. The Medic must be very familiar with war injuries. No doubt Razor's officer connections helped her obtain something as expensive as the healing salves she must have used on Day. I put out my open palm, and he puts his hand in mine.

"How does it feel?"

Day shakes his head incredulously. "It feels like nothing. Completely light and painless." A mischievous grin crosses his face. "Now you'll get to see how I can *really* run a building, darling. Not even a cracked knee to hold me back, yeah? What a nice birthday present."

"Birthday? I didn't know. Happy belated," I say with a smile. My eyes go to the paper clips strewn across his lap. "What are you doing?"

"Oh." Day picks up one of the things he's making, something that looks like a metal circle. "Just passing the time." He holds the circle up to the light, and then takes my hand. He presses it into my palm. "A gift for you."

I study it more closely. It's made of four unfurled paper clips carefully entwined around one another in a spiral, and pulled together end to end so they form a tiny ring.

Simple and neat. Artistic, even. I can see love and care in the twists of metal, the little bends where Day's fingers worked on the wire over and over until it formed the right curves. *He* made *it for me.* I push it onto my finger and it slides effortlessly into place. Gorgeous. I'm bashful, flattered into complete silence. Can't remember the last time anyone actually *made* something for me on his own.

Day seems disappointed by my reaction, but hides it behind a careless laugh. "I know you rich folks have all your fancy traditions, but in the poor sectors, engagements and gestures of affection usually go like this."

Engagements? My heart flutters in my chest. I can't help smiling. "With paper clip rings?"

Oh no. I'd meant it as an honest question of curiosity, but don't realize I sound sarcastic until the words are already out of my mouth.

Day blushes a little; I'm immediately angry at myself for slipping up again. "With something handmade," he corrects me after a beat. He's looking down, clearly embarrassed, and I feel horrible for having triggered it. "Sorry it's kind of stupid-looking," he says in a low voice. "Wish I could make something nicer for you."

"No, no," I interrupt, trying to fix what I just said. "I really like it." I run my fingers over the tiny ring, keeping my eyes fixed on it so I don't have to meet Day's eyes. *Does he assume that I don't think it's good enough? Say something, June. Anything.* My details come bubbling up. "Unplated galvanized steel wiring. This is good material, you know. Sturdier than the alloy ones, still bendy, and won't rust. It's —"

I stop when I see Day's withering stare. "I like it," I repeat. *Idiotic reply, June. Why don't you punch him in the face while you're at it.* I turn even more flustered when I remember that I *have* actually pistol-whipped him in the face before. Romantic.

"You're welcome," he says, shoving a couple of the unbent paper clips into his pockets.

There's a long pause. I'm not sure what he wanted me to say back, but it probably wasn't a list of a paper clip's physical properties. Suddenly unsure of myself, I draw closer and rest my head against Day's chest. He takes a quick breath, as if I'd caught him by surprise, and then he drapes his arm gently around me. *There, that's better.* I close my eyes. One of his hands combs through my hair, sending goose bumps down my arms, and I allow myself to in-

97

dulge in a little moment of fantasy — I imagine him running a finger along my jaw line, bringing his face down to mine.

Day leans over my ear. "How are you feeling about the plan?" he whispers.

I shrug, shoving my disappointment away. Stupid of me to fantasize about kissing Day at a time like this. "Has anyone told you what you're supposed to do?"

"No. But I'm sure there's going to be some kind of national broadcast to tell the country I'm still alive. I'm supposed to stir up trouble, right? Work the people into a frenzy?" Day laughs dryly, but his face doesn't look amused. "Whatever gets me to Eden, I guess."

"I guess," I say.

He pulls me upright then, so that I face him. "I don't know if they'll let us communicate with each other," he says. His voice drops so low I can barely hear it. "The plan *sounds* good, but if something goes wrong —"

"They'll keep a close eye on me, I'm sure," I interrupt him. "Razor's a Republic officer. He can find a way to get me out if it starts falling apart. As for communications . . ." I bite my lip, thinking. "I'll come up with something."

Day touches my chin, bringing me closer

until his nose brushes mine. "If anything goes wrong, if you change your mind, if you need help, you send a signal, you hear me?"

His words send shivers down my neck. "Okay," I whisper.

Day gives me a subtle nod, then pulls away and leans back against his pillows. I let out my breath. "Are you ready?" he asks. There's more to his sentence, I can tell, but he doesn't say it. *Are you ready to kill the Elector?*

I give him a forced grin. "Ready as I'll ever be."

We stay like that for a long time, until the light filtering in from the windows is bright and we hear the morning pledge blaring out across the city. Finally, I hear the front door swing open and close, and then Razor's voice. Footsteps approach the bedroom, and Razor peeks in right as I straighten and sit up.

"How's that leg of yours?" he asks Day. His face is as calm as ever, his eyes expressionless behind his glasses.

Day nods. "Good."

"Excellent." Razor smiles sympathetically. "I hope you've had enough time with your boy, Ms. Iparis. We're moving out in an hour."

"I thought the Medic wanted me to rest it

99

for —" Day starts to say.

"Sorry," Razor replies as he turns away. "We have an airship to catch. Don't push that leg too hard just yet."

DAY

The Patriots disguise me before we head out.

Kaede cuts my hair so it stops right below my shoulders, then she tints the white-blond strands a dark brownish red. She uses some sort of spray to do it, something they can remove with a special cleanser if they need to strip the color out. Razor gives me a pair of brown contact lenses that completely hide the bright blue of my eyes. Only I can tell that it's artificial; I can still see the tiny, tiny specks of deep purple dotting my irises. These contacts are a luxury in themselves — rich trots use them to change their eye color — for *fun.* They would've come in handy for me on the streets if I'd had access to them. Kaede adds a synthetic scar to my cheek, then finishes off my disguise with a first-year air force uniform; a full black suit with red stripes running along each pant leg.

Finally, she equips me with a tiny flesh-colored earpiece and mike — the first embedded discreetly in my ear, the second inside my cheek.

Razor himself is decked out in a custom Republic officer uniform. Kaede wears a flawless flight outfit — a black jumpsuit with silver wing stripes wrapped around both sleeves, matching white condor gloves, and wing goggles. She's not a Pilot in the Patriots for nothing — according to Razor, she can pull off a split-S in the air better than anyone he's ever seen. Kaede should have no trouble posing as a Republic fighter pilot.

Tess is already gone, whisked away half an hour ago by a soldier who Razor says is another Patriot. Tess is too young to pass as a soldier of any level, so getting her onto the RS *Dynasty* means dressing her in a simple brown collar shirt and trousers, the outfit of workers who operate the airship's hundreds of stoves.

And then there's June.

June quietly watches my transformation from the couch. She hasn't said much since our last conversation over my recovery bed. While the rest of us have our various getups, June is unchanged — no makeup, her eyes still dark and penetrating, her hair still pulled back in that shiny tail. She's dressed in the plain cadet uniform Razor gave us last night. In fact, June doesn't look all that different from the photo on her military ID. She's the only one of us who isn't equipped with a mike and earpiece, for obvious reasons. I try to catch her gaze a few times while Kaede works on my appearance.

Less than an hour later, we head down the main Vegas strip in Razor's officer jeep. We pass several of the first pyramids — the Alexandria dock, the Luxor, the Cairo, the Sphinx. All named after some ancient pre-Republic civilization, or at least that's what we were taught back when the Republic actually allowed me in school. They look different during the day, with their bright beacon lights off and edges unlit, looming like giant black tombs in the middle of the desert. Soldiers bustle in and out of their entrances. It's good to see so much activity — all the better for us to blend in. I go over our own uniforms again. Polished and authentic. I can't get used to it, even though June and I have technically been passing as soldiers for weeks. The collar scratches at my neck, and the sleeves feel way too stiff. I don't know how June could stand wearing this stuff all the time. Does she at least like how it looks on me? My shoulders *do* seem a little broader.

"Stop tugging on your uniform," June whispers when she sees me fiddling with the edges of my military jacket. "You're messing up its alignment."

It's the most I've heard her say in an hour. "You're just as nervous," I reply.

June hesitates, then turns away again. Her jaw is clenched as if to keep herself from blurting something out. "Just trying to help," she mutters.

After a while, I reach over to squeeze her hand once. She squeezes back.

Finally, we reach the Pharaoh, the landing dock where the RS *Dynasty* is resting. Razor ushers us out, then has us stand at attention. Only June falls out of line, stopping beside Razor and facing off to one side of the street. I watch her discreetly.

A second later, another soldier melts from the crowd and nods at Razor, then at June, who straightens her shoulders, joins up behind the soldier, and disappears back into the street crowd. Out of sight, just like that. I exhale, hollowed out by her sudden absence.

I won't see her again until the whole thing's over. If it all goes well. *Don't think like that. It will go well.*

We head inside with the tides of other soldiers filing into and out of the Pharaoh. The interior is huge; beyond the main entrance, the ceiling stretches all the way up to the top of the pyramid and ends with the base of the RS *Dynasty,* where I can see tiny figures boarding through a maze of ramps and walk-ways. Rows of barrack doors line each level of the pyramid's sides. Long marquees of text run across each wall with a never-ending onslaught of departure and arrival times. Diagonal elevators run along each of the pyramid's four main edges.

Here, Razor leaves us behind. One second he's walking ahead, and the next he takes an abrupt turn through the crowds and melts in with the sea of uniforms. Kaede continues walking without hesitation, but slows enough so we're side by side. I can barely see her lips move, but her voice echoes with razor-sharp clarity from my earpiece.

"Razor will board the *Dynasty* with the other officers, but we can't go in with the soldiers or we'll get ID'd. So sneaking in is our next best option —"

My eyes go up to the airship's base, skim-ming across the nooks and crannies lining its sides. I think back on the time when I broke into a grounded airship and stole two bags' worth of canned food. Or the time I sank a smaller airship in Los Angeles's lake by flood-ing its engines. For both cases, there was one easy way of getting in undetected. "The garbage chutes," I murmur back through my own mike.

Kaede gives me a quick, approving grin.

"Spoken like a true Runner."

We make our way through the crowds until we reach an elevator terminal at one of the pyramid's corners. Here we blend in with the small group clustered in front of the elevator door. Kaede clicks her mike off to make small talk with me, and I'm careful not to make eye contact with the other soldiers. So many of them are younger than I'd imagined, even close to my age, and several already have permanent injuries — metal limbs like my own, a missing ear, a hand covered with burn scars. I glance up again at the *Dynasty,* this time long enough to note all the garbage chute openings along the side of the hull. If we're going to shimmy our way up into this airship, we're going to have to do it fast.

Soon the elevator comes. We take the nauseating ride up the diagonal side of the pyramid, then wait at the top while everyone else files out. We exit last. As the others scatter to either side of the top hall leading toward the airship's entrance ramps, Kaede turns to me.

"One more flight for us," she says, nodding toward a narrower set of stairs at the end of the hall that lead up to the pyramid's inside ceiling. I study it quietly. She's right. These stairs go right up into the ceiling (and probably lead up to the roof), and all along this ceiling are mazes of metal scaffolding and crisscrossing support beams. From here, the docked airship's back side casts a shadow across the ceiling that swathes this part of it in darkness. If we can leap off the middle of this last flight of stairs and climb up into that mess of metal beams, we can make our way over to the airship undetected in the shadows and climb up the dark side of the hull. Plus, the air vents are noisy this close up. That, along with the noise and bustle of the base, should mask any sounds we make.

Here's hoping my new leg holds up. I stomp down on it twice to test it. It doesn't hurt, but there's a little pressure where my flesh meets the metal, like it hasn't completely fused yet. Still, I can't help smiling. "This'll be fun, yeah?" I say. I'm almost back in my element, at least for a moment, back where I'm at my best.

We make our way up into the shadowy stairs, and then each of us takes the short leap up into the scaffolding and climbs into the beams. Kaede's first. She struggles a little with her bandaged arm, but manages to get a good grip after some shuffling. Then it's my turn. I swing effortlessly up into the beams and weave my body into the shadows. Leg's good so far. Kaede watches me approvingly.

"Feeling mighty fine," I whisper.

"I can see that."

107

We travel in silence. My pendant slips out of my shirt a couple of times and I have to tuck it back in. Sometimes I look down or toward the airship; the floor of the landing base is packed with cadets of all ranks, and now that most of the *Dynasty*'s previous crew have rotated out of the ship, the new ones are starting to form long lines at the entrance ramps. I watch as each one passes through a quick inspection, ID check, and body scan. Far below us, more cadets are accumulating near the elevator doors.

Suddenly I pause.

"What's the problem?" Kaede snaps.

I hold up a finger. My eyes are fixed on the ground, frozen on a familiar figure who's cutting his way through the crowd.

Thomas.

This trot's tracked us all the way from Los Angeles. He stops now and then to question what seem like random soldiers. With him is a dog so white, it stands out like a beacon from this height. I rub my eyes to make sure I'm not hallucinating. Yep, he's still there. He continues to weave his way through the crowd, one hand on the gun at his waist, the other holding the leash to that enormous white shepherd. A small line of soldiers follows him. My limbs turn numb for an instant, and suddenly all I see is Thomas lifting his gun and pointing it at my mother, Thomas beating me to a pulp in a Batalla Hall interrogation room. My vision swims in red.

Kaede notices what's holding my attention and turns her head down to the ground floor too. Her voice snaps me back. "He's here for June," she whispers. "Keep moving."

Immediately I begin to crawl again, even though my whole body's shaking. "June?" I whisper back. I can feel my rage rising. "You guys put *him,* of all people, onto June's trail?"

"It was for a good reason."

"And what's that?"

Kaede sighs impatiently. "Thomas won't hurt her."

Stay calm, stay calm, stay calm. I force myself to keep going. No choice but to trust Kaede now. Eyes forward. Keep moving. My hands tremble and I fight to steady them, to push down my hatred. The thought of Thomas putting his hands on June is more than I can bear. If I focus on that now, I won't be able to concentrate on anything else.

Stay. Calm.

Below us, Thomas's patrol keeps making their way through the masses. He's gradually moving toward the elevators.

We reach the hull of the ship. From here, I can see the line of soldiers waiting to get in via the ramps. That's when I hear the white shepherd's first bark. Thomas and his soldiers are now gathered at one of the elevator terminals. The same one we went through. The dog is barking relentlessly, his nose pointed at the elevator door, his tail wagging. *Eyes forward. Keep moving.*

I glance back down at the ground level. Thomas has one hand pressed tightly against what must be his earpiece. He stands there for a minute, as if struggling to understand something he's hearing. Then, suddenly, he shouts at his men and they start heading away from the elevators. Back into the crowds of soldiers.

They must have found June.

We make our way across the shadows of the pyramid's ceiling until we're perched close enough to the dark side of the ship's hull. It looms a good dozen feet away from us, with only a lone metal ladder running vertically up its side to the top of the ship's deck. Kaede readjusts her balance on the metal beams, then turns back to me. "Make the first jump," she says. "You're better."

Time to move. Kaede shifts enough so I can get a good angle on the ship. I adjust my footing, brace myself, hope my leg stays intact, then take a giant leap. My body slams against the ladder bars with a muffled thud, and I grit my teeth to keep from yelling. Pain lances up and down my healing leg. I wait for a few seconds, letting the strain die down before I start climbing again. I can't see the patrol anymore from this back side, but that means — hopefully — that they can't see us either. Better yet, I hope they're gone. Behind me I hear Kaede take her own leap and hit the ladder several feet below me.

Finally, I reach the garbage chute opening. I launch off from the ladder — my hands catch the side of the chute and my arms swing me right into the darkness. There's another jolt of pain, but the leg still pulses with newfound energy, strong for the first time in a long time. I dust off my hands and stand up. The first thing I notice inside the chute is the cold air. They must have the insides of the ship cooled for the launch.

Moments later, Kaede swings inside too. She winces, rubbing at the cast of her still-injured arm, then shoves me in the chest. "Don't just stop like that in the middle of a climb," she snaps. "Always keep moving. We can't afford for you to be impulsive."

"Then don't give me a reason to be impulsive," I snap back. "Why didn't you tell me Thomas was coming for June?"

"I know your history with that captain," Kaede replies. She squints into the dark, then motions for us to start climbing up the chute.

"And Razor didn't think it would do you any good to worry about it in advance."

I'm ready to fire back, but Kaede shoots me a warning glance. With effort, I manage to swallow my anger. I remind myself of why I'm here. This is for Eden. If Razor thinks June is safest under Thomas's watch, then so be it. But what are they going to do with June once they've got her? What if something goes wrong, and Congress or the courts do something that Razor didn't plan for? How can he be so sure that everything will go smoothly?

Kaede and I make our way up the chute until we reach the lower levels of the *Dynasty*. We stay hidden behind a stairwell in a lonely back engine room until takeoff, when the steam pistons flare to life and we feel the pressure of the rising ship push against our feet as it lifts free from the landing base. I hear giant cables snapping loose from the ship's sides and the roar of applause from the base crew cheering another successful liftoff.

After a half hour passes, when my anger's finally had time to cool, we emerge from the stairwell. "Let's go this way," Kaede murmurs as we reach a tiny room with two paths — one leading to the engines and the other leading straight up to the lower floors. "Sometimes they run surprise inspections on the entrances to the base deck. We might have fewer problems in the engine rooms." She pauses, pressing a hand to her ear and frowning in concentration.

"What is it?"

"Sounds like Razor is in," she replies.

My leg feels a little sore as we continue, and I find myself walking with a very slight limp. We head up another stairwell that leads to the engine rooms, bumping into a couple of soldiers along the way, until we hit a floor marked "6" where the stairs stop. We wander down this hall for a while before pausing at a narrow door. A sign reads TO ENGINE ROOMS A, B, C, D.

A lone guard waits by the door. He glances up, sees us, and straightens from his slouch. "What do you two want?" he mutters.

We exchange casual salutes. "We were sent here to see someone," Kaede lies. "Engine room personnel."

"Yeah? Who?" He squints at Kaede in disapproval. "You're a pilot, aren't you? You should be on the upper deck. They're doing inspections."

Kaede's ready to protest, but I interrupt her and put on a sheepish face. I say the only thing I can think of that he probably won't question. "All right, soldier to soldier," I mutter to the guard, sneaking a sideways glance at Kaede. "We, ah . . . we were hunting for a good place to . . . you know. We figured the engine rooms should work." I give him an apologetic wink. "I've been trying to get a kiss out of this girl for weeks. Knee surgery got in the way." I pause here and demonstrate an exaggerated version of my limp for him.

The guard suddenly grins and lets out a surprised laugh, as if he's pleased to have a role in something naughty. "Ah, I see," he says, glancing sympathetically at my leg. "She's a cute one." I laugh with him, while Kaede plays along by rolling her eyes.

"Like you said," Kaede tells the guard as he unlocks the door for us. "I'm late for inspections. We'll be fast — we're heading up to the top deck in a few minutes."

"Good luck, you poor bastards," he calls to us as we head inside. We exchange lazy salutes with him.

"I had a really good story ready to tell him," Kaede whispers as we go. "Nice cover from you, though. You think of that one all by yourself?" She smiles slyly and looks me over from head to toe. "Too bad I got stuck with such an ugly sidekick."

I hold both hands up in mock defense. "Too bad I got stuck with such a liar."

We walk along a cylindrical corridor bathed in a dim, red light. Even down here, flat screens roll a stream of news and airship updates. They're displaying a list of where all the Republic's active airships are headed, along with their dates and schedules. Apparently twelve are airborne at the moment. As we pass one of the screens, my eyes skim down to the RS *Dynasty*.

REPUBLIC SHIP *DYNASTY* | DEPARTURE: 0851 OCEAN
STANDARD TIME, 01.13 FROM PHARAOH DOCK,
LAS VEGAS, NV | ARRIVAL: 1704 BORDER STANDARD TIME, 01.13 AT
BLACKWELL DOCK, LAMAR, CO

Lamar. We're headed for a warfront city up north. One step closer to Eden, I remind myself. June will be fine. This mission will all be over soon.

The first room we enter is enormous — rows and rows of giant boilers and hissing vents, with dozens of workers operating each one. Some are checking temperatures, while others are shoving something like white coal into furnaces. They're all dressed in the same outfit Tess had on right before she left us at the Venezia. We hurry along through one of the rows of boilers until we push through the next door. One more stairwell. Then we emerge onto the *Dynasty*'s lower deck.

This airship is enormous. I've been on board airships before, of course. When I was thirteen, I snuck onto the flight deck of the RS *Pacifica* and stole fuel from three F-170 fighter jets, then sold it on the black market for a good price. But I've never been inside one of this size. Kaede leads us out the door of the stairwell and onto a metal walkway that opens up into a view of all the floors above us. Soldiers are everywhere. We walk with them, careful to keep our faces expressionless. Here on the lowest floor, several formations of troops run through drills. Doors line the corridors, and in between every four doors is a flat screen displaying news. The new Elector's portrait hangs above each screen. They sure move fast, don't they?

Razor's office is one of a half dozen that line the walls of the fourth deck, with a silver Republic seal embedded in its door. Kaede knocks twice. When she hears Razor's voice calling for us to enter, she ushers us inside, then shuts the door carefully behind her and snaps to attention. I follow her lead. Our boots click against the hardwood floor. Something in the room smells faintly like jasmine, and as I take in the ornate, spherical wall lamps and the Elector's portrait on the back wall, I realize how chilly it is in here. Razor stands by his desk with his hands behind his back, all fancy in his formal commander uniform, talking to a woman dressed in a similar outfit.

It takes me a second to realize that the woman is Commander Jameson.

Kaede and I both freeze in our tracks. After the shock of seeing Thomas, I'd simply assumed that if Commander Jameson was anywhere in Vegas, she'd be at the pyramid dock, monitoring her captain's progress. I never thought she'd be on the ship. Why is she going to the warfront?

Razor nods in our direction as both Kaede and I salute him. "At ease," he says to us, then turns his attention back to Commander Jameson. Beside me, I can sense Kaede's tension. My street instincts kick in. If Kaede's anxious, that means the Patriots hadn't planned on Commander Jameson's being here. My eyes dart to the door's lock; I imagine myself whirling around, flinging the door open, and swinging over the balcony railings to the deck below. The ship's layout plays in my thoughts like a three-dimensional map. I need to be ready to bolt if she recognizes me. Gotta have my escape route ready.

"I've been advised to keep my eyes open," Commander Jameson says to Razor. He seems completely unfazed — his shoulders are relaxed, and he's wearing an easy smile. "And so should you, DeSoto. If you notice anything odd, come to me. I'll be ready."

"Of course." Razor tips his head respectfully at Commander Jameson, even though his uniform's insignias indicate that he's her senior. "All the best to you, and to Los Angeles."

They exchange casual salutes. Then Commander Jameson begins walking toward the door. I force myself to remain still, but every muscle is screaming at me to escape.

Commander Jameson passes me, and I wait quietly as she scans me from head to toe. From the corner of my eyes, I can see the hard lines of her face and the thin, scarlet slash of her lips. Behind her expression is an icy nothingness — a complete lack of emotion that injects both fear and hate into my blood. Then I notice that her hand is bandaged. Still injured from when she'd held me captive at Batalla Hall, when I'd bitten it almost down to the bone.

She knows who I am, I think. A bead of sweat trickles down my back. She must know. Even with this brief glance, she can see right through my disguise, this dark cropped hair and synthetic scar and brown contact lenses. I wait for her to raise the alarm. My boots tilt against the ground, ready to run. My healing leg pulses.

But the split second passes, and Commander Jameson's gaze swivels away as she reaches the door. I step back from the cliff. "Your uniform is rumpled, soldier," she calls back to me with distaste. "If I were Commander DeSoto, I'd give you a dozen laps as punishment."

She steps away, walks through the door, and disappears. Kaede locks the door again — her shoulders slouch, and I hear her let out a breath. "Nice one," she says to Razor as she plops down on the office's couch. Her voice drips sarcasm.

Razor motions for me to sit as well. "We have you to thank, Kaede," he says. "For our young friend's first-rate disguise." Kaede beams at his compliment. "I apologize for the unexpected surprise. Commander Jameson has gotten wind of June's arrest. She wanted to board the ship to see if anything else turned up." He sits down behind his desk. "She's taking a plane back to Vegas now."

I feel weak. As I rest on the couch beside Kaede, I can't help keeping an eye on the windows in case Commander Jameson comes back for something. The windows are made of frosted glass. Can anyone from below see us up here?

Kaede's already relaxed again, chatting up a storm with Razor about our next steps. What time we'll land, when we should regroup in

119

Lamar, whether decoy soldiers at the capital are in place. But I just sit and think about Commander Jameson's expression. Of all the Republic officers I've come across, except maybe for Chian, only Commander Jameson's eyes can freeze me to my core. I fight down the memory of how she'd ordered my mother's death — and John's execution. If Thomas has June under arrest, what will Commander Jameson do to her? Can Razor actually keep her protected? I close my eyes and try to send a silent thought to June.

Stay safe. I want to see you again when all this is done.

JUNE

I can't bring myself to look at Day again before leaving him behind. As Razor's Patriot walks me away from the front entrance of the Pharaoh pyramid, I keep my face pointed firmly away from him. *It's for the best,* I tell myself. If the mission goes well, it'll only be a short separation.

Day's concerns about my well-being really hit home now. Razor's plan for me *sounds* good, but something could go wrong. What if, instead of taking me to see the Elector, I'm shot the instant I'm found? Or they could strap me upside down in an interrogation room and beat me senseless. I've seen it happen plenty of times. I could be dead before this day is over, long before the Elector learns I've been found. A million things could go wrong.

That's why I have to focus, I remind myself. And I can't do that if I stare into Day's eyes.

Now the Patriot guides me inside the

pyramid and down a narrow walkway running along one side of a wall. It's loud and chaotic in here. Hundreds of soldiers are milling around on the ground level. Razor had told me they would put me in one of the empty barrack rooms on the first floor, where I would pretend to be hiding before trying to sneak on board the RS *Dynasty.* When Republic soldiers knock down the door and come for me, I'm supposed to make a run for it. To give it all I've got.

My steps quicken to match my guide's. Now we reach the end of the walkway, where a secure door (five feet six wide, ten feet high) leads away from the main floor and into the hallways of the first floor barracks. The guide swipes a card across the door. It beeps, then blinks green and slides open.

"Put up a fight when they come for you," the Patriot tells me in a voice I can barely hear. His appearance is no different from any of the other soldiers here, with slicked-back hair and a black uniform. "Make sure they believe you don't want to be caught. You were trying to turn yourself in near Denver. Okay?"

I nod.

His attention shifts away from me. He studies the hall, tilting his head up to inspect the ceiling. A row of security cams lines this corridor, eight in total, one facing the front of each barrack door. Before we step all the way into the hall, the guide pulls out a pocketknife and uses it to clip off one of the shiny buttons lining his jacket. Then he braces himself against the doorway, presses one foot against each side of the door frame, and leaps up.

I glance back down the hall. There are no other soldiers here at the moment, but what if one suddenly turns the corner? It's no surprise if they capture *me* here (that's our goal, after all), but what about my guide?

He reaches up toward the first security cam, then uses the knife to scrape away some of the rubber coating protecting the cam's wires. When a bit of the rubber comes off and exposes the wires underneath, he wraps his fingers in the length of his sleeve and presses the metal button against the wires.

A quiet burst of sparks. To my surprise, every security cam along the hall blinks off.

"How'd you break all of them with just one — ?" I start to whisper.

The guide jumps back down to the ground and motions for me to hurry up. "I'm a Hacker," he whispers back as we run. "I've worked the command centers here before. I rewired things a little to suit us." He smiles proudly, showing even white teeth. "But this is nothing. Just wait till you hear about what we've done to Denver's Capitol Tower."

Impressive. If Metias joined the Patriots, he'd be a Hacker too. *If he were alive.*

We sprint down the hall until he stops us at one of the doors. Barrack 4A. Here he pulls out a key card and swipes the door's access panel. It clicks and swings open a little — inside, eight rows of bunks and lockers sit in the dark.

The Hacker turns to face me. "Razor wants you waiting here to ensure that the right soldiers capture you. He has a specific patrol in mind."

Of course, makes perfect sense. It confirms that Razor doesn't want me beaten to a pulp by letting just any Republic patrol arrest me. "Who — ?" I start to ask.

But he taps the edge of his military cap before I can finish. "We'll all be watching your mission from the cams. Good luck," he whispers. Then he's gone, hurrying down the hall until he rounds a corner and I can't see him anymore.

I take a deep breath. I'm alone. Time to wait for soldiers to arrest me.

I quickly step inside the room and shut the barrack door. It's pitch-black in here —

no windows, not even a slit of light from under the door. Certainly a believable enough place for me to be hiding. I don't bother moving farther into the room; I already know what the layout is, rows of bunk beds and a communal bathroom. I just flatten myself against the wall right next to the door. Better to stay here.

I reach out in the darkness and find the doorknob. Using my hands to measure, I gauge how far the knob is from the ground (three feet six). That's probably how much space is between the doorknob and the top of the door frame too. I think back to when we were still standing out in the corridor, picturing how much space is between the door frame's top edge and the ceiling. It must've been a little less than two feet.

Okay. Now all my details are in place. I settle back against the wall, close my eyes, and wait.

Twelve minutes drag by.

Then, farther down the hall outside, I hear a dog's bark.

My eyes pop open. *Ollie.* I'd recognize that bark anywhere — my dog is still alive. *Alive, by some miracle.* Joy and confusion wash over me. What the hell is he doing here? I press an ear against the door and listen. Several more seconds of silence. Then, I hear the bark again.

My white shepherd is here.

Now thoughts are racing through my mind. The only reason why Ollie would be here is because he's with a patrol — the patrol that's hunting me down. And there's only one soldier who'd think to use my own dog to sniff me out: Thomas. The Hacker's words come back to me. Razor wanted "the right soldiers" to capture me. He had a specific patrol in mind.

Of course the patrol — the *person* — Razor had in mind would be Thomas.

Thomas must've been assigned by Commander Jameson to track me down. He's using Ollie to help. But of all the patrols I'd prefer to be arrested by, Thomas's ranks last on the list. My hands start to shake. I don't want to see my brother's murderer again.

Ollie's barking grows steadily louder. With it come the first sounds of footsteps and voices. I hear Thomas's voice out in the corridor, shouting to his soldiers. I hold my breath and remind myself of the numbers I'd calculated.

They're right outside the door. Their voices have gone quiet, replaced by clicks (safety on loaded guns, sounds like some M-series, some standard-issue rifles).

The following seems to happen in slow

motion. The door creaks open and light spills in. Immediately I make a small jump and step one leg up — my foot lands silently on the doorknob as the door swings toward me. As the soldiers enter the room with their guns drawn, I reach up and grab the top of the door frame by using the doorknob as a step. I pull myself up. Without a sound, I perch on top of the open door like a cat.

They don't see me. They probably can't see anything except the darkness in here. I count them all in a flash. Thomas leads the group with Ollie at his side (to my surprise, Thomas doesn't have his gun drawn), and behind him are a cluster of four soldiers. There are more soldiers outside the room, but I can't tell how many.

"She's in here," one of them says, with a hand pressed to his ear. "She hasn't had a chance to board any airships yet. Commander DeSoto just confirmed one of his men saw her enter."

Thomas says nothing. I watch him turn to observe the dark room. Then his gaze wanders up the door.

We lock eyes.

I leap down and knock him to the ground. In a moment of blind rage, I actually want to break his neck with my bare hands. It'd be so easy.

The other soldiers clamor for their guns, but in the chaos I hear Thomas choke out an order. "Don't fire! Don't fire!" He grabs my arm. I almost manage to break free and dart through the soldiers and out the doorway, but a second soldier shoves me down. They're all on me now, a whirlwind of uniforms seizing my arms and dragging me to my feet. Thomas keeps shouting at his men to be careful.

Razor was right about Thomas. He'll want to keep me alive for Commander Jameson.

Finally, they cuff my hands and push me so hard against the floor that I can't move. I hear Thomas's voice overhead. "Good to see you again, Ms. Iparis." His voice shakes. "You're under arrest for assaulting Republic soldiers, for creating a disturbance in Batalla Hall, and for abandoning your post. You have the right to remain silent. Anything you say can and will be used against you in a court of law." I notice he doesn't say anything about assisting a criminal. He still has to pretend the Republic executed Day.

They pull me to my feet and lead me back down the hall. By the time we're in the sunlight, more than a few passing soldiers stop to watch. Thomas's men shove me unceremoniously into a waiting patrol jeep's backseat, chain my hands to the door, and lock my arms down in metal shackles. Thomas sits next to me and points his gun at my head. Ridiculous. The jeep ushers us back through the streets. The other two soldiers sitting in the jeep's front watch me in the rearview mirror. They act like I'm some sort of untamed weapon — and in a way, I guess that's true. The irony of it all makes me want to laugh. Day is a Republic soldier on board the RS *Dynasty,* and I am the Republic's most valuable captive. We've switched places.

Thomas tries to ignore me as we travel, but my eyes never leave him. He seems tired, with pale lips and dark circles rimming his eyes. Stubble dots his chin, a surprise in itself — Thomas would normally never show his face without being perfectly clean shaven. Commander Jameson must've run him ragged for letting me escape from Batalla Hall. They probably interrogated him for it.

The minutes drag on. None of the soldiers talk. The one who drives us keeps his eyes firmly on the road, and all we can hear is the drone of the jeep's engine and the muffled sounds from the streets outside. I swear the others must be able to hear the hammering of my heart too. From here I can see the jeep driving ahead of us, and

129

through its back window I see occasional flashes of white fur that make me feel incredibly happy. Ollie. I wish he were in the same jeep as me.

Finally, I turn to Thomas. "Thank you for not hurting Ollie."

I don't expect him to answer. *Captains don't speak to criminals,* he'd say. But to my surprise, he meets my gaze. For me, it seems, he's still willing to break protocol. "Your dog turned out to be useful."

He's Metias's dog. My anger starts rising again, but I push it back down. Useless to rage over something that won't help my plans. It's interesting that he kept Ollie alive at all — he could have tracked me down without him. Ollie's not a police dog and has no training in sniffing down targets. He couldn't have helped when they were trying to track me across half the country; he's only useful in very close range. Which means that Thomas kept him alive for other reasons. Because he cares for me? *Or . . . maybe he still cares for Metias.* The thought startles me. Thomas's stare flickers away when I don't reply. Then there's another long silence. "Where are you taking me?"

"You'll be held in the High Desert Penitentiary until after your interrogation, and then the courts will decide where you'll go."

Time to put Razor's plans to work. "After my interrogation, I can guarantee that the courts are going to send me to Denver."

One of the guards sitting up front narrows his eyes at me, but Thomas holds up a hand. "Let her talk," he says. "All that matters is that we deliver her unharmed." Then he glances at me. He seems gaunter than the last time I saw him too — even his hair, combed neatly in a side part, is dull and limp. "And why is that?"

"I have information the Elector may be highly interested in."

Thomas's mouth twitches — he's hungry to question me now, to uncover whatever secrets I might hold. But that's outside of protocol, and he's already broken enough rules by conversing idly with me. He seems to decide against pressing me further. "We'll see what we can get out of you."

Then I realize that it's a little strange they're sending me to a Vegas penitentiary at all. I should be interrogated and tried in my home state. "Why am I being held *here*?" I ask. "Shouldn't I be on my way to Los Angeles?"

Thomas keeps his eyes forward now. "Quarantine," he replies.

I frown. "What, it's spread to Batalla now too?"

His answer sends a chill down my spine. "*Los Angeles* is under quarantine. All of it."

High Desert Penitentiary.
Room 416 (20 × 12 square feet).
2224 Hours; same day as my capture.

I sit a few feet away from Thomas. Nothing but a flimsy table separates us — well, if I don't count the number of soldiers standing guard beside him. They shift uncomfortably whenever I let my eyes rest on them. I sway a little in my chair, fighting back exhaustion, and clink the chains that keep my arms secured across my back. My mind is starting to wander — I keep thinking back on what Thomas said about Los Angeles and its quarantine. *No time to dwell on that now,* I tell myself, but the thoughts won't go away. I try to picture Drake University marked with plague signs, Ruby sector's streets crowded with plague patrols. How is that possible? How could the entire city be under quarantine?

We've been in this room for six hours, and Thomas has gotten nowhere with me. My answers to his questions lead us around in circles, and I've been doing it in a way so subtle that he doesn't realize I've been manipulating the conversation until he's wasted another hour. He's tried threatening

132

to kill Ollie. To which I threatened to carry any information I had to my grave. He's tried threatening *me.* To which I reminded him of the taking-information-to-my-grave factor. He's even tried some mind games — none of which went even remotely well. I just keep asking him why Los Angeles is under quarantine. I've been trained in interrogation tactics as much as he has, and it's backfiring on him. He hasn't gotten physical with me yet, the way he had with Day. (This is another interesting detail. It doesn't matter how much Thomas cares for me — if his superiors order him to use physical force, he'll do it. Since he hasn't hurt me yet, it means Commander Jameson told him not to. Odd.) Even so, I can tell his patience with me is wearing thin.

"Tell me, Ms. Iparis," he says after we're silent for a moment. "What will it take for me to get something useful out of you?"

I keep my face expressionless. "Already told you that. I'll trade you an answer for a request. I have information for the Elector."

"You're in no position to bargain. And you can't keep this up indefinitely." Thomas leans back in his chair and frowns. The fluorescent lights cast long shadows under his eyes. Against the undecorated white walls of the room (aside from two Republic flags and the Elector's portrait), Thomas stands out ominously in his black-and-red captain's uniform. Metias used to wear a uniform like that. "I know Day is alive, and *you* know how we can find him. You'll talk after a few days without food or water."

"Don't assume what I will and won't do, Thomas," I reply. "As for Day, I should think the answer's obvious. *If* he were alive, he'd head off to rescue his little brother. Any fool could guess that."

Thomas tries to ignore my jab, but I can see the irritation on his face. "*If* he's alive, he'll never find his brother. That location is classified. I don't need to know where Day *wants* to go. I need to know where he *is*."

"It makes no difference. You'd never catch him anyway. He won't fall for the same tricks twice."

Thomas folds his arms. Was it really just a few weeks ago that the two of us sat together, eating dinner at a Los Angeles café? The thought of LA brings me right back to the quarantine news, and I picture the café empty, covered with quarantine notices.

"Ms. Iparis," Thomas says, putting his palms flat on the table. "We can continue like this forever, and you can just keep being snide and shaking your head until you collapse from exhaustion. I don't want to hurt you. You have a chance to redeem yourself to the Republic. In spite of everything you've done, I've received word from my higher-ups that they still consider you to be quite valuable."

So. Commander Jameson *was* involved in making sure I'm not harmed during my interrogation. "How kind," I reply, letting sarcasm seep into my words. "I'm luckier than Metias."

Thomas sighs, bows his head, and squeezes the upper bridge of his nose in exasperation. He sits like that for a moment. Then he motions toward the other soldiers. "Everyone out," he snaps.

When the soldiers have left us alone, he turns back to me and leans forward to put his arms on the table. "I'm sorry you have to be here," he says quietly. "I hope you understand, Ms. Iparis, that I'm bound by my duty to do this."

"Where's Commander Jameson?" I reply. "She's your puppet master, isn't she? I would've thought she'd come interrogate me as well."

Thomas doesn't flinch at my taunt. "She's containing Los Angeles at the moment, organizing the quarantine and reporting the situation to Congress. With all due respect, the world does not revolve around you."

135

Containing Los Angeles. The words chill me. "Are the plagues really that bad right now?" I decide to ask yet again, keeping my eyes firmly fixed on Thomas's face. "Is LA quarantined because of illness?"

He shakes his head. "Classified."

"When will it be lifted? Are *all* the sectors quarantined?"

"Stop asking. I told you, the whole city is. Even if I knew when it would be lifted, I'd still have no reason to tell you."

I know instantly by his expression that what he actually means is: *Commander Jameson didn't tell me what's going on in the city, so I have no idea.* Why would she need to keep him in the dark? "What *happened* in the city?" I press, hoping to get more out of him.

"That's not relevant to your interrogation," Thomas replies, tapping his fingers impatiently against his arm. "Los Angeles is no longer your concern, Ms. Iparis."

"It's my *hometown,*" I reply. "I grew up there. Metias *died* there. Of course it's my concern."

Thomas is quiet. His hand comes up to push dark hair away from his face, and his eyes search mine. Minutes tick by. "That's what this is all about," he finally mutters. I wonder if he's saying this because he's weary too after six hours in this room. "Ms. Iparis, what happened to your brother —"

"I know what happened," I interrupt him. My voice trembles in rising anger. "You killed him. You sold him to the state." The words hurt so much that I can barely squeeze them out.

His expression quivers. He lets out a cough and straightens in his chair. "The order came directly from Commander Jameson, and the last thing I'd do is disobey a direct order from her. You should know this rule as well as I do — although I have to admit you've never been very good at following it."

"What, so you were just willing to hand him over like that, because he figured out how our parents died? He was your *friend*, Thomas. You grew up with him. Commander Jameson wouldn't have given you the time of day — you wouldn't be sitting across this table right now — if Metias hadn't recommended you for her patrol. Or have you forgotten that?" My voice rises. "You couldn't risk even a fraction of your own safety to help him?"

"It was a direct order," Thomas repeats. "Commander Jameson is *not* to be questioned. What don't you understand about that? She knew that he hacked into the

deceased persons' database, along with a host of other high security government catalogs. Your brother broke the law, multiple times. Commander Jameson couldn't have a well-respected captain of her patrol committing crimes right under her nose."

I narrow my eyes. "And that's why you killed him in a dark alley, then framed Day for it? Because you'd happily follow your commander's orders right off a cliff?"

Thomas slams his hand down on the table hard enough to make me jump. *"It was a signed order from the state of California,"* he shouts. "Do you understand what I'm saying? I had no better choice." Then his eyes widen — he hadn't expected those words to come out, not that way. They stun me too. He keeps talking, now at a quicker pace, seemingly determined to erase the words. A strange light glows in his eyes, something that I can't quite pinpoint. What is it? "I'm a soldier of the Republic. When I joined the military I took an oath to obey my superiors' orders at all costs. Metias took the same oath, and he broke it."

There's something odd about the way he refers to Metias, a sort of hidden emotion that throws me off. "The *state* is broken." I take a deep breath. "And you're a coward for leaving Metias at its mercy."

Thomas's eyes constrict as if I'd stabbed him. I study him closer, but he notices me analyzing him and jerks his face away, turning to the side and hiding his head in his hands.

I think about my brother again, this time flipping in my mind through his many years spent in Thomas's company. Metias had known Thomas since they were kids, long before I was born. Whenever his father, our apartment floor's janitor, would bring Thomas along to accompany him during his work shifts, Thomas and Metias would play for hours on end. Military video games. Toy guns. After I came into the picture, I remember the many quiet conversations the two of them would share in our living room, and how often they were together. I recall Thomas's Trial score: 1365. Great for a poor sector kid, but average for kids in Ruby sector. Metias was the first to pick up on Thomas's intense interest in being a soldier. He'd spend entire afternoons teaching Thomas everything he knew. Thomas would never have made it into Emerald sector's Highland University without my brother's help.

My breaths turn shallow as something falls into place. I remember the way Metias's gaze would linger on Thomas during their training sessions. I'd always assumed that was just my brother's way of studying Thomas's posture and performance for accuracy. I remember how patient and gentle Metias was when explaining things to Thomas. The way his hand would touch Thomas's shoulder. The night when I'd eaten *edame* at that café with Thomas and Metias, when Metias first stopped shadowing Chian. The way Metias's hand would sometimes rest on Thomas's arm for a beat longer than it had to. The chat I had with my brother when he took care of me on the day of his induction. How he'd laughed. *I don't need girlfriends. I've got a baby sister to take care of.* And it was true. He'd dated a couple of girls in college, but never for longer than a week, and always with polite disinterest.

So obvious. How could I not have seen this before?

Of *course* Metias never talked to me about it. Officer and subordinate relationships are strictly forbidden. Harshly punished. Metias had been the one to recommend Thomas for Commander Jameson's patrol . . . He must have done it for Thomas's sake, even though he knew that it meant any chance of a relationship would be impossible.

All of this flashes through my thoughts in

a matter of seconds. "Metias was in love with you," I whisper.

Thomas doesn't reply.

"Well? Is it true? You must have known."

Thomas still doesn't answer. Instead, he keeps his head in his hands and repeats, "I took an *oath.*"

"Wait a minute. I don't understand." I lean back against my chair and take a deep breath. My thoughts are now a whirling, jumbled mess. Thomas's silence tells me far more than anything he's said aloud.

"Metias loved you," I say slowly. My words are quivering. "And did so much for you. But you still turned him in?" I shake my head in disbelief. "How could you?"

Thomas looks up at me from his hands, a flash of confusion lighting his face. "I never *reported* him."

We face each other for a long time. Finally, I say through clenched teeth, "Tell me what happened, then."

Thomas stares off into space. "Security admins found traces he left behind when he hacked through a loophole in the system," he replies. "Into the deceased civilians' database. The admins reported it to me first, with the understanding that I would pass the message to Commander Jameson. I'd always warned Metias about hacking. You

141

cross the Republic too many times, and eventually you get burned. Stay loyal, stay faithful. But he never listened. Neither one of you do."

"So you kept his secret?"

Thomas drops his head back into his hands. "I confronted Metias about it first. He admitted it to me. I promised him I wouldn't tell anyone, but deep down, I *wanted* to. I have never kept anything from Commander Jameson." He pauses here for a second. "Turns out that my silence wouldn't have made a difference. The security admins decided to forward a message on to Commander Jameson anyway. That's how she found out. Then she tasked me with taking care of Metias."

I listen in shocked silence. *Thomas had never wanted to kill Metias.* I try to imagine a scenario that I can bear. Maybe he even tried to persuade Commander Jameson to assign the mission to someone else. But she refused, and he chose to do it anyway.

I wonder whether Metias ever acted on his attraction, and whether Thomas reciprocated. Knowing Thomas, I doubt it. Did he love Metias back? He *had* tried to kiss me that night after the celebration for Day's capture. "The celebratory ball," I muse, aloud this time. I don't need to explain that evening for Thomas to know what I'm talking about. "When you tried to . . ."

I trail off as Thomas continues to stare at the floor, his expression oscillating between blankness and pain. Finally, he runs a hand through his hair and mumbles, "I knelt over Metias and watched him die. My hand was on that knife. He . . ."

I wait, light-headed from the words he's saying.

"He told me not to hurt you," Thomas continues. "His last words were about you. And I don't know. At Day's execution, I tried to come up with a way to stop Commander Jameson from arresting you. But you make it *so* hard for people to protect you, June. You break so many rules. Just like Metias. That night at the ball — when I looked at your face —" His voice cracks. "I thought I could protect you, and that the best way might be to keep you close to me, to try to win you over. I don't know," he repeats bitterly. "Even Metias had trouble watching out for you. What chance did I have of keeping you safe?"

The evening of Day's execution. Had Thomas been trying to help me out when he escorted me down to see the electro-bomb storage basement? What if Commander Jameson was preparing to arrest

143

me, and Thomas tried getting to me first? To what, help me escape? I don't understand.

"I did care for him, you know," he says through my silence. He pretends bravado, some false professionalism. Still, I hear a tinge of sadness. "But I am also a soldier of the Republic. I did what I had to do."

I shove the table aside and lunge for him, even though I know I'm chained down to my chair. Thomas jumps back. I stumble against my restraints, fall to my knees, and then grab for his leg. For anything. *You're sick. You're so twisted.* I want to kill him. I've never wanted anything this much in my entire life.

No, that's not true. I want Metias to be alive again.

The guards outside must've heard the commotion because they come pouring in, and before I know it I'm pinned down by several soldiers, cuffed with an extra set of shackles, and untied from my chair. They drag me to my feet. I kick out furiously, running through a list in my head of every attack I've ever learned in school, trying frantically to free myself. Thomas is so close. He's only a few feet away.

Thomas just looks at me. His hands dangle at his sides. "It was the most merciful way for him to go," he calls out. It makes me nauseous I know he's right, and that Metias would've almost certainly been tortured to death had Thomas not taken him down in that alley. But I don't care. I'm blind, smothered by my anger and confusion. How could he do that to someone he loved? How could he possibly attempt to justify this? What is *wrong* with him?

After Metias's death, on nights when Thomas sat alone in his home, did he ever step out of his façade? Did he ever shed the soldier and let the civilian grieve?

I'm dragged out of the room and back down the corridor. My hands tremble — I fight to steady my breathing, to calm my racing heart, to push Metias back into a safe corner of my mind. A small part of me had hoped that I was wrong about Thomas. That he hadn't been the one to kill my brother.

By the next morning, all traces of emotion have disappeared from Thomas's face. He tells me the Denver court has gotten wind of my request for the Elector and has decided to transfer me to the Colorado State Penitentiary.

I'm off to the capital.

DAY

We touch down in Lamar, Colorado, on a cold, rainy morning, right on schedule. Razor leaves with his squadron. Kaede and I wait in the dark stairwell leading out from the back entrance of his office until the sounds outside have quieted and most of the ship's crew have left. This time there are no guards performing fingerprint scans or ID checks, so we can follow the last of the soldiers straight off the exit ramp. We melt right in with the troops that are actually here to fight for the Republic.

Sheets of icy rain pound the base as we step out of the pyramid dock and into the formidable grayness of this place. The sky's completely covered with churning storm clouds. Landing docks line the side of the cracked cement street, an ominous row of enormous black pyramids stretching off in either direction, slick and shiny with rain. The air smells stale, wet. Jeeps packed with soldiers drive back and forth, splashing mud and gravel across the pavement. The soldiers here all have a wide stripe of black painted across their eyes from one ear to the other. Must be some sort of crazy warfront style. The rest of the city looms in front of us — gray skyscrapers that probably serve as barracks for the soldiers, some new with smooth sides and tinted glass windows, others pockmarked and crumbling as if they've been fed a steady diet of grenades. A few are ash and ruins, some with just one wall left, pointing upward like a broken monument. No terraced buildings here, no grassy levels dotted with herds of cattle.

We hurry along the street with our stiff jacket collars turned up in a pitiful attempt to shield us from the rain. "This place has been bombed, yeah?" I mutter to Kaede. My teeth chatter with each word.

Kaede opens her mouth in mock surprise. "Wow. You're a cracked genius, you know that?"

"I don't get it." I study the crumbling buildings that dot the horizon. "What's with the shell-shocked look here? Isn't the actual fighting happening farther away?"

Kaede leans in so the other soldiers on the street don't hear us. "The Colonies have been pushing in along this part of the border since I was, what, seventeen? Anyway, for years.

They've probably gotten a good hundred miles in from where the Republic claims the Colorado line is."

After so many years of listening to the constant bombardment of Republic propaganda, it's jarring to hear someone tell me the truth. "What — so are you saying the Colonies are winning the war, then?" I ask in a low voice.

"They've been winning for a while now. You heard it from me first. Give it a few more years, kid, and the Colonies will be right in your backyard." She sounds kinda disgusted. Maybe there's some lingering resentment she has against the Colonies. "Make of that what you will," she mutters. "I'm just here for the money."

I fall silent. *The Colonies will be the new United States.* Can it really be possible that after all these years of war, it might finally come to an end? I try to imagine a world without the Republic — without the Elector, the Trials, the plagues. The Colonies as the victor. Man, too good to be true. And with the Elector's potential assassination, this might all come true even sooner. I'm tempted to press her more on it, but Kaede shushes me before I can start, and we end up walking in silence.

We make a turn several blocks down and follow a double row of railroad tracks for what feels like several miles. Finally, we stop when we reach a street corner far from the barracks, darkened by the shadows of ruined buildings alongside it. Lone soldiers walk by here and there. "There's a lull in the fighting right now," Kaede murmurs as she squints down the track. "Has been for a few days. But it'll pick up soon. You're gonna be so grateful to be hanging with us; none of these Republic soldiers will have the luxury of hiding underground when the bombs come raining down."

"Underground?"

But Kaede's attention is fixed on a soldier walking straight toward us along one side of the tracks. I blink water out of my eyes and try to get a better look at him. He's dressed no differently from us, in a soaked cadet jacket with a diagonal flap of cloth covering part of the buttons, and single silver stripes along each shoulder. His dark skin is slick behind the sheets of pouring rain, and his short curls are plastered to his head. His breath comes out in white clouds. When he gets closer, I can see that his eyes are a startling, pale gray.

He walks by without acknowledging us, and gives Kaede the subtlest gesture: two fingers of his right hand held out in a V.

We cross the tracks and continue for several more blocks. Here the buildings are crowded close together and the streets are so narrow that only two people can fit down an alley at a time. This must have once been an area where civilians lived. Many of the windows are blown out and others are covered with tattered cloth. I see a couple of people's shadows inside them, lit by flickering candles. Whoever isn't a soldier in this town must be doing what my father used to do — cooking, cleaning, and caring for the troops. Dad must've lived in squalor like this too whenever he headed out to the warfront for his tours of duty.

Kaede shakes me out of my thoughts by pulling us abruptly into one of the dark, narrow alleys. "Move fast," she whispers.

"You know who you're talking to, right?"

She ignores me, kneels down along the edge of one wall where there's a metal grating lining the ground, then takes out a tiny black device with her good arm. She runs it quickly along an edge of the grating. A second passes. Then the grating lifts off the ground on two hinges and silently slides open, revealing a black hole. It's purposely designed to be worn and dirty, I realize, but this thing's been modified into a secret entrance. Kaede stoops down and jumps into the hole. I follow suit. My boots splash into shallow water, and the grating above us slides shut again.

Kaede grabs my hand and leads me through

a tunnel. It smells stale here, like old stone and rain and rusted metal. Ice-cold water drips from the ceiling and through my wet hair. We travel only a few feet in before taking a sharp right turn, letting the darkness swallow us whole.

"There used to be miles of tunnels like this in almost every warfront city," Kaede whispers into the silence.

"Yeah? What were they for?"

"Rumor's that all these old tunnels used to be for eastern Americans trying to sneak west to get away from the floods. Even back before the war began. So each of these tunnels goes right under the warfront barricades between the Republic and the Colonies." Kaede makes a sliding motion with her hand that I can barely make out in the gloom. "After the war started, both countries started using them offensively, so the Republic destroyed all the entrances within their borders and the Colonies did the same on the other end. The Patriots managed to dig out and rebuild five tunnels in secret. We'll be using this Lamar one" — she pauses to gesture at the dripping ceiling — "and one in Pierra. A nearby city."

I try to imagine what it must've once been like, a time when there wasn't a Republic or Colonies and a single country covered the middle of North America. "And no one knows these are here?"

Kaede snorts. "You think we'd be using these if the Republic knew about them? Not even the Colonies know. But they're great for Patriot missions."

"Do the Colonies sponsor you guys, then?"

Kaede smiles a little at that. "Who else would give us enough money to maintain tunnels like this? I haven't met our sponsors over there yet — Razor handles those relationships. But the money keeps coming, so they must be satisfied with the job we're doing."

We walk for a while without talking. My eyes have adjusted enough to the darkness so that I can see rust crusting the tunnel's sides. Rivulets of water drip patterns across the metal walls. "Are you happy that they're winning the war?" I say after a few minutes. Hopefully she's willing to talk about the Colonies again. "I mean, since they practically kicked you out of their country? Why'd you leave in the first place?"

Kaede laughs bitterly. The sound of our boots sloshing through water echoes down the tunnel. "Yeah, I guess I'm happy," she says. "What's the alternative? Watching the Republic win? You tell me what's better. But you grew up in the Republic. Who knows what you'd think of the Colonies. You might think it's a paradise."

"Is there a reason I shouldn't?" I reply. "My father used to tell me stories about the Colonies. He said there were cities completely lit up by electricity."

"Your dad worked for a resistance or something?"

"I'm not sure. He never said it out loud. We all assumed he must've been doing *something* behind the Republic's back, though. He'd bring back these . . . trinkets related to the United States. Just odd things for a normal person to have. He would talk about getting us all out of the Republic someday." I pause there, lost for a moment in an old memory. My pendant feels heavy around my neck. "Don't think I'll ever really know what he was up to."

Kaede nods. "Well, I grew up along one of the Colonies' eastern coastlines, where it borders the South Atlantic. I haven't been back in years — I'm sure the water's gone at least a dozen more feet inland by now. Anyway, I got into one of their Airship Academies and became one of their top pilots in training."

If the Colonies don't have the Trials, I wonder how they choose who to admit into their schools. "So, what happened?"

"Killed a guy," Kaede replies. She says it like it's the most natural thing in the world. In the darkness, she draws closer to me and peers boldly at my face. "What? Hey, don't

153

give me that — it was an accident. He was jealous that our flight commanders liked me so much, so he tried to push me over the edge of our airship. I damaged one of my eyes good during that scuffle. I found him in his locker room later and knocked him out." She makes a disgusted sound. "Turned out I'd hit his head *too* hard, and he never woke up. My sponsor pulled out after that little incident tainted my reputation with the corps — and not because I killed him, either. Who wants an employee — a *fighter pilot* — with a bad eye, even after surgery?" She stops walking and points at her right eye. "I was damaged goods. My price went way down. Anyway, the Academy booted me out after my sponsor dropped me. It's a shame, honestly. I missed out on my last year of training because of that damn con."

I don't understand some of the terms Kaede uses — *corps, employees* — but I decide to ask her about them some other time. I'm sure I'll gradually get more info about the Colonies out of her. For now, I still want to know more about the people I'm working for. "And then you joined the Patriots?"

She flips her hand in a nonchalant gesture and stretches her arms out in front of her. I'm reminded of how tall Kaede is, how her shoulders line up with mine. "Fact of the matter is, Razor pays me. Sometimes I even get to fly. But I'm here for the money, kid, and as long as I keep getting my cash, I'll do whatever I can to help stitch the United States back together. If that means letting the Republic collapse, fine. If it means the goddy Colonies taking over, fine. Get this war over and the US thing going. Get people living normal lives again. That's what I care about."

I can't help feeling a little amused. Even though Kaede tries to seem uncommitted, I can tell that she's proud to be a Patriot. "Well, Tess seems to like you well enough," I reply. "So I guess you must be all right."

Kaede laughs in earnest. "Gotta admit, she's a sweet one. I'm glad I didn't kill her in that Skiz duel. You'll see — there's not a single Patriot who doesn't like her. Don't forget to show some love to your little friend now and then, okay? I know you've got the hots for June, but Tess is head over heels mad for you. In case you couldn't tell."

That makes my smile fade a little. "I guess I just never really thought about her like that," I murmur.

"With *her* past, she deserves some love, yeah?"

I put my hand out and stop Kaede. "She told you about her past?"

Kaede glances back at me. "She's never told you her stories, has she?" she says, genuinely bewildered.

"I could never get them out of her. She always sidestepped it, and after a while I just gave up trying."

Kaede sobers. "She probably doesn't want you to feel sorry for her," she finally says. "She was the youngest of five. She was nine at the time, I think. Parents couldn't afford to feed all of them, so one night they locked her out of the house and never let her back in. She said she pounded on the door for days."

I can't say I'm surprised to hear this. The Republic's so lazy when it comes to dealing with street orphans that none of us ever got a second glance — my family's love was all I had to hang on to in my early street years. Apparently, Tess didn't even have *that*. No wonder she was so clingy when I first met her. I must have been the only person in the world who cared about her.

"I didn't know," I whisper.

"Well, now you do," Kaede replies. "Stick by her — you two are a good match, y'know." It makes her snicker. "Both so damn optimistic. I've never met such a sunshine-and-rainbows pair of slum sector cons."

I don't respond. She's right, obviously — I'd never dwelled on the thought, but Tess and I *are* a good match. She understands intimately where I came from. She can cheer me up on my darkest days. It's as if she came from a perfectly happy home instead of what Kaede just told me. I feel a relaxing warmth at the thought, realizing suddenly how much I'm anticipating meeting up with Tess again. Where she goes, I go, and vice versa. Peas in a pod.

Then there's June.

Even the thought of her name makes it hard for me to breathe. I'm almost embarrassed by my reaction. Are June and I a good match? *No.* It's the first word to pop into my mind.

And yet, still.

Our conversation fizzles out. Sometimes I glance back over my shoulder, half hoping to see a hint of light, half hoping I don't. No light means that the tunnel doesn't run right under all the gratings in the city, visible to those walking by above. The ground also feels slanted. We're traveling deeper and deeper underground. I force myself to breathe evenly as the walls narrow, closing in around me. Goddy tunnel. What I wouldn't give to be back in the open.

It takes forever, but finally I feel Kaede come to an abrupt halt. The echo of our boots in the water sounds different now — I think we've stopped in front of a solid structure of some sort. Maybe a wall. "This used to be a rest bunker for fugitives," she mutters. "Near the back of this bunker the tunnel continues on, right over to the Colonies." Kaede tries opening the door with a small lever at one side, and when that fails, she taps her knuckles softly against it in a complicated series of ten or eleven taps. "Rocket," she calls out. We wait, shivering.

Nothing. Then, a dim little rectangle in the wall slides open, and a pair of yellow-brown eyes blinks at us. "Hi, Kaede. Airship was right on time, yeah?" the girl behind the wall says before narrowing her eyes at me. "Who's your friend?"

"Day," Kaede replies. "Now you better stop all this crap and let me in. I'm freezing."

"All right, all right. Just checking." The eyes search me up and down. I'm surprised she can see much of anything in this darkness. Finally, the little rectangle slides shut. I hear a few beeps and a second voice. The wall slides open to reveal a narrow corridor with a door at its other end. Before either of us make a move, three people step forward from behind the wall and point guns right at our heads.

"Get in," one of them barks at us. It's the girl who just opened the wall's peephole. We do as she says. The wall closes behind us. "This week's code?" she adds, cracking her gum loudly.

"Alexander Hamilton," Kaede replies impatiently.

Now the three guns are pointed at me instead of Kaede. "Day, eh?" the girl says. She blows a quick bubble. "You sure about that?"

It takes me a moment to realize that her second question is addressed to Kaede instead of me. Kaede sighs in exasperation and smacks the girl's arm. "*Yes,* it's him. So knock it off."

The guns lower. I let out a breath I didn't know I was holding. The girl who let us in gestures for us to walk toward the second door, and when we reach it, she slides a little device similar to the one Kaede had across the door's left side. A few more beeps. "Go on in," she tells us. Then she juts her chin at me. "Any sudden moves and I'll shoot you faster than you can blink."

The second door slides open. Warm air pours over us as we step into a large room full of people bustling around tables and wall-mounted monitors. Electric lights are on the ceiling; a faint but distinct scent of mold and rust lingers in the air. There must be twenty, thirty people down here, and the room still feels spacious.

A large projection of an insignia decorates the room's back wall, one that I immediately recognize as the abbreviated version of the official Patriot flag — a large silver star, with three silver V stripes below it. Smart to project it, I realize, so they can pick up and move out quickly if need be. Some of the monitors show the airship schedules I'd seen while onboard the *Dynasty*. Others show security cam–like footage streaming from officers' rooms or wide shots of Lamar's city streets or video from the flight decks of airships right in the warfront's skies. One even has a short rotation of morale-boosting Patriot propaganda that reminds me a little too much of the Republic's ads; it says BRING BACK THE STATES, followed by LAND OF THE FREE and then WE ARE ALL AMERICANS. Still others display views of continental America littered with multicolored dots — and two of them show world maps.

I gape at this for a while. Never in my life have I seen a world map. I'm not even sure if any *exist* in the Republic. But here I can see the oceans that wrap their way around North America, the cut-up island territories labeled SOUTH AMERICA, a tiny archipelago called the British Isles, gigantic landmasses called Africa and Antarctica, the country of China (with a bunch of little red dots sprinkled right in the ocean around the edge of its land).

This is the *actual* world, not the world the Republic shows to its civilians.

Everyone in the room is watching me. I turn away from the map and wait for Kaede to say something. She just shrugs and slaps me across the back. My wet jacket makes a squishing sound. "This is Day."

They all wait in silence, although I can see the recognition light up their eyes when they hear my name. Then somebody wolf-whistles. That breaks the tension — there's a chorus of snickers and laughs, then most people go back to whatever they were doing before.

Kaede guides me through the mess of tables. A couple of people are gathered around some diagram, another group is unpacking boxes; a few are just relaxing, watching reruns of some Republic soap opera. Two Patriots sitting in front of a corner monitor are tossing challenges back and forth as they play a video game, racing some sort of spiky blue creature across their screen by waving their hands in front of it. Even this must've been customized for the Patriots, as all the objects in the game are blue and white.

One boy snickers as I walk by. He has a shock of dyed blond hair spiked up into a faux hawk, dark bronze skin, and a slight hunch to his broad, hulking shoulders, as if he's permanently ready to pounce. A chunk of flesh is missing from his earlobe. I realize it's the same person who wolf-whistled earlier.

"So. You're the one who ditched Tess, huh?" There's an arrogance about him that annoys me. He looks me over in disdain. "Don't know why a girl like her hangs with a con like you. A few nights in the Republic's prisons squeeze all the air outta your chest?"

I take a step toward him and grin cheerfully. "With all due respect, I don't see the Republic tacking up wanted posters with *your* pretty face on them."

"Shut up." Kaede pushes between us and stabs a finger into the other boy's chest. "Baxter, shouldn't you be getting ready for tomorrow night's run?"

The boy just grunts at me and turns away. "Still don't understand why we're trusting a Republic lover," he grumbles.

Kaede taps my shoulder and keeps walking. "Don't mind that trot," she tells me. "Baxter's not the biggest fan of your girl June. He's probably gonna give ya some trouble, so just try to stay on his good side, yeah? You'll have to work with him. He's a Runner too."

"He is?" I say. I wouldn't have expected such a muscular person to be a fast Runner — but then again, his strength might help him reach places I can't.

"Yup. You bumped him down the hierarchy of Runners." Kaede smirks. "And you once messed up a Patriot mission that he was on.

You never even realized it."

"Oh? And what mission was that?"

"Bombing Administrator Chian's car, in Los Angeles."

Wow — it's been a long time since I faced off against Chian. No idea the Patriots had planned an attack at the same time. "How tragic," I reply, searching the faces in the room after Baxter's mention of Tess.

"If you're looking for Tess, she beat us here. She's with the other Medics." Kaede gestures toward the back of the room, where several doors line the walls. "Probably in the med ward watching someone sew up a wound. She's a fast learner, that Tess."

Kaede leads me past the tables and the other Patriots, then stops in front of the world map. "I bet you've never seen anything like this."

"Nope." I study the landmasses, still boggled by the idea that so many societies are functioning beyond the Republic's borders. In grade school we'd learned that the parts of the world not controlled by the Republic are just crumbling nations struggling to get by. Are *this* many countries struggling to get by? Or are they doing well — maybe even prospering? "What do you need world maps for?"

"Our movement here has spawned similar ones across the globe," Kaede replies, crossing her arms. "Wherever people are pissed at their governments. Kinda morale-boosting for us to see it on the wall." When she sees me continue to analyze the map with a concentrated frown, she runs a quick hand across the middle of North America. "There's the Republic we all know and love. And that's the Colonies." She points to a smaller, more broken-up spread of land sharing the Republic's eastern border. I study the red circles denoting cities in the Colonies. New York City, Pittsburgh, St. Louis, Nashville. Do they glow like my father said?

Kaede goes on, sweeping her hand up north and down south. "Canada and Mexico each keep a strict demilitarized zone between themselves and both the Republic and Colonies. Mexico's got her own share of Patriots. Then here's whatever's left of South America. This all used to be a huge continent too, y'know. Now it's Brazil" — she points to a large, triangular island far south of the Republic — "Chile, and Argentina."

Kaede cheerily points out what the continents are and what they used to be. What I see as Norway, France, Spain, Germany, and the British Isles used to be part of a larger place called Europe. The rest of Europe's people, she says, fled to Africa. Mongolia and Russia aren't extinct nations, contrary to

164

Republic teachings. Australia used to be one solid landmass. Then there are the superpowers. China's enormous, floating metropolises are built entirely over the water and have permanently black skies. "Hai Cheng," Kaede interjects. "Sea cities." I learn that Africa wasn't always the flourishing, technologically advanced continent it is today, gradually filling up with universities, skyscrapers, and international refugees. And Antarctica, believe it or not, was once uninhabited and completely covered in ice. Now, like China and Africa, it houses the world's tech capitals and attracts a fair share of tourists. "The Republic and the Colonies have such pathetic tech in comparison," Kaede adds. "I'd like to visit Antarctica someday. Supposed to be gorgeous."

She tells me the United States used to be one of those superpowers. "Then came the war," Kaede adds, "and all their top thinkers literally fled for higher ground. Antarctica caused the flooding, y'know. Things were already going downhill, but then the sun went haywire and melted all the Antarctic ice. Flooding like you and I couldn't even imagine. Millions dropped dead from the temperature changes. Now *that* must've been a spectacle, yeah? The sun reset itself eventually, but the climate never did. All that freshwater mixed up with seawater and nothing's been the same since."

"The Republic never talks about any of this."

Kaede rolls her eyes. "Oh, come on. It's the *Republic.* Why would they?" She points toward one small monitor in the corner that seems to be broadcasting news headlines. "You wanna see what the Republic is like from a foreigner's perspective? Here."

When I pay closer attention to the headlines, I realize that the voiceover is in a language I can't understand. "Antarctican," Kaede explains when I glance questioningly at her. "We're feeding in one of their channels. Read the captions."

The screen shows an aerial view of a continent, with the text REPUBLIC OF AMERICA hovering over the land. A woman's voice narrates, and right at the bottom of the screen is a running marquee of her translated words: "— to find new ways of negotiating with this heavily militarized rogue state, especially now that the transition of power to the Republic's new Elector is complete. African president Ntombi Okonjo proposed a halt today to the United Nations' aid for the Republic until there is enough evidence of a peace treaty between the isolationist country and its eastern neighbor —"

Isolationist. Militarized. Rogue. I stare at the words. To me, the Republic had been por-

166

trayed as the epitome of power, a ruthless, unstoppable military machine. Kaede grins at the expression on my face as she finally leads us away from the monitors. "Suddenly the Republic doesn't seem so powerful, does it? Puny little secretive state, groveling for international aid? I'm telling you, Day — all it takes is one generation to brainwash a population and convince them that reality doesn't exist."

We walk over to a table with two slim comps sitting on it. The young man hovering over one of the computers is the same guy who'd flashed Kaede a V sign on the railroad tracks, the one with dark skin and light eyes. Kaede taps him on the shoulder. He doesn't react right away. Instead, he types a few last lines into whatever's on the screen and then slides into a sitting position on the table. I catch myself admiring his grace. *A Runner for sure.* He crosses his arms and waits patiently for Kaede to introduce us.

"Day, this is Pascao," she says to me. "Pascao's the undisputed leader of our Runners — he's been eager to meet you, to put it lightly."

Pascao holds out a hand to me, his pale eyes fixed intensely on mine. He gives me a brilliant white smile. "A pleasure," he says in an excited, breathless rush. His cheeks flush red as I smile back at him. "Suffice it to say we've all heard a great deal about you. I'm your biggest fan. *Biggest* fan."

I don't think anyone's ever flirted with me so blatantly before, except maybe a boy I remember from Blueridge sector. "Nice to meet another Runner," I reply, shaking his hand. "I'm sure I'll pick up some new tricks from you."

He gives me a devilish grin when he sees how flustered I look. "Oh, you'll like what's coming. Believe me, you won't be sorry for joining up with us — we're gonna usher in a whole new era for America. The Republic won't know what hit it." He goes into a series of excited gestures, first spreading his arms wide and then pretending to untie knots in the air. "Our Hackers spent the last few weeks quietly rewiring things in Denver's Capitol Tower. Now, all we have to do is twist a wire on any of the building's speakers — and *bam,* we're broadcasting to the entire Republic." He claps once and snaps his fingers. "*Everyone* will hear you. Revolutionary, yeah?"

Sounds like a more elaborate version of what I did in the alley of the ten-second place, back when I first confronted June in an attempt to get plague cures for Eden. When I'd done a crude rewiring of the alley's speakers. But to rewire a capital building's speakers to broadcast to the entire Republic? "Sounds like fun," I say. "What are we broadcasting?"

Pascao blinks at me in surprise. "The Elector's assassination, of course." His eyes dart to Kaede, who nods, and then he pulls a small rectangular device from his pocket. He flips it open. "We're gonna need to record all the evidence, every last detail as we drag him out of his car and put some bullets in him. Our Hackers will be ready to go at the Capitol Tower, where they've set up the JumboTrons to broadcast the assassination. We'll declare our victory over the speakers to the entire Republic. Let's see them try and stop that."

The savagery of the plan sends chills down my spine. It reminds me of the way they'd taped and broadcasted John's death — *my* death — to the whole country.

Pascao leans toward me, puts his hand against my ear, and whispers, "That's not even the best part, Day." He pulls away long enough to give me another huge, toothy grin. "Want to know what the *best part* is?"

I stiffen. "What?"

Pascao crosses his arms in satisfaction. "Razor thinks *you* should be the one to shoot the Elector."

JUNE

Denver, Colorado.
1937 Hours.
24°F.

I arrive in the capital by train (Station 42B) in the midst of a snowstorm, where a crowd has gathered on the train platform to see me. I peer at them through my frosted window as we slow to a standstill. Even though it's freezing cold outside, these civilians are crowded behind a makeshift metal railing, pushing and shoving one another as if Lincoln or some other celebrity singer had just arrived. No less than two capital military patrols push back against them. Their muffled shouts reach me.

"Get back! Everyone's to move behind the barriers. *Behind* the barriers! Anyone with a camera will be arrested on sight."

It's odd. Most of the civilians here seem poor. Helping Day must have given me a good reputation in the slum sectors. I rub

170

at the thin wires of the paper clip ring on my finger. A habit I've already developed.

Thomas walks over to my aisle and leans over the seats to talk to the soldiers sitting alongside me. "Take her to the door," he says. "Quickly." His eyes flicker to me and then over the outfit I'm wearing (yellow prison vest, thin white collar shirt). He acts as though the conversation we had last night in the interrogation room never happened. I just concentrate on my lap. His face makes me sick to my stomach. "She'll be cold out there," he says to his men. "Make sure she has a coat."

The soldiers point their guns at me (Model XM-2500, 700m range, smart rounds, can shoot through two layers of cement), then haul me to my feet. During the train ride, I'd watched these two soldiers with such intensity that their nerves must be completely shot by now.

My hand shackles clank together. With guns like that, one hit and I'd likely die of blood loss no matter where on my torso the bullet struck me. They probably think I'm planning a way to grab a gun from them when they're not paying attention. (A ridiculous assumption, because with my shackles on I have no way of firing the rifle correctly.)

Now they lead me down the aisle and to the end of our train car, where four more soldiers wait at the open door that leads down to the station platform. A gust of cold wind hits us and I suck in my breath sharply. I've been near the warfront once, back when Metias and I went on our only mission together, but that was West Texas in the summer. I've never set foot in a city buried in snow like this. Thomas heads to the front of our little procession and motions for one of the soldiers to drape a coat over me. I take it gratefully.

The crowd (about ninety to a hundred people) goes completely silent when they see my bright yellow vest, and as I make my way down the steps I can feel their attention burning through me like a heat lamp. Most are shivering, thin and pale with threadbare clothes that can't possibly keep them warm in this weather, wearing shoes riddled with holes. I can't understand it. Despite the cold, they still came out here to see me *get off a train* — and who knows how long they've been waiting. Suddenly I feel guilty for accepting the coat.

We make it to the end of the platform and nearly into the station's lobby when I hear one of the onlookers shouting. I spin around before the soldiers can stop me.

"Is Day alive?" a boy calls out. He's probably older than I am, barely out of his teens, but so skinny and short that he could pass for my age if one didn't pay attention to his face.

I lift my head and smile. Then a guard hits him across the face with the butt of his rifle, and my own soldiers grab my arms and force me back around. The crowd breaks into an uproar; shouts instantly fill the air. In the midst of it all, I hear a few call out, *"Day lives! Day lives!"*

"Keep moving," Thomas barks. We push into the lobby and I feel the cold air cut abruptly off as the door shuts behind us.

I didn't say anything, but my smile was enough. *Yes. Day is alive.* I'm sure the Patriots will appreciate my enforcing this rumor for them.

We make our way through the station and into a trio of waiting jeeps. As we leave the station and head onto an arching freeway, I can't help gaping at the city that's streaming past my window. You usually need a good reason to come to Denver. No one but native civilians are allowed in without specific permission. The fact that I'm here and getting a glimpse of the city's interior is unusual. Everything's smothered under a blanket of white — but even through the snow I can see the faint outline of a vast dark wall that traps Denver like giant levees against floodwaters. The Armor. I read about it during grade school, of course, but to see it with my own eyes is something different. The skyscrapers here are so tall that they disappear into the fog of snow-laden clouds, each terraced level covered in thick sheets of snow, each side secured with giant metal support beams. Between buildings, I catch glimpses of the Capitol Tower. Now and then I see spotlights sweeping through the air and helicopters circling the skyscrapers. At one point, four fighter jets streak by above us. I pause to admire them for a moment (they're X-92 Reapers, experimental aircrafts that haven't gone into production outside the capital yet; but they must have passed their test runs if the engineers trust them to soar right over the center of downtown Denver). The capital is every bit the military city Vegas is, and is even more intimidating than I'd imagined.

Thomas's voice snaps me back to reality. "We're taking you to Colburn Hall," he says from the jeep's front passenger seat. "It's a dining hall in the Capital Plaza where the Senators sometimes convene for banquets. The Elector dines there frequently."

Colburn? From what I've heard, that's a

very fancy meeting spot, especially considering how I was originally meant to stay at the Denver penitentiary. This must all be new info for Thomas, too. I don't think he's ever been inside the capital, but like a good soldier, he doesn't waste any time gawking at the scenery. I find myself anxious to see what the Capital Plaza's like — if it's as large as I've imagined. "From there my patrol will leave you behind, and you'll be passed along to one of Commander DeSoto's patrols." *Razor's patrols,* I add to myself. "The Elector will meet you in the Hall's royal chamber. I suggest you behave appropriately."

"Thanks for the tip," I reply, smiling coldly at Thomas's reflection in the rearview mirror. "I'll be sure to give him my best curtsy." In reality, though, I'm starting to feel nervous. The Elector is someone I've been taught to revere since birth, someone I thought I'd never hesitate to give my life for. Even now, even after everything I know about the Republic, I still feel that deep-rooted commitment trying to resurface, a familiar blanket I want to wrap myself with. Strange. I didn't feel this when I heard about the Elector's death, or when I saw Anden's first televised speech. It's been hidden until now, when I'm only a few hours from seeing him in person.

I'm not the prized prodigy I was when we first met. What will he think of me?

Colburn Hall, Royal Dining Chamber.
It echoes in here. I sit alone at one end of a long table (twelve feet of dark cherrywood, hand-carved legs, ornate gold trim probably painted on with a fine-detail millimeter brush), my back straight against the chair's red velvet cushioning. Far against the opposite wall, a fireplace crackles and pops, with a giant portrait of the new Elector hanging above it, and eight gold lamps light the sides of the chamber. Capital patrol soldiers are *everywhere* — fifty-two line the walls, shoulder to shoulder, and six stand at attention to either side of me. It's still bitterly cold outside, but in here it's warm enough for the servants to have clothed me in a light dress and thin leather boots. My hair has been washed, dried, and brushed, and it falls straight and shining down to the middle of my back. It's been adorned with strands of tiny cultivated pearls (easily worth two thousand Notes apiece). At first I admire them with ginger touches — but then I recall the poor people gathered at the train station in their threadbare clothes, and I pull my fingers away from my hair, dis-

176

gusted with myself. Another servant had dabbed translucent powder across my eyelids so they gleam in the low firelight. My dress, a creamy white accented by stormy grays, flows down to my feet in layers of chiffon. The inner corset makes me short of breath. An expensive dress, no doubt; fifty thousand Notes? Sixty?

The only things that seem out of place in this picture are the heavy metal shackles that bind my ankles and wrists, chaining me down to my chair.

A half hour passes before another soldier (wearing the distinctive black-and-red coat of the capital's patrols) enters the chamber. This one holds the door open, stands at attention, and lifts his chin. "Our glorious Elector Primo is in the building," he announces. "Please rise."

He tries to look like he's talking to no one in particular, but I'm the only one sitting. I push up from my chair and stand with a clink of my chains.

Five more minutes pass. Then, just as I'm starting to wonder whether anyone's going to come at all, a young man steps quietly through the door and nods to the soldiers at the entrance. The guards snap to a salute. I can't salute with these shackled hands, and I can't bow or curtsy properly either —

so I just stay the way I am and face the Elector.

Anden looks almost exactly like he did when I first met him at the celebratory ball — tall and regal and sophisticated, his dark hair tidy, his evening coat a handsome charcoal gray with gold pilot stripes on the sleeves and gold epaulettes on the shoulders. His green eyes are solemn, though, and there's a very slight slouch to his shoulders, as if a new weight had settled there. It seems as though his father's death has affected him after all.

"Sit, please," he says, holding a white gloved hand (condor flight gloves) out in my direction. His voice is very soft, but still carries in the large room. "I hope you've been comfortable, Ms. Iparis."

I do as he says. "I have. Thank you."

Once Anden has seated himself at the other end of the table and the soldiers have all gone back to their regular stances, he speaks again. "I received word that you requested to see me in person. I imagine you don't mind wearing the clothes I've provided." He pauses here for a split second, just enough time for a coy smile to light up his features. "I thought you might not want to spend dinner in a prison uniform."

There's something patronizing about his

tone that grates on my nerves. *How dare he dress me like a doll?* an indignant part of me thinks. At the same time, I'm impressed by his air of command, his ownership of his new status. He has suddenly come into power, a great deal of it, and he wears it so confidently that my old feelings of loyalty press heavily against my chest. The uncertainty he'd once had is quickly disappearing. This man was born to rule. *Anden seems to have developed an attraction to you,* Razor had told me. So I tilt my face down and look up at him through my lashes. "Why are you treating me so well? I thought I was an enemy of the state now."

"I would be ashamed to treat our Republic's most famous prodigy like a prisoner," he says as he carefully straightens his forks, knives, and champagne glass into perfect alignment. "You don't find this unpleasant, do you?"

"Not at all." I glance around the chamber again, memorizing the positions of the lamps, the wall décor, the location of each soldier, and the weapons they carry. The elaborate elegance of this encounter makes me realize that Anden hasn't arranged the dress and the dinner just to be flirtatious. *He wants news about how well he's treating me to leak to the public,* I think. *He wants people to know that the new Elector is taking good care of Day's savior.* My initial distaste wavers — this new thought intrigues me. Anden must be very aware of his poor public reputation. Perhaps he's hoping for the people's support. If that's the case, then he's taking pains to do something that our last Elector cared little about. It also makes me wonder: If Anden is actually looking for public approval, what does he think of Day? He certainly won't win people over by announcing a manhunt for the Republic's most celebrated criminal.

Two servants bring out trays of food (a salad with real strawberries, and exquisitely roasted pork belly with hearts of palm), while two others place fresh white cloth napkins across our laps and pour champagne into our glasses. These servants are from the upper class (they walk with the signature precision of the elite), although probably not of the rank that my family had.

Then the most curious thing happens.

The servant pouring Anden's champagne brings the bottle too close to his glass. It tips over, and the liquid spills all over the tablecloth, then the glass rolls off the table and shatters on the floor.

The servant lets out a squeak and drops to her hands and knees. Red curls tumble out of the neat bun tied behind her head; a few strands fall across her face. I notice how dainty and perfect her hands are — definitely an upper-class girl. "So sorry, Elector," she says over and over. "So sorry. I'll have the cloth changed right away and get you a new glass."

I don't know what I expected Anden to do. Scold her? Give her a stern warning? Frown, at least? But to my shock, he pushes back his chair, stands up, and holds out his hand to her. The girl seems to have frozen. Her brown eyes go wide, and her lips tremble. In one motion Anden leans down, takes both her hands in his, and pulls her up. "It's just a glass of champagne," he says lightly. "Don't cut yourself." Anden waves a hand at one of the soldiers near the door. "A broom and tray, please. Thank you."

The soldier nods in a hurry. "Of course, Elector."

While the servant rushes away for a new glass and a janitor comes in to sweep the broken one safely away, Anden takes his seat again with all the grace of royalty. He picks up a fork and knife with impeccable etiquette, then cuts a small piece of pork. "So tell me, Agent Iparis. Why did you want to see me in person? And *what happened* on the evening of Day's execution?"

I follow his lead, picking up my own fork and knife and cutting into my meat. The chains on my wrists are exactly long enough for me to eat, as if someone had taken the trouble to measure them out. I push the surprise of the champagne incident out of my mind and start planting the story that Razor made up for me. "I *did* help Day escape his execution, and the Patriots helped me. But after it was over, they wouldn't let me go. It seemed like I'd finally gotten away from them when your guards arrested me."

Anden blinks slowly. I wonder if he believes anything I'm saying. "You've been with the Patriots for the last two weeks?" he says after I've finished chewing a slice of pork. The food's exquisite; the meat so tender, it practically melts in my mouth.

"Yes."

"I see." Anden's voice tightens with distrust. He dabs his mouth with a cloth napkin, then puts his silverware down and leans back. "So. Day is alive, or he was when you left him? Is he also working with the Patriots?"

"When I left, he was. I don't know about now."

"Why is he working with them, when he always avoided them in the past?"

I shrug a little, trying to feign puzzlement. "He needs help finding his brother, and he's indebted to the Patriots for fixing his leg. He had an infected bullet wound from . . . all this."

Anden pauses long enough to take a small sip of champagne. "Why did you help him escape?"

I flex my wrist so that the cuffs don't leave imprints against my skin. My shackles clank loudly against each other. "Because he didn't kill my brother."

"Captain Metias Iparis." The sound of my brother's full name sends a wave of anguish through me. Does he know how my brother died? "I'm sorry for your loss." Anden bows his head a little, an unexpected sign of respect that makes a lump rise in my throat.

"I remember reading about your brother when I was younger, you know," he continues. "I read about his grades in school, how well he performed on his Trial, and *especially* how good he was with comps."

I spear a strawberry, chew it thoughtfully, then swallow. "I never knew my brother had such an esteemed fan."

"I wasn't a fan of *him,* per se, although he was certainly impressive." Anden picks up his new champagne glass and sips. "I was a fan of *you.*"

Remember, be obvious. Make him think you're flattered. And attracted to him. He *is* handsome, for sure — so I try to focus on that. The light from the wall lamps catches the wavy edges of his hair, making it shine; his olive skin has a warm, golden glow; his eyes are rich with the color of spring leaves. Gradually I feel a blush growing on my cheeks. *Good, keep going.* He's some mix of Latin blood, but the ever-so-slight slant of his large eyes and the delicateness of his brow reveal a hint of Asian heritage. *Like Day.* Suddenly, my attention scatters, and all I can see is me and Day kissing in that Vegas bathroom. I remember his bare chest, his lips against my neck, his intoxicating defiance that makes Anden pale by comparison. The subtle blush on my cheeks flares into bright heat.

The Elector tilts his head to the side and smiles. I take a deep breath and compose myself. Thank goodness I still managed to get the reaction I was aiming for.

"Have you thought about why the Republic has been so lenient, given your betrayal of the state?" Anden says, toying idly with his fork. "Anyone else would already have been executed. But not you." He straightens in his chair. "The Republic has been watching you since you scored that perfect fifteen hundred on your Trial. I've heard about your grades, and your performance in Drake's afternoon drills. Several Congressmen nominated you for political assignment before you even finished your freshman year at Drake. But they ultimately decided to assign you to the military instead, because your personality has 'officer' written all over it. You're a celebrity in the inner circles. Your being convicted of disloyalty would be a tremendous loss to the Republic."

Does Anden know the *truth* of how my parents and Metias were killed? That their disloyalty cost them their lives? Does the Republic value me so much that they're hesitant to execute me despite my recent crime *and* traitorous family ties? "How did you see me around the Drake campus?" I say. "I don't remember hearing that you visited the university."

Anden cuts into a heart of palm on his plate. "Oh no. You wouldn't have heard it."

I give him a quizzical frown. "Were you . . . a student at Drake while I was there?"

Anden nods. "The administration kept my identity a secret. I was seventeen — a sophomore — when you came to Drake at twelve. We all heard a lot about you, obviously — and your antics." He grins at that, and his eyes sparkle mischievously.

The Elector's son had been walking amongst the rest of us at Drake, and I didn't even know it. My chest swells with pride at the thought of the Republic's leader taking notice of me on campus. Then I shake my head, guilty for liking the attention. "Well, I hope not *everything* you heard was bad."

Anden reveals a dimple in his left cheek when he laughs. It's a soothing sound. "No. Not *everything.*"

Even I have to smile. "My grades were good, but I'm pretty sure my dean's secretary is happy I won't be haunting her office anymore."

"Miss Whitaker?" Anden shakes his head. For a moment he drops his formal façade, ignoring etiquette by slouching back in his chair and making a circular gesture with his fork. "I'd been called in to her office too, which was funny because she had no idea who I was. I'd gotten into trouble for switching out the heavy practice rifles in the gym for foam ones."

"That was *you*?" I exclaim. I remember that incident well. Freshman year, drill class. The foam rifles had looked so real. When the students had bent down in unison to pick up what they thought were heavy guns, they'd all yanked the foam ones up so hard that half the students toppled over

186

backward from the force. The memory gets a real laugh out of me. "That was *brilliant.* The drill captain was so mad."

"Everyone needs to get in trouble at least once in college, right?" Anden smirks and drums his fingers against his champagne glass. "*You* always seemed to cause the most trouble, though. Didn't you force one of your classes to evacuate?"

"Yes. Republic History Three-oh-two." I try to rub my neck in momentary embarrassment, but my shackles stop me. "The senior sitting next to me said I wouldn't be able to hit the fire alarm lever with his training gun."

"Ah. I can see you've always made good choices."

"I was a junior. Still kind of immature, I admit," I reply.

"I disagree. All things considered, I'd say you were well beyond your years." He smiles, and my cheeks turn pink again. "You have the poise of someone much older than fifteen. I was glad to finally meet you at the celebratory ball that night."

Am I really sitting here, eating dinner and reminiscing about good old Academy days with the Elector Primo? Surreal. I'm stunned by how easy it is to talk to him, this discussion of familiar things in a time when so much strangeness surrounds my life, a conversation where I can't accidentally offend anyone with an offhand class-related remark.

Then I remember why I'm really here. The food in my mouth turns to ash. *This is all for Day.* Resentment floods through me, even though I'm wrong for feeling it. Am I? I wonder if I'm really ready to murder someone for his sake.

A soldier peeks through the chamber entrance. He salutes Anden, then clears his throat uncomfortably as he realizes that he must've cut the Elector off in the middle of our conversation. Anden gives him a good-natured smile and waves him in. "Sir, Senator Baruse Kamion wants a word with you," the soldier says.

"Tell the Senator I'm busy," Anden replies. "I'll contact him after my dinner."

"I'm afraid he insisted that you speak to him now. It's about the, ah . . ." The soldier considers me, then hurries over to whisper in Anden's ear. I still catch some of it, though. "The stadiums. He wants to give . . . message . . . should end your dinner right away."

Anden raises an eyebrow. "Is that what he said? Well. I'll decide when my own dinner ends," he says. "Deliver *that* message back

188

to Senator Kamion whenever you see fit. Tell him that the next Senator to send me an impertinent message will answer to me directly."

The soldier salutes vigorously, his chest puffed out a little at the thought of delivering a message like this to a Senator. "Yes, sir. Right away."

"What's your name, soldier?" Anden asks before he can leave.

"Lieutenant Felipe Garza, sir."

Anden smiles. "Thank you, Lieutenant Garza," he says. "I will remember this favor."

The soldier tries to keep a straight face, but I can see pride in his eyes and the smile right below the surface. He bows to Anden. "Elector, you honor me. Thank you, sir." Then he steps out.

I observe the exchange with fascination. Razor had been right about one thing — there is definitely tension between the Senate and their new Elector. But Anden is no fool. He's been in power for less than a week, and already he's doing exactly what he should be: trying to cement the military's loyalty to him. I wonder what else he's doing to win their trust. The Republic army had been fiercely faithful to his father; in fact, that loyalty was probably what made the late Elector so powerful. Anden knows this, and he's making his move as early as possible. The Senate's complaints are useless against a military that backs Anden without question.

But they don't *back Anden without question,* I remind myself. There's Razor, and his men. Traitors in the military's ranks are moving into place.

"So." Anden delicately cuts another slice of pork. "You brought me all the way here to tell me that you helped a criminal escape?"

For a moment there's no sound except the clinking of Anden's fork against his plate. Razor's instructions echo in my mind — the things I need to say, the order I need to say them in. "No . . . I came here to tell you about an assassination plot against you."

Anden puts his fork down and holds two slender fingers up in the direction of the soldiers. "Leave us."

"Elector, sir," one of them starts to say. "We're not to leave you alone."

Anden pulls a gun from his belt (an elegant black model I've never seen before) and places it on the table next to his plate. "It's all right, Captain," he says. "I'll be quite safe. Now, please, everyone. Leave us."

The woman Anden called Captain gestures to her soldiers, and they file silently from the room. Even the six guards standing next to me leave. I am alone in this chamber with the Elector himself, separated by twelve feet of cherrywood.

Anden leans both of his elbows on the table and tents his fingers together. "You came here to warn me?"

"I did."

"But I heard you were *caught* in Vegas. Why didn't you turn yourself in?"

"I was on my way here, to the capital. I wanted to get to Denver before turning myself in so I'd have a better chance of talking to you. I definitely wasn't planning to be arrested by a random patrol in Vegas."

"And how did you get away from the Patriots?" Anden gives me a hesitant, skeptical look. "Where are they now? Surely they must be pursuing you."

I pause, lower my eyes, and clear my throat. "I hopped a Vegas-bound train the night I managed to get away."

Anden stays quiet for a moment, then puts down his fork and dabs his mouth. I'm not sure if he believes my escape story or not. "And what were their plans for you, if you hadn't gotten away?"

Keep it vague for now. "I don't know all the details about what they had planned for me," I reply. "But I do know they're planning some sort of attack at one of your morale-boosting stops along the warfront, and that I was supposed to help them. Lamar, Westwick, and Burlington were places they mentioned. The Patriots have people in place too, Anden — people here in your inner circle."

I know I'm taking a risk by using his first name, but I'm trying to keep our new rapport going. Anden doesn't seem to notice — he just leans over his plate and studies me. "How do you know this?" he says. "Do the Patriots *realize* you know? Is Day involved in all this too?"

I shake my head. "I was never supposed to find out. I haven't spoken to Day since I left."

"Would you say that you're friends with him?"

A bit of an odd question. Maybe he wants to find Day? "Yes," I reply, trying not to distract myself with memories of Day's hands entwined in my hair. "He has his reasons for staying — I have mine for leaving. But yes, I think so."

Anden nods his thanks. "You said there are people in my inner circle that I need to know about. Who?"

I put my fork down and lean forward

across the table. "There are two soldiers in your personal guard who are going to make an attempt."

Anden blanches. "My guards are carefully chosen for me. Very carefully."

"And who chooses *them*?" I cross my arms. My hair falls over one shoulder, and I can see the pearls gleaming from the corner of my eye. "It doesn't matter if you believe me or not. Investigate. Either I'm right, and you won't be dead, or I'm wrong, and then *I'll* be dead."

To my surprise, Anden gets out of his chair, straightens, and walks over to my end of the table. He sits in the chair next to mine and scoots it closer to me. I blink as he studies my face.

"June." His voice is so soft, barely above a whisper. "I want to trust you . . . and I want you to trust me."

He knows I'm hiding something. He can see through my deception, and he wants me to know it. Anden leans against the table and tucks his hands into his trouser pockets. "When my father died," he begins, saying each word slowly and very quietly, as if he were treading dangerous waters, "I was completely alone. I sat at his bedside as he passed. Still, I'm grateful for it — I never had that chance with my mother. I know how it feels, June, being the only one left."

My throat tightens painfully. *Win his trust.* That's my role, my sole reason for being here. "I'm sorry to hear that," I whisper. "And about your mother."

Anden inclines his head, accepting my condolences. "My mother was the Senate's Princeps. My father never once talked about her . . . but I'm glad they're together now."

I'd heard rumors about the late Princeps. How she'd died of some autoimmune disease right after giving birth. Only the Elector can name a leader for the Senate — so there hasn't been one in two decades, not since Anden's mother died. I try to forget the comfort I'd felt while talking to him about Drake, but it's harder to do than I thought. *Think of Day.* I remind myself how excited he'd been about the Patriots' plan, and about a new Republic. "I'm glad your parents are at peace," I say. "I *do* understand how it feels to lose loved ones."

Anden contemplates my words with two fingers pressed to his lips. His jaw looks tight and uncomfortable. *He may have taken ownership of his role, but he's still a boy,* I realize. His father cut a fearsome figure, but Anden? *He's not strong enough to hold this country together by himself.* Suddenly I'm reminded of the early nights after Metias's murder, when I wept until the dark hours before dawn with my brother's lifeless face burned into my thoughts. Does Anden have the same sleepless nights? What must it feel like to lose a father that you aren't allowed to publicly mourn, however evil that father was? *Did* Anden love him?

I wait as he watches me, my dinner long forgotten. After what feels like hours, Anden lowers his hands and sighs. "It's no secret that he'd been ill for a long time. When you've been waiting for a loved one to die . . . for years . . ." He winces visibly here, allowing me to see very naked pain. "Well, I'm sure it is a different feeling from when that passing comes . . . unexpectedly." He looks up at me right as he says the last word.

I'm not sure whether he's referring to my parents or to Metias — perhaps to both — but the way he says it leaves little doubt in my mind. He's trying to say that he knows what happened to my family. And that he *disapproves.*

"I know what your experience with *assumptions* is. Some people think I poisoned my father, so I could take his place."

It's almost like he's trying to talk to me in code. *You'd once assumed that Day had killed your brother. That your parents' deaths were accidents. But now you know the truth.*

"The people of the Republic *assume* that I'm their enemy. That I'm the same man my father was. That I don't want this country to change. They think I'm an empty figurehead, a puppet who simply inherited a throne through my father's will." After a brief hesitation, he turns his eyes on me with an intensity that takes my breath away. "I'm *not*. But if I stay alone . . . if I remain the only one left, then I can't change anything. If I stay alone, I *am* the same as my father."

No wonder he wanted to have this dinner with me. Something groundbreaking is stirring in Anden. *And he needs me.* He doesn't have the people's support, and he doesn't have the Senate's. He needs someone to win over the people for him. And the two people in the Republic with the most power over the people . . . are me and Day.

The turn in this conversation confuses me. Anden isn't — *doesn't seem to be* — the man the Patriots described; a figurehead standing in the way of a glorious revolution. If he actually wants to *win over* the people, if Anden is telling the truth . . . why would the Patriots want him dead? *Maybe I'm missing something. Maybe there's something*

196

about Anden that Razor knows and that I don't.

"Can I trust you?" Anden says. His expression has changed into something earnest, with lifted eyebrows and widened eyes.

I lift my chin and meet his gaze. Can *I* trust *him*? I'm not sure, but for now, I whisper the safe answer. *"Yes."*

Anden straightens and pushes away from the table. I can't quite tell if he believes me. "We'll keep this between us. I'll tell my guards about your warning. I hope we find your pair of traitors." Anden smiles at me, then tilts his head and smiles. "If we do find them, June, I'd like for us to talk again. We seem to have a lot in common." His words make my cheeks burn.

And that's it. "Please, finish dinner at your leisure. My soldiers will bring you back to your cell quarters when you're ready."

I murmur a quiet thanks. Anden turns away and heads out of the chamber as soldiers file back inside, the echoing clatter of their boots breaking the silence that had permeated this space only moments earlier. I turn my head down and pretend to pick at the rest of my food. There's more to Anden than I'd first thought. Only now do I realize that my breath is coming out shorter than usual, and that my heart is racing. Can I

197

trust Anden? Or do I trust Razor? I steady myself against the edge of the table. Whatever the truth is, I'll have to play this all very carefully.

After dinner, instead of being taken to a typical prison cell, I'm delivered to a clean, luxurious apartment, a carpeted chamber with thick double doors and a large, soft bed. There are no windows. Aside from the bed, there's no furniture in the room at all, nothing for me to pick up and turn into a weapon. The only decoration is the ever-present portrait of Anden, embedded into the plaster of one wall. I locate the security cam immediately — it's right above the double doors, a small, subtle knob in the ceiling. A half-dozen guards stand ready outside.

I doze fitfully throughout the night. Soldiers rotate shifts. Early in the morning a guard taps me awake. "So far, so good," she whispers. "Remember who the enemy is." Then she steps out of the chamber and a new guard replaces her.

I dress silently in a warm velvet nightgown, my senses now on high alert, my hands shaking ever so slightly. The shackles on my wrists clank softly. I couldn't have been sure before, but now I *know* that the

Patriots are watching my every step. Razor's soldiers are slowly getting into position and closing in. I might never see that guard again — but now I study the face of every soldier around me, wondering who is loyal, and who is a Patriot.

DAY

Another dream.

I'm up *way* too early on the morning of my eighth birthday. Light has just started filtering in through our windows, chasing away the navy and gray of a disappearing night. I sit up in bed and rub my eyes. A half-empty glass of water balances near the edge of the old night table. Our lone plant — an ivy that Eden dragged home from some junkyard — sits in the corner, vines snaking across the floor, searching for sun. John's snoring loudly in his corner. His feet stick out from under a patched blanket and hang off the end of the cot. Eden's nowhere to be seen; he's probably with Mom.

Usually if I wake up too early I can lie back down and think of something calming, like a bird or a lake, and eventually relax enough to snooze a little longer. But it's no good today. I swing my legs over the side of the bed and pull mismatched socks over my feet.

The instant I step into the living room, I know something's off. Mom lies asleep on the couch with Eden in her arms, the blanket pulled up to her shoulders. But Dad isn't here. My eyes dart around the room. He just got back from the warfront last night, and he usually stays home for at least three or four days. It's too soon for him to be gone.

"Dad?" I whisper. Mom stirs a little and I fall silent again.

Then I hear the faint sound of our screen door against wood. My eyes widen. I hurry over to the door and poke my head outside. A rush of cool air greets me. "Dad?" I whisper again.

At first, no one's there. Then I see his shape emerge from the shadows. *Dad.*

I start running — I don't care if the dirt and pavement scratch me through the threadbare fabric of my socks. The figure in the shadows walks a few more steps, then hears me and turns around. Now I see my father's light brown hair and narrow, honey-colored eyes, that faint scruff on his chin, his tall frame, his effortlessly graceful stance. Mom always said he looked like he stepped right out of some old Mongolian fable. I break into a sprint.

"Dad," I blurt out when I reach him in the shadows. He kneels down and scoops me into his arms. "You're leaving already?"

201

"I'm sorry, Daniel," he whispers. He sounds tired. "I've been called back to the warfront."

My eyes well up with tears. "Already?"

"You need to get back in the house right now. Don't let the street police see you causing a scene."

"But you just got here," I try to argue. "You — it's my birthday today, and I —"

My father puts a hand on each of my shoulders. His eyes are two warnings, full of everything he wishes he could say out loud. *I want to stay,* he's trying to tell me. *But I have to go. You know the drill. Don't talk about this.* Instead, he says, "Go back home, Daniel. Kiss your mother for me."

My voice starts to shake, but I tell myself to be brave. "When will we see you again?"

"I'll come back soon. I love you." He puts a hand on my head. "Keep an eye out for when I come back, all right?"

I nod. He lingers with me for a moment, then gets up and walks away. I go home.

That was the last time I ever saw him.

A day's passed. I'm sitting alone on my assigned Patriot bed in one of the bunk rooms, studying the pendant looped around my neck. My hair falls around my face, making me feel like I'm looking at the pendant through a bright veil. Before my shower earlier, Kaede had

202

given me a bottle of gel that stripped the fake color from my hair. *For the next part of the plan,* she'd told me.

Someone knocks on the door.

"Day?" The voice sounds muffled from the other side of the wood. It takes me a second to reorient myself and recognize Tess. I'd woken up from a nightmare about my eighth birthday. I can still see everything like it happened yesterday, and my eyes feel red and swollen from crying. When I woke up, my mind started producing images of Eden strapped to a gurney, screaming as lab techs inject him with chemicals, and John standing blindfolded before a squad of soldiers. And Mom. I can't stop all this goddy stuff from replaying in my head, and it pisses me off so much. If I find Eden, what then? How the hell do I take him from the Republic? I have to assume that Razor will be able to help me get him back. And in order to get him back, I've absolutely *got* to make sure Anden dies.

My arms are sore from spending most of the morning under Kaede's and Pascao's supervision, learning how to shoot a gun. "Don't worry if you miss the Elector," Pascao said as we worked on my aim. He ran his hands along my arm enough to make me blush. "Won't matter. There will be others with you who will finish the job, regardless. Razor just wants the *image* of you pointing a gun at the Elector. Isn't it perfect? The Elector, at the warfront to give morale-boosting speeches to the soldiers, gunned down with hundreds of troops in the vicinity. Oh, the irony!" Pascao then gave me one of his signature grins. "The people's hero kills the tyrant. What a story that will be."

Yeah — what a story, indeed.

"Day?" Tess says from behind the door. "Are you in there? Razor wants to talk to you." Oh, right. She's still out there, calling for me.

"Yeah, you can come in," I reply.

Tess pokes her head inside. "Hey," she says. "How long have you been in here?"

Be good to her, Kaede had told me. *You two match.* I shoot Tess a small smile in greeting. "No idea," I reply. "I was getting some rest. Couple hours, maybe?"

"Razor's asking for you out in the main room. They're running a live feed of June. I thought you might be —"

Live feed? *She must have made it. She's still okay.* I jump to my feet. Finally, an update on June — the thought of seeing her again, even if it's on a grainy security cam, makes me dizzy with anticipation. "I'll be right out."

As we head down the short hall toward the main room, a number of other Patriots greet Tess. She smiles each time, exchanging gentle jokes and laughs as if she's known them forever. Two boys give her good-natured pats on her shoulder.

"Hurry the hell up, kids. Don't wanna keep Razor waiting." We both turn to see Kaede jog past us in the direction of the main room. She pauses to swing one arm around Tess's neck, then ruffles her hair lovingly and plants a playful kiss on her cheek. "I swear — you're the slowest of the bunch, sweetheart."

Tess laughs and shoves her off. Kaede winks back before picking up her pace, disappearing around the corner into the main room. I look on, a little surprised at Kaede's display of affection. Not something I'd expect from her. I'd never thought about it before, but now I realize just how good Tess is at forming new bonds — I sense the Patriots' ease around her, the same ease I'd always felt with her on the streets. That's her strength, no doubt. She heals. She's comforting.

Then Baxter passes us. Tess turns her eyes downward as he brushes her arm, and I notice him give her a brief nod before glaring at me. When he's out of earshot, I lean over to Tess. "What's his deal?" I whisper.

She just shrugs and brushes my arm with her hand. "Don't mind him," she replies, repeating what Kaede had said back when I first arrived at the tunnel. "He has mood swings."

Tell me about it, I think darkly. "If he gives you a hard time, let me know," I mutter.

Tess shrugs again. "It's okay, Day. I can handle him."

I suddenly feel a little stupid, offering my help like an arrogant knight in shining armor when Tess probably has dozens of new friends eager to help her out. When she can help herself.

By the time we've made it out to the main room, a small crowd has gathered in front of one of the larger wall screens, where a tape of security cam footage is playing. Razor is near the front of the crowd with his arms casually crossed, while Pascao and Kaede stand beside him. They see me and motion me over.

"Day," Razor says, clapping me on the shoulder. Kaede gives me a quick nod in greeting. "Good to see you here. Are you okay? I heard you've been a little down this morning."

His concern's actually kinda nice — it reminds me of the way my father used to talk to me. "I'm fine," I reply. "Just tired from the trip."

"Understandable. It was a stressful flight." He gestures up to the screen. "Our Hackers got us footage of June. The audio's separated out, but you'll get to hear it soon enough. I thought you'd want to see the video regardless."

My eyes are glued to the screen. The images are crisp and colorful, as if we're hovering right there in the corner of the room. I see an ornate dining chamber with an elegantly decorated dinner table and soldiers lining the walls. The young Elector is seated at one end of the table. June sits at the other, wearing a gorgeous dress that makes my heartbeat speed up. When *I'd* been the Republic's prisoner, they'd beaten me to a pulp and thrown me in a dirty cell. June's incarceration seems more like a vacation. I'm relieved for her, but at the same time, I'm a little bitter. Even after betraying the Republic, people with June's pedigree get to coast, while people like me suffer.

Everyone watches me watching June. "Glad she's doing good," I say to the screen. Already I'm disgusted with myself for dwelling on such mean thoughts.

"Clever of her to start talking to the Elector about their college years at Drake," Razor says, summarizing the audio as the video plays. "She planted the story. They're going to have her take a lie detector test next, I'd imagine, and we'll have a straight path to Anden if she's good enough to pass it. Our

207

next phase tomorrow night should run smoothly."

If *she's good enough to pass it.* An early bond. "Good," I reply, trying not to let my face betray my thoughts. But as the footage continues, and I see Anden order the soldiers out of the chamber, I feel a knot tighten in my throat. This guy's all sophistication, power, and authority. He leans close to say something to June, and they laugh and drink champagne. I can picture them together. They match.

"She *is* doing a good job," Tess says, tucking her hair behind her ears. "The Elector's completely into her."

I want to dispute this, but Pascao chimes in brightly. "Tess's totally right — see that glow in his eyes? That's a man won over right there, I can tell you that. He's head over heels for our girl. She'll have him completely hooked in a couple days."

Razor nods, but his enthusiasm is more subdued. "True," he says. "But we'll need to make sure Anden doesn't get into June's head too. He's a born politician. I'll find a way to have a word with June."

I'm glad that Razor speaks sense and caution during a time like this, but I have to turn away from the screen now. I never considered the idea that he might be able to get into June's head.

Everyone's comments fade as I stop listening. Tess is right, of course; I can see the desire on the Elector's face. He gets up now and walks to where June sits shackled to the chair, then leans in close to talk to her. I wince. How could anyone resist June? She's perfect in too many ways. Then I realize that I'm not upset over Anden's attraction to her — he's gonna be dead soon anyway, right? What makes me sick is that June doesn't look like she's faking her laughter in this video. She almost seems to be having a good time. She's on par with men like him: aristocrats. Made for the Republic's upper-class life. How can she ever be happy with someone like me, someone with nothing but a handful of paper clips in his pockets? I turn and start to walk away from the crowd. I've seen all I want to see.

"Wait up!"

I look over my shoulder to see Tess hurrying after me, her hair flying into her face. She skids into step beside me. "Are you okay?" she asks, studying my expression as we head back down the hall toward my room.

"I'll be fine," I reply. "Why shouldn't I be? Everything's going just . . . perfectly." I give her a tense smile.

"Okay. I know. I just want to make sure." Tess gives me a dimpled grin, and I soften toward her again.

"I'm fine, cousin. Seriously. You're safe, I'm safe, the Patriots are on track, and they'll help me find Eden. That's all I can ask for."

Tess brightens at my words, and her lips curl up into a teasing smirk. "There's been some gossip about you, you know."

I lift my eyebrows playfully. "Oh, really? What kind of gossip?"

"Rumors that you're alive and well are spreading like wildfire — it's all anyone's talking about. Your name's spray-painted on walls all over the country, even over the *Elector's* portraits in some places. Can you believe that? Protests are popping up everywhere. They're all chanting your name." Tess's energy wanes some. "Even the quarantined folks in Los Angeles. I guess the whole city's under quarantine now."

"They've sealed *Los Angeles*?" This takes me aback. We'd learned about the gem sectors being fenced off, but I've never heard of such a large-scale quarantine. "What for? The plagues?"

"Not for the plagues." Tess's eyes get wider with excitement. "For *riots.* The Republic's broadcasting it officially as a plague quarantine, but the truth is that the whole city's rebelling against the new Elector. Rumors are spreading that the Elector is hunting you down with everything he's got, and some Patriots are telling people that Anden was the one who ordered — er, who ordered your family's . . ." Tess hesitates, turning bright red. "Anyway, the Patriots are trying to make Anden sound bad, worse than his father. Razor says the LA protests are a great opportunity for us. The capital has had to call in thousands of extra troops."

"A great opportunity," I echo, remembering how the Republic had put down the last protest in Los Angeles.

"Yep, and it's all thanks to you, Day. You triggered it — or, at least, the rumor that you're alive did. They're inspired by your escape, and *pissed* about how you're being treated. You're the one thing the Republic can't seem to control. Everybody's looking to you, Day. They're waiting for your next move."

I swallow, not daring to believe it. That can't be possible — the Republic would never let rebellions get that far out of control in one of the country's biggest cities. Would they? Are the people actually overwhelming the local military there? And are they rebelling because of me? *They're waiting for your next move.* But hell if *I* even know what that's supposed to be. I'm just trying to find my brother — that's it, that's all. I shake my head, forcing down a sudden tide of fear. I'd *wanted* the power to fight back, yeah? That's what I was *trying* to do for all these years, wasn't I? Now they're handing the power to me . . . but I don't know what to do with it. "Yeah, right," I manage to reply. "Are you kidding me? I'm just a street con from LA."

"Yeah. A famous one." Tess's infectious smile instantly lightens my mood. She nudges me in the arm as we reach the door to my room. We step inside. "Come on, Day. Don't you remember why the Patriots agreed to recruit you in the first place? Razor said you could become as powerful as the new Elector himself. Everybody in the country knows who you are. And most of them actually *like* you. Something to be proud of, yeah?"

I just walk over to my bed and sit down. I don't even notice right away that Tess seats herself beside me.

She sobers at my silence. "You really care about this one, don't you?" she says, smoothing the covers over the bed with one hand. "She's not like the girls you used to fool around with in Lake."

"What?" I reply, confused for a second. Tess thinks I'm still brooding about Anden's infatuation with June. Tess's own cheeks are turning pink now, and I suddenly feel uncomfortably warm sitting alone with her, her big eyes fixed on me, her crush unmistakable. I've always been smooth at handling girls who've liked me, but they were strangers. Girls who'd pass in and out of my life without consequence. Tess is different. I don't know what to do with the idea that we could be more than friends. "Well, what do you want me to say?" I ask. I want to hit myself as soon as it comes out of my mouth.

"Stop worrying — I'm sure she'll be *fine.*" She spits out that last word with sudden venom, then goes quiet again. Yeah, I definitely said the wrong thing.

"I didn't join the Patriots because I *wanted* to, you know." Tess rises from the bed and stands over me, her back stiff, her hands clenching and unclenching. "I joined the Patriots because of *you.* Because I was worried sick about you after *June* took you away and arrested you. I thought I could talk them into saving you — but I don't have the bargaining power June has. June can do whatever she wants to you, and you'd still take her back. June can do anything she wants to the *Republic,* and they'll take her back too." Tess raises her voice. "Whenever *June* needs something, she gets results, but my needs aren't worth a bucket of pig's blood. Maybe if *I* were the Republic's darling, you'd care about *me* too."

Her words cut deep. "That's not true," I say,

213

getting up and grabbing her hands. "How could you even say that? We grew up on the streets together. You have any idea what that means to me?"

She purses her lips tight and looks up, trying not to cry. "Day," she begins again, "have you ever wondered *why* you like June so much? I mean — well — given how you were arrested and all —"

I shake my head. "What do you mean?"

She takes a deep breath. "I've heard of this thing somewhere before, on the JumboTrons or something, where they were talking about prisoners from the Colonies. About how kidnapping victims fall for their captors."

I frown. The Tess I know is fading away into a cloud of suspicion and dark thoughts. "You think I like June because she *arrested* me? You really think I'm that twisted in the head?"

"Day?" Tess says carefully. "June turned you in."

I throw down Tess's hands. "I don't want to talk about this."

Tess shakes her head mournfully, her eyes glossy with unshed tears. "She killed your mother, Day."

I take a step back from Tess. I feel like I've been slapped in the face. "*She* didn't do it," I say.

"She may as well have," Tess whispers.

I can feel my defenses rising up again, closing me off. "You're forgetting that she also helped me escape. She saved me. Look, are you —"

"I've saved you dozens of times. But if *I* turned you in, and your family *died* for it, would you forgive me?"

I swallow. "Tess, I'd forgive you for just about anything."

"Even if I was responsible for your mom's *death*? No, I don't think you would." She fixes her eyes on mine. Her voice carries a hint of harshness now, armored with an edge of steel. "That's what I mean. You treat June differently."

"Doesn't mean I don't care about you."

Tess ignores my reply and barrels on. "If you had to choose between saving either me or June, and you had no time to waste . . . what would you do?"

I can feel my face going red as my frustration builds.

"Who would you save?" Tess uses a sleeve to wipe her face and waits for my answer.

I sigh impatiently. Just tell her the goddy truth. "You, all right? I'd save *you*."

She softens, and in that moment the ugliness of jealousy and hate is smoothed away. All it takes is a little sweetness for Tess to turn back into an angel. "Why?"

215

"I don't know." I run a hand through my hair, unable to figure out why I can't take control of this conversation. "Because June wouldn't need my help."

Stupid, so stupid. I almost couldn't have said anything worse. The words spilled out before I could stop myself, and now it's too late to take them back. *That's not even the right reason.* I would've saved Tess because she's *Tess,* because I can't bear to imagine something happening to her. But I don't have time to explain that. Tess turns and starts walking away from me. "Thanks for your pity," she says.

I hurry over to her, but when I take her hand, she jerks away. "I'm sorry. That's not what I meant. I don't pity you. Tess, I —"

"It's fine," she snaps. "It's just the truth, yeah? Well, you'll be reunited with June soon enough. If she decides not to go back to the Republic." She knows how cold her words are, but she doesn't try to sugarcoat them. "Baxter thinks you're going to betray us, you know. That's why he doesn't like you. He's been try- ing to convince me of that ever since I first joined. I dunno . . . maybe he's right."

She leaves me standing alone in the hall. Guilt slices through my skin, opening veins as it goes. A part of me is angry — I want to defend June, and tell Tess all the things June had given up for my sake. But . . . *is Tess right*? Am I just deluding myself?

JUNE

I had a nightmare last night. I dreamt that Anden pardoned Day for all his crimes. Then I saw the Patriots dragging Day onto a dark street and putting a bullet in his chest. Razor turned to me and said, *"Your punishment, Ms. Iparis, for working with the Elector."* I jerked awake in a sweat, trembling uncontrollably.

A day and night (more specifically, twenty-three hours) pass before I see the Elector again. This time I meet him in a lie detection room.

As guards lead me down the hall to an ensemble of waiting jeeps outside, I go over all the things I've learned at Drake about how lie detectors work. The examiner's going to try to intimidate me; they're going to use my weaknesses against me. They'll use Metias's death, or my parents, or maybe even Ollie. They'll certainly use Day. So I concentrate on the hall we're walking down, think about each of my weaknesses in turn, and then press each one deep into the back of my mind. I silence them.

We drive through the capital for several blocks. This time I see the city smothered in the gray half glow of a snowy morning, soldiers and workers hurrying along the sidewalks through the spots of light that streetlamps cast on the slick pavement. The JumboTrons here are enormous, some towering fifteen stories, and the speakers lining the buildings are newer than those in LA — they don't make the announcer's voice crackle. We pass the Capitol Tower. I study its slick walls, how sheets of glass protect each balcony so anyone giving a speech will be properly shielded. The old Elector had once been attacked that way, back before the glass went up — someone had tried to shoot at him all the way up on the fortieth floor. The Republic had been quick to put up the barriers after that. The Tower's JumboTrons have wet streaks distorting the images on their screens, but I can still read some of the headlines as we pass them.

A familiar one catches my attention.

DANIEL ALTAN WING EXECUTED DEC. 26 BY FIRING SQUAD

Why are they still broadcasting that, when all the other headlines from the same time have long since made way for more recent news? *Maybe they're trying to convince people that it's true.*

Another one flashes by.

ELECTOR TO ANNOUNCE FIRST LAW OF NEW YEAR TODAY AT DENVER CAPITOL TOWER

I want to pause and read this headline again — but the car speeds past and then the ride's over. My car door opens. Soldiers grab my arms and pull me out. I'm instantly deafened by shouts from the crowd of onlookers and dozens of federal press reporters clicking their little square camera screens at me. When I take in the people surrounding us, I notice that in addition to those who are here just to see me, there are others. A *lot* of others. They're protesting in the streets, shouting slurs about the Elector, and being dragged off by police. Several wave homemade signs over their heads even as guards take them away.

June Iparis Is Innocent! says one.

Where Is Day? says another.

One of the guards nudges me forward. "Nothing for you to see," he snaps, hurrying me up a long series of steps and into the giant corridor of some government building. Behind us, the noise from outside fades away into the echoes of our footsteps. Ninety-two seconds later, we stop before a set of wide glass doors. Then someone scans a thin card (about three by five inches large, black, with a reflective sheen and a gold Republic seal logo in one corner) across the entry screen, and we step in.

The lie detection room is cylindrical, with a low domed roof and twelve silver columns lining the rounded wall. Guards strap me standing into a machine that encircles my arms and wrists with metal bands, and press cold metal nodes (fourteen of them) onto my neck and cheeks and forehead, my palms and ankles and feet. There are so many soldiers in here — twenty in total. Six of them are the examination team, with white armbands and transparent green shades. The doors are made of flawlessly clear glass (it's imprinted with a faint symbol of a circle cut in half, which means it's one-way bulletproof glass, so if I somehow broke free, soldiers outside the room could shoot me through the glass but I wouldn't be able to shoot back at them or break out). Outside the room, I see Anden standing with two Senators and twenty-four more guards. He looks unhappy, and is deep in conversation with the Senators, who try to cloak their displeasure with fake, obedient smiles.

"Ms. Iparis," the lead examiner says. Her eyes are a very pale green, her hair blond, her skin porcelain white. She scrutinizes my face calmly before pressing on a small black device she's holding in her right hand. "My name is Dr. Sadhwani. We're going to ask you a series of questions. As you are a former Republic agent, I'm sure you understand as well as I do how capable these machines are. We'll catch the smallest twitch of movement from you. The slightest trembling of your hands. I strongly advise you to tell us the truth."

Her words are all just pretest hype — she's trying to convince me of the complete power of this lie detection device. She thinks the more I fear it, the more reaction I'll show. I meet her eyes. *Take slow, normal breaths. Eyes relaxed, mouth straight.* "Fine with me," I reply. "I have nothing to hide."

The doctor busies herself studying the nodes stuck to my skin, then the projections of my face that are probably being broadcast around the room behind me. Her own eyes are darting around nervously, and tiny beads of sweat are dotting the very top of her forehead. She's probably never tested such a well-known enemy of the state before, and certainly not in front of someone as important as the Elector.

As expected, Dr. Sadhwani starts with simple, irrelevant questions. "Is your name June Iparis?"

"Yes."

"When is your birthday?"

"July eleventh."

"And your age?"

"Fifteen years, five months, and twenty-eight days." My tone stays flat and emotionless. Each time I answer, I pause for several seconds and let my breathing become shallower, which in turn makes my heart pump faster. If they're measuring my physical rates, then let them see fluctuations during the control questions. It'll make it harder to tell when I'm actually lying.

"What grade school did you attend?"

"Harion Gold."

"And after that?"

"Be specific," I reply.

Dr. Sadhwani recoils slightly, then recovers. "All right, Ms. Iparis," she says, this time with irritation in her voice. "What high school did you attend after Harion Gold?"

I face the audience watching me behind the glass. The Senators avoid my stare by pretending fascination with the wires snaking around me, but Anden looks back at me without hesitation. "Harion High."

"For how long?"

"Two years."

"And then —"

I let my temper go up, so that they might think I'm having trouble controlling my emotions (and my exam results). "And then I spent three years at Drake University," I snap. "I got accepted when I was twelve and graduated when I was fifteen, because I was just *that* good. Does that answer your question?"

She hates me now. "Yes," she says tightly.

"Good. Then let's move on."

The examiner purses her lips and looks back down at her black device so she doesn't have to meet my eyes. "Have you ever lied before?" she asks.

She's moving on to more complicated questions. I speed up my breathing again. "Yes."

"Have you lied to any military or government officials?"

"Yes."

Right after I answer this question, I see a strange series of sparks at the edges of my vision. I blink twice. They disappear, and the room comes back into focus. I hesitate for a second — but when Dr. Sadhwani notices this and types something on her device, I force myself to turn back into a blank slate.

"Have you ever lied to any of your professors at Drake?"

"No."

"Have you ever lied to your brother?"

Suddenly the room vanishes. A shimmering image replaces it — a familiar living room bathed in warm afternoon light comes into focus, and a white puppy sleeps next to my feet. A tall, dark-haired teenager sits next to me with his arms crossed. It's Metias. He frowns and leans forward with his elbows resting on his knees.

"Have you ever lied to me, June?"

I blink in shock at the scene. *This is all fake,* I tell myself. *The lie detector is conjuring up illusions that are designed to break me down.* I'd heard of devices like this being used near the warfront, where a machine can simulate sequences to play out in your mind by copying the brain's ability to create vivid dreams. But Metias looks so real, it's like I could reach out and tuck his dark hair behind his ear, or feel my tiny hand in his large one. I can almost believe that I'm right there in the room with him. I close my eyes, but the image stays embedded in my mind, bright as daylight.

"Yes," I say. It's the truth. Metias's eyes go wide with surprise and sadness, then he vanishes along with Ollie and the rest of the apartment. I'm back in the middle of the gray lie detector room, standing before Dr. Sadhwani as she jots down more notes. She gives me an approving nod for answering correctly. I try to steady my hands as they stay clenched and trembling at my sides.

"Very good," she murmurs a moment later.

My words sound as cold as ice. "Do you plan on using my brother against me for the rest of these questions?"

She looks away from her notes again. "You saw your brother?" She seems more relaxed now, and the sweat on her forehead has faded away.

So. They can't control what visions pop up, and they can't see what I see. But they're able to trigger something that forces these memories up to the surface. I keep my head high and my eyes on the doctor. "Yes."

The questions continue. *Which grade did you skip during your time at Drake?* Sophomore year. *How many conduct warnings did you receive when you were at Drake?* Eighteen. *Prior to your brother's death, had you ever had negative thoughts about the Republic?* No.

On and on. She's trying to desensitize my brain, I realize, to make me lower my guard so she'll be able to see a physical reaction when she does ask something relevant. Twice more I see Metias. Each time it happens, I take a deep breath and force myself to hold it in for several seconds. They grill me about how I escaped from the Patriots, what the bombing mission was for. I repeat what I'd told Anden at our dinner. So far, so good. The detector says I've told the truth.

"Is Day alive?"

And then Day materializes in front of me. He's standing only a few feet away, with blue eyes so reflective that I can see myself in them. An easy grin lights up his face when he sees me. Suddenly I ache for him so much that I feel like I'm falling. *He's not real. This is all a simulation.* I let my breathing steady. "Yes."

"Why did you help Day escape, when you knew that he's wanted for so many crimes against the Republic? Might you have feelings for him?"

A dangerous question. I harden my heart against it. "No. I simply didn't want him to die at my hands for the one crime he didn't commit."

The doctor pauses in her note-taking to raise an eyebrow at me. "You risked an awful lot for someone you hardly know."

I narrow my eyes. "*That* doesn't say much about your character. Perhaps you should wait until someone's about to be executed for a mistake *you* made."

She doesn't respond to the acid in my words. The illusion of Day vanishes. I get a few more irrelevant control questions, then: "Are you and Day affiliated with the Patriots?"

Day appears again. This time he leans in close enough for his hair to brush, light as silk, against my cheeks. He pulls me toward him for a long kiss. The scene vanishes, replaced abruptly by a stormy night and Day struggling through the rain, blood dripping from his leg and leaving a trail behind him. He collapses onto his knees in front of Razor before the whole scene disappears again. I fight to keep my voice steady. *"I was."*

"Is there going to be an assassination attempt on our glorious Elector?"

No need for me to lie on this one. I let my gaze wander to Anden, who nods at me in what I assume is encouragement. "Yes."

"And are the Patriots aware that you know

about their assassination plans?"

"No, they are not."

Dr. Sadhwani looks over at her colleagues, and after several seconds she nods and turns back to me. *The detector says I've told the truth.* "Are there soldiers close to the Elector who may support this assassination attempt?"

"Yes."

Several more seconds of silence while she checks with her colleagues on my answer. Again, she nods. This time she turns around to face Anden and his Senators. "She's telling the truth."

Anden nods back. "Good," he says, his voice muffled through the glass. "Continue, please." The Senators keep their arms crossed and their lips tight.

Dr. Sadhwani's questions are ceaseless, drowning me in their never-ending torrent. *When will the assassination attempt take place?* On the Elector's planned route to the warfront city of Lamar, Colorado. *Do you know where the Elector will be safe?* Yes. *Where should he go instead?* A different border city. *Is Day going to be a part of this assassination attempt?* Yes. *Why is he involved?* He's indebted to the Patriots for fixing his injured leg.

229

"Lamar," Dr. Sadhwani murmurs as she types more notes into her black device. "I guess the Elector will be switching his route."

Another piece of the plan falls into place.

The questions finally come to an end. Dr. Sadhwani turns away from me to talk with the others, while I let a breath out and sag against the detector machine. I've been in here for exactly two hours and five minutes. My eyes meet Anden's. He's still standing near the glass doors, surrounded on both sides by soldiers, his arms crossed tightly over his chest.

"Wait," he says. The examiners pause in their deliberations to look over at their Elector. "I have a last question for our guest."

Dr. Sadhwani blinks and waves at me. "Of course, Elector. Please."

Anden walks closer to the glass separating us. "Why are you helping me?"

I push back my shoulders and meet his eyes. "Because I want to be pardoned."

"Are you loyal to the Republic?"

A final collage of memories comes into focus. I see myself holding my brother's hand on the streets of our Ruby sector, our arms raised in salute to the JumboTrons as we recite the pledge. There's Metias's face, his smile and also his strained look of worry

230

on the last night I saw him. I see the Republic flags at my brother's funeral. Metias's secret online entries scroll past my eyes — his words of warning, his anger at the Republic. I see Thomas pointing his gun at Day's mother; I see her head snap backward at the bullet's impact. She crumples. It's my fault. I see Thomas clutching his head in the interrogation room, tortured, blindingly obedient, forever captive to what he did.

I'm not loyal anymore. Am I still loyal? I am right here in the Republic's capital, helping the Patriots assassinate the new Elector. A man I once pledged my allegiance to. I am going to kill him, and then I'm going to run away. I know that the lie detector is going to reveal my betrayal — I'm distracted, consumed with the conflict of needing to make things right with Day, but hating to leave the Republic at the mercy of the Patriots.

A shudder runs through me. *They're just images. Just memories.* I remain silent until my heartbeat steadies. I close my eyes, take a deep breath, and then open them again. "Yes," I say. "I am loyal to the Republic."

I wait for the lie detector to flare red, to beep, to reveal that I'm lying. But the machine is quiet. Dr. Sadhwani keeps her head down and types in her notepad.

"She's telling the truth," Dr. Sadhwani finally says.

I've passed. I can't believe it. The machine says I'm telling the truth. But it's only a machine.

Later that night, I sit on the edge of my bed with my head in my hands. Shackles still hang from my wrists, but otherwise I'm free to move around. I can still hear the sounds of occasional muffled conversation outside my room, though. *Those* guards are still there.

I'm so exhausted. I shouldn't be, technically, since I haven't done anything physically straining since I was first arrested. But Dr. Sadhwani's questions whirl in my mind and combine with the things Thomas had said to me, haunting me until I have to clutch my head in an attempt to ward off the headache. Somewhere out there, the government is debating whether or not they should pardon me. I'm shivering a little, even though I know the room is warm.

Classic signs of an oncoming illness, I think darkly. *Maybe it's the plague.* The irony of that sends a hint of sadness — and fear — through me. *But I'm vaccinated.* It's probably just a cold — after all, Metias had always said I was a little sensitive to changes in weather.

Metias. Now that I'm alone, I let myself worry. My last answer during the lie detector test should have thrown a red flag. But it didn't. Does that mean I *am* still loyal to the Republic, without even being aware of it? Somewhere, deep down, the machine could sense my doubts about carrying out the assassination.

But if I decide not to play out my role, what will happen to Day? I'll need a way to contact him without Razor finding out. *And then what?* Day's certainly not going to see the Elector the way I see him. And besides, I have no backup plan. *Think, June.* I have to come up with an alternative that will keep us all alive.

If you want to rebel, Metias had told me, *rebel from* inside *the system.* I keep dwelling on this memory, although my shivering makes it hard to concentrate.

Suddenly I hear a commotion outside the door. There's the sound of heels clicking smartly together, the telltale sign of an official coming to see me. I wait quietly. The doorknob finally turns. Anden steps in.

"Elector, sir, are you sure you don't want a few guards with you —"

Anden just shakes his head and waves a

hand at the soldiers outside the door. "Please, don't trouble yourselves," he says. "I'd like a private word with Ms. Iparis. It'll only take a minute." His words remind me of the ones I spoke when I'd visited Day in his cell at Batalla Hall.

The soldier gives Anden a quick salute and closes the door, leaving the two of us alone. I look up from where I'm sitting on the edge of my bed. The shackles that bind my hands clink in the silence. The Elector isn't in his usual formal garb; instead he wears a full-length black coat with a red stripe that runs down the front, and the rest of his clothes are elegantly simple (black collar shirt, a dark waistcoat with six shining buttons, black trousers, black pilot boots). His hair is glossy and neatly combed. A lone gun hangs at his waist, but he wouldn't be able to draw it fast enough to shoot me if I decided to attack him. He's genuinely trying to show his faith in me.

Razor had told me that if I was to find a moment when I could assassinate Anden on my own, I should do it. Take the opportunity. But now here he is, unexpectedly vulnerable before me, and I don't make a single gesture. Besides, if I try to kill him here, there's zero chance I'll see Day again — or survive.

Anden sits down beside me, careful to leave some distance between us. Suddenly I'm embarrassed by my appearance — slouched and weary, with undone hair and nightclothes, seated next to the Republic's handsome prince. But I still straighten and tilt my head up as gracefully as I can. *I am June Iparis,* I remind myself. I'm not going to let him see the chaos I'm feeling.

"I wanted to let you know that you were right," he starts. There's genuine warmth in his voice. "Two soldiers in my guard went missing this afternoon. Ran away."

The two Patriot decoys have escaped, as planned. I sigh and give him a rehearsed look of relief, just in case Razor is watching. "Where are they now?"

"We're not sure. Scouts are trying to track them." Anden rubs his gloved hands together for a moment. "Commander DeSoto has instated a new rotation of soldiers that will accompany us."

Razor. He is putting his own soldiers in place, gradually moving in for the kill.

"I'd like to thank you for your help, June," Anden goes on. "I want to apologize for the lie detector test you had to undergo. I know it must have been unpleasant for you, but it was necessary. At any rate, I'm grateful for your honest answers. You'll stay here with us for a few more days, until we're sure the danger of the Patriots' plans is past. We may still have some questions for you. After that, we will figure out how to integrate you back into the Republic's ranks."

"Thank you," I say, even though the words are completely hollow.

Anden leans in. "I meant what I said at our dinner," he whispers, his words rushed and his mouth barely moving. He's nervous. A sudden paranoia seizes me — I tap a finger against my lips and give him a pointed look. His eyes widen, but he doesn't shy away. He gently touches my chin, then pulls me toward him as if he were going to kiss me. He stops his lips right beside my own, letting them rest ever so slightly against the skin of my lower cheek. Tingles run down my spine and along with them, an undercurrent of guilt.

"So the cams don't pick it up," he whispers. This is a better way to talk in private; if a guard were to poke his head inside the door, it would seem like Anden's stealing a kiss instead of whispering with me. A safer rumor to spread. And the Patriots would just think I'm going along with their plans.

Anden's breath is warm against my skin. "I need your help," he murmurs. "If you were pardoned of all crimes against the

Republic and set free, would you be able to contact Day? Or is your relationship with him over now that you're not with the Patriots?"

I bite my lip. The way Anden says *relationship* makes it sound like he thinks there was once something between Day and me. Once. "Why do you want me to contact him?" I ask.

His words have a quiet, commanding urgency that gives me goose bumps. "You and Day are the most celebrated people in the Republic. If I can form an alliance with you both, I can win the people. Then instead of quelling rebellions and trying to keep things from falling apart, I can concentrate on implementing the changes this country needs."

I feel light-headed. This is sudden, startling, and for a moment I can't even think of a good response. Anden is taking a huge risk talking to me like this. I swallow, my cheeks still burning from his proximity. I shift a little so I can see his eyes. "Why should we trust you?" I say, my voice steady. "What makes you think Day wants to help you?"

Anden's eyes are clear with purpose. "I'm going to change the Republic, and I'm going to start by releasing Day's brother."

My mouth turns dry. Suddenly I wish we were talking loud enough for Day to hear. "You're going to release Eden?"

"He never should have been taken in the first place. I'll release him along with any others being used along the warfront."

"Where is he?" I whisper. "When are you —"

"Eden has been traveling along the warfront for the past few weeks. My father had taken him, along with a dozen others, as part of a new war initiative. They're basically being used as living biological weapons." Anden's face darkens. "I'm going to stop this mad circus. Tomorrow my order will go out — Eden will be taken from the warfront and cared for in the capital."

This is new. This changes everything.

I have to find a way to tell Day about Eden's release, before he and the Patriots kill the one person with the power to free him. What's the best way to communicate with him? *The Patriots must be watching all of my moves from the cams,* I think, letting my mind spin. I'll need to signal him. Day's face appears in my thoughts and I want to run to him. I want so much to tell him this good news.

Is it good news? My practical side pulls at me, warning me to take this slowly. Anden might be lying, and this could all be a trap. But if it was just another attempt to arrest Day, then why wouldn't he just threaten to kill Eden? That would bring Day out of hiding. Instead, he's letting Eden go.

Anden waits patiently through my silence. "I need Day to trust me," he murmurs.

I put my arms around his neck and move my lips closer to his ear. He smells like sandalwood and clean wool. "I'll need to find a way to contact him, and convince him. But if you release his brother, he *will* trust you," I whisper back.

"I'm going to win your trust too. I want you to have faith in me. I have faith in *you*. I've had faith in you for a very long time." He's quiet for a second. His breathing has quickened, and his eyes change abruptly. Gone is that sense of distant authority, and in this moment he's just a young man, a human being, and the electricity between us is too much. In an instant, he turns his face and his lips meet mine.

I close my eyes. It is so light. Barely there, yet I can't help but want a little more. With Day, there's a fire and a hunger between us, even anger, some deep desperation and need. With Anden, though, the kiss is all delicacy and refined grace, aristocratic manners, power, and elegance. Pleasure and shame wash through me. Can Day see this through the cams? The thought stabs at me.

It lasts for mere seconds, then Anden pulls away. I let out a breath, open my eyes, and let the rest of the room come back into focus. He's spent enough time here — any longer and the guards outside might start to worry. "I'm sorry to disturb you," he says, bowing his head slightly before standing up and straightening his coat. He's pulled back into the shelter of formality, but there's a slight awkwardness in his stance, and a faint smile on the edges of his lips. "Get some rest. We'll talk tomorrow."

Once he's gone and the room has fallen back into a thick silence, I curl up with my knees at my chin. My lips burn from his touch. I let my mind wrap around what Anden just said to me, and my fingers run repeatedly over the paper clip ring on my hand. The Patriots had wanted Day and me to join them in assassinating this young Elector. By assassinating him, they claimed, we'd be stoking the fires of a revolution that would free us from the Republic. That we could bring back the glory of the old United States. But what does that *mean,* really? What will the United States have that Anden can't give the Republic? Freedom? Peace? Prosperity? Will the Republic become a country full of beautifully lit sky-scrapers and clean, wealthy sectors? The Patriots had promised Day that they would find his brother and help us escape to the Colonies. But if Anden can do all of these things with the right support and the right determination, if we won't *need* to flee into the Colonies, then *what is this assassination accomplishing*? Anden isn't remotely like his father. In fact, his first official act as the Elector is undoing something his father had put in place — he's going to free Eden, maybe even stop the plague experiments. If we keep him in power, would he change the Republic for the better? Wouldn't he be the catalyst that Metias had wished for in his defiant journal entries?

There's a bigger problem I can't wrap my head around. Razor *must* know, on some level, that Anden isn't a dictator like his father was. After all, Razor's high enough of a rank to hear any rumors of Anden's rebellious nature. He'd told Day and me that Congress disliked Anden . . . but he never told us *why* they were clashing.

Why would he want to murder a young Elector who would help the Patriots establish a new Republic?

In the midst of my churning thoughts, though, one stays clear.

I know for certain where my loyalties lie now. I won't help Razor assassinate the Elector. But I have to warn Day, so he doesn't follow through with the Patriots' plans.

I need a signal.

Then I realize that there might be one way to do it, as long as he's watching footage of me along with the rest of the Patriots. He won't know why I'm doing it, but it's better than nothing. I lower my head slightly, then lift my hand with Day's paper clip ring on it and press two fingers against the side of my brow. Our agreed signal when we'd first arrived on the streets of Vegas.

Stop.

DAY

Later that night, I head out to the main conference room and join the others to hear about the next phase of the mission. Razor's back again. Four Patriots continue to work in a smaller cluster at one corner of the room, mostly Hackers from what I can tell, analyzing how speakers are mounted on some building or other. I'm starting to recognize a few of them — one of the Hackers is bald and built like a tank, if a bit short; another has a giant nose set between half-moon eyes on a very thin face; a third one is a girl missing an eye. Almost everyone has a scar of some sort. My attention wanders to Razor, who's addressing the crowd at the front of the room, his figure outlined in light with all the world map screens behind him. I crane my neck to see if I can catch Tess milling around with the others, to take her aside and try to apologize. When I finally catch sight of her, though, she's standing with a few other Medics in training, hold-

243

ing out some sort of green herb in her palm and patiently explaining how to use it. Or so I think. I decide to save my apology for later. It doesn't seem like she needs me right now. The thought makes me sad and oddly uncomfortable.

"Day!" Tess finally notices me. I give her a quick wave in return.

She makes her way over to me, then pulls out two pills and a small roll of clean bandages from her pocket. She pushes them into my hands. "Stay safe tonight, okay?" she says breathlessly, fixing me with a firm stare. There's no sign of the earlier tension between us. "I know how you get when your adrenaline's pumping. Don't do anything too crazy." Tess nods at the blue pills in my hand. "They'll warm you up if it's too cold out there."

Acts old enough to be my caretaker, I swear. Tess's concern leaves a warm feeling in my stomach. "Thanks, cousin," I reply, tucking her gifts away in my own pockets. "Hey, I —"

She stops my apology with a hand on my arm. Her eyes are as wide as ever, so comforting that I find myself wishing she could come with me. "Whatever. Just . . . promise me you'll be careful."

So quick to forgive, in spite of everything. Had she said those things to me earlier in the heat of the moment? Is she still angry? I lean over and give her a brief hug. "I promise. And *you* be safe too." She squeezes my waist in response, then heads off to rejoin the other young Medics before I can attempt my apology again.

After she's gone, I turn my attention back on Razor. He points to a grainy video that shows some street near the Lamar train tracks Kaede and I had passed earlier. A pair of soldiers hurry across the screen, their collars flipped up against the falling sleet, each of them munching on steaming empanadas. My mouth waters at the sight. The Patriots' canned food is a luxury, but, *man,* what I wouldn't give for a hot meat pastry. "First of all, I'd like to reassure everyone that our plans are on the right track," he says. "Our Agent has successfully met with the Elector and told him about our decoy assassination plan." He circles an area of the screen with his finger. "Originally the Elector had planned to visit San Angelo on his morale-boosting tour, then head here to Lamar. Now word is that he'll be coming to Pierra instead. A few of our soldiers will be accompanying the Elector instead of his original troop." Razor's eyes sweep over me, then he gestures to the screen and falls silent.

A video replaces the grainy Lamar train track scene; we're seeing footage of a bedroom. The first thing I notice is a slender figure seated on the edge of a bed, her knees tucked up to her chin. June? But the room is a nice one — certainly doesn't look like a prison cell to me — and the bed looks soft and thickly layered with blankets I would've killed to have back in Lake.

Someone grabs my arm. "Hey. There you are, hotshot." Pascao's standing beside me, that permanently cheery grin plastered all over his face and those pale gray eyes pulsing with excitement.

"Hey," I reply, giving him a quick nod in greeting before turning my attention back to the screen. Razor has started giving the group a general overview of the next phase of the plans, but Pascao tugs on my sleeve again.

"You, me, and a few other Runners are heading out in a couple of hours." His eyes flicker to the video before settling back on me. "Listen up. Razor wanted me to give my crew a more specific rundown than the one he's delivering to the group. I just briefed Baxter and Jordan."

I'm barely paying attention to Pascao anymore because now I can tell that the small figure on the bed is June. It must be her, what with the way she pushes her hair behind her shoulders and analyzes the room with a sweeping gaze. She's dressed in pretty cozy-looking nightclothes, but she's shivering as if the room's cold. Is this elegant bedchamber really her prison cell? Tess's words come back to me.

Day, have you forgotten? June killed your mother.

Pascao tugs on my arm again and forces me to face him, then leads me to the back of the group. "Listen *up,* Day," he whispers again. "There's a shipment coming into Lamar tonight, by train. It'll have cartloads of guns, gear, food, and whatever else for the warfront soldiers, along with a whole ensemble of lab equipment. We're going to steal some supplies and destroy a railcar's worth of grenades on it. That's our mission tonight."

Now June's talking to the guard standing near the door, but I can barely hear her. Razor's done addressing the room and has fallen deep into conversation with two other Patriots, both of them occasionally gesturing up at the screen, then drawing out something on their palms. "What's the point of blowing up a cartload of grenades?" I ask.

"This mission is the decoy assassination. The Elector was originally scheduled to come here to Lamar, at least before June had a talk with him. Our mission tonight should convince the Elector, if he isn't convinced already, that June was telling him the truth. Plus, it'll be a nice chance to steal a few grenades." Pascao rubs his hands together with almost maniacal glee. "Mmmm. Nitroglycerin." I raise an eyebrow. "Me and three other Runners are gonna do the train job, but we'll need a special Runner to distract the soldiers and guards."

"What do you mean, *special*?"

"What I *mean*," Pascao says pointedly, "is that this is why Razor decided to recruit you, Day. This is our first chance to show the Republic that you're *alive.* It's why Kaede had you strip the dye from your hair. When word gets out that you were seen in Lamar, taking down a Republic train, people are gonna go nuts. The Republic's notorious little criminal, still up and about even after the government's attempt to execute him? If *that* doesn't stir up people's sense of rebellion, nothing will. That's what we're aiming for — chaos. By the time we're done, the public will be so pumped about you that they'll be salivating for revolution. It's the perfect atmosphere for the Elector's assassination."

Pascao's excitement makes me smile a little. Messing with the Republic? This is what I was born to do. "Give me more details," I say, moving my hand in a come-hither gesture.

Pascao checks to make sure Razor's still going through the plans with the others, then winks at me. "Our team is gonna unhook the grenade railcar a couple of miles from the station — by the time we get there, I don't want there to be more than a handful of soldiers guarding the train. Be careful, now. There usually aren't many troops near those train tracks, but tonight's different. The Republic will be on the hunt for us after hearing June's warning about the decoy assassination. Watch for extra soldiers. Buy us the time we need, and make sure they spot you."

"Fine. I'll get you your time." I cross my arms and point at him. "You just tell me where I need to go."

Pascao grins and slaps me hard on the back. "Great. You're the best Runner out of us by far — you'll throw those soldiers off without a hitch. Join up with me in two hours near the entrance where you came in. We're gonna have a ball." He snaps his fingers. "Oh, and don't mind Baxter. He's just sore that you get special treatment from both me *and* Tess."

As soon as he walks away, my eyes go back to the video screen and stay frozen on June's figure. As it continues playing, pieces of Razor's conversation with the other Patriots reach me. " — enough to hear what's going on," he's saying. "She has him in position."

On the video, June seems to be dozing, with her knees tucked up to her chin. There's no sound at all this time, but I don't think much of it. Then I see someone step inside her cell, a young man with dark hair and an elegant black cloak. It's the Elector. He bends down and starts talking to her, but I can't make out what he's saying. When he gets close to her, June tenses up. I can feel the blood draining from my face. All the chatter and bustle around me fades into the distance. The Elector puts a hand under June's chin and brings her face toward his own. He is taking something that I thought was just for me, and I feel a sudden, shattering sense of loss. I want to rip my eyes away, but even from the corner of my vision, I can still see him kissing her. It seems to last forever.

I watch numbly as they finally pull away from each other and the Elector steps out of the room, leaving June alone, curled up on the bed. What's going through her mind right now? I can't watch any longer. I'm about to turn my back, ready to follow Pascao out of the crowd and away from this scene.

But then something catches my eye. I look up at the monitor. And just in time, I see June hold up two fingers to her brow in our signal.

It's past midnight when Pascao, me, and three other Runners paint wide black stripes across our eyes and suit ourselves up in dark warfront uniforms and military caps. Then we head out of the Patriots' underground hideout

250

for the first time since I arrived. A couple of soldiers wander by now and then, but we see more clusters of troops as we head farther out of our neighborhood and cross the train tracks. The sky's still completely covered with clouds, and under the dim streetlights, I can see thin sheets of sleet falling. The pavement's slick with drizzle and icy slush, and the air smells stale, like a mix of smoke and mold. I pull my stiff collar higher, swallow one of Tess's blue pills, and actually wish I was back with her in Los Angeles's humid slums. I tap the dust bomb hidden inside my jacket, double-checking that it's dry. In the back of my mind, the scene between June and the Elector plays on repeat.

June's signal was for me. Which part of the plan does she want me to stop? Does she want me to forfeit the Patriots' mission and escape? If I defect now, what will happen to her? The signal could've meant a million things. It could even mean she's decided to stay with the Republic. I shake the thought furiously from my mind. No, she wouldn't do that. *Not even if the Elector himself wanted her?* Would that make her stay?

I also remember that the video footage of them didn't have sound on it. Every other video we've seen has had crisp sound — Razor even insisted on making sure the volume was turned up. Had the Patriots stripped it from this one? Are they hiding something?

Pascao stops us in the shadows of an alley not far from the train station. "Train arrives in fifteen minutes," he says, his breath rising in clouds. "Baxter, Iris, you two come with me." The girl named Iris — long and lean, with deep-set eyes that constantly dart around — smiles, but Baxter glowers and tightens his jaw. I ignore him and try not to think about whatever he's trying to put in Tess's mind about me. Pascao points to the third Runner, a petite girl with copper-colored braids who keeps sneaking glances at me. "Jordan, you're going to pinpoint the right railcar for us." She gives Pascao a thumbs-up.

Pascao's eyes shift to me. "Day," he whispers. "You know your drill."

I tug the edge of my cap. "Got it, cousin." Whatever June means, this is no time for me to leave the Patriots behind. Tess is still back there in the bunker, and I have no idea where Eden is. No way I'm going to put both of them in jeopardy.

"Keep those soldiers busy, yeah? Make them hate you."

"That's my specialty." I gesture up at the slanted roofs and crumbling walls towering around us. To a Runner, those roofs are like

252

giant slides made smooth by ice. I say a silent thanks to Tess — already the blue pill is warming me up from the inside out, as soothing as a bowl of hot soup on an icy evening.

Pascao gives me a wide grin. "Well then. Let's show them a good time."

I watch the others hurry away along the railroad tracks through the veil of sleet. Then I step farther into the shadows and study the buildings. Each one is old and pockmarked with footholds — and to make things even more fun, they all have rusted metal beams crisscrossing their walls. Some have top floors that are completely blown off and open to the night sky. Others have slanted, tiled roofs. In spite of everything, I can't help feeling a twinge of anticipation. These buildings are a Runner's paradise.

I turn back down the street toward the train station. There are at least two clusters of soldiers, maybe more that I can't see on the other side. Some are lined up along the tracks in expectation, their rifles hoisted, the black stripes across their eyes gleaming wetly in the rain. I reach up to my face and check my own stripe. Then I pull my military cap down tighter on my head. Showtime.

I get a good foothold on one wall and shimmy my way up toward the roof. Every time I tuck my leg in, my calf brushes against my artificial leg implant. The metal is freezing cold, even through fabric. Several seconds later, I'm perched behind a crumbling chimney three stories up. From here I can see that, just as I expected, there's a third group of soldiers on the other side of the train station. I make my way to the other end of the building and then leap silently from building to building until I'm on top of a slanted roof. Now I'm close enough to see expressions on soldiers' faces. I reach into my jacket, make sure my dust bomb is still mostly dry, and then crouch there on the roof to wait.

A few minutes pass.

Then I stand up, pull out the dust bomb, and fling it as far from the train station as I can.

Boom. It explodes in a giant cloud the moment it hits the ground. Instantly the dust swallows up that entire block and races down the streets in rolling waves. I hear shouts from the soldiers near the train station — one of them yells out, "There! Three blocks down!" *Way to state the obvious, soldier.* A group of them breaks away from the station and starts hurrying toward where the dust cloud has blanketed the streets.

I slide down the slanted roof. Shingles break off here and there, sending showers of ice mist into the air, but through all the shouting and running below me I can't even hear myself. The roof itself is slippery as wet glass. I pick up speed. The sleet whips harder against my cheeks — I brace myself as I reach the bottom of the roof and then launch into the air. From the ground I probably look like some sort of phantom.

My boots hit the slanted roof of the next building, this one right next to the train station. The soldiers still there are distracted, staring down the street toward the dust. I do a little hop at the bottom of this second roof, then grab on to the side of a streetlight and slide all the way down the pole to the ground. I land with a quick, muffled crunch on the pavement's streaks of ice.

"Follow me!" I shout at the soldiers. They see me for the first time, just another nondescript soldier with a dark uniform and black stripe across the eyes. "There's an attack on one of our warehouses. Could be the Patriots finally showing their faces." I gesture to both of the groups left. "*Everyone.* Commander's orders, hurry!" Then I turn on my heels and start running away from them.

Sure enough, the sound of their pounding boots soon follows. No way would these soldiers dare risk disobeying their commander, even if it means leaving the station momentarily unguarded. Sometimes you gotta love the Republic's iron discipline.

I keep running.

When I've led the soldiers four or five blocks down, past the dust cloud and several ware-houses, I suddenly veer off down a narrow corridor. Before they can turn the corner, I run straight at one of the alley's walls — and when I'm several feet away I jump up and kick off against the brick. My hands shoot out. I grab on to the second floor's ledge and it's only the work of the moment to spring up to it. My feet land solidly on the ledge.

By the time the soldiers have rushed into the same alley, I've melted into the shadowed crevice of a second-floor window. I hear the first ones pause, then their bewildered excla-mations. *Now's as good a time as any,* I think. I reach up and pull my cap off, letting my white-blond hair tumble loose. One of the soldiers turns his head up fast enough to see me dart out of the window crevice and turn the corner from the second-floor ledge. "Did you see that?" someone shouts incredulously. "Was that Day?" As I jam my feet into the spaces of old bricks and pull myself up to the third floor, the soldiers' tones go from confused to angry. Someone shouts at the others to shoot me down. I just grit my teeth and leap up to the third floor.

The first bullets ricochet off the wall. One hits inches away from my hand. I don't stop

— instead I lunge up toward the top floor and swing up onto the slanted rooftop in one move. More sparks light up the bricks below me. Off in the distance I see the station — the train's arrived, half hidden behind steam, and parked unattended except for several soldiers who have stepped off the train itself.

I scamper up the roof and slide down its other half, then take another flying leap to the next roof. Down below, some of the soldiers have started rushing back toward the train. Maybe they've finally realized that this is all a diversion. My eyes leave the station only when I go flying onto another rooftop.

Two blocks away.

Then, an explosion. A bright, furious cloud rolls up from farther down the railroad tracks, and even my rooftop vantage point shudders. The impact makes me lose my balance and fall to my knees. *There's the blast Pascao had mentioned.* I take in the inferno for a moment, pondering. A lot of soldiers are going to be heading over there — it's dangerous, but if my job is to let the Republic know I'm alive, I better make sure I'm seen by as many people as possible. I push myself back onto my feet and run faster, stuffing my hair back up into my cap as I go. The soldiers below have split into two groups — one dashing toward the explosion, the other continuing to trail me.

Suddenly I skid to a stop. The soldiers rush right past the building I'm on. Without wasting another second, I slide down the roof and swing down from the edge of the gutter. Boot into foothold. One after another. I jump down to the pavement. The soldiers probably *just* realized they'd lost me, but I'm already blending into the shadows on the ground. Now I'm running steadily along the street as if I'm just another soldier. I head for the train.

The sleet's coming down harder. The blaze left over from the explosion lights up the night sky, and I'm close enough to the train to hear shouts and pounding feet. Did Pascao and the others get out safely? I quicken my steps. Other soldiers materialize through the sleet, and I fall smoothly into line with them as we jog alongside the train. They're rushing toward the fire.

"What happened?" one of them shouts at another.

"Don't know — I heard some spark set off the cargo."

"That's impossible! The railcars are all covered —"

"Somebody get ahold of Commander DeSoto. The Patriots made their move — send word to the Elector — they're —"

They continue on; I miss the last half of the sentence. I gradually slow until I'm at the back of the line, then I dart away into the tiny slit between two railcars. All the soldiers I can see are still headed for the blaze. Others are in the area where I'd set off the dust bomb, and the ones who'd been chasing me are probably still bewildered, combing the streets I was running. I wait until I'm certain there's no one else near me. Then I slide out from between the railcars and run along the opposite side of the tracks that the other soldiers were on. I let my hair loose again. Now I just need to choose the right moment to make my grand appearance.

There are small markings on each railcar that I pass. Coal. Tracked guns. Ammunition. Food. I'm tempted to stop at the last one, but that's just the Lake part of me talking. I remind myself that I'm not scavenging on the streets anymore and that the Patriots have a full pantry in their headquarters. I force myself to keep going. More markings. More warfront supplies.

Then I pass a marking that forces me to stop. A shiver runs down my arms and legs. I quickly jog back to see the marked railcar again, just in case I'd imagined it.

Nope. There it is, embossed into the metal. The one I'd recognize anywhere.

The three-lined X. My mind whirls — I see the red spray-painted symbol scarring my mother's door, the plague patrols making their way from house to house in Lake, Eden being taken away. There's no way this symbol could mean anything other than the fact that my brother, or something related to him, is on this train. All my interest in the Patriots' plan goes right out of my head. *Eden might be in here.*

I can tell the two sliding car doors are locked, so I take a few steps back, then run at it. When I'm close enough, I jump, take three fast steps against the car's side, grab the top edge of the car, and pull myself up.

There's a circular metal seal in the middle of this railcar's roof that they're probably using to access the interior. I crawl over to it, run my fingers along the edges, and find four latches holding the seal down. Feverishly I pry them loose. The soldiers should be coming back any second now. I push against the seal with all the strength I've got. It slides open a crack, just enough for me to jump in.

I land with a soft thud. It's dark enough so I can't see anything at first. I reach out my hands and touch what feels like a round glass surface. Slowly I begin to make out my surroundings.

I'm standing in front of a glass cylinder almost as tall and wide as the railcar, with smooth metal casing on top and bottom. It emits a very faint blue glow. A small figure is lying on the floor inside, with tubes poking out of one of his arms. I know right away that it's a boy. His hair is short and clean and a mess of soft waves, and he's dressed in a white jumpsuit that makes him stand out against the darkness.

A loud buzzing in my ears blocks out anything and everything. It's Eden. *It's Eden.* It must be him. I've hit the jackpot — I can't believe my luck. He's right here, I've found him in the middle of nowhere, in all the vastness of the Republic, in a stroke of insane coincidence. I can get him out. We can escape into the Colonies sooner than I ever thought possible. We can escape *tonight.*

I rush over to the cylinder and pound my fist on the glass, half hoping it shatters even though I can tell that it's at least a foot thick and almost certainly bulletproof. For an instant I don't know if he can hear it. But then his eyes open. They dart around in a weird, unfocused way before attempting to settle on me.

It takes me a long moment to process the fact that this boy is not Eden.

The bitter taste of disappointment stings my tongue. He's so small, *so* close in age to my brother, that I can't stop the image of Eden's face from overwhelming me. *Others exist who were also marked with unusual strains of*

261

plague? Well, of course there would be. Why would Eden be the only one in the entire country?

The boy and I just face each other for a while. I *think* he can see me, but he can't seem to fix his gaze; he keeps squinting in a way that reminds me of Tess's nearsightedness. *Eden.* I think back to the way his irises had bled from the plague . . . from the way this boy's trying to gauge me, I can tell that he's almost entirely blind. A symptom my brother probably has too.

He suddenly snaps out of his trance and crawls over to me as fast as he can. He presses both his hands against the glass. His eyes are a pale, opaque brown, not the creepy black that Eden's had been when I last saw him, but the bottom halves of both irises are dark purple with blood. Does that mean this boy — that Eden — is getting better, because the blood is draining *away,* or worse, because the blood is draining *in*? Eden's irises had been completely filled with blood the last time I saw him.

"Who's there?" he says. The glass muffles his voice. He still can't focus on me even at this close range.

I snap out of my trance too. "A friend," I reply hoarsely. "I'm going to get you out." At that, his eyes pop open — hope instantly blossoms on his small face. My hands run along the glass and search for something, *anything,* that can open this goddy cylinder. "How do you operate this thing? Is it safe?"

The boy pounds frantically against the glass. He's terrified. "Help me, please!" he exclaims, his voice trembling. "Get me out — please get me out of here!"

His words break my heart. Is this what Eden's doing, terrified and blind, waiting in some dark railcar for me to save him? *I have to get this boy out.* I steady myself against the cylinder. "You have to stay calm, kid. All right? Don't panic. What's your name? What city is your family from?"

Tears have started to run down the boy's face. "My name's Sam Vatanchi — my family's in Helena, Montana." He shakes his head vigorously. "They don't know where I went. Can you tell them I want to come home? Can you —"

No, I can't. I'm so goddy helpless. I want to punch straight through the railcar's metal sides. "I'll do what I can. How do you open this cylinder?" I ask again. "Is it *safe* to open?"

The boy points frantically to the cylinder's other side. I can tell he's trying hard to contain his fright. "Okay — okay." He pauses in an attempt to think. "Um, it's safe. I think. There's something over there that they type into," he replies. "I can hear the beeps and then it makes the tube open."

I rush to where he's pointing. *Is it my imagination, or do I hear the faint sounds of boots pounding against pavement?* "It's some sort of glass screen," I say. The word LOCKED stretches across it in red type. I turn back to the boy and knock on the glass. His eyes swivel toward the sound. "Is there a password? How do they type it in?"

"I don't know!" The boy throws his hands up; his words contort with a sob. "Please, just —"

Damn it, he reminds me *so much* of Eden. His tears are making my own eyes water. "Come on," I coax, fighting to keep my words strong. Gotta stay in control. "*Think.* Any other way this thing opens, aside from the keypad?"

He shakes his head. "I don't know. I *don't know!*"

I can already imagine what Eden would say, if he was this boy. He'd say something technical, thinking like the little engineer that he is. Something like, *"Do you have a sharp edge? Try finding a manual trigger!"*

Steel yourself. I pull out the knife that's always at my belt. I'd seen Eden take gadgets apart before and reconfigure all the inner wires and circuit boards. Maybe I should try the same thing.

I place the blade against the tiny slit running along the keypad's edge and carefully apply some pressure. When nothing happens, I push harder until the blade bends. Doesn't help at all. "It's too tight," I mutter. If only June were here. She'd probably figure out how this thing works in half a second. The boy and I share a brief moment of silence. His chin drops to his chest and his eyes close; he knows there's no way to open it.

I need to rescue him. *I need to save Eden.* It makes me want to scream.

It's not my imagination — I *do* hear the soldiers getting closer. They must be checking the compartments. "Talk to me, Sam," I say. "Are you still sick? What are they doing to you?"

The boy wipes his nose. The light of hope has already faded from his face. "Who are you?"

"Someone who wants to help," I whisper. "The more you tell me, the easier it will be for me to fix this."

"I'm not sick anymore," Sam replies in a rush, like he knows we're running out of time, "but they say I've got something in my blood. They call it a *dormant virus.*" He stops to think. "They give me medicine to keep me from getting sick again." He rubs at his blind eyes, wordlessly begging me to save him. "Every time the train stops, they take a blood sample from me."

"Any idea what cities you've already been to?"

"Dunno . . . I heard the name Bismarck once . . ." The boy trails off as he thinks. "And Yankton?"

Both are warfront cities up in Dakota. I think about the transport they're using for him. It probably maintains a sterile environment, so people can go in and take a blood sample, then mix them with whatever activates the dormant virus. The tubes in his arms might just be for feeding.

My best guess is that they're using him as a bioweapon against the Colonies. *He's been turned into a lab rat.* Just like Eden. The thought of my brother being shipped around like this threatens to drown me. "Where are they taking you next?" I demand.

"I don't know! I just . . . I want to go home!"

Somewhere along the warfront. I can only imagine how many others are being paraded up and down the warfront line. I picture Eden huddled in one of these trains. The boy has started to wail again, but I force myself to cut him off. "Listen to me — do you know of a boy named Eden? Have you heard that name mentioned anywhere?"

His cries grow louder. "No — I don't — know

who — !"

I can't linger anymore. Somehow I manage to tear my eyes away from the boy's and run to the railcar's sliding doors. The soldiers' footsteps are louder now — they can't be more than five or six cars away. I take one last glance back at the boy. "I'm sorry. I have to go." It *kills* me to say these words.

The boy starts to cry again. His hands pound against the cylinder's thick glass. "No!" His voice breaks. "I told you everything I know — *please don't leave me here!*"

I can't bear to listen anymore. I force myself to step up the side latches of one sliding door and get close enough to the railcar's ceiling to grab the edge of the top circular seal. I pull myself out into the night air again, back into the sleet that stings my eyes and whips ice against my face, and struggle to regain my composure. I'm so ashamed of myself. This boy had given me whatever help he could, and this is how I repay him? By running for my life?

Soldiers are inspecting the cars some fifty feet away. I slide the seal back into place and shimmy flat against the roof until I've reached the edge. I swing down and land on the ground.

Pascao materializes out of the shadows, his pale gray eyes flashing in the dark. He must've been looking for me. "Why the *hell* are you here?" he whispers. "You were supposed to make a scene near the explosion, yeah? Where were you?"

I'm in no mood to play nice. *"Not now,"* I snap as I start running alongside Pascao. Time to head back to our underground tunnel. Everything whizzes past us in a surreal fog.

Pascao opens his mouth to say something else, hesitates when he sees my face, and decides to drop it. "Er . . . ," he starts again, this time more quietly, "well, you did good enough. Probably got the word out that you're alive, even without all the extra fireworks. Your run up there on the roofs was pretty amazing. We'll see tomorrow morning how the public reacts to your appearance here." When I don't reply, he bites his lip and leaves it at that.

I have no choice but to wait until Razor's finished with the assassination before they help me rescue Eden. A tide of rage against the young Elector swells up in me. *I hate you. I hate you with everything I've got, and I swear I'm going to put a bullet in you the first chance I get.* For the first time since I joined the Patriots, I actually find myself excited for the assassination. I'm going to do everything to make sure the Republic can never touch my brother again.

In the chaos of the burning fire and shouting

of troops, we slip away down the other side of
the town and back into the night.

Less than two days before the Elector's actual assassination. Thirty hours for me to stop it.

The sun has just set when the Elector, along with six Senators and at least four guard patrols (forty-eight soldiers), boards a train headed for the warfront city of Pierra. I'm riding with them too. This is the first time I'm traveling as a passenger instead of a prisoner, so tonight I'm dressed in warm winter tights and soft leather boots (no heels or steel toes, so I can't use them as weapons) and a hooded duffle cape that's deep scarlet with silver trim. No more shackles. Anden even makes sure I have gloves (soft leather, black and red), and for the first time since arriving in Denver, my fingers don't feel cold. My hair is the way it's always been, clean and dry, pulled back into a high ponytail. In spite of all this, my head feels warm and my muscles ache. All the lamps along the station platform are off, and no one besides the Elector's ensemble is in sight. We board the train in complete silence. Anden's sudden detour from Lamar to Pierra is probably something most of the Senators don't even know about.

My guards lead me into my own private railcar, a car so luxurious that I know I'm in here only because Anden insisted on it. It's twice as long as the standard railcars (a good nine hundred square feet, with six velvet curtains and Anden's ever-present portrait hanging against the right wall). The guards lead me to the center table of the car, then pull out a seat for me. I feel a strange detachment from it all, like none of it is quite real — it's as if I were exactly where I used to be, a wealthy girl taking her rightful place amongst the Republic's elite.

"If you need anything, let us know," one of them says. He sounds polite, but the tightness of his jaw gives away how nervous he is around me.

There are no sounds now except for the subtle rattle of the train on tracks. I try not to focus directly on the soldiers, but from the corner of my eye, I watch them closely. Are there any Patriots disguised as soldiers on this train? If so, do they suspect my shifting loyalties?

We wait together in a thick silence. The snow has started up again, piling against my window's outside corners. Curls of white frost decorate the glass. It reminds me of Metias's funeral, of my white dress and Thomas's polished white suit, the white lilacs and white carpets.

The train picks up speed. I lean toward the window until my cheek almost touches the cold glass, watching silently as we approach the looming Armor wall that surrounds Denver. Even in the darkness I can see the train tunnels carved into the Armor; some of them are completely sealed with solid metal gates while others remain open for night freight to pass through. Our train hurtles into one of the tunnels — I guess trains leaving the capital don't need to stop for inspection, especially if the Elector has approved them. As we leave the enormous wall behind, I see an inbound train slowing for inspection at a checkpoint.

We continue on, melting away into the night. The rain-worn skyscrapers of slum sectors stream past the windows, the now-familiar view of how people live on the outskirts of a city. I'm too tired to pay much attention to the details. My mind goes over what Anden said to me the last night, which leads me back to the endless problem of how to warn Anden *and* keep Day safe at the same time. The Patriots will know I've betrayed them if I reveal the assassination plot to Anden too early. I need to time my steps so any plan deviations happen right before the assassination, when I can reach Day easily.

I wish I could tell Anden now. Tell him everything, get it over with. In a world without Day, that's what I would do. *In a world without Day, many things would be different.* I think about the nightmares I've been having, the haunting thought of Razor putting a bullet in Day's chest. The paper clip ring sits heavy on my finger. Again, I lift two fingers to my brow. If Day didn't catch my first signal, I hope he sees this one. The guards don't seem to think I'm doing anything unusual; it looks like I'm just resting my head. The railcar sways to one side and a wave of dizziness washes over me. Maybe this cold I have coming on — if it really is a cold, that is, and not something more serious — is starting to affect my logic. Still, I don't raise a request for doctors or medicine. Medicine inhibits the real immune system, so I've always preferred fighting illnesses on my own (much to Metias's exasperation).

Why do so many of my thoughts lead back

to Metias?

An aggravated man's voice distracts me from my wandering thoughts. I turn from the window and back to the inside of my railcar. It sounds like an older man. I sit straighter in my chair and can see two figures walking toward me through the tiny window on my railcar door. One is the man I'd just heard, short and pear-shaped, with a scruffy gray beard and small, bulbous nose. The other is Anden. I strain to hear what they're saying — at first, all I can make out are broken hints of their conversation, but their words sharpen as they draw closer to my railcar.

"Elector, please — I'm telling you this for your own good. Acts of rebellion need to be met with severe punishment. If you don't react appropriately, it'll only be a matter of time before everything is thrown into upheaval."

Anden listens patiently with his hands behind his back and his head tilted down toward the man. "Thank you for your concern, Senator Kamion, but my mind is made up. Now is hardly the time to meet the unrest in Los Angeles with military force."

My ears perk up at this. The older man spreads his arms wide in a gesture of irritation. "Push the people back in line. You *need* that right now, Elector. Demonstrate your will."

Anden shakes his head. "It'll push the people over the edge, Senator. Using fatal force before I have a chance to publicize all the changes I have in mind? No. I won't issue such a command. *That's* my will."

The Senator scratches at his beard in irritation and puts a hand on Anden's elbow. "The public is already up in arms against you, and your leniency will look like weakness — not just externally, but internally too. The LA Trial admins are complaining about our lack of response — the protests have forced them to cancel several days' worth of examinations."

Anden's mouth tightens into a stern line. "I think you know how I feel about the Trials, Senator."

"I do," the Senator replies sullenly. "That's a discussion for another time. But if you don't issue orders that allow us to stop the rioting, I can guarantee that you'll be getting an earful from the Senate *and* the Los Angeles patrols."

Anden pauses to raise an eyebrow at him. "Is that so? I'm sorry. I was under the impression that our Senate and our military understand *exactly* how much weight my words carry."

The Senator wipes sweat from his brow. "Well, that is — of course the Senate will bow to your wishes, sir, but I just meant — well —"

"Help me convince the other Senators that this is the wrong time for us to come down on the public." Anden pauses to face the man and claps him on the shoulder. "I don't want to make enemies in Congress, Senator. I want your fellow delegates and the national court to respect my decisions as they did with my father's. Using fatal force to put down rioters will only incite more anger toward the state."

"But, sir —"

Anden stops outside my railcar. "We'll finish this discussion later," he says. "I'm tired." Even though his reply is muffled by the doors between us, I can hear the steel in his words.

The Senator mumbles something and bows his head. When Anden nods, the man turns around and hurries away. Anden watches him go, then opens the door to my railcar. The guards salute him.

We nod at each other.

"I've come to deliver your release terms, June." Anden speaks to me with a distant formality, perhaps due to the chilly conversation he just had with the Senator. The kiss he'd given me last night feels like a hallucination. Even so, seeing him gives me a peculiar sense of comfort, and I catch myself relaxing against my chair as if I were in the company of an old friend. "Last night we received word that there *was* an attack in Lamar. A train was destroyed in an explosion — the train I was supposed to be on. I don't know the final word on who's responsible, and we failed to catch any of the attackers, but we assume that they were the Patriots. We have teams hunting for them there now."

"Glad to be of service, Elector," I say. My hands grip each other tightly in my lap, reminding me of the luxurious softness of my gloves. Should I feel so safe and secure in this elite railcar while Day is probably on the run with the Patriots?

"If you can think of any other details, Ms. Iparis, please feel free to share them. You're back in the Republic now; you're one of us, and I give you my word that you have nothing to fear. Once we arrive in Pierra, your record will be scrubbed clean. I'll personally see to it that you're reinstated to your former rank — although you'll be placed in a different city patrol." Anden puts a hand to his mouth and clears his throat. "I've recommended you for a Denver team."

"Thank you," I reply softly. Anden is falling right into the Patriots' trap.

"Some Senators feel that we've been too generous with you, but everyone agrees that you're our best hope of tracking down the Patriots' leaders." Anden walks closer and takes a seat before me. "I'm sure they'll try to strike again, and I want you to lead my men in intercepting future attempts."

"You are too kind, Elector. I'm honored," I reply, lowering my head in a half bow. "And if you don't mind my asking, will my dog be pardoned as well?"

Anden chuckles a little. "Your dog is being cared for in the capital; he'll be waiting for you when you arrive."

I meet Anden's eyes and hold them for a moment. His pupils dilate and his cheeks flush slightly. "I can see why the Senate would be unhappy with your leniency," I finally say. "But it's true that no one can keep you safer than I can." I need a minute alone with him. "But there must be another reason you're being so kind to me. Isn't there?"

Anden swallows and looks up at his own portrait. My eyes dart to the guards standing at the railcar's doors. As if he knows what I'm thinking, Anden waves a hand at the soldiers, then motions up at the cams in the railcar. The soldiers leave, and a moment later the cams' red, blinking lights flick off. For the first time, no one is watching us. We are truly alone. "The truth is," Anden continues, "you've become *very* popular with the public. If word gets out that the country's most gifted prodigy is being convicted of treason — or even demoted for disloyalty — well, you can see how poorly that would reflect on the Republic. And on me. Even Congress knows this."

My hands curl back and retreat into my lap. "Your father's Senate and you have somewhat different moral codes," I say, mulling over the conversation I'd overheard between Anden and Senator Kamion moments ago. "Or so I gather."

He shakes his head and smiles bitterly. "To put it lightly."

"I didn't know you disliked the Trials so much."

Anden nods. He doesn't seem surprised that I overheard his conversation. "The Trials are an outdated way of choosing our country's best and brightest."

It's odd to hear this coming from the Elector's own mouth. "Why is the Senate so intent on keeping them? What's their investment in the Trials?"

Anden shrugs. "It's a long story. Back when the Republic first implemented them, they were . . . somewhat different."

I lean forward. I've never heard any stories about the Republic that weren't filtered through the country's school or public messaging systems — and now the Elector himself is going to tell me one. "How were they different?" I ask.

"My father was . . . very charismatic." Anden actually sounds a bit defensive.

Weird reply. "I'm sure he must have had his ways," I say, careful to keep neutral.

Anden crosses his legs and leans back. "I don't like what the Republic has become," he says, forming each word slowly and thoughtfully. "But I cannot say that I don't understand *why* things are like this. My father had his reasons for doing what he did."

I frown at him. Puzzling. Hadn't I just heard him arguing against cracking down on rioters? "What do you mean?"

Anden opens and closes his mouth as if trying to find the right words. "Before my father became the Elector, the Trials were voluntary." He pauses when he hears me suck my breath in. "Hardly anyone knows that — it was a long time ago."

The Trials were once voluntary. The idea is

completely foreign to me. "Why did he change it?" I say.

"Like I said, it's a long story. Most people will never know the truth about the Republic's formation, and for good reason." He runs a hand through his wavy hair, then leans one elbow on the windowsill. "Do you want to know?"

What a perfectly rhetorical question. Behind Anden's words is a certain loneliness. I hadn't thought about it before, but now I realize that I might be one of the only people he's ever talked freely with. I lean forward, nod, and wait for him to continue.

"The Republic was originally formed in the middle of the worst crisis North America — and the world, for that matter — had ever seen," he begins. "Floodwaters had destroyed America's eastern coastline, and millions of people from the east were pouring into the west. There were far too many people for our states to take in. No jobs. No food, no shelter. The country had lost its mind to fear and panic. Rioting was out of control. Protesters were dragging soldiers, policemen, and peacekeepers out of their cars, then beating them to death or setting them on fire. Every shop was looted, every window broken." He takes a deep breath. "The federal government tried their best to maintain order, but one disaster after another made it impossible. They had no money to handle all these crises. It became absolute anarchy."

A time when the Republic had no control over its people? Impossible. I have a hard time picturing it, until I realize that Anden might instead be referring to the government of the old United States.

"Then our first Elector seized power. He was a young officer in the military, just a few years older than I am now, and ambitious enough to win the support of unhappy troops in the west. He declared the Republic a separate country, seceded from the Union, and placed the west under martial law. Soldiers could fire at will, and after seeing their comrades tortured and killed in the streets, they took every advantage of their newfound power. It became *us versus them* — the military versus the people." Anden looks down at his shiny loafers, as if ashamed. "Many people were killed before the soldiers were able to win control of the Republic."

I can't help wondering what Metias would've thought of this. Or my parents. Would they have approved? Would they have forced order out of chaos like that? "What about the Colonies?" I ask. "Did they take advantage of all this?"

"The eastern half of North America was even worse off at the time. Half their land was underwater. When the Republic's first Elector sealed the borders, their people had no place to go. So they declared war on us." Anden straightens. "After all this, the Elector vowed never to let the Republic fall that way again, so he and the Senate gave the military an unprecedented level of power, which has lasted to this day. My father and the Electors before him have made sure it stays that way."

He shakes his head and rubs his face with his hands before continuing. "The Trials were supposed to encourage hard work and athleticism, to produce more military-quality people — and they did. But they were also used to weed out the weak — and the defiant. And gradually, they were also used to control overpopulation."

The weak and the defiant. I shiver. Day had fallen into the latter category. "So, you know what happens to the children who fail the Trial?" I say. "It was done to control the population?"

"Yes." Anden winces even as he tries to explain it. "The Trials made sense in the beginning. They were meant to entice the best and fittest to join the military. Over time, they shifted to being offered in all schools. That wasn't enough for my father, though . . . he wanted only the best to survive. Anyone else was, frankly, considered a waste of space and resources. My father always told me that the Trials were absolutely necessary for the Republic to flourish. And he won a lot of support in the Senate for making the examinations mandatory, especially after we started winning more battles because of it."

My hands are clasped so tightly in my lap that they're starting to feel numb. "Well, do you think your father's policies worked?" I ask quietly.

Anden lowers his head. He searches for the right words. "How can I answer that? His policies *did* work. The Trials *did* make our armies stronger. Does that make what he did *right,* though? I think about it all the time."

I bite my lip, suddenly understanding the confusion Anden must feel, his love for his father warring with his vision for the Republic. "What's right is relative, isn't it?" I ask.

Anden nods. "In some ways, it doesn't matter why it all started, or if it was ever right. The thing is — over time, the laws evolved and twisted. Things changed. At first the Trials weren't given to children, and they didn't favor the wealthy. The plagues . . ." He hesitates at this, then shies away from the subject altogether. "The public is angry, but the Senate is afraid to change things that might lead to them losing control again. And to them, the Trials are a way to reinforce the Republic's power."

There's a profound sadness in Anden's face. I can sense the shame he feels for belonging to such a legacy. "I'm sorry," I say in a low voice. I feel a sudden urge to touch his hand, to find a way to comfort him.

Anden's lips tug upward into a hesitant smile. I can clearly see his desire, his dangerous weakness, the way he longs for me. If I ever doubted it before, I know for certain now. I quickly turn away, half hoping that gazing at a snowy landscape might bring some of its coolness to my cheeks.

"Tell me," he murmurs. "What would you do if you were me? What would your first action be as the Elector of the Republic?"

I answer without hesitation. "Win over the people," I say. "The Senate would have no power over you if the public could threaten them with revolution. You need the people at your back, and they need a leader."

Anden leans back in his chair; some of the railcar's warm lamplight catches against his coat and outlines him in gold. Something in our conversation has inspired an idea in him; maybe it's an idea he had all along. "You'd make a good Senator, June," he says. "You'd be a good ally to your Elector — and the public loves you."

My mind starts spinning. I *could* stay here in the Republic and help Anden. Become a Senator when I'm old enough. Get my life back. Leave Day behind with the Patriots. I know how selfish this thinking is, but I can't stop myself. *What's so wrong with being selfish, anyway?* I think bitterly. I could just tell Anden everything about the Patriots' plans right now — without caring whether word will get back to the Patriots or whether they'll hurt Day because of it — and return to living a wealthy, secure life as an elite government worker. I could honor my brother's memory by slowly changing the country from the inside. Couldn't I?

Horrible. I release this dark fantasy. The thought of leaving Day behind in such a way, of betraying him so completely, of never wrapping my arms around him again, of *never ever seeing him again,* makes me clench my teeth in pain. I close my eyes for a second and remember his gentle, calloused hands, his passionate ferocity. No, I could never do it. I know this with such blinding certainty that it frightens me. After everything we've both sacrificed, surely we deserve a life — or *something* — together after this is all over? Escaping to the Colonies, or rebuilding the Republic? Anden wants Day's help; we can all work together. How could I bear to turn away from that light at the end of the tunnel? *I need to get back to him. I need to tell Day everything.*

First things first. I try to formulate the best way to warn Anden now that we're finally alone. There's not much I can safely say. Tell him too much and he might do something that tips off the Patriots. Still, I decide to try my best. At the very least, I need him to trust me without question. I need him behind me when I sabotage the Patriots' detour.

"Do you believe in me?" This time I do brush his hand with my own.

Anden stiffens, but doesn't pull away. His eyes search my face, perhaps wondering what had gone through my mind when I closed my eyes. "Perhaps I should ask you the same question," he replies, a hesitant smile on his lips.

Both of us are speaking on two levels, referring to secrets shared. I nod at him, hoping he'll take my words seriously. "Then do what I say when we get to Pierra. Prom-

287

ise? Everything I say."

He tilts his head, his eyebrows furrowed in puzzlement, then shrugs and nods yes. He seems to understand that I'm trying to tell him something without saying it aloud. When the time comes for the Patriots to act, I hope Anden remembers his promise.

DAY

Me, Pascao, and the other runners spend a full half day aboveground after the train job, huddled in alleys or on top of abandoned roofs, dodging the soldiers that comb the streets near the station. Not until the sun begins to set do we finally get a chance to return, one by one, to the Patriots' underground quarters. Neither Pascao nor I bring up what happened by the train. Jordan, the shy Runner with the copper braids, asks me twice if I'm okay. I just shrug her off.

Yeah, something's wrong. Isn't *that* the understatement of the year.

By the time we make our way back, everyone is getting ready to leave for Pierra — some are destroying documents, while others are wiping the comps clean of data. Pascao's voice is a welcome distraction.

"Well done, Day," he says. He's sitting at a table against the shelter's back wall. He opens the side of his jacket, where he's stashed dozens of packed grenades stolen from the train. He carefully packs each one into a box stacked with empty egg crates. He gestures up at a monitor on the far right of the back wall. It's showing footage from a large city square, where a group of people have crowded around something spray-painted against the side of a building. "Check it out."

I read what the people have painted on the wall. *Day lives!* is scrawled across the building at least three or four times. The onlookers are cheering — some are even holding handmade signs with the same phrase written on them.

If my thoughts weren't on Eden's whereabouts or June's cryptic signal or Tess, I would be excited to see what I've stirred up.

"Thanks," I reply, maybe a little too sharply. "Glad they liked our stunt."

Pascao hums cheerfully under his breath, oblivious to my tone. "Go see if you can help Jordan."

As I make my way to the hall, I pass Tess. Baxter is walking beside her — it takes me a second to realize that he's trying to put an arm around her neck and murmur something in her ear. Tess brushes him away when she sees me. I'm about to say something to her when Baxter bumps me hard in the shoulder, hard enough to knock me back a couple of steps and send the cap flying off my head. My hair tumbles down.

Baxter smirks at me, the black soldier stripe still obscuring most of his face. "Make some room," he snaps. "Think you own this place?"

I clench my teeth, but Tess's wide eyes make me hold back. *He's harmless,* I tell myself. "Just get the hell out of my way," I reply stiffly, turning away.

Behind me I hear Baxter mutter something under his breath. It's enough to make me stop and face him again. My eyes narrow. "Say that again."

He grins, shoves his hands into his pockets, and lifts his chin. "I *said,* jealous that your girl's whoring around with the Elector?"

I'm almost able to swallow that. Almost. But at that moment, Tess breaks her silence and shoves Baxter with both hands. "Hey," she says. "Leave him alone, all right? He's had a rough night."

Baxter grunts something in irritation. Then he shoves Tess unceremoniously back. "*You're* an idiot for believing in this Republic lover, little girl."

My rage explodes. I've never been fond of fistfights — I always tried to steer clear of them on the streets of Lake. But all the anger that's been building inside me floods my veins when I see Baxter lay hands on Tess.

I lunge forward and punch him in the jaw as hard as I can.

He crashes into one of the tables and onto the ground. Instantly the others nearby burst into whoops and hollers, forming a makeshift circle around the two of us. Before Baxter can get to his feet, I leap on him. My fist connects twice with his face.

He lets out a snarl. Suddenly his weight advantage takes over. He pushes me hard enough to send me flying into the side of a comp desk, then pulls me up, grabs my jacket, and slams me against the wall. He lifts me clear off my feet, then drops me and smashes his fist into my stomach, knocking the breath out of me. "You ain't one of us. You're one of *them,*" he hisses. "Did you detour from our train mission on purpose?" I feel a knee ram into my side. "Well, I'm gonna kill you, you dirty damn trot. I'm gonna skin you alive."

I'm too furious to feel the pain. I manage to tuck one of my legs up, then kick him in the chest as hard as I can. From the corner of my eye I notice some Patriots quickly exchanging bets. An improvised Skiz duel. For an instant Baxter reminds me of Thomas, and suddenly all I see is my old street in Lake, with Thomas pointing his gun at my mother and soldiers dragging John away into a waiting jeep. Strapping Eden into that lab gurney. Arresting June.

Hurting Tess. The edges of my vision turn scarlet. I lunge for him again and swing at his face.

But Baxter's ready for me. He knocks my arm out of the way and throws his full weight against me. My back slams down hard on the ground. Baxter grins, then grabs my neck and gets ready to shove his fist into the side of my face.

Abruptly he lets go. I suck in a deep breath as his weight leaves my chest, then clutch my head as one of my headaches erupts in full-scale agony. Somewhere above me I can hear Tess, then Pascao shouting at Baxter to back off. Everyone's talking at once. *One . . . Two . . . Three . . .* I count off numbers in my head, hoping this little exercise distracts me from the pain. It used to be so much easier to ward off these headaches. Maybe Baxter had hit me in the head and I don't even know it.

"Are you okay?" Now Tess's hands are on my arm and pulling me to my feet.

I'm still dizzy with pain from my headache, but the rage has passed. Abruptly I'm aware of the burning soreness in my side. "Fine," I reply hoarsely, inspecting her face. "Did he hurt you?" Baxter is glaring at me from where Pascao's trying to talk him down. Already the others around us have returned to their business, probably disappointed that the fight

293

didn't last longer. I wonder who they've decided the winner is.

"I'm okay," Tess says. She runs a hand hurriedly through her bobbed hair. "Don't worry."

"Tess!" Pascao calls out to us. "See if Day needs any patching up. We're on a schedule here."

Tess leads me down the hall and away from the common room. We walk into one of the bunker rooms that's been turned into a makeshift hospital, then shut the door. We're surrounded by shelves piled high with an assortment of pill bottles and boxes of bandages. A table sits in the middle of the room, leaving only a narrow space to walk around. Now I lean against the table as Tess rolls up her sleeves. "Do you hurt anywhere?" she asks.

"I'm fine," I repeat. But the moment I say that, I wince and clutch at my side. "Okay, maybe a little banged up."

"Let me see," Tess says firmly. She bats my hand aside, then unbuttons my shirt. It's not like Tess has never seen me shirtless (I've lost count of how many times she's had to patch me up), but now there's an awkwardness that hangs heavily between us. Her cheeks burn bright pink as she runs her hand across my chest, along my stomach, then presses her fingers against my sides.

I inhale sharply when she touches a sensi-

294

tive spot. "Yeah, that's where his knee got me."

Tess studies my face. "Feel nauseous?"

"No."

"You shouldn't have done that," she says as she works. "Say 'ah.'" I open my mouth for her. She touches a tissue to my nose, inspects both my ears, and then hurries out for a moment. She comes back with an ice pack. "Here. Hold this on the spot."

I do what she tells me. "You've become very professional."

"I've learned a lot from the Patriots," Tess replies. When she stops inspecting my chest long enough to face me, she holds my gaze with her own. "Baxter just doesn't like your . . . attraction to a former Republic soldier," she mutters. "But don't let him get to you like that, okay? No point in getting yourself killed."

I remember Baxter's arm around Tess's neck; my temper flares again, and suddenly I feel a need to guard Tess the way I did back on the streets. "Hey, cousin," I say softly. "I'm really sorry about what I said to you. About . . . you know."

Tess's blush deepens.

I struggle to find the right words. "You don't need me to take care of you," I say with an embarrassed laugh, then tap her nose once. "I mean, you've probably fussed over me a thousand times. I've always needed your help more than you've needed mine."

Tess draws closer and lowers her eyes shyly, a gesture that helps me forget my troubles. Sometimes I forget how nice Tess's steady devotion is, a rock I could always lean on during the worst of times. Even though our days in Lake were a struggle, right now they seem so much simpler. I catch myself wishing we could go back to that, sharing scraps of food and whatever else we could scrounge up. If June were here, what would've happened? She probably would've attacked Baxter herself. And she probably would've done a hell of a better job than I did, just like everything else. She wouldn't have needed me at all.

Tess's hand lingers on my chest, but she's not checking for bruises anymore. I become aware of how close she is. Her eyes wander back up to mine, large and liquid brown . . . and unlike June's, so easy to read. The image of June kissing the Elector pops into my mind again, a recollection that twists in my stomach like a knife. Before I can think about anything else, Tess leans forward and presses her lips against mine. My mind is blank, completely taken aback. A brief tingle runs through me.

In my numbness, I let her linger.

Then I wrench away. My palms break out in

a cold sweat. What was *that*? I should have seen this coming and stopped myself right away. I put my hands on her shoulders. When I see the hurt pass across her eyes, I realize just how big of a mistake I've made.

"I can't, Tess."

Tess blows out an irritated breath. "What, are you married to June now?"

"No. I just . . ." My words flitter away, sad and powerless. "I'm sorry. I shouldn't have done that — at least, not now."

"What about the fact that *June* is kissing *the Elector*? What about that? Are you really going to be so loyal to someone you don't even have?"

June, always June. I hate her for a moment, and wonder if everything would've been better if we'd never met. "This isn't about June," I say. "June is playing a role, Tess." I edge away from Tess until we're separated by a good foot. "I'm not ready for this to happen between us. You're my best friend — I don't want to mislead you when I don't even know what I'm doing."

Tess throws up her hands in indignation. "You kiss random girls on the street without a second thought. But you won't even —"

"You're not a random girl on the street," I snap. "You're *Tess*."

Her eyes flash at me and she takes her

frustration out on her lip, biting it so hard that she draws blood. "I don't understand you, Day." Each word hits me with measured force. "I don't understand you at all, but I'm going to try to help you anyway. Can you really not see how your precious June has changed your life?"

I shut my eyes and press both hands against my temples. "Stop."

"You think you're in love with a girl you've known for less than a month, a girl who — who's responsible for *your mother's death*? For *John's*?"

Echoes of what she'd said to me in the bunker room. "Damn it, Tess. It wasn't her fault —"

"Wasn't it?" Tess spits out. "Day, *they shot your mother because of June*! But you act like you love *her*? I've done nothing but *help* you — I have been at your side ever since the day we met. You think I'm being childish? Well, I don't care. I've never said a word about the other girls you've been with, but I can't bear to watch you choose a girl who has done nothing but *hurt* you. Has June even apologized to you for what happened, has she had to work for your forgiveness? What's the matter with you?" At my silence, she puts her hand on my arm. "Well, do you love her?" she says more quietly. "Does she love *you*?"

Love her? I'd told her so in that Vegas bathroom, and I'd meant it. *But she didn't say it back, yeah?* Maybe she never felt the same way — maybe I'm just deluding myself. "I don't know, okay?" I reply. My words sound angrier than I actually am.

Tess is trembling. Now she nods, silently takes the ice pack from my side, and buttons my shirt back up. The chasm between us widens. I wonder if I'll ever be able to reach the other side again. "You should be fine," she says in a monotone as she turns her back on me. She stops in front of the door, her back to me. "Trust me, Day. I'm saying this for your sake. June *will* break your heart. I can see it already. She'll shatter you into a million pieces."

JUNE

Pierra's Olan Court Hall.
Sometime around 0900 Hours.
29°F outside.

The day has finally arrived for Anden's assassination, and I have three hours before the Patriots make their move.

The night before, I had another visit from the same guard who had once given me a message from the Patriots. "Good work," she whispered in my ear as I lay in bed, wide awake. "Tomorrow you'll be pardoned by the Elector and his Senators, and they'll release you at Pierra's Olan Court Hall. Now, listen closely. When you're all finished at the court hall, the Elector's jeeps will escort all of you back to Pierra's main military quarters. The Patriots will be waiting along that route."

The soldier paused to see if I had any questions. But I just stared straight ahead. I could guess what the Patriots wanted me to do, anyway — they'll want me to separate Anden from his guards. Then the Patriots will drag him out of his jeep and shoot him. They'll record it, then announce it to the whole Republic using the rewired speakers and JumboTrons on Denver's Capitol Tower.

When I didn't say anything, the soldier cleared her throat and went on in a hurried voice, "Watch for an explosion on the road. When you hear it go off, have Anden order his convoy to take a different route. Make sure you separate the Elector from his guards — tell him to trust you. If you've done your job, he'll follow your lead." The soldier smiled briefly at me. "Once Anden is separated from the other jeeps, leave the rest to us."

I spent the rest of that night in a fitful state.

Now, as I'm escorted into the main court hall building, I check the rooftops and alleys of the other buildings along the street, watching for Patriot eyes, wondering if one pair of them will be bright blue. Day will be amongst the Patriots out here today. Inside my black gloves, my hands are cold with sweat. Even if he saw my signal, will he understand what I meant by it? Will he know to drop what he's doing and make a run for it? As I head toward the courtroom's grand arched entrance, I memorize street names and locations out of habit — where the main military base is, where Pierra's hospital rises in the distance. I feel like I can sense the Patriots getting into position. There's a stillness in the air, even though the buildings here are tightly packed and the streets are narrow; both soldiers and civilians (most of them poor and assigned to tend to the troops) bustle noisily along the roads. Some of the uniformed soldiers on the street look at us a little too long. I note them carefully. There must be Patriots watching us. Even inside the hall, it's cold enough for my breath to cloud, and I tremble nonstop. (The ceiling's at least twenty feet high, and the floors are polished synthetic — judging from the sound of boots against it — wood. Not very conducive to retaining heat in winter.)

"How long is this going to take?" I ask one of the guards as they escort me to my seat at the front of the courtroom. My boots (warm, waterproof leather) echo harshly against the floors. I shiver in spite of the double-breasted coat I have on.

The guard I spoke to gives me an uncomfortable nod. "Not long, Ms. Iparis," she replies with practiced politeness. "The Elector and Senators are in final deliberations. Probably going to take at least another half hour." It's interesting, really. Because the Elector himself will be pardoning me today, the guards aren't sure exactly how to behave. Guard me like a criminal? Or kiss up like I'm a high-ranking Agent in one of the capital's patrols?

The waiting drags on. I feel slightly dizzy. I'd been given some medicine after finally mentioning my symptoms to Anden earlier in the day, but it hasn't helped. My head still feels warm, and I'm having trouble keeping count of the time in my head.

Finally, when I've counted off twenty-six minutes (possibly off by three or four seconds), Anden emerges from the doors at the far end of the room with a team of officials behind him. It's clear that not everyone is happy; some Senators hang back, their mouths pulled into tight lines. I recognize Senator Kamion amongst them, the man Anden had been arguing with on the train here. His graying hair looks disheveled today. Another Senator I remember from occasional headlines, Senator O'Connor, a blubbery woman with limp red hair and a mouth not unlike a frog's. I don't know the others. Aside from the Senators, two young journalists flank Anden's sides.

One has his head down, taking dictation furiously on a notepad, while the second struggles to keep his voice recorder close enough to Anden.

I rise when they reach me. The Senators who were bickering amongst themselves fall silent. Anden nods at my guards. "June Iparis, Congress has pardoned you of all crimes against the Republic on the condition that you will continue to serve your nation to the best of your capabilities. Do we have an understanding, Ms. Iparis?"

I nod. Even this slight movement makes me light-headed. "Yes, Elector." The scribe beside Anden frantically jots our words down. His notepad's screen flickers under his flying fingers.

Anden takes in my listlessness. He can tell that my condition hasn't improved. "You will enter a period of probation as advised to me by my Senators, during which time you'll be *closely* surveyed until we can all agree that you're ready to return to duty. You'll be assigned to the capital's patrols. We'll discuss which patrol you'll be joining once we're all settled at Pierra's base this afternoon." He raises his eyebrows and turns to his right and left. "Senators? Any comments?"

They remain silent. One of them finally

speaks through a thinly veiled sneer. "Understand that you are not yet in the clear, Agent Iparis. You will be watched at all times. You should consider our decision an act of enormous mercy."

"Thank you, Elector," I reply, tapping my head in a brief salute as any soldier would. "Thank you, Senators."

"Thank *you* for all of your help," Anden says with a subtle bow. I keep my head lowered so I don't have to meet his eyes, to see the double layer of meaning in his words — he's thanking me for the help I supposedly gave in protecting him, and the help he wants from both Day and me.

Somewhere outside, Day is in position with the others. The thought makes me nauseous with anxiety.

The soldiers begin escorting our party back to the front of the conference hall and toward our respective rides. I take each step deliberately, trying hard to maintain my focus. Now is not the moment to fail because of illness. I keep my eyes on the hall's entrance. Since our last train ride, this is the one idea I've settled on that just might work. Something to throw off all the Patriots' timing — something I can do to prevent us from heading back toward Pierra's main military hall.

I hope this works. I don't think I can afford any mistakes.

With ten feet to the doors, I stumble. Instantly, I right myself again and continue walking, but then stumble again. Murmurs from the Senators rise up behind me. One of them snaps, "What is it?"

Then Anden is there, his face hovering above me. Two of his guards jump in front of him. "Elector, sir," one says. "Please stay back. We'll take care of this."

"What happened?" Anden asks, first to the soldiers, then to me. "Are you injured?"

It's not too hard to pretend I'm about to faint. The world around me fades, then sharpens again. My head hurts. I raise my head and make eye contact with Anden. Then I let myself collapse to the ground.

Startled exclamations buzz around me. Then my ears perk up when I hear Anden above them all, saying exactly what I'd hoped he would say: "Take her to the hospital. Immediately." He remembers my last piece of advice to him, what I'd said to him on the train.

"But, Elector —" protests the same guard who had barred him earlier.

Anden takes on a steely tone. "Are you questioning me, soldier?"

Strong hands help me back to my feet. We

go through the doors and back out into the light of an overcast morning. I squint at the surroundings, still searching for suspicious faces. Are the guards holding me up potentially Patriots in disguise? I cast glances at them, but their expressions are completely blank. Adrenaline is rushing through me — I've made my move. The Patriots know I've deviated from the plan, but they don't know if I did it intentionally. The important thing is that the hospital is on a route opposite the one leading to the Pierra base, where the Patriots are ready and waiting. Anden's going to follow me. The Patriots won't have time to readjust their positions.

And if the other Patriots hear about this, so should Day. I close my eyes and hope that he can follow through. I try sending a silent message to him. *Run away. When you hear that I've deviated from the plan, run away as fast as you can.*

A guard hoists me up into the backseat of one of the waiting jeeps. Anden and his soldiers get into the jeep in front of us. The Senators, bewildered and indignant, go to their regular cars. I have to force a smile off my face as I sit limply in my seat, peering out the windows. The jeep roars to life and pulls forward. Through the windshield, I see Anden's jeep leading us away from the conference hall.

Then, just as I'm congratulating myself for such a stellar plan, I realize that our jeeps are still headed for the base. They're not going toward the hospital at all. My momentary joy vanishes. Fear replaces it.

One of my guards notices too. "Hey, chauffeur," he snaps at the soldier who's driving. "Wrong way. Hospital's on the left side of town." He sighs. "Somebody get the Elector's driver on his mike. We're —"

The driver waves him off, presses one thick, gnarly hand against his ear in concentration, then glances back at us with a frown. "Negative. We just got orders to stay on our original course," he replies. "Commander DeSoto says the Elector wants Ms. Iparis taken to the hospital afterward, instead."

I freeze. Razor must be lying to Anden's driver — I seriously doubt that Anden would have let him give the drivers such an order. Razor's going ahead with the plan; he's going to force us to take the intended route in any way that he can.

It doesn't matter what the reason is. We're still heading straight toward the Pierra base . . . straight into the Patriots' waiting arms.

DAY

The day of the Elector's assassination is finally here. It arrives like a looming hurricane of change, promising everything I'm anticipating and dreading. Anticipating: the Elector's death. Dreading: June's signal.

Or maybe it's the other way around.

I still don't know what to make of it. It leaves me on edge when I would otherwise feel nothing but a rising sense of enthusiasm. I tap restlessly on the hilt of my knife. *Be careful, June.* That's the only certain thought running through my head. *Be careful — for your sake, and for ours.*

I'm perched precariously at the edge of a crumbling windowsill in an old shell of a building, four stories up and hidden from the street, with two grenades and a gun tucked securely at my belt. Like the rest of the Patriots, I'm dressed in a black Republic coat, so from a distance I look like a Republic soldier. A black stripe runs across my eyes again. The only thing distinguishing us is a white band on our left (instead of right) arms. From here, I can see the railroad tracks that run right along a neighboring street, slicing Pierra in half. Off to my right, in a small alley three buildings down, lies the entrance to the Patriots' Pierra tunnel. Its underground bunker is empty now. I'm alone in this abandoned building, although I'm pretty sure Pascao can see me from his vantage point on a roof across the street. The thud of my heart against my ribs can probably be heard for miles.

I start thinking, for the hundredth time, about why June wants to stop the assassination. Did she uncover something the Patriots are keeping a secret from me? Or did she do what Tess had guessed she might do — did she betray us? I shake the thought stubbornly away.

June would never do that. Not after what the Republic did to her brother.

Maybe June wants to stop the assassination because she's falling for the Elector. I shut my eyes as the image of them kissing flares up in my mind. No way. *Would the June I know be that sentimental?*

All the Patriots are in position — Runners on the roofs, poised with explosives; Hackers one building away from the tunnel entrance, ready to record and broadcast the Elector's assassination; fighters positioned along the street below us in soldier or civilian garb, prepared to take the Elector's guards down. Tess and a couple of Medics are scattered, ready to bring the injured into the tunnel. Tess specifically is hiding in the narrow street bordering the left side of my building. After the assassination, we'll need to be ready to escape, and she'll be the first one I'll get.

And then there's me. According to the plan, June's supposed to steer the Elector away from the protection of his guards. When we see his jeep speed by alone, the Runners will cut off his escape routes with explosions. Then I head down to the street. After the Patriots have dragged Anden out of his car, I'm going to shoot him.

It's the middle of the afternoon, but clouds keep the world around me a cold, ominous gray. I check my watch. It's set on a timer for when the Elector's jeeps are expected to come whizzing around the corner.

Fifteen minutes until showtime.

I'm shaking. Is the Elector really going to be dead in fifteen minutes — by my hand? Is this plan really going to work? After it's all over, when are the Patriots going to help me find and rescue Eden? When I'd told Razor about seeing that boy on board the train, he'd given me a sympathetic response and said that he's

311

already started working to track Eden down. All I can do is believe him. I try to picture the Republic thrown into complete chaos, with the Elector's assassination publicly broadcast on every JumboTron in the nation. If the people are already rioting, I can only imagine how they'll react when they see me shoot the Elector. What then? Will the Colonies take advantage of the situation and surge right into the Republic, breaking past the warfront that's held the two sides apart for so long?

A new government. A new order. I shiver with pent-up energy.

Of course, this doesn't factor in June's signal. I try to flex my fingers — my hands are clammy with cold sweat. Hell if I know what's *really* going to happen today.

Static buzzes in my earpiece, and I pick up a few broken words from Pascao. "— Orange and Echo streets — clear —" His voice sharpens. "Day?"

"I'm here."

"Fifteen minutes," he says. "Quick review. Jordan's setting off the first explosion. When the Elector's jeep caravan reaches her street, she'll toss her grenade. June will separate the Elector's car from the others. I toss my grenade, then they'll turn right down your street. *You* toss yours down when you see the caravan. Corner that jeep in — and then head down to the ground. Got it?"

"Yeah. Got it," I reply. "Just hurry the hell up and get into your own position."

Waiting here gives me a sick feeling in my stomach, taking me back to that evening when I'd waited for the plague patrols to show up at my mother's door. Even that night seems better than today. My family was alive back then, and Tess and I were still on good terms. I practice taking several deep breaths and slowly letting them back out. In less than fifteen minutes, I'm going to see the Elector's caravan — and June — come down this street. My fingers run along the edges of the grenades at my belt.

One minute passes, then another.

Three minutes. Four minutes. Five minutes. Each one drags by slower than the last. My breaths quicken. What will June do? Is she right? What if she's *wrong*? I think I'm ready to kill the Elector — I've been talking myself into this over the last few days, even getting excited over it. Am I ready to save his life, someone I can't think about without feeling enraged? Am I ready to have his blood on my hands? What does June know that I don't? What does she know that makes him *so worth saving*?

Eight minutes.

Then, suddenly, Pascao comes back on.

"Stand by. We've got a delay."

I tense up. "Why?"

There's a long pause. "Something's wrong with June," Pascao says in a hushed whisper. "She fainted while leaving the courthouse. But don't freak out — Razor says she's fine. We're resetting the clocks for a two-minute delay. Got it?"

I rise a little from my crouch. *She's making her move.* I know this instantly. Something tingles at the back of my mind, a sixth sense, warning me that whatever I'd planned to do to the Elector will shift depending on what June does next. "Why did she collapse?" I ask.

"Don't know. Scouts say it looks like she got dizzy or something."

"So she's back on track now?"

"Sounds like we're still moving forward."

Still moving forward? Was June's plan foiled? I get up, pace for a few steps, and then return to my crouch. Something's not right about this scenario. If we're going ahead with the plan, will I still see her come by in the same jeep as expected — and against her will? Are the Patriots going to know she tried to deviate? The bad feeling refuses to go away, no matter how hard I try to ignore it. Something's *really* off.

Two agonizing minutes pass. In my anxiety, I've chipped away a large chunk of paint from

314

the hilt of my knife. My thumb's covered in black flakes.

Several streets away, the first grenade explodes. The ground trembles, the building shudders, and a cloud of dust rains down from the ceiling. The Elector's jeeps must've made an appearance.

I leave my vantage point at the windowsill, then head into the stairwell up to the roof. I keep low, careful to stay out of sight. From here, I get a better view of where smoke from the first explosion is rising, and I can hear the startled shouts of soldiers near it. They're about three blocks away. I flatten myself onto the broken tiles of the roof as several guards come dashing down the street. They're yelling something incomprehensible — I'm willing to bet they're bringing reinforcements over to the bombing area. Too late. By the time they get there, the Elector's jeep will have turned the corner that we wanted it to turn.

I take out one of my grenades and hold it gingerly in my hand, reminding myself how it works, reminding myself that if I throw it on time, I'll be going against June's warning. *"It's an impact grenade,"* Pascao had said. *"Blows the second it hits. Depress the strike lever. Pull the pin. Throw, and brace yourself."* Off in the distance, another explosion rocks the streets and an accompanying cloud rises.

Baxter was in charge of that one — now he's somewhere on ground level over there, hiding in an alley.

Two blocks away. The Elector is getting closer.

A third explosion goes off. This one's much closer — the jeep must only be a block away. I steady myself as the ground shakes from the impact. My turn's coming up. *June,* I think. *Where are you?* If she makes a sudden move, what will *I* do? Over my earpiece, Pascao sounds urgent. "Steady," he says.

And then I see something that makes me forget everything I've promised to do for the Patriots. The door on the second jeep flies open, and out rolls a girl with a long dark ponytail. She tumbles a few times, then struggles to her feet. She looks up to the rooftops and waves her hands frantically in the air.

It's June. She's here. And there's no doubt now that she does not want me to separate the Elector from his guards.

Pascao's voice comes on again. "Stay the course," he hisses. "Ignore June — stay the course, do you hear me?"

I don't know what comes over me — an electric shudder runs down my spine. *No — June, you can't stop now,* a part of me says. *I*

316

want *the Elector dead. I want to get Eden back.*

But then there's June, waving her arms in the middle of a street full of danger, risking her life to raise the alarm for me. Whatever her reason, it must be good. It *must* be. What do I do? *Trust her,* something deep inside of me says. I squeeze my eyes shut and bow my head.

Each second that ticks by now is a bridge between life and death.

Trust her.

Suddenly I jump up and run across the roof. Pascao shouts something angry at me over the earpiece. I ignore him. As the vehicles pass next to the building I'm on, I pull the pin from my grenade and throw it as far as I can down the block. Right in front of where the Patriots want them to go.

"Day!" Pascao's frantic voice. "No — what are you — !"

The grenade hits the street. I cover my ears and am instantly thrown off my feet as a blast shakes the earth. The jeeps screech to a halt right in front of the explosion — the Elector's jeep tries to swerve around the rubble, but one of its tires bursts and forces it to a stop. I've completely blocked off the street they were supposed to go down, where the Patriots are waiting for the Elector. And the rest of the

Elector's jeeps are still there, the entire caravan of them.

Now June's sprinting toward the Elector's vehicle. If she's trying to save him, then I have no time to waste. I hop back to my feet, swing over the side of the roof, and grab on to the gutter at the edge of the building. Then I slide down. The gutter pipe pops off the building, throwing me off balance, but I fling myself off it and grab the edge of a nearby windowsill. My feet land on the second floor's ledge. I hop down to the first floor and roll.

The street's absolute chaos. Through the shouts and smoke, I can see Republic soldiers running toward the jeeps while the soldiers in the other jeeps rush out to get to the Elector. Some of the Patriots in disguise are hesitating, confused over my mistimed blast. It's too late to separate the Elector's jeep from the others now — there are simply too many soldiers. Swarms of them are coming down the street. I feel numb, in some ways as bewildered as they are, still unsure of why I'm going against everything I planned to do.

"Tess!" I shout. She's right where she's supposed to be, frozen against the shadows of my building. I reach her and grab her shoulders.

"What's going on?" she shouts back, but I just whirl her around.

"Tunnel entrance, okay? Don't ask!" I point her in the direction of the Patriots' bunker. Where we were supposed to hide after the assassination. Tess's mouth is open in naked fear, but she does what I say, darting into the security of the building's shadows and disappearing from view.

Another explosion rocks the street behind me. The grenade must have come from one of the other Runners. Even though they won't get the Elector to their planned location, they're trying to block in the jeeps to make an attempt. Patriots must be running around everywhere. They're literally going to kill me for what I did. Me and Tess have to reach the tunnel before they find us.

I run up to June right as she reaches the Elector's jeep. There's a man inside with dark, wavy hair, and she's shouting at him as she presses her hands against his window. Another explosion goes off somewhere, forcing June to her knees. I throw myself over her as debris and rubble rain down on us from every direction. A block of cement hits my shoulder, making me shudder in pain. The Patriots are definitely trying to make up for lost time, but the delay has already cost them dearly. If they get desperate, I know they'll just forget about broadcasting an actual kill and blow up the Elector's jeep instead. Republic soldiers are pouring into the street. I'm sure they've seen me by now too. I hope Tess is safe in the hideout.

"June!" She looks dazed and bewildered, but then she recognizes me. No time for greetings now.

A bullet zips overhead. I duck and shield June again; one of the soldiers near us gets shot in the leg. *Please, for the love of — Please let Tess make it safely to the tunnel entrance.* I whirl around and meet the Elector's wide eyes through the window. So, this is the guy who kissed June — he's tall and good-looking and rich, and he's going to uphold all of his father's laws. He's the boy king who symbolizes everything the Republic is; the war with the Colonies that led to Eden's illness, the laws that put my family in the slums and led to their deaths, the laws that sent me off to be executed because I'd failed some stupid goddy test when I was ten. This guy *is* the Republic. I should kill him right now.

But then I think of June. If June knows a reason we should protect him from the Patriots, and believes it enough to risk her life — and mine — then I'm going to trust her. If I refused, I'd be breaking ties with her forever. *Can I live with that?* The thought of that chills me to the bone. I point down the street toward the explosion and do something I never thought I'd do in my whole life. I yell as loud as I can for the soldiers. *"Back up the jeeps! Barricade the street! Protect the Elector!"* Then, as other soldiers reach the Elector, I shout frantically at them, "Get the Elector out of this car! Get him away from here — they're going to blow it up!"

June yanks us down as another bullet hits the ground near us. "Come on," I shout. She follows me. Behind us, dozens of Republic soldiers have arrived on the scene. We catch a quick glimpse of the Elector getting out of his jeep, then being hurried away behind the protection of his soldiers. Bullets fly. Did I just see one hit the Elector in the chest? No — just his upper arm. Then he disappears, lost behind a sea of soldiers.

He's saved. He's going to make it. I can hardly breathe at the thought — I don't know if I should be happy or furious. After all that buildup, the Elector's assassination has failed because of me and June.

What have I done?

"That's Day!" someone calls out. *"He's alive!"* But I don't dare turn around again. I squeeze June's hand tighter and we dart around the rubble and smoke.

We bump into our first Patriot. Baxter. He stops short for a second when he sees us, then seizes June's arm. *"You!"* he spits out.

She's too quick for him, though. Before I can draw the gun at my waist, June's slipped right out of his grasp. He grabs for us again — but someone else knocks him flat on his face before we can make another move. I meet Kaede's burning eyes.

She waves her hands furiously at us. "Get to safety!" she yells. "Before the others find you!" There's deep shock on her face — is she stunned that the plan fell apart? Does she know we had anything to do with it? She must know. *Why is she turning on the Patriots too?* Then she runs away. I let my eyes follow her for an instant. Sure enough, Anden is nowhere to be seen and Republic soldiers have started firing back up at the roofs.

Anden is nowhere to be seen, I think again. Has the assassination attempt officially failed?

We keep running until we're on the other side of the explosion. Suddenly there are Patriots everywhere; some are running toward the soldiers and looking for a way to shoot the Elector, and others are fleeing for the tunnel. Running after *us.*

Another explosion shakes the street — someone has tried in vain to stop the Elector with another grenade. Maybe they finally managed to blow up his jeep. *Where's Razor?* Is he out for our blood now? I picture his calm, fatherly face alight with rage.

We finally reach the narrow alley that leads to the tunnel, barely ahead of the Patriots hot on our tail.

Tess is there, huddled in the shadows against the wall. I want to scream. Why didn't she jump down into the tunnel and head for the hideout? "Inside, now," I say. "You weren't supposed to wait for me."

But she doesn't move. Instead she stands in front of us with her fists clenched, her eyes flickering back and forth between me and June. I rush over and grab her hand, then pull her along with us to one of the small metal gratings that line where the alley's walls meet the ground. I can hear the first signs of Patriots behind us. *Please,* I beg silently. *Please let us be the first ones to reach the hideout.*

"They're coming," June says, her eyes fixed on a spot down the alley.

"Let them try to catch us." I run my hands frantically across the metal grating, then pry it open.

The Patriots are getting closer. Too close.

I stand up. "Get out of the way," I say to Tess and June. Then I pull a second grenade from my belt, yank out the pin, and toss it toward the alleyway's opening. We throw ourselves to the ground and cover our heads with our hands.

Boom! A deafening blast. It should slow the Patriots down some, but I can already see silhouettes coming through the debris and toward us.

June runs to the open tunnel entrance by my side. I let her jump in first, then turn to Tess and extend my hand. "Come *on,* Tess," I say. "We don't have much time."

Tess looks at my open hand and takes a step back. In that instant, the world around us seems to freeze. She's not going to come with us. There's anger and shock and guilt and sadness all wrapped up in her thin little face.

I try again. "Come on!" I shout. "*Please,* Tess — I can't leave you here."

Tess's eyes rip through me. "I'm sorry, Day," she gasps. "But I can take care of myself. So don't try to come after me." Then she tears her eyes away from me and runs back toward the Patriots. *She's rejoining them?* I watch her go, stunned into silence, my hand still outstretched. The Patriots are so close now.

Baxter's words. He'd warned Tess this whole time that I would betray them. And I did. I did exactly what Baxter said I'd do, and now Tess has to live with it. *I've let her down so bad.*

June's the one who saves me. "Day, *jump!*" she yells up at me, snapping me out of the moment.

I force myself to turn away from Tess and

jump into the hole. My boots splash into shallow, icy water right as I hear the first Patriot reach us. June grabs my hand. "Go!" she hisses.

We sprint down the black tunnel. Behind us I hear someone else drop down and start running after us. Then another. They're all coming.

"Got any more grenades?" June shouts as we run.

I reach down to my belt. "One." I pull the last grenade out, then toss the pin. If we use this, there's no going back. We could be stuck down here forever — but there's no other choice, and June knows it.

I shout a warning behind us, and throw the grenade. The closest Patriot sees me do it and scrambles to a stop. Then he starts yelling at the others to get back. We keep sprinting.

The blast lifts us clear off our feet and sends us flying. I hit the ground hard, skidding through icy water and slush for several seconds before coming to a stop. My head rings — I press my palms hard against my temples in an attempt to stop it. No luck, though. A headache bursts my mind wide open, drowning out all of my thoughts, and I squeeze my eyes shut at the blinding pain. *One, two, three . . .*

Long seconds drag by. My head throbs with the impact of a thousand hammers. I struggle to breathe.

Then, mercifully, it starts to fade. I open my eyes in the darkness — the ground has settled again, and even though I can still hear people talking behind us, they're muffled, as if coming from the other side of a thick door. Gingerly I pull myself up into a sitting position. June's leaning against the side of the tunnel, rubbing her arm. We're both facing the space we'd come from.

A hollow tunnel stood there just seconds ago, but now a pile of concrete and rubble have completely sealed off the entrance.

We've made it. But all I feel is emptiness.

JUNE

When I was five years old, Metias took me to see our parents' graves. It was the first time he'd been to the site since the actual funeral. I don't think he could stand being reminded of what had happened. Most of Los Angeles's civilians — even a good number of the upper class — are assigned a one-square-foot slot in their local cemetery high-rise and a single opaque glass box in which to store a loved one's ashes. But Metias paid off the cemetery officials and got a four-square-foot slot for Mom and Dad, along with engraved crystal headstones. We stood there in front of the headstones with our white clothes and white flowers. I spent the whole time staring at Metias. I can still remember his tight jaw, his neatly brushed hair, his cheeks damp and glistening. Most of all I remember his eyes, heavy with sadness, too old for a seventeen-year-old boy.

Day looked that way when he learned about his brother John's death. And now, as we make our way along the underground tunnel and out of Pierra, he has those eyes again.

We spend fifty-two minutes (or fifty-one? I'm not sure. My head feels feverish and light) jogging through the dark wetness of the tunnel. For a while we'd heard angry shouts coming from the other side of the mountain of twisted concrete that separates us from the Patriots and the Republic's soldiers. But eventually those sounds faded to silence as we rushed deeper and deeper into the tunnel. The Patriots probably had to flee from the oncoming troops. Maybe the soldiers are trying to excavate the rubble out of the tunnel. We have no idea, so we keep going.

It's quiet now. The only sounds are our ragged breathing, our boots splashing into shallow, slushy puddles, and the *drip, drip, drip* of ice-cold water from the ceiling that runs down our necks. Day grips my hand tightly as we run. His fingers are cold and rubbery with wetness, but I still cling to them. It's so dark down here that I can barely see Day's outline in front of me.

Did Anden survive the assault? I wonder.

Or did the Patriots manage to assassinate him? The thought makes the blood rush in my ears. The last time I played the role of double agent, I'd gotten someone killed. Anden had put his faith in me, and because of that, he could've died today — maybe he *did* die. The price people seem to pay for crossing my path.

This thought triggers another. *Why didn't Tess come down with us?* I want to ask, but oddly enough, Day hasn't said a word about her since we entered this tunnel. They'd had an argument, that much I know. *I hope she's okay.* Had she chosen to stay with the Patriots?

Finally, Day stops in front of a wall. I nearly collapse against him, and a sudden wave of relief and panic hits me. I should be able to run farther than this, but I'm exhausted. Is this a dead end? Has part of the tunnel collapsed on itself, and now we're trapped from both sides?

But Day puts his hand against the surface in the darkness. "We can rest here," he whispers. They're the first words he's spoken since we got down here. "I stayed in one of these in Lamar."

Razor had mentioned the Patriots' getaway tunnels once. Day runs his hand along the edge of the door where it meets the wall.

Finally, he finds what he's searching for, a small sliding lever sticking out from a thin twelve-inch slot. He pulls it from one end to the other. The door opens with a click.

At first, we just step into a black hole. Although I can't see anything, I listen closely to how our footsteps are echoing around the room and guess that there's a low ceiling, probably only a few feet taller than the tunnel itself (ten, maybe eleven feet high), and when I put a hand along one wall I can tell it's straight, not curved. A rectangular room.

"Here it is," Day mutters. I hear him press and release something, and artificial light floods the space. "Let's hope it's empty."

It's not a large chamber, but it would be big enough to fit twenty or thirty people comfortably, even up to a hundred if they were crammed in. Against the back wall are two doors leading off into dark hallways. All the walls have monitors, thick and clunky along the edges, with clumsier design than the ones used in most Republic halls. I wonder if the Patriots installed these or if they're old tech left over from when these tunnels were first built.

While Day wanders through the first hall at the back of the main room, his gun drawn, I check the second one. There are two smaller rooms here, with five sets of bunk beds in each one, and at the far end of the hall is a small door that leads back into the dark, endless tunnel. I'm willing to bet that the hall Day is in also has a tunnel entrance. As I wander from bunk to bunk, I run my hand along the wall where people had scrawled their names and initials. *This way to salvation. J. D. Edward,* one says. *The only way out is death. Maria Márques,* says another.

"All clear?" Day says from behind me.

I nod at him. "Clear. I think we're safe for now."

He sighs, lets his shoulders slump, then runs a hand wearily through his tangled hair. It's only been a few days since the last time I saw him, but somehow it feels like so much longer. I walk over to him. His eyes wander across my face as if taking me in for the first time. He must have a million questions for me, but he just lifts a hand and pushes a lock of my hair into place. I'm not sure if I feel dizzy from illness or emotion. I'd almost forgotten how his touch makes me feel. I want to fall into the purity that is Day, soaking in his simple honesty, his heart that sits open and beating on his sleeve.

"Hey," he murmurs.

I wrap my arms around him, and we hold

each other tightly. I close my eyes, letting myself sink against Day's body and the warmth of his breath on my neck. His hands brush through my hair and run down my back, holding on to me like he's afraid to let go. He pulls away enough to meet my eyes. He leans forward as if to kiss me . . . but then, for some reason, he stops himself, and pulls me back into a hug. Holding him is comforting, but still.

Something has changed.

We make our way into the kitchen (two hundred twenty-five square feet, judging by the number of tiles on the square floor), dig up two cans of food and bottles of water, squeeze onto the counters, and settle in for a break. Day's silent. I wait expectantly as we share a can of pasta drowning in tomato sauce, but he still doesn't utter a word. He seems to be thinking. About the foiled plan? About Tess? Or perhaps he's not thinking at all, but still stunned into silence. I stay quiet too. I would prefer not to put words in his mouth.

"I saw your warning signal from one of the security cam videos," he finally says after seventeen minutes have passed. "I didn't know exactly what you wanted me to do, but I got the general idea."

I notice he doesn't mention the kiss

between Anden and me, even though I'm sure he saw it. "Thanks." My vision darkens for a second and I blink rapidly to try to focus. Maybe I need more medicine. "I'm . . . sorry for forcing you into a tough spot. I'd tried to make the jeeps take a different route in Pierra, but it didn't work out."

"That was the whole delay when you collapsed, right? I was afraid you might've gotten hurt."

I chew thoughtfully for a moment. Food should taste great right now, but I'm not hungry at all. I should tell him about Eden's freedom right away, but Day's tone — somehow like a thunderstorm on the horizon — holds me back. Had the Patriots been able to hear all of my conversations with Anden? If so, then Day might already know. "Razor's lying to us about why he wants the Elector dead. I don't know why yet — but the things he's told us just don't add up." I pause, wondering if Razor has already been detained by Republic officials. If not now, then soon. The Republic should know by the end of today that Razor specifically instructed the jeep drivers to stay on course, leading Anden right into the trap.

Day shrugs and concentrates on the food. "Who knows *what* he and the Patriots are doing now?"

I wonder if he says this because he's thinking about Tess. The way she'd looked at him before we escaped into the tunnel . . . I decide not to ask about what might have happened between them. Still, my imagination conjures up a vision of them on the couch together, so comfortable and relaxed like they'd been when we first met the Patriots in Vegas, Day resting his head in Tess's lap. Tess leaning down to brush her lips over his. My stomach tightens in discomfort. *But she didn't come,* I remind myself. What happened between them? I picture Tess arguing with Day about me.

"So," he says in a monotone. "Tell me what you found out about the Elector that made you decide that we should betray the Patriots."

He doesn't know about Eden, after all. I put down my water and purse my lips. "The Elector freed your brother."

Day's fork stops in midair. "What?"

"Anden let him go — on the day after I gave you the signal. Eden is under federal protection in Denver. Anden hates what the Republic did to your family . . . and he wants to win back our trust — yours and mine." I reach over for Day's hand, but he snatches it away. My breath escapes me in a

334

disappointed sigh. I wasn't sure how he'd take this news, but a part of me hoped that he would just be . . . happy.

"Anden is completely opposed to the late Elector's politics," I go on. "He wants to stop the Trials, and the plague experiments." I hesitate. Day is still staring at the can of pasta, fork in hand, but he's not eating any longer. "He wants to make all these radical changes, but he needs to win the public's favor first. He basically begged me for our help."

Day's expression quivers. "That's it? *That's* why you decided to throw the Patriots' entire plan out the window?" he replies bitterly. "So the Elector can bribe me in exchange for my support? Sounds like a damn joke, if you ask me. How do you know he's telling the truth, June? Did you actually get proof that he released Eden?"

I put my hand on his arm. This is exactly what I feared from Day, but he has every right to be suspicious. How can I explain the gut instinct I have about Anden's personality, or the fact that I'd seen the honesty in his eyes? I know Anden released Day's brother. I *know* it. But Day wasn't there in the room. *He* doesn't know Anden. He has no reason to trust him. "Anden is different. You have to believe me, Day. He released

Eden, and not just because he wants us to do something for him."

Day's words are cold and distant. "I *said*, do you have any proof?"

I sigh, taking my hand off his arm. "No," I admit. "I don't."

Day snaps out of his daze and digs his fork back into the can. He does it so hard that the fork's handle bends. "He played you. *You*, of all people. The Republic is *not* going to change. Right now the new Elector's young, stupid as hell, and full of it, and he just wants to make people take him seriously. He'll say anything. Once things settle down, you'll see his true colors. I guarantee it. He's no different from his father — just another goddy rich trot with deep pockets and a mouthful of lies."

It irritates me that Day thinks I'm so gullible. "Young and full of it?" I give Day a little shove, trying to lighten the mood. "Reminds me of someone."

Once this would have made Day laugh, but now he just glares at me. "I saw a boy in Lamar," he continues. "He was my brother's age. For a minute, I thought he *was* Eden. He was being shipped around in a giant glass tube, like some sort of science experiment. I tried to get him out, but I couldn't. The boy's blood is being used as a bioweapon that they're trying to launch into the Colonies." Day throws his fork into the sink. "*That's* what your pretty Elector's doing to my brother. Now, you still think he released him?"

I reach over and put my hand over his. "Congress had sent Eden to the warfront before Anden was Elector. Anden just released him the other day. He's —"

Day shrugs me off, his expression a mix of frustration and confusion. He readjusts the sleeves of his collar shirt back up to his elbows. "Why do you believe in this guy so much?"

"What do you mean?"

He gets angrier as he goes. "I mean, the only reason I didn't smash your Elector's car window and put a knife through his throat was because of *you.* Because I knew *you* must've had a good reason. But now it seems like you just take his words on faith. What happened to all that logic of yours?"

I don't like the way he calls Anden *my* Elector, as if Day and I were still on opposing sides. "I'm telling you the truth," I say quietly. "Besides, last time I checked, you're not a murderer."

Day turns away from me and mutters something under his breath that I can't quite catch. I cross my arms. "Do you remember when I trusted *you,* even though everything I'd ever known told me that you were an enemy? I gave you the benefit of the doubt, and I sacrificed everything for what I believed. I can tell you right now that assassinating Anden will solve nothing. He's the one person the Republic actually needs — someone inside the system with enough power to change things. How could you live with yourself after killing a person like that? Anden is *good.*"

"*So what* if he is?" Day says coldly. He's gripping the countertop so tightly that his knuckles have turned white. "Good, bad — what does it matter? He's the *Elector.*"

I narrow my eyes. "Do you *really* believe that?"

Day shakes his head and laughs mirthlessly. "The Patriots are trying to start a revolution. That's what this country needs — not a *new* Elector, but *no* Elector. The Republic is broken beyond repair. Let the Colonies take over."

"You don't even know what the Colonies are like."

"I know they've got to be better than this hellhole," Day snaps.

I can tell that he's not angry at just me, but he's starting to sound childish and it rubs me the wrong way. "You know why I agreed to help the Patriots?" I put a hand on his upper arm, feeling the faint outline of a scar under the fabric. Day tenses up at my touch. "Because I wanted to help *you*. You think everything's my fault, don't you? It's my fault that your brother's being experimented on. It's my fault that you had to leave the Patriots. It's my fault that Tess refused to come."

"No . . ." Day trails off as he wrings his hands in frustration. "It's not all your fault. And Tess . . . Tess is definitely my fault." There's genuine pain on his face — at this point, I can't tell who it's for. So much has happened. I feel a curious pang of resentment that makes blood rush in my ears even as it shames me. It's not fair for me to be jealous. After all, Day has known Tess for years, much longer than he's known me, so why shouldn't he feel attached to her? Besides, Tess is sweet, selfless, healing. I am not. Of course I know why Tess had abandoned him. It *is* because of me.

I study his face. "What happened between you and Tess?"

Day stares at the wall across from us, lost in thought, and I have to tap his foot with mine to snap him out of it. "Tess kissed me," he mutters. "And she feels like I betrayed her . . . for you."

My cheeks redden. I close my eyes, forcing the image of them kissing out of my thoughts. *This is so stupid. Isn't it?* Tess has known Day for years — she has every right to kiss him. And hadn't the Elector kissed me too? Hadn't I liked it? Anden suddenly feels a million miles away, like he doesn't matter at all. The only thing I can see is Day and Tess together. It's like a punch to the stomach. *We're in the middle of a war. Don't be pathetic.* "Why would you tell me that?"

"Would you rather I kept it a secret?" He looks ashamed, and he purses his lips.

I don't know why, but Day never seems to have a problem making me feel like a fool. I try pretending that it doesn't bother me. "Tess will forgive you." My words, meant to be comforting and mature, sound hollow and fake instead. I passed the lie detector test without a hitch while I was under arrest — why's it so hard for me to deal with *this*?

After a while, he says in a quieter voice, "What do you think of him? Honestly?"

"I think he's real," I say, impressed with how calm I sound. Glad to steer our conversation in a different direction. "Ambitious and compassionate, even if it makes him a little impractical. Definitely not the brutal dictator the Patriots said he'll become. He's

340

young, and he needs the Republic's people on his side. And he's going to need help if he's going to change things."

"June, we barely got away from the Patriots. Are you trying to say we should help Anden *more* than we already have — that we should keep risking our lives for this goddy rich stranger you barely know?" The venom in his eyes as he spits out the word *rich* startles me, making me feel like he's insulting me too.

"What does class have to do with this?" Now I'm irritated too. "Are you really saying you'd be glad to see him dead?"

"Yes. I *would* be glad to see Anden dead," Day says through gritted teeth. "And I'd be glad to see every single person in his government dead too, if it meant I could have my family back."

"That's not like you. Anden's death *won't* fix things," I insist. *How can I make him see?* "You can't lump everyone into the same category, Day. Not everyone working for the Republic is evil. What about me? Or my brother and parents? There *are* good people in the government — and they're the ones who can spearhead permanent changes for the Republic."

"How can you possibly defend the government after everything they've done to you?

How could you not want to see the Republic collapse?"

"Well, I *don't*," I say angrily. "I want to see it *change* for the better. The Republic had its reasons in the beginning for controlling the people —"

"Whoa. Wait a minute." Day holds up his hands. His eyes are now alight with a rage I've never seen. "Say that to me again. I dare you. The Republic had its *reasons* in the beginning? The Republic's actions are *reasonable*?"

"You don't know the whole story about how the Republic was formed. Anden told me how the country started from anarchy, and that the people were the ones who —"

"So now you believe everything he says? Are you trying to tell me that it's the *people's* fault that the Republic's the way it is?" Day's voice rises. "That we brought all this goddy crap on ourselves? *That's* the justification for why his government tortures the poor?"

"No, I'm not trying to justify that —" Somehow, the history sounds much less viable than it did when Anden was telling it.

"And now you think Anden can *fix* us with his half-wit ideas? This rich boy's going to save us all?"

"Stop calling him that! It's his *ideas* that

might do it, not his *money*. Money doesn't mean anything when —"

Day points a finger right at me. "Don't ever say that to my face again. Money means *everything*."

My cheeks flush. "No, it doesn't."

"Because you've never been without it."

I wince. I want so desperately to respond, to explain that that's not what I meant. *Money doesn't define me, or Anden, or any of us.* Why couldn't I have said *that*? Why is Day the only person I have trouble making a coherent argument to? "Day, please —" I begin.

He jumps off the counter. "You know, maybe Tess was right about you."

"Excuse me?" I snap back. "What is Tess right about?"

"You might have changed a little over the last few weeks, but deep down, you're still a Republic soldier. Through and through. You're still loyal to those murderers. Have you forgotten how my mother and brother died? Have you forgotten who killed your family off?"

My own anger flares. *Are you purposely refusing to see things from my point of view?* I hop off the counter to face him. "I never forget anything. I'm here for *your* sake, I gave up *everything* for you. How *dare* you

343

bring my family into this?"

"*You* brought *my* family into this!" he yells. "Into *all* of this! You and your beloved Republic!" Day spreads his arms out. "How dare *you* defend them, how dare *you* try to reason with yourself over why they are the way they are? It's so easy for you to say that, isn't it, when you've lived your entire life in one of their high-rise palaces? I bet you wouldn't be so quick to logic it all out if you'd spent your life digging up trash to eat in the slums. *Would you?*"

I'm so furious and hurt that I'm having trouble catching my breath. "That's not fair, Day. I didn't *choose* to be born into this. I never wanted to hurt your family —"

"Well, you did." I feel myself tremble and fall apart under his glare. "*You* led the soldiers right to my family's door. *You're* the reason they're dead." Day turns his back on me and storms out of the kitchen. I stand there alone in the sudden silence, for once at a loss over what to do. The lump in my throat threatens to choke me. My vision swims with tears.

Day thinks I'm being blindly faithful to the Elector instead of being logical. That I can't possibly be on his side and still loyal to the state. *Well,* am *I still loyal?* Hadn't I answered that question correctly in the lie detector chamber? Am I jealous of Tess? Jealous because she is a better person than I am?

And then, the thought so painful I can hardly bear it, no matter how angry his words made me: He's right. I can't deny it. I *am* the reason Day lost everything that matters to him.

DAY

I shouldn't have yelled at her. Kinda terrible thing to do, and I know it.

But instead of apologizing, I go back around the shelter and check the rooms again. My hands are still unsteady; my mind is still fighting down the rush of adrenaline. I'd said it — the words that have been stewing in my head for weeks. They're out now, and there's no going back. Well, so what? I'm glad she knows. She *should* know. And to say that money means nothing — that phrase just flowed from her mouth, natural as water. Memories fill my head of all the times we needed more, of everything that could've been better with *more.* There was one afternoon, during a particularly bad week, when I came home early from grade school to find four-year-old Eden rummaging in the fridge. He jumped when he saw me step inside the house. In his hands was an empty can of beef hash. It'd been half full that morning, precious leftovers from the night before that Mom had carefully wrapped in foil and stored away for the next night's supper. When Eden saw me staring at the empty can in his hand, he dropped it on the kitchen floor and burst into tears. "Please don't tell Mom," he begged.

I ran over to him and took him in my arms. He gripped my shirt with baby hands, burying his face against me. "I won't," I whispered to him. "I promise." I can still remember how thin his arms were. Later that night, when Mom and John finally came home, I told Mom that I'd caved in and eaten the leftover food. She slapped me hard, told me I was old enough to know better. John gave me a disappointed speech. But who cares? I didn't mind.

I slam a door in the corridor in anger. Has June ever had to worry about stealing half a can of beef hash? If she'd been poor, would she be so quick to forgive the Republic?

The gun that the Patriots gave me sits heavily against my belt. The Elector's assassination would have given the Patriots the opportunity to take down the Republic. We would have been the spark that lit a powder keg — but because of us — because of June — it fizzled out. And for *what*? To watch this Elector go on to become just like his father? I want to laugh at the idea that he'd free Eden. What a Republic lie. And now I'm no closer to saving him, and I've lost Tess, and I'm right back to square one. On the run.

That's the story of my life, yeah?

When I go back to the kitchen half an hour later, June's not there anymore. Probably off in one of the hallways, making mental notes to herself about every goddy crack in the wall.

I throw open the kitchen's drawers, empty out one of the burlap sacks, and start sorting stacks of each type of food into it. Rice. Corn. Potato and mushroom soups. Three boxes of crackers. (How nice — everything's going to hell, but at least I can fill my stomach.) I grab several bottles of water for each of us and then close up the sack. Good enough for now. Soon we'll have to be on our way again, and who knows how long the rest of this tunnel is or when we'll hit another shelter. We have to move forward into the Colonies. Maybe they'll be willing to help us when we get to the other side. Then again, we might have to keep a low profile. We *did* ruin the assassination that the Colonies were sponsoring. I sigh deeply, wishing I had more time to chat with Kaede, to coax out all her stories about living on the other side of the warfront.

How did our plans turn into such a mess?

There's a faint knock on the kitchen's open door. I turn around to see June standing there with her arms crossed. She's unbuttoned her

Republic coat, and the collar shirt and vest underneath look rumpled. Her cheeks are more flushed than usual, and her eyes are red, like she's been crying. "The electric circuits in here aren't feeding into the Republic," she says. If she *had* shed any tears, I sure as hell don't hear them in her voice. "Their cables run down through the other end of the tunnel, the part we haven't covered yet."

I go back to stacking cans. "So?" I mutter.

"That means they must be getting their power from the Colonies, right?"

"Guess so. Makes sense, yeah?" I straighten my back and pull the two burlap sacks I've prepared tightly shut. "Well, at least it means the tunnel will lead out to the surface somewhere, hopefully in the Colonies. When we're ready to go we can just follow the cables. We should probably get some rest first."

I'm just about to walk out of the kitchen and past June when she clears her throat and speaks up. "Hey — did the Patriots teach you anything about fighting while you were with them?"

I shake my head. "No. Why?"

June turns to face me. The kitchen entrance is narrow enough that her shoulders brush past mine, raising goose bumps on my arms. I'm annoyed that she still has this effect on me, in spite of everything. "While we were getting into the tunnel I noticed that you were swinging at the Patriots from your arms . . . but that's not very effective. You should be swinging from your legs and hips."

Her critique grates on my nerves, even though she's giving it in a strangely hesitant tone. "I don't want to do this right now."

"When are we going to do it if not now?" June leans against the door frame and points toward the shelter's entrance. "What if we bump into some soldiers?"

I sigh and put my hands up for a second. "If this is your way of apologizing after a fight, then you really *suck* at it. Listen. I'm sorry I got angry earlier." I hesitate, remembering my words. I'm *not* sorry. But telling her that now won't help anything. "Just give me a few minutes, and I'll feel better."

"Come on, Day. What'll happen when you find Eden and you need to protect him?" She *is* trying to apologize, in her own subtle way. *Well. At least she's giving it a shot, however crappy she is at it.* I glare at her for a few seconds.

"All right," I finally say. "Show me some moves, soldier. What you got up your sleeves?"

June gives me a small smile, then walks me over to the center of the shelter's main room. She stands beside me. "Ever read Ducain's

The Art of the Fight?"

"Does it look like I've had free time in my life to read?"

She ignores me, and I immediately feel bad for saying it. "Well, you're already light on your feet and you have flawless balance," she continues. "But you don't use those strengths when you attack. It's like you panic. You forget all about your speed advantage and your center of mass."

"My center of what?" I start to say, but she just taps the outside of my leg with her boot.

"Stay on the balls of your feet and keep your legs shoulder width apart," she goes on. "Pretend you're standing on train tracks with one foot forward."

I'm a little surprised. June's been watching my attacks closely, even though it usually happens when all sorts of chaos is going on around us. And she's right. I hadn't even realized that all my instincts of balance go right out the window when I try to fight. I do as she says. "Okay. Now what?"

"Well, keep your chin down, for one." She touches my hands, then lifts them up so one fist stays close to the side of my cheek and the other hovers out in front of my face. Her hands run along my arms, checking my posture. My skin tingles. "Most people lean back and keep their chins high and jutted," she says, her face close beside mine. She taps my chin once. "That's what you do too. And it's just asking for a knockout."

I try to focus on my own posture by putting two fists up. "How do you punch?"

June gently touches the tip of my chin, then the edge of my brow. "Remember, it's all about how *accurately* you can hit someone, not how *hard.* You'll be able to knock out someone much larger if you catch them in the right spots."

Before I know it, half an hour's gone by. June teaches me one tactic after another — keeping my shoulder up to protect my chin, catching my opponent off guard with fake moves, overhand hits, underhand hits, leaning back and following through with kicks, leaping out of the way with speed. Aiming for the vulnerable spots — eyes, neck, and so on. I lunge out with everything I've got. When I try to catch her by surprise, she slips from my grasp like water between rocks, fluid and constantly moving, and if I blink, she's behind me and twisting my arm up behind my back.

Finally, June trips me and pins me to the floor. Her hands push my wrists down. "See?" she says. "Tricked you. You're always staring at your opponent's eyes — but that gives you a bad peripheral view. If you want to track my arms and legs, you have to focus on my chest."

I raise my eyebrow at that. "Say no more." My eyes shift downward.

June laughs, then turns a little red. We pause there for an instant, her hands still holding my arms down, her legs across my stomach, both of us breathing heavily. Now I understand why she suggested the impromptu sparring — I'm tired, and the exercise has drained my anger. Even though she doesn't say it, I can see her apology plainly on her face, the tragic slant of her eyebrows and the slight quiver of unspoken words on her lips. The sight finally softens me, albeit only a little. I'm still not sorry about what I'd said to her earlier, true, but I'm also not being fair. Whatever I lost, June has lost equally. She used to be rich, then she threw it away to save my life. She'd played her part in my family's deaths, but . . . I run a hand through my hair, feeling guilty now. I can't blame her for everything. And I can't be alone at a time like this, with no allies, *no* one I can turn to.

She sways.

I prop myself up on my elbows. "You okay?"

She shakes her head, frowns, and tries to shrug it off. "Fine. I think I picked up a bug or something. Nothing big."

I study her under the artificial light. Now that

I'm paying closer attention to the color of her face, I can see that she's paler than usual, and that her cheeks look flushed because her skin is so wan. I sit up higher, forcing her to slide off. Then I press a hand to her forehead. Immediately I pull it away. "Man, you're burning up."

June starts to protest, but as if our training session has weakened her, she sways again and steadies herself with one arm. "I'll be fine," she mumbles. "We should be heading out, anyway."

And here I've been angry with her, forgetting all she's been through. Trot of the year. I ease one of my arms around her back and wrap the other under her knees, then scoop her up. She slumps against my chest, the heat of her brow startling against my cool skin. "You need to rest."

I carry her into one of the bunker rooms, pull off her boots, lay her down carefully on a bed, and cover her with the blankets. She blinks at me. "I didn't mean what I said earlier." Her eyes are dazed, but the emotion's still there. "About money. And . . . I didn't —"

"Stop talking." I smooth stray hairs from her forehead. What if she caught something serious while under arrest? A plague virus? . . . But she's upper class. She should have vaccines. *I hope.* "I'm going to find you some medicine, okay? Just close your eyes." June shakes her head, frustrated, but she doesn't try to argue.

After upending the entire shelter, I finally manage to hunt down an unopened bottle of aspirin and return to June's bedside with it. She takes a couple of pills. When she starts shivering, I grab two more blankets from the other beds in the room and cover her with them, but it doesn't seem to help. "It's okay. I'll manage," she whispers right as I'm about to go hunting for more blankets. "Won't really matter how high you stack them — I just need my fever to break." She hesitates, then reaches for my hand. "Can you stay here?"

The weakness of her voice worries me more than anything. I climb into the bed, lie beside her on top of the blankets, and pull her to me. June smiles a little, then closes her eyes. The feel of her body's curves against mine sends warmth coursing through me. I've never thought of describing her beauty as delicate, because *delicate* just isn't a word that fits June . . . but here, now that she's sick, I realize just how fragile she can be. Pink cheeks. Small, soft lips against large, closed eyes fringed with the curve of dark lashes. I don't like seeing her this delicate. The heat of our argument lingers in the back of my mind, but for now I need to forget about it. Fighting will only slow us down. We'll deal with the problems between us later.

Slowly, we both doze off.

Something jerks me out of my sleep. A beeping sound. I listen to it for a while, trying to pinpoint its location through my grogginess, and then crawl out of bed without waking June. Before leaving the room, I lean over to touch her forehead again. Still no better. Sweat beads on her brow, so her fever must've broken at least once, but she's as warm as ever.

When I follow the beeping sound out into the kitchen, I see a tiny beacon blinking above the door that we'd come into the shelter from. Words flash below it in bright, menacing red.

APPROACHING — 400 FT

A cold fear seizes me. Someone must be coming down the tunnel toward the shelter — Patriots, maybe, or Republic soldiers. Can't decide which would be worse. I whirl on my heels and hurry to where I'd stacked our burlap sacks of food and water, then empty some cans out of one of them. When the bag's light enough, I pull my arms through both sack strings like it's a backpack and then rush to June's bedside. She stirs with a soft moan.

"Hey," I whisper, trying to sound calm and

reassuring. I bend down and stroke her hair. "It's time to go. Come here." I push the blankets aside, keeping one to wrap around her, pull her boots onto her feet, and hoist her into my arms. She struggles for a moment as if she thinks she's falling, but I just hang on tighter. "Easy," I murmur against her hair. "I've got you."

She settles into my embrace, half-conscious.

We leave the shelter and head back into the darkness of the tunnel, my boots splashing through puddles and mud. June's breath is shallow and quick, hot with fever. Behind us, the alarm grows quieter until we round several bends, then it fades to a soft hum. I half expect to hear footsteps coming after us, but soon the hum of the alarm fades away too, and we're left to travel in silence. To me, it feels like hours have passed — although June mutters that "it's been forty-two minutes and thirty-three seconds." We trudge on.

This stretch of tunnel is much longer than the first, and dimly lit with the occasional flickering fixture. At some point I finally stop and slump down in a dry section, sipping on water and canned soup (at least, I think it's soup — I can't see much in this darkness so I just pop the lid off the first tin I grab). June's shivering again, which is no surprise. It's cold down here, cold enough for me to see the faint clouds of my breath. I wrap the blanket tighter around June, check her forehead one more time, and then try to feed her some soup. She refuses it.

"I'm not hungry," she mutters. When she shifts her head against my chest, I feel the heat of her brow through my shirt.

I squeeze her hand. My arms are so numb that even this seems difficult. "Fine. But you're going to have some water, okay?"

"Fine." June huddles closer to me and rests her head in my lap. I wish I could figure out a way to keep her warm. "Are they still following us?"

I squint down into the black depths we came from. "No," I lie. "We lost them a long time ago. Just relax and don't worry, but try to stay awake."

June nods. She fiddles with something on her hand, and when I look closer, I realize it's the paper clip ring. She rubs it as if it can give her strength. "Help me out. Tell me a story." Her eyes are half-closed now, even though I can tell she's struggling to keep them open. She's speaking so softly that I have to lean over her mouth to hear it.

"What kind of story?" I reply, determined to keep her from fading into unconsciousness.

"I don't know." June tilts her head slightly to face me. After a pause, she says sleepily, "Tell me about your first kiss. How was it?"

Her question confuses me at first — no girl I've ever known has liked me talking about other girls in front of her. But then I realize that this is June, and that she might be using jealousy to keep herself from dozing off. I can't help smiling in the dark. Always so goddy clever, this one. "I was twelve," I murmur. "The girl was sixteen."

June's eyes become more alert. "You must've been quite the smooth talker."

I shrug. "Maybe. I was clumsier back then — almost got myself killed a few times. Anyway, she was working a pier in Lake with her dad, and she caught me trying to smuggle food out of their crates. I talked her out of turning me in, and as part of our deal, she led me off to a back alley near the water."

June tries to laugh, but it comes out as a coughing fit. "And she kissed you there?"

I grin. "You could say that."

She manages to raise a curious eyebrow at my short reply, which I take as a good sign. At least she's awake now. I lean closer to her and put my lips next to her ear. My breath stirs soft wisps of her hair. "The first time I saw you, when you stepped into that Skiz ring against Kaede, I thought you were the most beautiful girl I'd ever seen. I could've watched you forever. The first time I kissed *you* . . ."

That memory overpowers me now, taking me by surprise. I remember every last detail of it, almost enough to push away the lingering images of the Elector pulling June to him. "Well, that might as well have been my first kiss ever."

Even in the dark, I see hints of a smile creep onto her face. "Yeah. You *are* a smooth talker."

I give her a wounded frown. "Sweetheart, would I ever lie to you?"

"Don't try. I'd see right through it."

I give her a low laugh. "Fair enough."

Our words sound light and almost carefree, but we can both feel the strain behind them. The effort of trying to forget, to push down. The consequence of things neither of us can ever take back.

We linger there for a few more minutes. Then I wrap up our belongings, carefully pick her up, and continue down the tunnel. My arms are shaking now, and each breath I take sounds ragged. There are no signs of any shelters ahead. Despite the tunnel's wetness and the cold, I'm sweating as if it's the middle of a Los Angeles summer — my breaks become more and more frequent, until I finally stop at another dry stretch of tunnel and collapse against the wall.

"Just taking a quick breather," I reassure June as I give her some water. "I think we're almost there."

Just as she said earlier, she can see right through my lie. "We can't go any farther," she says weakly. "Let's rest. You'll never last another hour like this."

I brush off her words. "This tunnel's got to end somewhere. We must have gone right under the warfront by now, which means we're already on Colonies land." I pause — the realization hits me at the same time my words come out, sending a thrill down my spine. *Colonies land.*

As if on cue, a sound comes from somewhere beyond the tunnel, somewhere far above us. I fall silent. We listen for a while, and soon the sound comes back — a whirring, humming noise muffled through the earth, coming from some massive object.

"Is that an airship out there?" June asks.

The sound fades away, but not before it brings an icy cold breeze into the tunnel. I glance up. I'd been too exhausted to notice earlier, but now I can just make out a tiny, rectangular sliver of light. An exit to the surface. In fact, there are several of them lining the ceiling in sporadic intervals; we've probably been passing them for a good while. I force myself back to my feet and reach up to run my finger along the edge of that sliver.

Smooth, frozen metal. I give it a tentative push.

It shifts. I push harder on the metal and start sliding it to one side. Even though I can tell that it's nighttime outside, the light coming into the tunnel is more than we've been getting for the past few hours, and I actually find myself squinting. It takes me a second to realize that something cold and light is falling gently onto my face. I swat at it, confused for a second, until I realize that they're — I think — snowflakes. My heartbeat quickens. When I've slid the metal as far as it will go, I shrug off my Republic military jacket. No fun getting shot by soldiers right when we've reached the promised land.

When I've stripped down to my collar shirt and waistcoat, I jump up and grab the sides of the opening, arms trembling, then pull myself up halfway to see where we are. Some sort of dark corridor. Nobody around. I jump back down and take June's hands, but she's starting to fade away into sleep again.

"Stay with me," I murmur, gathering her in my arms. "See if you can pull yourself up." June unwinds the blanket. I kneel and help her step up onto my shoulders. She wobbles, breathing heavily, but manages to pull herself to the surface. I follow with her blanket tucked under an arm, then pop up through the ground with one thrust.

We come up into a dark, narrow alley not unlike where we came from, and for a second I wonder if somehow we've come all the way back around into the Republic again. Wouldn't *that* be something. But after a while, I can tell that this isn't the Republic at all. The ground is even and nicely paved under a patchy layer of snow, and the wall is completely covered with brightly colored posters of grinning soldiers and smiling children. On the corner of each poster is a symbol that I recognize after a few seconds. A gold, falconlike bird. With a shiver of excitement, I realize how closely it resembles the bird imprinted on my pendant.

June's notices the posters too. Her eyes are wide and hazy with fever, her breath rising in faint clouds of steam. All around us are what appear to be military barracks, covered from top to bottom with the same bright posters. Streetlights line both sides of the road in neat, orderly patterns. This must be where the tunnel and those underground shelters get their electricity. A cold wind blows more snow in our faces.

June suddenly grabs my hand. She sucks in her breath at the same time I do. "Day . . . *over there.*" She's trembling uncontrollably against me, but I can't tell if it's from the cold or from what we're seeing.

Stretching out before us, peeking through the gaps between the military buildings, is a city: tall, shining skyscrapers reaching up through low clouds and delicate snow, and each building illuminated by beautiful blue lights that pour from almost every window and every floor. Fighter jets line the skyscrapers' rooftops. The entire landscape is aglow. My hand tightens around June's. We just stand there, unable for a second to do anything else. It's exactly how my father described it.

We've reached a glittering city in the Colonies of America.

JUNE

Metias had always told me that whenever I do get sick, I pull out all the stops.

I know it's cold, but I can't tell what the temperature is. I know it's night, but I can't tell what time it is. I know Day and I have somehow made it across the border and into the Colonies, but I'm too tired to figure out which of their states we crossed into. Day's arm is wrapped tightly around my waist, supporting me even though I can feel him shaking from the effort of carrying me for so long. He whispers encouragingly to me, urging me on. *Just a little longer,* he says. *There must be hospitals this close to the war-front.* My legs are trembling from the effort of keeping me up, but I refuse to faint now. We crunch through light snow, our eyes fixed on the sparkling city before us.

The buildings range between five stories and hundreds of stories tall, some of them disappearing into low clouds. The sight is familiar in some ways and entirely new in others: The walls are lined with foreign flags shaped like swallowtails, colored navy blue and gold; the buildings have archway designs carved into their sides; and fighter jets line each rooftop. They're distinctly different models from the ones in the Republic, with a strange reverse-swept-wing structure that makes them tridentlike in appearance. The jets' wings are all painted with ferocious gold birds, as well as a symbol I don't recognize. No wonder I always heard that the Colonies had a better air force than the Republic — these jets are newer than the ones I'm used to and, considering their rooftop placements, must all be able to perform vertical takeoffs and landings effortlessly. This warfront city seems more than prepared to defend itself.

And the people. They're everywhere, both soldiers and civilians crowding the streets, huddled under hooded coats to shield themselves from the snow. As they pass under the neon glow of lights, their faces are tinted shades of green, orange, and purple. I'm too exhausted to do a proper analysis of them, but the one thing I notice is that all of their clothes — boots, pants, shirts, coats — have a variety of emblems and words on them. I'm shocked by the sheer number of ads on the walls — they stretch on as far as the eye can see, sometimes bunched so closely together that they completely hide the walls beneath them. They seem to be advertising anything and everything under the sun, things I've never seen or heard of before. Corp-sponsored schools? Christmas?

We pass one window where a bunch of miniature screens are displayed, each broadcasting news and videos. SALE! the window display reads. 30% OFF UNTIL MONDAY! Some channels' broadcasting programs are familiar — headlines from the warfront, political conferences. DESCON CORP SCORES ANOTHER VICTORY FOR COLONIES ON DAKOTA/MINNESOTA BORDER. REPUBLIC RUBBLE AVAILABLE FOR PURCHASE AS SOUVENIRS! Others broadcast movies, something the Republic only shows in rich sector theaters. Most screens are showing commercials. Unlike the Republic's propaganda commercials, it's as if these ads were trying to persuade their population to buy things. I wonder what kind of government runs a place like this. Maybe they don't have a government at all.

"My father once told me that the Colonies' cities are like glitter from far away," Day says. His eyes skip from one brightly

367

colored ad to the next as he helps me through the shuffle of people. "It's exactly like he described, but I can't figure out all these ads. Aren't they strange?"

I nod back. In the Republic, ads have organized displays with a consistent, distinct government style that remains the same no matter where in the country you are. Here, the ads don't follow any sort of color theory. They're jumbled, a mishmash of neon and flashing lights. As if they weren't made by any sort of central government, but by a number of smaller, independent groups.

One ad shows a video of a smiling officer in a uniform. The voiceover says: *"Tribune Police Department. Need to report a crime? Only 500 Note deposit needed!"* Underneath the officer, in small print, are the words: TRIBUNE POLICE DEPARTMENT IS A SUBSIDIARY OF DESCON CORP.

Another ad says NEXT NATIONWIDE EHL* CHECK SPONSORED BY CLOUD — JAN. 27. NEED SOME HELP TO PASS? NEW MEDITECH JOYENCE PILLS NOW AVAILABLE AT ALL STORES! Below this, another small asterisk is followed by the text: EHL, EMPLOYEE HAPPINESS LEVEL.

A third ad actually makes me do a double take. It shows a video of rows of young children, all dressed in the exact same clothes, smiling the biggest smiles I've ever seen. When the text comes up, it reads FIND YOUR PERFECT SON, DAUGHTER, OR EMPLOYEE. SWAPSHOP FRANCHISE STORES ARE A SUBSIDIARY OF EVERGREEN ENT. I frown, puzzled. Maybe this is how the Colonies run orphanages or the like. Isn't it?

As we move along, I notice that there's one unchanging image in the bottom right-hand corner of each ad. It's a giant symbol of a circle split into four quadrants, with a smaller symbol inside each of the quadrants. Underneath it in block letters is the following:

THE COLONIES OF AMERICA
CLOUD.MEDITECH.DESCON.EVERGREEN
A FREE STATE IS A CORPORATE STATE

Abruptly I feel Day's breath warm against my ear. "June," he whispers.

"What is it?"

"Someone's following us."

Another detail I should've noticed first. I've lost count of the number of things I'm failing to catch. "Can you see his face?"

"No. But judging from the figure, it's a girl," he replies. I wait for a few more seconds, then chance a look back. Nothing but a sea of Colonians. Whoever it was, she's already disappeared into the crowds.

"Probably just a false alarm," I mutter. "Some Colonies girl."

Day's eyes sweep the street, perplexed, then he shrugs it off. I wouldn't be surprised if we were starting to see things, especially amongst all these strange new glittering lights and fluorescent ads.

A person approaches us right as we turn our attention back to the street. Five foot seven, droopy cheeks, tannish pink skin, a few strands of black hair peeking out from a heavy snow cap, a flat tablet in her hand. She has a scarf wrapped tightly around her neck (synthetic wool, judging from the uniform texture), and little ice crystals cling to the fabric under her chin where her breath has frozen on it. Her sleeve has the words *Street Proctor* sewn on, right above another strange symbol. "You're not showing up. Corp?" she mutters to us. Her eyes stay fixed on the tablet, which has a map-like image and moving bubbles on it. Each bubble seems to correspond to a person on the street. She must mean we're not showing up on there. Then I realize that there are many people like her dotting the street, all wearing the same dark blue coat.

"Corp?" she repeats impatiently.

370

Day's about to reply when I stop him. "Meditech," I blurt out, remembering the four names from the ads we've seen.

The woman pauses to give our outfits (dirty collar shirts, black trousers, and boots) a disapproving once-over. "You must be new," she adds to herself, tapping something out on her tablet. "You're a long way from where you're supposed to be, then. Don't know if you've had your orientations yet, but Meditech will dock you hard if you're late." Then she gives us a fake smile and launches into an oddly perky routine. "I'm sponsored by Cloud Corp. Stop in Tribune Central Square to buy our newest line of bread!" Her mouth snaps back into the sullen line it was in before, and she hurries away. I watch as she stops a person farther down the street, launching into the same performance.

"There's something off about this city," I whisper to Day as we struggle on.

Day's grip on me is tight and tense. "That's why I didn't ask her where the closest hospital was," he replies. Another wave of dizziness hits me. "Hang in there. We'll figure something out."

I try to respond, but now I can barely see where I'm going. Day says something to me, but I can't understand a word — it sounds like he's underwater. "What did you say?" The world is spinning now. My knees buckle.

"I said, maybe we . . . stop one . . . hospital . . ."

I feel myself falling, and my arms and legs are coming up around me in a protective ball, and somewhere overhead Day's beautiful blue eyes hold me. He puts his hands on my shoulders, but it feels like he's a million miles away. I try to speak, but my mouth feels like it's full of sand. I sink into darkness.

A flash of gold and gray. Someone's cool hand against my forehead. I reach up to touch it, but the instant my fingers brush against the skin, the hand melts away. I can't stop shivering — it's unimaginably cold in here.

When I finally manage to open my eyes, I find myself lying on a simple white cot with my head in Day's lap, and Day has one of his arms draped around my waist. A moment later I realize that he's watching another person — another *three* people — standing in the room with us. (They're wearing the distinctive uniforms of warfront Colonies soldiers: navy military peacoats studded with gold buttons and epaulettes, with gold and white stripes running along the bottom edge and that signature gold falcon embroidered on each sleeve.) I shake my head. A pretty generic breakdown. I'm so slow right now.

"Through the tunnels," Day says. Lights on the ceiling blind me. I hadn't noticed them there earlier.

"How long have you been in the Colonies?" one of the other men asks. His accent sounds strange. He has a pale mustache and limp, greasy hair, and the lighting gives him a sickly complexion. "Better be honest, boy. DesCon doesn't tolerate liars."

"We just got here tonight," Day replies.

"And where did you come from? Do you work for the Patriots?"

Even in my haze, I know this is a dangerous question. They are not going to be happy if they find out that we're the ones who botched their plans for the Elector. Maybe they don't even know what happened yet. Razor did say that they update the Colonies only sporadically.

Day realizes the question's danger too, because he evades it. "We came here alone." He pauses, and then I hear him speak with a hint of impatience. "Please, she's burning up with fever. Take us to a hospital, and I'll tell you anything you want. I didn't come all this way to see her die in a police station."

"Hospital's going to cost you, son," the man answers.

Day pats one of my pockets and digs out our little wad of Notes. I notice that his gun is now gone, probably confiscated. "We have four thousand Republic —"

The soldiers cut him off with snickers. "Boy, four thousand Republic Notes won't buy you a bowl of soup," one of them says. "Besides, you're both going to wait here until our commander shows up. Then you'll be sent to our POW compound for standard interrogation."

POW compound. For some reason this triggers the memory of when Metias took me on a mission over a year ago, when we'd tracked that Colonies prisoner of war deep through the Republic's states and killed him in Yellowstone City. I remember the blood on the ground, soaking that soldier's navy uniform. A moment of panic seizes me and I reach up to grab Day's collar. The other men in the room make a startled noise. I hear several metallic clicks.

Day's arm tightens protectively around me. "Easy there," he whispers.

"What's the girl's name?"

Day turns back to the men. "Sarah," he

lies. "She's not a threat — she's just really sick."

The men say something that makes Day angry, but my world is becoming a wild chaos of colors again, and I sink back into a delirious half sleep. I hear loud voices, then the swinging sound of a heavy door, and then nothing for a long time. Sometimes I think I see Metias standing in the corner of the barrack, watching me. Other times he changes into Thomas, and I can't decide if I should feel anger or grief at the sight of him. Sometimes I recognize Day's hands against mine. He tells me to relax, that everything will be okay. The visions disappear.

After what seems like hours, I start to hear faint, broken snippets of conversation again.

"— from the Republic?"

"Yes."

"You're Day?"

"That's me."

Some shuffling sounds, then expressions of incredulity. "No, I recognize him," someone keeps saying. "I recognize him, I recognize him. He's the one."

More shuffling. Then I feel Day rise, and I collapse alone onto the cold sheets of the cot beneath me. *They've taken him somewhere. They've taken him away.*

I want to cling to this thought, but my

feverish delirium takes over and I drift back to black.

I'm in my Ruby sector apartment, my head on a pillow damp with sweat, my body covered by a thin blanket and bathed in golden light from the afternoon sun filtering in through our windows. Ollie sleeps nearby, his enormous puppy paws resting lazily on the cool marble tiles. I realize that this doesn't make any sense, because I'm almost sixteen and Ollie should be nine years old. I must be dreaming.

A wet towel touches my forehead — I look up to see Metias sitting beside me, carefully placing the towel so water doesn't drip in my eyes.

"Hey, Junebug," he says with a smile.

"Aren't you going to be late for something?" I whisper. There's a nagging feeling in my stomach that Metias isn't supposed to be here. Like he's late for something.

But my brother just shakes his head, making several chunks of dark hair fall across his face. The sun lights up his eyes with glints of gold. "Well, I can't just leave you alone here, can I?" He laughs, and the sound fills me with so much happiness that I think I might burst. "Face it, you're stuck with me. Now eat your soup. I don't care how gross you think it is."

I take a sip. I swear I can almost taste it. "Are you really going to stay here with me?"

Metias bends down and kisses my forehead. "Forever and ever, kid, until you're sick and tired of seeing me."

I smile. "You're always taking care of me. When will you ever have time for Thomas?"

Metias hesitates at my words, and then chuckles. "I can't keep anything secret with you here, can I?"

"You could have told me about you guys, you know." The words are painful for me to say, but I'm not entirely sure why. I feel like I'm forgetting something important. "I wouldn't have told anyone. Were you just worried Commander Jameson would find out and split you and Thomas into different patrols?"

Metias lowers his head, and his shoulders fall. "I never really had a reason to bring it up."

"Do you love him?"

I remember that I'm dreaming, and whatever Metias might say is simply my own thoughts projected into his image. Still, I ache when he looks down and answers with a slight nod of his head.

"I thought I did," he replies. I can barely hear him.

"I'm so sorry," I whisper. He meets my gaze with eyes full of tears.

I try to reach up and wrap my arms around his neck. But then the scene shifts, the light fades, and suddenly I'm lying in a dim whitewashed room on a bed that isn't my own. Metias disappears into wisps. Caring for me in his place is Day, his face framed by hair the color of light, his hands readjusting the towel on my forehead, his eyes studying mine intensely.

"Hey, Sarah," he says. He's using the fake name he made up for me. "Don't worry, you're safe."

I blink at the sudden change in scene. "Safe?"

"Colonies police picked us up. They took us to a small hospital after they found out who I am. I guess they've all heard about me over here, and it's working out to our benefit." Day gives me a sheepish grin.

But this time I'm so disappointed to see Day, so bitterly sad that I've lost Metias to the shallows of my dreams again, that I have to bite my lip to keep myself from crying. My arms feel so weak. I probably couldn't have wrapped them around my brother's neck anyway, and because I didn't, I couldn't keep Metias from floating away.

Day's grin fades — he senses my grief.

He reaches over and touches my cheek with one hand. His face is so close, radiant in the soft evening glow. I lift myself up with what little strength I have and let him pull me close. "Oh, Day," I whisper into his hair, my voice breaking with all the sobs I've been holding back. "I really miss him. I miss him so much. And I'm so sorry, I am *so sorry for everything.*" I repeat it over and over again, the words I said to Metias in my dream and the words I will say to Day for the rest of my life.

Day tightens his embrace. His hand brushes through my hair, and he rocks me gently like I'm a child. I cling to him for dear life, unable to catch my breath, drowning in my fever and sorrow and emptiness.

Metias is gone again. He is always gone.

DAY

It takes June a half hour to finally fall back asleep, loaded up on whatever drugs a Colonies nurse injected into her arm. She'd been sobbing over her brother again, and it was like she'd fallen down a hole and crumpled in on herself, her bleeding heart torn open for all to see. Those strong dark eyes of hers — now, their expression was just . . . broken. I wince. Of course, I know exactly what it feels like to lose an older brother. I watch as her eyes dance around behind closed lids, probably deep in another nightmare that I can't help her out of. So I just do what she always does for me — I smooth down her hair and kiss her damp forehead and cheeks and lips. It doesn't seem to help, but I do it anyway.

The hospital is relatively quiet, but a few sounds form a blanket of white noise in my head: There's a faint whir coming from the ceiling lights, and some sort of dim commotion on the streets outside. Like in the Republic, a screen mounted to the wall broadcasts a stream of warfront news. Unlike the Republic, the news is peppered with commercials the way the streets outside had been, for things that I don't comprehend. I stop watching after a while. I keep thinking about the way my mother comforted Eden when he first got the plague, how she whispered soothing words and touched his face with her poor bandaged hands, how John would come to the bedside with a bowl of soup.

I'm so sorry for everything, June had said.

Several minutes later, a soldier opens the door to our hospital room and walks over to me. It's the same soldier who'd realized who I was and had us delivered to this twenty-story hospital. She halts in front of me and gives me a quick bow. Like I'm an officer or something. Just as surprising is the fact that she's the only soldier in the room with us. These guys must not see me and June as threats. No handcuffs, not even a guard to watch our door. Do they know that we're the ones who botched the Elector's assassination? If they're sponsoring the Patriots, they're bound to find out sooner or later. Maybe they don't know we worked for the Patriots at all. Razor *had* added us fairly late in the game.

"Your friend is stable, I presume?" Her eyes rest on June. I just nod. Best if no one here figures out that June is the Republic's beloved prodigy. "Given her condition," the soldier adds, "she'll need to stay here until she's well enough to move around on her own. You're welcome to stay with her in here, or DesCon Corp would be happy to sponsor an additional room for you."

DesCon Corp — more Colonies lingo I don't understand. But far be it from me to start questioning the source of their generosity. If I'm famous enough over here to get star treatment in a hospital, then I'll take it for all it's worth. "Thanks," I reply. "I'm fine staying in here."

"We'll have an extra bed brought in for you," she says, motioning toward the room's empty space. "We'll come check on you again in the morning."

I go back to my vigil over June. When the guard doesn't leave, I look up at her and raise my eyebrows. She turns red. "Anything else I can do for you?"

She shrugs it off and tries to look nonchalant. "No. I just . . . so, you're Daniel Altan Wing, eh?" She says my name like she's trying it on for size. "Evergreen Ent keeps printing stories about you in their tabs. The Republic Rebel, the Phantom, the Wild Card — they probably come up with a new name and photo for you every day. Say you escaped a Los

Angeles prison all by yourself. Hey, did you really date that singer Lincoln?"

The idea is so ludicrous that I have to laugh. I didn't know Colonians kept up with the Republic's government-appointed propaganda singers. "Lincoln's a little old for me, don't you think?"

My laugh breaks the tension, and the soldier laughs along with me. "Well, this week you are. Last week Evergreen Ent reported that you'd dodged all the bullets from a Republic firing squad and escaped your execution." The soldier goes back to laughing again, but I fall silent.

No, I didn't dodge any bullets. I let my older brother take them for me.

The soldier's laugh trickles away awkwardly when she sees my expression. She clears her throat. "As for that tunnel you two came through, we've sealed it up. Third one we've sealed in a month. Every now and then Republic refugees come in just like you did, you know, and the people living in Tribune have gotten really tired of dealing with them. No one likes civilians from an enemy territory suddenly taking up residence in one's home-town. We usually end up kicking them back over the warfront. You're a lucky one." The soldier sighs. "Back in the day, this all used to be the United States of America. You know that, yes?"

My quarter pendant suddenly feels heavy around my neck. "I know."

"Well, do you know about the floods? Came fast, in less than two years, and wiped out half of the low-lying south. Places Reps like you have probably never even heard of. Louisiana, gone. Florida, Georgia, Alabama, Mississippi, Carolinas, gone. So fast you'd swear they never existed in the first place, at least if you couldn't still see some of their buildings peeking out far off in the ocean."

"And that's why you guys came here?"

"More land in the west. You have any idea how many refugees there were? Then the west built a wall to keep the easterners from overcrowding their states, from the top of the Dakotas down through Texas." The soldier slams one fist into the palm of her other hand. "So we had to build tunnels to get in. There used to be thousands of them back when the migration was at its peak. Then the war started. When the Republic started using the tunnels to launch surprise assaults on us, we sealed them all off. The war's been going on for so long that most people don't even remember that the fight's about land. But when the floodwaters finally settled, things over here stabilized. And we became the Colonies of America." She says this with her chest puffed out. "This war won't go on for much longer — we've been winning for a while now."

I remember Kaede telling me that the Colonies were winning the war when we first touched down in Lamar. I hadn't thought too much of it then — after all, what's one person's assumption? Rumor? But now this soldier's saying it like it's the truth.

Both of us pause as the commotion outside the building gets louder. I tilt my head. There have been crowds of people coming and going from the hospital ever since we got here, but I hadn't thought about it. Now I think I hear my name. "Do you know what's going on out there?" I ask. "Can we move my friend to a quieter room?"

The soldier crosses her arms. "Want to see all the commotion for yourself?" She gestures for me to get up and follow her.

The shouting outside has reached a thunderous pitch. When the soldier swings the balcony's doors open and leads us out into the night air, I'm greeted by a gust of icy wind and a huge chorus of cheers. Flashing lights blind me — for a second all I can do is stand there against the metal railings and take in the scene. It's some insanely late hour of the night, but there must be hundreds of people below our window, oblivious to the snow-packed ground. All of their eyes are turned up to me. Many of them hold up homemade signs. *Welcome to our side!* one says.

The Phantom Lives, says another.

Take Down the Republic, says a third. There are dozens of them. *Day: Our Honorary Colonian! Welcome to Tribune, Day! Our home is your home!*

They know who I am.

Now the soldier points at me and smiles for the crowd. "This is Day," she shouts.

Another eruption of cheers. I stay frozen where I am. What're you supposed to do when a bunch of people are yelling your name like they're completely cracked? I have no goddy clue. So I raise my hand and wave, which brings their shrieks to a higher pitch.

"You're a celebrity here," the soldier says to me over the noise. She seems to be much more interested in this than I am. "The one rebel the Republic can't seem to get their hands on. Trust me, you'll be plastered all over the tabs by morning. Evergreen Ent is going to be dying to interview you."

She keeps talking, but I'm not paying attention to her anymore. One of the people holding up signs has caught my attention. It's a girl with a scarf wrapped around her mouth and a hoodie covering part of her face.

But I can tell it's Kaede.

My head feels light. Instantly I think back on the blinking red alarm down in the bunker, warning June and me of someone approaching the hideout. I recall the person I thought had been following us down the Colonies' streets. *Was it Kaede?* Does that mean that other Patriots are here too? She's holding up a sign that's almost lost in the sea of others.

The sign says: *You have to go back. Now.*

JUNE

I'm dreaming again. I'm sure of it because
Metias is here, and I know he's supposed to
be dead. This time I'm ready for it, and I
keep a tight rein on my emotions.

Metias and I are walking in the streets of
Pierra. All around us, Republic soldiers run
around rubble and explosions, but to the
two of us, everything seems quiet and slow,
like we're watching a movie in extreme slow
motion. Showers of dirt and shrapnel from
grenades bounce harmlessly off of us. I feel
invincible, or invisible. One or the other,
maybe both.

"Something's just not right here," I say to
my brother. My eyes go up to the roofs, then
back down to the chaotic streets. Where is
Anden?

Metias gives me a thoughtful frown. He
walks with his hands behind his back, graceful as any captain ought to be, and the gold
tassels on his uniform clink softly together

as he goes. "I can tell this scene is bothering you," he replies, scratching at the faint scruff on his chin. Unlike Thomas, he'd always been a bit lax about the military's grooming rules. "Talk to me."

"This scene," I say, pointing around us. "This whole plan. Something's off."

Metias steps over a pile of concrete rubble. "What's off?"

"Him." I point up to the roof. For some reason, Razor is standing there in plain sight, watching everything happen. His arms are crossed. "Something's not right about *him*."

"Well, Junebug, reason it out," Metias says.

I count off on my fingers. "When I got into the jeep behind the Elector's, the drivers' instructions were clear. The Elector told them to take me to the hospital."

"And then?"

"And then Razor ordered the drivers to take the assassination route anyway. He completely ignored the Elector's command. He must've told Anden that *I* insisted on the assassination route. It's the only way Anden would've gone with it."

Metias shrugs. "What does it mean? That Razor simply wanted to force the assassination through?"

"No. If the assassination happened, everyone would know who ignored the Elector's order. Everyone would know that Razor was the one who ordered the jeeps forward." I grab Metias's arm. "The Republic would *know* that Razor tried to kill Anden."

Metias tightens his lips. "Why would Razor put himself in such obvious danger? What else was strange?"

I turn back to the street's slow-moving chaos. "Well, right from the beginning, he was able to bring Patriots into his Vegas officer quarters so easily. He got his Patriots on and off that airship as if it were nothing. It's like he has superhuman abilities to hide out."

"Maybe he does," Metias says. "After all, he has the Colonies sponsoring him, doesn't he?"

"That's true." I run a hand through my hair in frustration. In this dream state, my fingers are numb and I can't feel the strands running against my skin. "It doesn't make sense. They should have called off the assassination. Razor shouldn't have gone through with it at all, not after I disrupted it. They would've gone back to their quarters, thought things through again, and then attempted another strike. Maybe in a month or two. Why would Razor put his position at risk if the assassination was in danger of failing?"

Metias watches as a Republic soldier runs past us. The soldier tilts his head up at Razor standing on the roof and salutes.

"If the Colonies are behind the Patriots," my brother says, "and they know who Day is, shouldn't you both have been taken straight to talk with whomever is in charge?"

I shrug. I think back on the time I spent with Anden. His radical new laws, his new way of thinking. Then I remember his tension with Congress and the Senators.

And that's when the dream breaks apart. My eyes snap open. I've figured out why Razor bothers me so much.

The Colonies aren't sponsoring Razor — in fact, the Colonies have no idea what the Patriots are up to. That's why Razor went ahead with the plan — of course he had no fear of the Republic finding out that he worked for the Patriots.

The Republic had hired Razor to assassinate Anden.

DAY

After the soldier and I left the balcony and the throng of people outside our hospital room, I made sure guards stood outside our door ("In case any fans come barging in," the soldier said before she left), then requested extra blankets and medicine for June. I didn't want to get up and see Kaede still standing below the balcony. Gradually, the shouts outside started to die down. Eventually, everything sank into silence. Now we're completely alone, except for the guards standing outside our door.

Everything's ready to go, but I stand unmoving at June's bedside. There's nothing in here I can make into a weapon, so if we really do need to make a run for it tonight, all we can hope for is that we won't have to fight anyone. That no one will notice we're gone until morning.

I get up and walk to the balcony. The snow on the ground below is completely trampled and dark with the dirt of boots. Kaede isn't there anymore, of course. I soak in the Colonies landscape for a while, puzzling once again over Kaede's sign.

Why would Kaede tell me to return to the Republic? Is she trying to trap me or warn me? Then again — if she wanted to hurt us, why did she hit Baxter and let us go in Pierra? She'd even urged us to escape before the other Patriots could get to us. I turn to June, who's still sleeping. Her breathing is more even now, and the flush on her cheeks is less pronounced than it was several hours ago. Still, I don't dare disturb her.

More minutes drag by. I wait to see if Kaede will try again. After the dizzying speed of everything that's happened to us, I'm not used to being stuck here like this. Suddenly there's too much time.

A thud sounds out against the balcony doors. I jump to my feet. Maybe a branch broke off a tree, or a shingle fell from the roof. I wait now, alert. Nothing happens for a while. Then there's another thud against the glass.

I get up from June's bed, walk over to the balcony doors, and carefully peek out through the glass. No one's there. My eyes skip to the balcony floor. There, in plain sight, are two small rocks — one with a note tied to it.

I unlock the balcony door, slide it open a

little, and grab the note from the rock. Then I lock the door again and open the note up. The words are hastily scrawled.

Come outside. I'm alone. Emergency. Here to help. We have to talk. — K

Emergency. I crumple the note in my hand. What does she think is an emergency? Isn't everything an emergency right now? She *had* helped us escape — but that doesn't mean I'm ready to trust her.

Not a minute has passed before a third rock hits the door. This time, its message reads:

If you don't talk to me now, you're gonna regret it. — K

My temper rises at the threat. Kaede does have the power to turn us in for messing up the Patriots' plans. I stay where I am, reread-ing the note in my hands. *Maybe just for a few minutes,* I tell myself. *That's it. Just long enough to see what Kaede wants. Then I'm coming back inside.*

I grab my coat, take a deep breath, and step back over to the balcony doors. My fingers quietly undo the latch. A cold wind hits my face as I sneak out onto the balcony, crouch low, lock the balcony doors, and push them closed. If anyone's going to break in to hurt June, they're going to have to make enough noise to alert the guards outside. I leap down the side of the balcony, twist around, and grab on to the ledge with my hands. I lower myself down until I'm dangling halfway between the first and second floors. Then I let go.

My boots land in powdered snow with a soft crunch. I take a last look at the second floor ledge, memorize where this hospital building is on the street, then tuck my hair into my coat and flatten myself against the wall.

The streets are empty and silent at this hour. I wait against the side of the building for a minute before I step out. *Come on, Kaede.* My breath comes out in short bursts of steam. My eyes scour the nooks and crannies around me, checking for danger. But I'm all alone. *You wanted me to meet you out here? Well, I'm here.*

"Talk to me," I whisper under my breath as I walk alongside the building. My eyes search for street patrols, but no one's out here.

Suddenly I pause. There's a subtle shadow crouched in one of the nearby alleys. I tense up. "Come out," I whisper loud enough for the person to hear me. "I know you're there."

Kaede materializes out of the shadows, then waves me over. "Walk with me," she whispers back. "Hurry." She scurries off into a narrow alley hidden behind a row of snow-laden bushes. We go down the alleyway until it crosses a wider street, which Kaede turns onto sharply. I hurry after her. My eyes search every corner. I gauge all the spots where I can shimmy up to a higher floor in case anyone tries to take me by surprise. Every hair on my neck stands on end, rigid with tension.

Kaede gradually slows her walk until we're side by side. She's wearing the same pants and boots that she had on during the attempt earlier in the day, but has switched out her military jacket for a wool cloak and scarf. Her face is scrubbed clean of the black stripe.

"All right, be fast about this," I say to her. "I don't want to leave June for too long. What are you doing here?" I make sure to keep a good distance between us, just in case she decides to get happy with a knife or something. We do seem to be alone, I'll give her that much, but I still make sure we stay on a main street where I can get away if I need to. A few Colonies workers hurry past us, aglow from the lights of building ads. Kaede's eyes glitter with near-frantic anxiety, a look that's completely foreign on her face.

"I couldn't climb up to your room," she says. The scarf around her mouth muffles her words, and she pushes it down impatiently.

"Damn guards would hear me. That's why you're the Runner, not me. I swear that I'm not here to harm your precious June. If she's just by herself up there, she's gonna be fine. We'll be quick."

"Did you follow us down through the tunnel?"

Kaede nods. "Managed to clear enough rubble away to squeeze through."

"Where are the others?"

She pulls her gloves on tighter, blows warm air on her hands, and mutters in disgust about the weather. "They're not here. Just me. I needed to warn you."

A sick feeling rises in my stomach. "About what? Is it Tess?"

Kaede stops what she's doing to poke me hard in the ribs. "Assassination was botched." She holds up two hands before I can interrupt. "Yeah, yeah, I know *you're* already aware of this. A lot of Patriots have been arrested. Some of them got away too — our Tess did, at least. She ran with a few of our Pilots and Runners. Pascao and Baxter too." I spit out a curse. Tess. I feel a sudden compulsion to chase her, to make sure she's safe — and then I remember the last thing she said to me. Kaede plunges on as we continue to walk. "I don't know where they are now. But here's what you don't know. *I* didn't even know, until

397

you and June stopped the assassination. Jordan — the Runner girl, you remember, right? — uncovered all this info from a comp drive and handed it off to one of our Hackers." She takes a deep breath, stops, and turns her head down to the ground. Her voice's usual strength fades. "Day, Razor played all of us. He lied to the Patriots, then handed them over to the Republic."

I halt in my walk. "What?"

"Razor told us that the Colonies hired us to kill the Elector and start a revolution," Kaede says. "But that's not true. Found out on the day of the assassination that the Republic's *Senate* is sponsoring the Patriots." She shakes her head. "Do you believe that? *The Republic hired the Patriots to assassinate Anden.*"

I'm silent. Stunned. June's words echo in my mind, how she'd told me that Congress dislikes their new Elector, how she thought Razor was lying. *The things he's told us don't add up,* she'd said.

"Blindsided all of us — except for Razor," Kaede says when I don't respond. We start walking again. "The Senators want Anden dead. They figured they could use us and pin the blame on us too."

My blood is racing so fast I can barely hear myself speak. "Why would Razor sell out the

Patriots like that? Hasn't he been with them for a decade? And I thought Congress was trying *not* to cause a revolution."

Kaede slumps her shoulders and lets out a breath of steam. "He got caught working for the Patriots a couple of years ago. So he made a deal with Congress: He leads the Patriots into killing Anden, the young revolutionary spitfire, and Congress forgets about his traitorous ties. At the end of it all, *Razor* gets to be the new Elector — and with you and June working for him, he comes off like the people's hero or something. The public would think that the Patriots took over the government, when it's really only the Republic all over again. Razor doesn't want the United States to be restored — he just wants to preserve himself. And he'll join whatever side's most convenient to achieve that."

I close my eyes. My world is spinning. Hadn't June warned me about Razor? All this time, I've been working for the Republic's Senators. They're the ones who want Anden dead. No wonder the Colonies don't seem to have any idea what the Patriots are up to. Then I open my eyes. "But they failed," I say. "Anden is still alive."

"Anden is still alive," Kaede repeats. "Thankfully."

I should have trusted June all along. My

anger toward the young Elector shudders and trembles, grows weak. Does this mean . . . that he actually *did* release Eden? Is my brother free and safe? I study Kaede. "You came all the way here to tell me that?" I whisper.

"Yup. Know why?" She leans closer, until her nose is almost touching mine. "Anden is about to lose his grip on the country. The people are *this* close to revolting against him." She holds two fingers close together. "If he falls, we're gonna have a lot of trouble stopping Razor from taking over the Republic. Right now, Anden's fighting for control of the military while Razor and Commander Jameson are trying to wrestle it away from him. The government's about to split in two."

"Wait — Commander Jameson?" I ask.

"There was a chat transcript recorded between her and Razor on that comp drive. Remember how we ran into her on board the RS *Dynasty*?" Kaede replies. "Razor made it sound like he had no idea she'd be there. But *I* think she totally recognized you. She must've wanted to see you with her own eyes. To know that you were truly a part of Razor's plans." Kaede grimaces. "I should've sensed something off about Razor. I was wrong about Anden too."

"Why do you care what happens to the

Republic?" I say. The wind whips snow flurries up from the street, echoing the coldness in my words. "And why now?"

"I was in it for the money — I admit that." Kaede shakes her head and sets her mouth in a tight line. "But first of all — I didn't get paid, because the plan didn't go off. Second, I didn't sign up to destroy the country, to hand all the Republic's civilians right back to another goddy Elector." Then she trails off a little, and her eyes go misty. "I don't know . . . maybe I was hoping that the Patriots could give me a nobler goal than making money. Joining these two cracked nations back together. That would've been nice."

The winter wind stings my face. Kaede doesn't need to tell me why she came all the way here to get me. After hearing this, I know why. I remember what Tess said to me back in Lamar. *They're all looking to you, Day. They're waiting for your next move.* I might be the only person who can save Anden now. I am the only person that the Republic's people will listen to.

We fall silent and sink farther into the shadows as a pair of Colonies police guards rush by. Snow flies underneath their boots. I watch until they disappear down the last alley we'd come through. Where are they going?

When Kaede just continues walking with her

scarf covering her mouth again, I say, "What about the Colonies?"

"What *about* them?" she mutters through fabric.

"What about letting the Republic collapse and the Colonies take over? What about that idea?"

"It was never about letting the Colonies *win.* The Patriots are about re-creating the United States. However that can be accomplished." Kaede pauses, then motions for us to turn down a different street. We walk two more blocks before she stops us in front of an enormous row of dilapidated buildings.

"What's this?" I ask Kaede, but she doesn't respond. I turn back to the building in front of me. It's about thirty or so stories tall, but stretches unbroken for several city blocks. Every few dozen yards, tiny, dark entrances are carved into the compound's bottom floor. Water drips from the sides, from windows and decaying balconies, carving ugly lines of fungus into the walls. The structure stretches on down the street from where we stand — from the sky it must look like a gigantic black cinder block.

I gape at it. After seeing the lights of the Colonies' skyscrapers, it's shocking to know that a building like this exists over here. I've seen abandoned *Republic* complexes that look better than this. The windows and corridors are squeezed so closely together that no light could possibly get down to the bottom. I peer inside one of the black entrances.

Darkness, nothing. The sound of dripping water and faint footsteps echoes from inside. Now and then, I see a flickering light go by, as if someone's in there with a lantern. I peer up at the higher floors. Most of the windows are cracked and shattered, or missing altogether. Some of them have plastic taped across the opening. Old pots on the balconies catch dripping water, and several have lines of tattered clothing hanging off the ledges. There must be people living in there. But the thought makes me shiver. I look back once at the glittering skyscrapers on the block right behind us, then forward at this rotting cement structure.

A commotion at the end of the street catches our attention. I tear my eyes away from the compound. A block down, there's a middle-aged woman in men's boots and a shabby coat pleading at the top of her lungs with a pair of men dressed in heavy plastic gear. Both have clear visors covering their faces and large, wide-brimmed hats on their heads.

"Watch," Kaede whispers. Then she drags us into one of the dark entrances between two doors on the compound's ground level.

We lean our heads slightly so that we can hear what's going on. Even though they're fairly far away, the woman's voice carries clearly across the quiet, icy air.

"— just missed one payment this year," the woman's saying. "I can run to the bank first thing in the morning and give you as many Notes as I have —"

One of the men interrupts her. "DesCon policy, ma'am. We cannot investigate crimes for customers who have been delinquent on payments to their local police."

The woman is in tears, wringing her hands so hard that I feel like she's going to rub her skin right off. "There must be something you can do," she says. "Something I can give you or another police department I —"

The second man shakes his head. "All police departments share DesCon's policy. Who's your employer?"

"Cloud Corp," the woman says hopefully. As if this info might persuade them to help her.

"Cloud Corp discourages its workers from being out past eleven P.M." He nods up at the compound. "If you don't return to your home, DesCon Corp will report you to Cloud and you might lose your job."

"But they've stolen everything I have!" The woman breaks into loud sobs. "My door is completely — completely bashed in — all of my food and clothes are gone. The men who did it live on my floor — if you please come with me, you can catch them — I know which apartment they live in —"

The two men have already started walking away. The woman scampers behind them, begging for help, even as they keep ignoring her.

"But my home — if you don't do something — how will I —" she keeps saying. The men repeat their warnings to report her.

After they're gone, I turn back to Kaede. "What was that?"

"Wasn't it obvious?" Kaede replies sarcastically as we step out from the building's darkness and back into the street.

We're quiet. Finally, Kaede says, "The working class gets shafted everywhere, don't they? My point is this: The Colonies are better than the Republic in some ways. But believe it or not, the reverse is also true. No such thing as the stupid utopia you've been fantasizing about, Day. Doesn't exist. There was no point trying to tell you that before. It's just something you had to see for yourself."

We start heading back to the hospital. Two more Colonies soldiers hurry past us, neither of them bothering to take us in. A million thoughts whirl through my head. My father must never have set foot inside the Colonies

— or if he did, he only skimmed the surface of it, the way June and I had when we first arrived. A lump rises in my throat.

"Do you trust Anden?" I say after a moment. "Is he worth saving? Is the *Republic* worth saving?"

Kaede makes several more turns. Finally, she stops next to a shop with miniature screens in its window, each one broadcasting different Colonies programming. Kaede guides us into the store's tiny side street, where the darkness of the night swallows us. She pauses to motion at the broadcasting screens inside the store. I remember passing a shop like this on our way into the city. "The Colonies always show news snatched from Republic airwaves," she says. "They have a whole channel for it. This news bite has been on repeat ever since the failed assassination."

My eyes wander over to the headlines on the monitor. At first I just stare blankly, lost in my churning thoughts about the Patriots, but a moment later I realize that the broadcast isn't about warfront skirmishes or Colonies news, but about the Republic's Elector. A surge of dislike instinctively courses through me at the sight of Anden on the screen. I strain to hear the newscast, wondering how differently the Colonies would interpret the same events.

A caption runs under Anden's recorded address. I read it in disbelief.

ELECTOR FREES YOUNGER BROTHER OF NOTORIOUS REBEL "DAY"; TO ADDRESS PUBLIC TOMORROW FROM CAPITOL TOWER.

"As of today," the Elector says in a prerecorded video, "Eden Bataar Wing is officially freed from military service and, as thanks for his contributions, exempt from the Trials. All others being transported along the warfront have been released to their families as well."

I have to rub my eyes and read the captions again.

They're still there. The Elector has freed Eden.

Suddenly I can't feel the cold air anymore. I can't feel *anything.* My legs feel weak. My breath keeps time with the hammering of my heart. This can't be right. The Elector is probably announcing this publicly so he can lure me back into the Republic and into his service. He's trying to trick me and make himself look good. There's no way he would've released Eden — and all the others, the boy I'd seen on the train — of his own accord. No possible way.

No possible way? Even after everything June had told me, even after what Kaede just said? Even now, I don't trust Anden? What's wrong with me?

Then, as I continue watching, the Elector's recorded address makes way for a video showing Eden being escorted out of a courthouse, shackle-free and dressed in clothes that usually belong on the child of an elite family.

His blond curls are neatly brushed. He searches the streets with blind eyes, but he's *smiling*. I push my hand deeper into the snow in an attempt to steady myself. Eden looks healthy, well taken care of. When was this filmed?

Anden's newscast finally ends, and now the video shows footage of the failed assassination attempt followed by a reel of warfront battles. The captions are wildly different from what I'd see in the Republic.

FAILED ASSASSINATION ATTEMPT ON REPUBLIC'S NEW ELECTOR PRIMO, THE LATEST SIGN OF UNREST IN REPUBLIC

The caption is wrapped up by a smaller line in the corner of the screen that says THIS BROADCAST BROUGHT TO YOU BY EVERGREEN ENT. The now-familiar circular symbol is beside it.

"Make up your own mind about Anden," Kaede mutters. She stops to wipe snowflakes off her eyelashes.

I was wrong. The certainty of this sits in my stomach like a dead weight, a rock of guilt for

408

turning so viciously on June when she'd tried to explain all of it to me in the underground shelter. The awful things I'd said to her. I think of the strange, unsettling ads I've seen here, the crumbling living quarters of the poor, the disappointment I feel in knowing that the Colonies aren't the shining beacon my father imagined. His dream of glittering skyscrapers and a better life was just that.

I remember my dream of what I'd do after all this was over . . . run into the Colonies with June, Tess, Eden . . . start a new life, leave the Republic behind. Maybe I've been trying to escape to the wrong place and run away from the wrong things. I think of all the times I clashed with soldiers. The hatred I had for Anden and everyone who grew up rich. Then I picture the slums that I'd grown up in. I despise the Republic, don't I? I want to see them collapse, yeah? But only now do I make the distinction — I despise the Republic's laws, but I love the Republic itself. I love the *people.* I'm not just doing this for the Elector; I'm doing this for *them.*

"Are the speakers at the Capitol Tower still hooked up to the JumboTrons?" I ask Kaede.

"As far as I know, yeah," she replies. "With all the commotion over the last forty-eight hours, no one's noticed the modified wiring."

My eyes go to the rooftops, where fighter

jets lie in wait. "Are you as good of a pilot as you say?" I ask.

Kaede shrugs her shoulders and grins. "Better."

Slowly, a plan starts to form in my mind.

Another pair of Colonies soldiers runs by. This time, an unsettling feeling creeps down my neck. These soldiers, like the last ones, also turn down the alley we'd come through. I make sure there are no more coming, then hurry out into the darkness of the street. *No, no. Not now.*

Kaede follows close behind. "What is it?" she whispers. "You just turned as white as a goddy snowstorm."

I'd left her alone and vulnerable in a place I once thought would be our safe haven. I'd left her to the wolves. And if something happens to her now because of me . . . I break into a run. "I think they're heading toward the hospital," I say. "For June."

JUNE

I snap out of my dream, lift my head, and my eyes sweep the area. The illusion of Metias vanishes. I'm in a hospital room, and Day is nowhere to be seen. It's the middle of the night. Hadn't we been in here earlier? I have a vague recollection of Day at my bedside, and Day stepping out onto the balcony to greet a cheering crowd. Now he's not here. Where did he go?

It takes me another second, light-headed as I am, to figure out what woke me up. I am not alone in the room. There are half a dozen Colonies soldiers in here. A tall soldier with long red hair hoists her gun and points it at me.

"That's the one?" she asks, keeping me in her line of fire.

An older male soldier nods. "Yup. Didn't know Day was hiding a Republic soldier. This girl is none other than June Iparis. The Republic's most well-known prodigy.

411

DesCon Corp will be happy. This prisoner's going to be worth a lot of money." He gives me a cold smile. "Now, my dear. Tell us where Day went."

Sixteen minutes have passed. The soldiers have secured my hands behind my back with a temporary set of cuffs. My mouth is gagged. Three of them stand near the room's open door, while the others guard the balcony. I groan. Even though my fever is gone and my joints don't ache, my head still feels dizzy. (Where *did* Day go?)

One of the soldiers talks into an earpiece. "Yes," he says. A pause, and then, "We're moving her to a cell. DesCon's going to get a lot of good info out of this one. We'll send Day along for questioning once we get hold of him." Another soldier is holding the door open with his boot. They're waiting for a gurney to arrive, I realize, so they can take me away. That means I probably have less than two or three minutes to get myself out of this.

I clench down on my gag, force down my nausea, and swallow. My thoughts and memories are getting jumbled up. I blink, wondering if I'm hallucinating. The Patriots are being sponsored by the Republic. Why didn't I see that earlier? It was so obvious, right from the beginning — the elaborate furnishings in the apartment, how easily Razor could get us from place to place without getting caught.

Now I watch the soldier continue to talk into his earpiece. How do I warn Day now? He must have left through the balcony doors — when he comes back, I'll be gone and they'll be here, ready to question him. They might even think we're Republic spies. I run a finger repeatedly across my paper clip ring.

The paper clip ring.

My finger stops moving. Then I inch it gradually off my ring finger behind my back and try to unfurl its spiraling metal wires. A soldier glances at me, but I close my eyes and let out a soft moan of pain through my gag. He returns to his conversation. I let my fingers run down the spiraling ring and pull it straight. The paper clips were twisted six times. I unfurl the first two. Then I straighten out the rest of the paper clip and bend it into what I hope is a stretched-out Z shape. The movement makes both of my arms cramp painfully.

Suddenly one of the balcony soldiers stops talking to check the streets below. He stays like that for a while, his eyes searching. If he heard Day, Day must have vanished again. The soldier scrutinizes the roofs, then loses interest and goes back into his stance. Far down the hospital corridor, I hear people talking and the unmistakable sound of wheels against the tiled floor. They're bringing the gurney.

I have to hurry. I insert one, then two of the bent paper clips into the lock on my cuffs. My arms are killing me, but I don't have time to rest them. Gingerly I push one of the wires around in the lock, feeling it scrape against the lock's interior until it finally hits the tumbler. I twist the paper clip, pushing the tumbler aside.

"DesCon's on their way with some backup," one soldier murmurs. As he says it, I move the second paper clip and hear the pin in the lock give a tiny, almost imperceptible click. Two soldiers and a nurse wheel the gurney into my room, stop for a moment inside the doorway, then roll it in my direction. The lock on my chains opens — I feel the cuffs coming off my hands with a soft clank. One soldier fixes milky blue eyes on me and pulls his thick lips into a frown. He notices the subtle change in my expression, and heard the clicking sound as well. His eyes flick to my arms.

If I'm going to make a break for it, now's

my only chance.

Suddenly I twist to the side of the bed and jump off. The chains fall back into the bed and my feet hit the floor. Dizziness hits me like a wall of water, but I manage to keep it at bay. The soldier with his gun pointed at me shouts out a warning, but he's too slow. I kick out at the gurney as hard as I can — it topples over, taking down one soldier with it. Another soldier grabs at me, but I duck and manage to slip out of his grasp. My eyes focus on the balcony.

But there are still three soldiers standing over there. They rush at me. I avoid two of them, but the third catches me around my shoulders and wraps an arm across my neck. He throws me down, knocking the breath out of me. I struggle frantically to free myself.

"Stay down!" one exclaims, while another tries to snap a new set of cuffs on my wrists. He lets out a howl as I twist around and sink my teeth deep into his arm.

No good. I'm captured, I'm arrested.

Suddenly the balcony's glass door shatters into a million pieces. The soldiers spin around, bewildered. Everything is whirling. In the midst of shouts and footsteps, I see two people breaking into the room from the balcony. One's a girl I recognize. *Kaede?* I

415

think incredulously.

The other is Day.

Kaede kicks one soldier in the neck —
Day barrels into the soldier holding me
down and knocks him to the floor. Before
anyone can react, Day's up again. He grabs
my hands and yanks me to my feet.

Kaede's already at the balcony ledge.
"Don't shoot them!" I hear a soldier call
out behind us. "They're valuable property!"
Day rushes us onto the balcony, then leaps
onto the railing's ledge in one bound. He
and Kaede try to pull me upright as two
other guards run toward us.

But I start sinking to my knees. My sudden burst of energy is no match for my
lingering illness — I'm too weak. Day jumps
back down from the ledge and kneels beside
me. Kaede lets out a whoop, tackling one of
the soldiers to the ground. "See you there!"
she yells back at us. Then she rushes inside
the room amid all the confusion, throwing
the guards off. I see her slip out of their
grasp and vanish down the corridor.

Day takes my arms, then wraps them
around his neck. *Don't let go.* When he
straightens, I tighten my legs around him
and cling to his back as hard as I can. He
climbs onto the balcony ledge, boots
crunching through broken glass, and leaps

onto the outcropping that wraps around the second floor. Immediately I understand where we're going. We're all heading for the roof, where fighter jets lie in wait. Kaede is taking the stairs. We're traveling by a more direct route.

We edge out onto the second-floor ledge. I hang on for dear life. Strands of Day's hair brush against my face as he pulls us up to the third floor's outcropping. I feel his rapid breathing, his muscles hard against my skin. Two more floors to go. A soldier attempts to follow us, decides against it, then rushes back inside to take the stairs.

Day struggles with his footing as he pulls us up one more floor. We're almost at the roof. The soldiers start spilling out onto the lawn below. I can see them pointing their guns up at us. Day grits his teeth and sets me down on the ledge. "Go first," he whispers, then gives me a boost. I grab the top ledge, gather all my strength, and pull. When I finally make it over the edge, I whirl around and grab Day's hand. He leaps onto the roof too. My eyes go to a streak of dark red staining his hand. He must've injured it in the climb.

I feel so light-headed. "Your hand," I start to say, but he just shakes his head at me, wraps his arm around my waist, and guides us toward the nearest of the fighter jets lining the roof. Soldiers start flooding out of the roof's entrance door — I get a good look at the one running fastest toward us. Kaede.

DAY

Kaede wastes no time. She gestures toward the fighter jet closest to us and sprints up the ramp to its cockpit. Shots ring out. June leans heavily against me. I can feel her strength fading, so I pick her up and carry her close to my chest. The soldiers who have reached the roof move faster once they see what Kaede's up to. But she's too far ahead of them. I rush us toward the ramp.

The jet's engine roars to life as we reach the ramp's first step, and right below the aircraft, two large exhausts slowly tilt downward to face the ground. We're gearing up for a straight shoot into the sky. "Hurry the *hell* up!" Kaede screams from the cockpit. Then she ducks back out of view and spits out a string of curses.

"Let me down," June says. She hops back onto her own feet, stumbles, and then straightens to take the first two steps. I stay behind her, my eyes fixed on the soldiers. They're almost here. June manages to reach the top of the ramp and climb into the cockpit. I hurry halfway up the ramp before a soldier grabs my pant leg and yanks me back down. *Remember balance. Stay on the balls of your feet. Catch him at the right spots.* June's fighting lesson rushes through my head all at once. When the soldier swings at me, I duck down, move to his side, and hit him as hard as I can right below his rib cage. He collapses onto one knee. *Liver blow.*

Another two soldiers reach me and I brace myself. But then one of them shrieks, falling backward off the ramp with a bullet wound to his shoulder. I glance up at the cockpit. June has Kaede's gun and is taking aim at the soldiers. I turn back to the steps and hop up to the top, where June's already buckled in the middle seat right behind Kaede. "Get in, already!" Kaede snaps. The engines let out another high-pitched roar. Behind me, several guards have started climbing up the first few steps.

I leap onto the metal railing lining the edge of the ramp, grab the side of the cockpit, and push with all my strength. The ramp teeters for a second — then starts toppling over. Soldiers shout warnings and fling themselves out of the way. By the time it smashes onto the roof, I'm already in the jet and buckling myself into the last seat. Kaede slides the cockpit shut. I feel my stomach drop as we shoot straight up off the roof and above the buildings. Through the cockpit's glass, I can see pilots rushing into the jets on nearby buildings as well as the second one sitting on the hospital's roof.

"Damn it all," Kaede spits out from the front. "I'm gonna *kill* them — they got me in my side." I feel the jet's exhausts shift. "Hang on. This is gonna be a wild ride."

We stop rising. The engines grow to a deafening roar. Then we shoot forward. The world rushes at us and pressure in my head builds as Kaede pushes the jet faster and faster. She lets out a whoop. Almost immediately I hear a voice crackling through the cockpit.

"Pilot, you are ordered to land your aircraft immediately." The speaker sounds nervous. Must be a jet following us. "We will open fire. I repeat, land immediately, or we will open fire."

"Only one jet in the air after us. Let's fix that. Suck in your breath, guys." Kaede turns violently, and I almost black out from the pressure change.

"All you all right?" I call out to June. She says something back, but I can't hear her over the roar of the engines.

Suddenly Kaede yanks a knob back and

pushes a lever all the way forward. My head slams into the side of the cockpit. We spin a full hundred-eighty degrees in less than a second. I see a jet flying straight for us at a terrifying speed. Instinctively I throw my hands up.

Even June yells out, "Kaede, that —"

Kaede opens fire. A shower of bright light streaks from our jet to the one in front of us. The engines yank us forward and up. An explosion sounds behind us — the other jet must've gotten hit in the fuel tank or taken a shot straight through its cockpit.

"They'll be hard-pressed to tail us now," she shouts. "We're too far ahead and they won't want to cross the warfront. I'm gonna push this baby to its max — we'll be in the Republic in a couple of minutes." I don't ask how she's planning to pass through the warfront without getting shot down.

When I look through the cockpit at the Colonies' towering buildings, I let out a breath and slump in my seat. Glittering lights, shining skyscrapers, everything my father had de-scribed to me on the few nights a year that we were able to see him. It's so lovely from a distance.

"So," Kaede says, "I'm not just burning up fuel for nothing, am I? Day — we're still head-ing for Denver?"

"Yes," I reply.

"What's the plan?" June still sounds weak, but there's a burning purpose behind it, the sense that we're about to do something pivotal. She can tell that something has changed inside me.

I feel strangely calm. "We're headed for the Capitol Tower," I reply. "I'm going to announce my support of Anden to the Republic."

JUNE

A couple of minutes to get into the Republic's border. That means, at the speed we're going (easily more than eight hundred miles per hour; we all felt a sudden pressure change as we broke the sound barrier, like being dragged out of deep mud), we're only two dozen or so miles from the warfront and several hundred from Denver. Day tells me everything that Kaede shared with him, about the Patriots and the true colors of Razor, about Eden, then Congress's determination to oust the Elector. Everything I'd discovered and then some. My head was in a fog when we'd bolted from the room and made our way up to the hospital roof. Now, after the cold outside air and the speed of Kaede's air maneuver, I can calculate details a little more clearly.

"We're closing in on the warfront," Kaede says. The instant those words come out of her mouth, I hear the distant sound of explosions. They're muffled, but we must be thousands of feet in the air and I can still feel the shock each time they go off. There's a sudden lift and I press into my seat. She's trying to push the jet as high as it can go so we don't get shot out of the sky by ground missiles. I force myself to take deep, calming breaths as we continue to climb. My ears pop endlessly. I watch as Kaede falls into formation with a squadron of Colonies jets. "We're gonna need to break from them soon," she mutters. There's pain in her voice, probably from her gunshot wound. "Hang tight."

"Day?" I manage to call out.

I don't hear anything, and for a second I think he blacked out. Then he replies, "Still here." He sounds detached, like he's fighting to stay conscious.

"Denver's a few minutes away," Kaede says.

We stabilize again. When I peer out of the cockpit down at the pockets of clouds far below us, I catch my breath. Airships (easily more than a hundred and fifty, as far as the eye can see) dot the sky like miniature daggers soaring through the air, stretching in lines off into the horizon. The Colonies' ships all have a distinct gold stripe down the middle of their runways that we can see even from way up here. Not far in front of them is a wide strip of empty airspace where sparks of light and smoke fly back and forth, and on the other side are rows of airships I can recognize: Republic ships, marked with a bloodred star on the side of each hull. Jets are raging in dogfights all over the place. We must be a good five hundred feet above them — but I'm not sure if that's a safe enough distance.

An alarm on Kaede's control board beeps. A voice rings out in the cockpit. "Pilot, you are not cleared for this area," it says. (Male, Colonies accent.) "This is not your squadron. You're ordered to land on DesCon Nine immediately."

"Negative," Kaede replies. She pulls our jet up and keeps climbing.

"Pilot, you are *ordered* to land on DesCon Nine immediately."

Kaede turns off her mike for an instant and looks back at us. She seems a little too happy about our situation. "Goddy talker's following us," she says in a mock authoritative tone. "We got two hot on our tail." Then she flips the mike on again and replies brightly, "Negative, DesCon. I'm gonna shoot you out of the sky."

The person in the other plane sounds shocked and angry this time. "Change

426

course and get this one —"

Kaede lets out an ear-piercing shout. "Split the sky, boys!" She rockets us forward and up at blinding speed, then goes into a spin. Streaks of light shoot past the cockpit window — the two jets tailing us must've gotten close enough to open fire. I feel my stomach drop as Kaede goes into a sudden nosedive, killing our engine in the process. We drop at a pace that turns my vision black and white. I feel myself fading away.

An instant later I jolt awake. I must've blacked out.

We're falling. We're plummeting to the earth. The airships below us grow in size — it looks like we're heading straight at the deck of one of them. No, we're going way too fast; we'll be smashed into pieces. More streaks of light rush past us. The jets following are diving after us.

Then, without warning, Kaede fires the engines again. They roar to life. She pulls back hard on a lever and the whole jet spins in a half circle so the nose is facing up again. I'm almost sucked into my chair at the sudden change. My vision blacks out again, and this time I have no idea how much time has passed. A few seconds? Minutes? I realize we're charging back up into the sky.

The other jets zoom down. They're trying

to pull up, but it's too late. Behind us, a huge explosion shakes us hard in our seats — the jets must've struck the deck of the airship with the force of a dozen bombs. Orange-and-yellow fire churns upward from one of the Colonies ships. We're now zooming across the empty airspace between the two countries, and Kaede sends us into another spin that saves us from a barrage of fire. We cross the airspace and cut through the sky over the Republic's airships. *One lone Colonies jet, lost in the chaos.* I gape at the scene outside, wondering if the Republic is confused that the Colonies attacked one of their own jets. If anything, that's what bought us enough time to cross the warfront space.

"Best split-S you've ever seen, I bet," Kaede says with a laugh. It sounds more strained than usual.

Not far from us now are the looming towers of Denver and its forbidding Armor, shrouded in a permanent sea of smog and haze. Behind us, I hear the first sounds of gunfire as Republic jets start tailing us in an attempt to shoot us down.

"How are we going to get inside?" Day shouts as Kaede spins the jet, sends a missile backward, and pushes us to go faster.

"I'll get us in," she shouts back.

"We can't make it if we go overhead," I reply. "The Armor has missiles lining every side of that wall. They'll shoot us down before we ever get across into the city."

"No city's impenetrable." Kaede sends the jet lower even as the Republic jets continue to pursue us. "I know what I'm doing."

We're closing in fast on Denver. I can see the looming gray walls of the Armor rising up before us, a barricade like nothing else in the Republic, and the heavy gray pillars (each a hundred feet apart from the next) lining its sides. I close my eyes. No way — no *way* — Kaede can get us over that. A squadron of jets could get over, maybe, and even then it'll be a long shot. I picture a missile hitting us and our seats ejecting us out over the city's skies, the shots they'll fire up at our parachutes, our bodies plummeting to the ground. The Armor is close now. They must've seen us approaching for a while, and their weapons will be trained on us. I bet they've never seen a rogue Colonies jet before.

Then Kaede dives. Not just any dive — she's headed down at almost ninety degrees, ready to send us smashing into the earth. Behind me, Day sucks in his breath. The buildings below rush up at us. *She's lost control of the jet. I know it. We've been hit.*

At the last second, Kaede pulls up. We skim above the buildings at mach speed, so close that the roofs seem like they're going to rip the bottom right off our jet. Immediately Kaede starts slowing down the jet, until we're cruising at a speed barely fast enough to keep us airborne. Suddenly I realize what she's going to do. It's completely stupid. She's not taking us over the Armor at all — she's going to try to squeeze the jet through the opening that the trains use to pass in and out of Denver. The same tunnels I'd seen when I'd taken that train ride with the Elector. *Of course.* The surface-to-air missile systems mounted along the Armor's wall aren't designed to take down anything like us from the ground, because they can't shoot at such a low angle. And machine guns on the wall aren't powerful enough. But if Kaede doesn't aim exactly right, we'll explode against the wall and burst into flames. We're close enough for me to see soldiers running back and forth on top of the wall of the Armor. Their communications must be flying fast.

But it doesn't matter at this rate. One second the Armor's several hundred feet in front of us, and the next, we're hurtling toward the dark entrance of an open train tunnel.

"Hold on!" Kaede shouts. She pushes the jet lower, as if that were possible. The entrance yawns at us with its gaping mouth.

We're not going to make it. The tunnel is way too small.

Then we're inside, and for an instant the tunnel's pitch-black. Bright sparks burst from each end of the jet as the wings tear through the entrance's sides. A rumbling sound comes from above us. They're rushing to shut the entrance, I realize, but they're too late.

Another second. We zoom out of the entrance and into Denver. Kaede slams the jet's lever the opposite way in an attempt to slow us down even more.

"Pull up, pull *up*!" Day yells. Buildings zip past us. We're too low to the ground — and heading straight for the side of a tall barrack.

Kaede veers sharply to one side. We miss the building by a hair. Then we're down, *really* down. The jet slams into the ground and skids, flinging our bodies forward hard against our seat belts. I feel like my limbs are ripping off. Civilians and soldiers alike run out of the way on either side of the street. A few sparks crack the cockpit; it's random gunfire, I realize, from shocked soldiers. Crowds line the roads several blocks away from us — they gape at the jet careening across the pavement.

We finally come to a halt when one of the wings catches the side of a building, sending us crashing sideways into an alley. I jerk roughly back against my seat. Our canopy pops open before I can even catch my breath. I manage to undo my seat belt and leap dizzily up onto the edge of the cockpit. "Kaede." I'm squinting to see her and Day through the smoke. "We have to —"

My words die on my tongue. Kaede's slumped against the pilot seat, her buckle still wrapped around her. Her pilot goggles sit on top of her head — I guess she never even bothered to put them on. Her eyes point vacantly at the buttons on her control panel. A small bloodstain soaks the front of her shirt, not far from the wound she'd received when we first got into the jet. One of the stray bullets had gone straight through the canopy and into her when we crash-landed. Kaede, who just minutes ago had seemed invincible.

For a moment, I'm frozen. The sounds of chaos around me dull, and the smoke covers everything except me and Kaede's body strapped into the pilot seat. A small voice manages to echo through my mind, penetrating the black-and-white fog of numbness, a familiar, pulsing light that gets me going again.

Move, it tells me. *Now.*

I tear my eyes away, then search frantically for Day. He's not sitting in the jet anymore. I scramble onto the edge of the wing and slide down blindly through the smoke and wreckage until I hit the ground on my hands and knees. I can't see a thing.

Then, through the smoke, Day rushes up to me. He pulls me to my feet. I'm suddenly reminded of the first time I'd ever seen him, materializing out of nothingness with his blue eyes and dust-streaked face, holding out his hand to me. His face is slashed with agony. *He must've seen Kaede too.*

"There you are — I thought you'd already gotten out," he whispers as we stumble through the jet's wreckage. "Make for the crowd." My legs ache. Our crash landing must have given me head-to-toe bruises.

We pause underneath one of the wrecked wings just as the first soldiers rush to the jet. Half of them form a makeshift barrier to keep civilians out, their backs turned to us. Other soldiers shine lights across the smoke and twisted metal, scanning for survivors. One of them must've spotted Kaede because he shouts something at the others and motions them over. "It's a

Colonies *jet,*" he shouts, sounding incredulous. "A jet made it past the Armor and right into Denver." We're temporarily hidden from view under this wing, but they'll see us any second now. The makeshift soldier barricade separates us from the crowds.

All around us and throughout the city are the sounds of breaking glass, roaring fires, screaming, chanting people — only those closest to our jet's wreckage seem to realize that a Colonies jet crashed at all. I glance at where the Capitol Tower looms. Anden's voice is ringing from every city block and from every speaker — a live feed of his image must be broadcasting to every JumboTron in the city . . . and in the nation. I look on as several furious rioters fling Molotov cocktails at the soldiers. The people have no idea that Congress is sitting back, waiting for their anger to spill enough to put Razor in Anden's place. There's no way Anden will be able to calm this crowd. I imagine the same protests sparking up across the country, in every street and city. If the Patriots had succeeded in publicly broadcasting the Elector's death from the Capitol Tower's speakers, there would already have been a revolution.

"Now," Day says.

We rush out from under the wing, taking the soldier barricade completely off guard. Before any of them can grab or shoot at us, we're through, ducking into the crowd and melting in with the people. Instantly Day lowers his head and pulls us through the thick pockets of arms and legs. His hand is clenched fiercely around mine. My breath comes out ragged and forced, but I refuse to slow us down now. I push on. People shout in surprise as we barrel through.

Behind us, the soldiers raise the alarm. "There!" one yells. A few shots ring out. They're after us.

We barrel ahead through the crowd. Now and then I hear people exclaim, *"Is that Day?" "Did Day come back in a Colonies jet?"* When I glance behind us, I can tell that half the soldiers are heading the wrong way, unable to tell which direction we took. A couple of others are still hot on our trail. We're only a block away from the Capitol Tower now, but to me it seems like miles. Occasionally, I get a glimpse of it through all the bodies pushing and shoving around. The JumboTrons show Anden standing on a balcony, a tiny, lone figure dressed in black and red, holding his hands out in a gesture of appeal.

He needs Day's help.

Behind us, four soldiers are gradually catching up. The chase saps away the last of my strength. I'm panting, struggling to breathe. Day is already slowing down to keep pace with me, but I can tell we'll never make it at this rate. I squeeze his hand and shake my head.

"You have to go ahead," I tell Day firmly.

"You're cracked." He purses his lips and pulls us forward faster. "We're almost there."

"No." I lean closer to him as we continue to make our way through the people. "This is our one shot. Neither of us will make it if I keep slowing us down."

Day hesitates, torn. We've already been separated once before — now he's wondering if letting me go means he'll never see me again. But we don't have time for him to dwell on this. "I can't run fast, but I can hide in the crowd. Trust me."

Without warning, he grabs my waist, pulls me into a tight embrace, and kisses me hard on the lips. They're burning hot. I kiss him back fiercely and run my hands along his back. "I'm sorry I didn't believe you," he breathes. "Hide, stay safe. See you soon." Then he squeezes my hand and vanishes. I suck in a breath of icy cold air. *Move it, June. No time to waste.*

436

I stop where I am, turn around, and crouch down right as the soldiers reach me. The first one doesn't even see me coming. One second he's running — the next I've tripped him and he's flat on his back. I don't dare stop to look — instead, I stagger back into the furious crowd, weaving my way through people with my head down until the soldiers have fallen far behind. I can't believe how many people are here. Fights between civilians and street police are breaking out everywhere. Above it all, the JumboTrons display live feeds of Anden's face, his expression grave; he's pleading from behind the protective glass.

Six minutes pass. I'm only a dozen yards from the base of the Capitol Tower when I notice that the people around me are slowly falling silent. They're no longer focused on Anden.

"Up there!" one person shouts.

They're pointing at a boy with torch-bright hair, who's perched on a Tower balcony on the opposite side of the same floor as Anden. The balcony's protective glass catches some of the street's light, and from here, the boy is glowing. I catch my breath and pause. It's Day.

DAY

By the time I reach the Capitol Tower, I'm soaked in sweat. My body burns with pain. I go around to one of its sides that isn't facing the main square, then survey the crowd as people shove roughly past me in both directions. All around us are blinding JumboTrons, each displaying the exact same thing — the young Elector, pleading in vain with the people to return home and stay safe, to disperse before things get out of hand. He's trying to console them by dictating his plans for reforming the Republic, doing away with the Trials and changing the way their career assignments are given. But I can tell this goddy political talk isn't going to come close to satisfying the crowd. And even though Anden is older and wiser than June and me, he's missing that crucial piece.

The people don't believe him, and they don't believe *in* him.

I bet Congress is watching all this with

delight. Razor too. Does Anden even know that Razor was the one behind the plot? I narrow my eyes, then leap up to grab the second floor ledge of the wired building. I try to pretend that June is right behind me, cheering me on.

The speakers do seem to be wired up the way Kaede had described back when we were in Lamar. I bend down at the ledge right below the rooftop to study the wires. Yep. Wired in almost the same way I'd done it on the night I first met June in that midnight alley, where I'd asked her for plague cures through the speaker system. Except this time, I'll be speaking not to an alleyway but to the Republic's entire capital. To the country.

The wind stings my cheeks and whistles past my ears in gales, forcing me to constantly adjust my footing. I could die right now. I have no way of knowing if the soldiers on the rooftops will shoot me down before I can reach relative safety behind a balcony's wall of glass, dozens of feet above the rest of the crowd. Or maybe they'll recognize who I am and hold their fire.

I climb until I reach the tenth floor, the same floor that the Elector's balcony is on, then crouch for a second to look down. I'm high enough — the instant I turn the corner of this building, everyone will see me. The masses are most concentrated on this side, their faces turned up to the Elector, their fists raised in anger. Even from here, I can see how many of them have that scarlet streak painted into their hair. Apparently the Republic's attempts to outlaw it don't work so well when *everyone* wants to do it.

On the edges of the square, street police and soldiers are striking out mercilessly with their batons, pushing people back with rows of transparent shields. I'm surprised there's no shooting. My hands start shaking in rage. There are few things as intimidating as hundreds of Republic soldiers decked out in faceless riot gear, standing in grim, dark lines against a mass of unarmed protesters. I flatten myself against the wall and take a few breaths of cold night air, struggling to stay calm. Struggling to *remind* myself of June and June's brother and the Elector, and that behind some of those faceless Republic masks are good people, with parents and siblings and children. I hope Anden is the reason no shots have rung out — that he has told his soldiers not to fire on this crowd. *I have to believe that.* Otherwise, I'll never convince the people of what I'm about to say.

"Don't be afraid," I whisper to myself, my eyes squeezed shut. "You can't afford it."

Then I step out from the shadows, hurry

along the ledge until I turn the corner of the building, and hop into the closest balcony I can find. I face the central square. The protective balcony glass cuts off about a foot over my head, but I can still feel the wind siphoning in from above. I take off my cap and toss it over the top edge. It floats down to the ground, carried sideways by the wind. My hair streams out all around me. I bend down, twist one of the speakers' wires, and hold the speaker up like a megaphone. Then I wait.

At first no one notices me. But soon one face turns up in my direction, probably attracted by the brightness of my hair, and then another face, and then another. A small group. It grows into several dozen, all of them pointing up at me. The roars and angry chants below begin to subside. I wonder if June sees me. The soldiers lining other roofs have their guns fixed on me — but they don't shoot. They're stuck with me in this awkward, tense limbo. I want to run. To do what I always do, have always *done,* for the last five years of my life. Escape, flee into the shadows.

But this time, I stand my ground. I'm tired of running.

The crowd grows quieter as more and more turn their faces up to see me. At first, I hear incredulous chatter. Even some laughs. *That can't be Day,* I imagine them muttering to one another. *Some imposter.* But the longer I stay here, the louder they get. Everyone has turned toward me now. My eyes wander over to where Anden is on his balcony; even he's looking at me now. I hold my breath, hoping that he doesn't decide to order me shot. *Is he on my side?*

Then they're all chanting my name. *Day! Day! Day!* I can hardly believe my ears. They're chanting for me, and their voices echo down every block and reach every street. I stay frozen where I am, still clinging to my makeshift megaphone, unable to tear my eyes away from the crowds. I lift the speaker to my lips.

"People of the Republic!" I shout. "Do you hear me?"

My words blare out from every speaker in the square — probably every speaker in the country, for all I know. It startles me. The people below let out a cheer that makes the ground tremble. The soldiers must've gotten a hurried order from someone in Congress, because I see some of them hoist their weapons higher. A single bullet zips through the air and hits the glass, sparking as it goes. I don't move.

The Elector makes a quick gesture at the guards standing with him, and they all press a hand to their ears and talk into their mikes.

Maybe he's telling them not to harm me. I force myself to believe it.

"I wouldn't do that," I shout in the direction that the lone bullet had come from. *Keep yourself steady.* The people's cheers turn into a roar. "You don't want an uprising, do you, Congress?"

Day! Day! Day!

"Today, Congress, I give you an ultimatum." My eyes shift to the JumboTrons. "You've arrested a number of Patriots for a crime *you* are responsible for. Release them. *All* of them. If you don't, I will call your people to action, and you *will* have a revolution on your hands. But probably not the kind you were hoping for." The civilians scream out their approval. The chants continue at a feverish pitch.

"People of the Republic." They cheer me on as I continue. "Listen to me. Today, I give all of *you* an ultimatum."

Their chants go on until they realize that I've fallen silent, and then they too begin to quiet down. I hold the speaker closer. "My name is Day." My voice fills the air. "I've fought the same injustices that you're here to protest right now. I've suffered the same things you've suffered. Like you, I've watched my friends and family die at the hands of Republic soldiers." I blink away the memories that threaten to overtake me. *Keep going.* "I've been starved, beaten, and humiliated. I've been tortured, insulted, and suppressed. I've lived in the slums with you. I've risked my life for you. And you've risked *your* lives for me. *We* have risked our lives for our country — not the country we live in now, but the country we hope to have. You are all, every single one of you, a *hero.*"

Joyful cheers answer me, even as guards below try in vain to bring down and arrest stragglers, while other soldiers are trying fruitlessly to disable the rewired speaker system. Congress is afraid, I realize. They're afraid of me, like they've always been. So I keep going — I tell the people what had happened to my mother and brothers, and what had happened to June. I tell them about the Patriots, and about the Senate's attempt to assassinate Anden. I hope Razor's listening to all this and seething. Throughout it all, the crowd's attention never wavers.

"Do you trust me?" I shout. The crowd answers with a unified voice. The sea of people and their deafening roars are overwhelming. If my mother was still here, if Dad and John were here, would they be smiling up at me right now? I take a deep, shuddering breath. *Finish what you came here to do.* I focus on the people, and on the young Elector. I gather my strength. Then I say the words

I never ever thought I'd say.

"People of the Republic, *know your enemy.* Your enemy is the Republic's way of life, the laws and traditions that hold us down, the government that brought us here. The late Elector. *Congress.*" I raise my arm and point toward Anden. "But the new Elector is . . . *Not. Your. Enemy!*" The people grow silent. Their eyes are forever fixed on me. "You think your Congress wants to end the Trials, or help your families? It's a *lie.*" I point at Anden when I say this, willing myself, for the first time, to trust him. "The Elector is young and ambitious, and he is *not his father.* He wants to fight for you, just as *I* fight for you, but first he needs you to give him that chance. And if you put your might behind him and lift him up, he will lift us up. He will change things for us, one step at a time. He can build that country we all hope we can have. I came here tonight for you all — and for *him.* Do you trust me?" I lift my voice: *"People of the Republic, do you trust me?"*

Silence. Then, a few chants. More join in. They raise their eyes and fists to me, their shouts ceaseless, a tide of change. "Then raise your voices for your Elector, as I have, and he will raise his for you!"

The cheers are deafening, drowning out anything and everything. The young Elector keeps his eyes on me, and I realize, at last, that June is right. I don't want to see the Republic collapse. I want to see it change.

JUNE

Two days have passed. Or, more precisely, fifty-two hours and eight minutes have passed since Day climbed to the top of the Capitol Tower and announced his support for our Elector. Whenever I close my eyes, I can still see him up there, his hair gleaming like a beacon of light against the night, his words ringing out clear and strong across the city and the country. Whenever I dream, I can feel the burn of his last kiss on my lips, the fire and fear behind his eyes. Every person in the Republic heard him that night. He gave power back to Anden and Anden won over the country, all in one blow.

This is my second day in a hospital chamber on the outskirts of Denver. The second afternoon without Day at my side. In a room several doors down, Day is undergoing the same tests, both to ensure his health and make sure the Colonies didn't implant any monitoring devices in his head. He's going to be reunited with his brother at any minute. My doctor has arrived to check on my recovery — but he won't be doing it in any sort of privacy. In fact, when I study my room's ceiling, I see security cameras at every corner, broadcasting my image live to the public. The Republic is afraid to give people even the slightest sense that Day and I aren't being taken care of.

A monitor on the wall shows me Day's chamber. It is the *only* reason I agreed to be separated from him for this long. I wish I could talk to him. As soon as they stop running X-rays and sensors on me, I'm putting on a mike.

"Good morning to you, Ms. Iparis," my doctor says to me as nurses dot my skin with six sensors. I mumble a greeting in return, but my attention stays on the cam footage of Day talking to his own doctor. His arms are crossed in a defiant stance and his expression's skeptical. Now and then his attention focuses on a spot on the wall that I can't see. I wonder if he's watching me through a cam too.

My doctor notices what's distracting me and wearily answers my question before I can ask it. "You'll see him soon, Ms. Iparis. Okay? I promise. Now, you know the drill. Close your eyes and take a deep breath."

I bite down my frustration and do as he says. Lights flicker behind my eyelids, and then a cold, tingly sensation runs through my brain and down my spine. They put a gel-like mask over my mouth and nose. I always have to tell myself not to panic during this sequence, to fight down the claustrophobia and feeling of drowning. *They're just testing me,* I repeat quietly. They're testing me for any remnants of Colonies brainwashing, for mental stability, for whether or not the Elector — the Republic — can trust me fully. That's all.

Hours go by. Finally, it stops, and the doctor tells me I can open my eyes again.

"Well done, Iparis," he says as he types something out on his notepad. "Your cough may linger, but I think you've survived the worst of your illness. You can stay longer if you'd like" — he smiles at the exasperated frown on my face — "but if you'd prefer to be discharged to your new apartment, we can arrange that today as well. At any rate, the glorious Elector is anxious to speak with you before you leave here."

"How is Day?" I ask. It's difficult for me to keep the impatience out of my voice. "When can I see him?"

The doctor frowns. "Didn't we just discuss this? Day will be released shortly after you.

449

First he'll need to see his brother."

I study his face carefully. There's a reason the doctor hesitated just now — something about Day's recovery. I can see the subtle twitch under the doctor's facial muscles. He knows something I don't.

The doctor snaps me back to reality. He drops his notepad to his side, straightens, and plants an artificial smile on his face. "Well, that's all for today. Tomorrow we'll begin your formal integration back into the Republic, with your new career assignment. The Elector will arrive in a few minutes, and you'll have some time beforehand to regain your bearings." With that, he and the nurses take their sensors and machines and leave me alone.

I sit on my bed and keep my eyes on the door. A dark red cloak is wrapped around my shoulders, but I still don't feel entirely warm in this room. By the time Anden comes in to see me, I'm shivering.

He steps inside with his signature grace, wearing silent dark boots and black scarf and uniform, his curls of hair perfectly trimmed, thin-rimmed glasses sitting neatly on his nose. When he sees me, he smiles and salutes. The gesture reminds me painfully of Metias, and I have to focus down on my feet for a few seconds to compose myself. Fortunately, he seems to think I'm bowing.

"Elector," I greet him.

He smiles; his green eyes sweep over me. "How are you feeling, June?"

I smile back. "Well enough."

Anden laughs a little and lowers his head. He steps closer, but he doesn't try to sit next to me on the bed. I can still see the attraction in his eyes, the way he lingers on every word I say and every move I make. Surely he must have heard rumors by now about my relationship with Day? If he knows, though, he doesn't reveal it. "The Republic," he continues, embarrassed that I've caught him staring, "that is, the government has decided that you are fit to return to the military with your original rank intact. As an Agent, here in Denver."

So, I'm not going back to Los Angeles. The last I heard, LA's quarantine had been lifted after Anden began an investigation into the Senate's traitors — and both Razor and Commander Jameson were arrested for treason. I can only imagine how much Jameson hates Day and me now . . . even the thought of what the fury on her face must look like sends a chill down my spine.

"Thank you," I say after a while. "I'm very grateful."

Anden waves a hand in the air. "No need. You and Day have done me a great service."

I give him a quick, casual salute. Already Day's influence is being felt — after his impromptu speech, Congress and the military obeyed Anden in allowing protesters to return unpunished to their homes and releasing the Patriots who had been arrested during the assassination attempt (under monitored conditions). If the Senate didn't fear Day before, they do now. He has the power for the time being to ignite a full-scale revolution with only a few choice words.

"But . . ." Anden's volume drops and he pulls his hands out of his pockets to cross them in front of his chest. "I have a different proposition for you. I think you deserve a more important position than *Agent.*"

A memory surfaces of when I was on that train with him, of the unspoken offer hanging on his lips. "What kind of position?"

For the first time, he decides to sit down with me on the edge of my bed. He's so close now that I can feel the light whisper of his breath on my skin and see the stubble shadowing his chin. "June," he begins, "the Republic has never been more unstable than it is now. Day brought it back from the brink of collapse, but I'm still ruling during dangerous times. Many of the Senators are battling for control amongst themselves, and many people in the country are hoping for me to make a wrong move." Anden falls silent for a second. "One moment won't keep me in the people's favor forever, and I can't hold the country together alone."

I know he's telling the truth. I can see the exhaustion in his face, and the frustration that comes with being responsible for his country.

"When my father was a young Elector, he and my mother ruled together. The Elector and his Princeps. He was never more powerful than he was during that time. I'd like an ally too, someone smart and strong whom I can trust with more power than anyone else in Congress." My breathing turns shallow as I take in the offer he's circling around. "I want a partner who has her finger on the pulse of the people, someone extraordinarily talented at everything she does, and someone who shares my ideas about how to create a nation. Of course, one couldn't go from Agent to Princeps in the blink of an eye. One would need intense training, instruction, and education. An opportunity to grow into the position over the course of many years, *decades,* to first learn as a Senator and then as the Senate's leader.

This is not training to bestow lightly, especially upon someone without Senate experience. Of course, there would be other Princeps-Elects shadowing me as well." He pauses here; his tone shifts. "What do you think?"

I shake my head, still not quite sure of what exactly Anden is offering. There's the chance to be the Princeps — a position second only to the Elector. I would spend almost every waking moment of my life in Anden's company, shadowing his every step for at least ten years. I would never see Day. This offer makes the life I'd imagined with him waver unsteadily. Is Anden offering this promotion purely based on what he thinks of my capabilities — or is he letting his emotions influence him, promoting me in the hopes that he might get a chance to spend more time with me? And how can I possibly compete with other potential Princeps-Elects, some of whom will probably be decades my senior, perhaps already Senators? I take a deep breath, then try to ask him in a diplomatic way. "Elector," I begin. "I don't think —"

"I won't pressure you," he interrupts, then swallows and smiles hesitantly. "You are absolutely free to turn this down. And you can be a Princeps without . . ." Is Anden blushing? "You don't have to," he says instead. "I — the Republic — would only be grateful if you did."

"I don't know if I have that kind of talent," I say. "You need someone so much better than I could ever be."

Anden takes both of my hands in his. "You were born to shake the Republic. June, there is no one better."

DAY

The doctors didn't like me in the beginning. The feeling was pretty mutual, of course — I haven't exactly had the best experiences in hospitals.

Two days ago, when they finally managed to get me off the balcony of Denver's Capitol Tower and calm the massive throngs of people cheering me on, they strapped me into an ambulance and took me straight to the hospital. There, I shattered a doctor's glasses and kicked over my room's metal trays when they tried to check me for injuries. "You put a hand on me," I'd snapped at them, "and I'll break your goddy necks." The hospital staff had to tie me down. I screamed myself hoarse for Eden, demanding to see him, threatening to burn down the entire hospital if they didn't deliver him. I shouted for June. I yelled for proof that the Patriots were released. I asked to see Kaede's body, begging them to give her a proper burial.

They broadcasted my reactions live to the public because of the crowds that had gathered by the hospital, demanding to see I was being treated properly. But gradually I calmed down, and after seeing me alive, the crowds in Denver began to calm down too.

"Now, this doesn't mean you won't be closely watched," my doctor says as I'm given a set of Republic collar shirts and military trousers. He mumbles so the security cameras can't pick up what he's saying. I can barely see his eyes through the glare across his tiny, round glasses. "But you've been fully pardoned by the Elector, and your brother Eden should be arriving at the hospital any minute now."

I'm quiet. After everything that's happened since Eden was first stricken by the plague, I can barely comprehend that the Republic is going to give him back to me. All I can do is smile at the doctor through gritted teeth. He smiles back at me with an expression full of dislike as he goes on about my test results and where I'm going to live after all this is over. I know he doesn't want to be here, but he doesn't say it aloud, not with all these cameras on. From the corner of my eye I can see the one monitor on the wall that shows me what they're doing to June. She appears safe, undergoing the same inspections as me.

But the anxiety in my throat refuses to go away.

"There's one last thing I'd like to tell you in private," the doctor goes on. I listen halfheartedly. "Quite important. Something we've discovered in your X-rays that you should know about."

I lean forward to hear him better. But at that instant, the room's intercom blares to life. "Eden Bataar Wing is here, Doctor," it says. "Please inform Day."

Eden. *Eden is here.*

Suddenly I couldn't care less about whatever my goddy X-ray results are. Eden is outside, right beyond my cell's door. The doctor tries to tell me something, but I just push past him, throw the door open, and stumble out into the corridor.

At first I don't see him. There are too many nurses wandering through the halls. Then I notice the small figure swinging his legs on one of the hall's benches, his skin healthy and his head full of wayward, white-blond curls, dressed in an overly large school uniform and kid-size boots. He seems taller, but maybe that's because he's able to sit up straighter now. When he turns toward me, I realize that he's wearing a thick pair of black-rimmed glasses. His eyes are a light, milky purple, reminiscent of the young boy I'd seen in the railcar on that cold, sleet-filled night.

"Eden," I call out hoarsely.

His eyes stay unfocused, but an amazing smile blooms on his face. He gets up and tries to walk toward me, but he stops when he can't seem to tell where exactly I am. "Is that you, Daniel?" he says with shaky hesitation.

I run to him, scoop him up in my arms, and hold him tight. "Yeah," I whisper. "It's Daniel."

Eden just cries. Sobs wrack his body. He tightens his arms around my neck so fiercely that I don't think he'll ever let go. I take a deep breath to contain my own tears. The plague has taken most of his vision, but he's *here,* alive and well, strong enough to walk and talk. That's enough for me. "Good to see you again, kid," I choke out, ruffling his hair with one hand. "Missed you."

I don't know how long we stay there. Minutes? Hours? But it doesn't matter. Time ticks by one long second after another, and I make the moment stretch out as much as I can. It's as if I'm standing here and hugging my entire family. He is everything that means anything. At least I have this.

I hear a cough behind me.

"Day," the doctor says. He's leaning against the open door of my cell, his face grave and shadowy under the fluorescent light. I gently put Eden down, keeping one hand on his shoulder. "Come with me. This will be quick, I promise. I, ah . . ." He pauses at the sight of Eden. "I recommend you keep your brother out here. Just for now. I *assure* you that you'll be back in a few minutes, and then you'll both be driven to your new apartment."

I stay where I am, unwilling to trust him.

"I *promise*," he says again. "If I'm lying, well, you have enough power to ask the Elector to arrest me for it."

Well, that's basically true. I wait a while longer, chewing on the inside of my cheek, and then I pat Eden's head. "I'll be right back, okay? Stay on the bench. Don't go *anywhere.* If someone tries to make you move, you scream. Got it?"

Eden wipes a hand across his nose and nods.

I guide him back to the bench, then follow the doctor into my cell. He shuts the door with a soft click.

"What is it?" I say impatiently. My eyes can't stop turning toward the door, like it'll vanish into the wall if I don't stay vigilant. Against the corner wall, June's monitor shows her waiting alone in her room.

But the doctor doesn't seem annoyed with me this time. He clicks a button on the wall and mutters something about turning the sound off on the cameras. "Like I was saying before you left . . . As part of your tests, we scanned your brain to see if it had been altered by the Colonies. We didn't find anything to worry about . . . but we ran across something else." He turns around, clicks a small device, and points to an illuminated screen on the wall. It's displaying an image of my brain. I frown at it, unable to make sense of what I'm seeing. The doctor points to a dark splotch near the bottom of the image. "We saw this near your left hippocampus. We think it's old, probably years old, and has been slowly worsening over time."

I puzzle over it for a while, then turn back to the doctor. It still seems trivial to me, especially when Eden is waiting out in the hall. Especially when I'll be able to see June again. "And? What else?"

"Have you had any severe headaches? Lately, or within the last few years?"

Yes. Of course I have. I've had headaches ever since the night that the Los Angeles Central Hospital ran tests on me, the night I was supposed to die, when I ran away. I nod.

He folds his arms. "Our records show that you had been . . . experimented on after you failed your Trial. There were some tests conducted on your brain. You . . . ah" — he coughs, struggling for the right words — "were meant to succumb rather quickly, but you survived. Well, it seems that the effects have finally started catching up to you." He switches to a low whisper. "Nobody knows about this — not even the Elector. We don't want the country to be thrown back into a revolutionary state. Initially we thought that we could cure it with a combination of surgery and medication, but when we studied the problem areas closer, we realized that everything is so entwined with healthy matter in your hippo-campus that it would be impossible to stabilize the situation without *severely* impairing your cognitive capacity."

I swallow hard. "So? What does that mean?"

The doctor removes his glasses with a sigh. "It means, Day, that you're dying."

JUNE

2007 Hours.
Two days since my release.
Oxford High-Rise, Lodo sector, Denver.
72°F inside.

Day was released yesterday at seven a.m. I'd called him three times since then, each time with no answer. It wasn't until a couple of hours ago that I finally heard his voice over my earpiece. "Are you free today, June?" I'd shivered at the softness of his voice. "Mind if I stop by? I want to talk to you."

"Come on over," I'd replied. And that was pretty much all we said to each other.

He'll be here soon. I'm embarrassed to admit that even though I tried busying myself for the last hour by tidying the apartment and brushing Ollie's coat, all I can really think about is what Day wants to discuss.

It's strange to have a living space that's

my own again, furnished with myriad new and unfamiliar things. Sleek couches, elaborate chandeliers, glass tables, hardwood floors. Luxurious items that I no longer feel entirely comfortable owning. Outside my window, a light spring snow falls. Ollie sleeps beside me on one of the two sofas. After my release from the hospital, soldiers escorted me by jeep here to the Oxford High-Rise — and the first thing I saw when I stepped inside was Ollie, his tail wagging like crazy, his nose pushing eagerly into my hand. They told me the Elector had long ago requested that my dog be sent to Denver and taken care of. Right after Thomas had arrested me. Now they've returned him, this small piece of Metias, to me. I wonder what Thomas thinks of all this. Will he just follow protocol as always and bow the next time he sees me, pledging his undying loyalty? Maybe Anden has ordered *his* arrest alongside those of Commander Jameson and Razor. I can't decide how that would make me feel.

Yesterday they buried Kaede. They would have given her a cremation and a tiny plain marking on the wall of a funeral tower, but I insisted on something nicer. A real plot. A square foot of her own space. Anden, of course, obliged. If Kaede were still alive,

464

where would she be? Would the Republic have eventually inducted her into their air force? Has Day visited her gravesite yet? Does he blame himself for her death, as *I* blame myself? Is this perhaps why he's waited so long after his hospital release to contact me?

What happens now? Where do we go from here?

2012 hours. Day's late. I keep my eyes glued to the door, unable to do anything else, afraid I'll miss him if I blink.

2015 hours. A soft bell echoes through the apartment. Ollie stirs, perks up his ears, and whines. *He's here.* I practically leap off the couch. Day is so light on his feet that even my dog can't hear him walking down the hall outside.

I open the door — then freeze. The hello I'd prepared halts in my throat. Day is standing before me, hands in his pockets, breathtaking in a brand-new Republic uniform (black, with dark gray stripes running down the sides of his trousers and around the bottoms of his sleeves, a thick diagonal collar on his military coat that's cut in the style of Denver's capital troops, and elegant white neoprene gloves that I can see peeking out from his trouser pockets, each decorated with a thin gold chain).

His hair spills past his shoulders in a shining sheet and is sprinkled with the delicate spring snow falling outside. His eyes are bright, startlingly blue, and lovely; a few snowflakes glimmer on the long lashes that fringe them. I can hardly bear the sight. Only now do I realize that I've never actually seen him dressed up in any kind of formal attire, let alone formal *soldier* attire. I hadn't thought to prepare myself for a vision like this, for what his beauty might look like under circumstances that would actually show it off.

Day notices my expression and offers me a wry grin. "It was for a quick photo," he says, pointing at his outfit, "of me shaking hands with the Elector. Not my choice. Obviously. I better not regret throwing my support behind this guy."

"Evaded the crowds gathered outside your place?" I finally say. I compose myself long enough to quirk my lips into a return smile. "Rumor has it that people are calling for *you* to be the new Elector."

He scowls in exasperation and makes a grumpy sound. "Day for Elector? Right. I don't even like the Republic yet. That'll take some getting used to. Now, the *evading* I can do. I'd rather not face people right now." I hear a hint of sadness there, something that tells me he did indeed visit Kaede's grave. He clears his throat when he notices me studying him, then hands me a small velvet box. There's a polite distance in his gesture that puzzles me. "Picked it up on my way here. For you, sweetheart."

A small murmur of surprise escapes me. "Thanks." I take the box gingerly, admiring it for a moment, and then tilt my head at him. "What's the occasion?"

Day tucks his hair behind one ear and tries to appear uncaring. "Just thought it looked pretty."

I open the box carefully, then take a sharp breath when I see what's inside — a silver chain with a small teardrop-shaped ruby pendant bordered with tiny diamonds. Three slender silver wires are wrapped around the ruby itself. "It's . . . gorgeous," I say. My cheeks burn. "This must have been so expensive." Since when did I start using cordial social niceties when talking to Day?

He shakes his head. "Apparently the Republic is throwing money at me to keep me happy. Ruby's your birthstone, yeah? Well, I just figured you should have a nicer keepsake from me than a ring made out of goddy paper clips." He pats Ollie on the head, then makes a show of admiring my apartment. "Nice place. A lot like mine."

Day's been given a similar, heavily guarded apartment a couple of blocks down the same street.

"Thank you," I say again, gingerly setting the box on my kitchen counter for the time being. Then I wink at him. "I still liked my paper clip ring best, though."

For a split second, happiness crosses his face. I want to throw my arms around him and pull his lips to my own, but — there's a weight to his posture that makes me feel like I should keep my distance.

I venture a hesitant guess at what's bothering him. "How's Eden?"

"He's doing well enough." Day gazes around the room one more time, then lets his eyes settle on me again. "All things considered, of course."

I lower my head. "I'm . . . sorry to hear about his vision. He's —"

"He's alive," Day cuts me off gently. "I'm happy enough about that." I nod in awkward agreement, and we lapse into a long pause.

Finally, I say, "You wanted to talk."

"Yes." Day looks down, fidgets with his gloves, then shoves his hands into his pockets. "I heard about the promotion Anden offered you."

I turn away and sit on my couch. It hasn't even been forty-eight hours and already I've seen the news pop up twice on the city's JumboTrons:

JUNE IPARIS TAPPED TO TRAIN FOR PRINCEPS POSITION

I should be happy that Day's the one who brought it up — I'd been trying to figure out a good way to approach the subject, and now I don't have to. Still, my pulse quickens and I find myself feeling as nervous as I feared. Maybe he's upset that I didn't mention it right away. "How much have you already heard?" I ask as he comes over to sit beside me. His knee gently grazes my thigh. Even this light touch sends butterflies dancing in my stomach. I glance at his face to see if he did it on purpose, but Day's lips are drawn into an uncomfortable line, as if he knows where he's going to take this conversation but doesn't want to do it.

"I heard through the grapevine that you'd have to shadow Anden's every step, yeah? You'd train to become his Princeps. That all true?"

I sigh, slump my shoulders, and let my head sink into my hands. Hearing Day say this makes me feel the gravity of the commitment I'd have to make. Of course I understand the practical reasons why Anden

469

would tap me for this — I hope I *am* someone who can help transform the Republic. All of my military training, everything Metias ever told me — I *know* I'm a good fit for the Republic's government. But . . . "Yes, all true," I reply, then add hastily, "It's not a marriage proposal — nothing like that. It's a professional position, and I'd be one of several competing for the position. But it'd mean weeks . . . well . . . *months* away at a time. Away from . . ." *Away from you,* I want to say. But it sounds too cheesy, and I decide not to finish the sentence. Instead, I give him all the details that have been running through my mind. I tell him about the grueling schedule of a Princeps-Elect, how I'd plan to give myself breathing room if I were to agree to it all, that I'm unsure how much of myself I want to give to the Republic. After a while I know I've started rambling, but it feels so good to get everything off my chest, to bare my troubles to the boy I care about, that I don't try to stop myself. If anyone in my life deserves to hear everything, it's Day.

"I don't know what to tell Anden," I finish. "He hasn't pressured me, but I need to give him an answer soon."

Day doesn't reply. My flood of words hangs in the silence between us. I can't describe the emotion on his face — something lost, something ripped from his gaze and strewn across the floor. A deep, quiet sadness that tears me apart. What's going through Day's mind? Does he believe me? Does he think, like I did when I first heard it, that Anden is offering this because of a personal interest in me? Is he sad because it would mean ten years of barely seeing each other? I watch him and wait, trying to anticipate what he'll say. Of course he's going to be unhappy with the idea, of course he'll protest. I'm not happy myself with —

Day suddenly speaks up. "Take the offer," he murmurs.

I lean toward him, because I don't think I heard him correctly. "What?"

Day studies me carefully. His hand twitches a little, as if he wants to lift it and touch my cheek. Instead, it stays at his side. "I came here to tell you to take his offer," he repeats softly.

I blink. My throat hurts; my vision swims in a haze of light. That can't be the right response — I had expected a dozen different answers from Day except for that one. Or perhaps it's not his answer that shocks me so much as the *way* he said it. Like he's letting go. I stare at him for a moment, wondering if I've imagined it. But his expression — sad, distant — stays the same. I turn away and shift to the edge of the couch, and through the numbness in my mind I can only remember to whisper, "Why?"

"Why *not?*" Day asks. His voice is detached, crumpled like a dead flower.

I don't understand. Maybe he's being sarcastic. Or maybe he's going to say that he still wants to find a way to be together. But he doesn't add anything else to his answer. *Why would he ask me to accept this offer?* I'd thought he would be so happy that all this was finally over, that we could try our hand at some semblance of normal life again, whatever that is. It'd be so easy for me to figure out some compromise with Anden's offer, or even to just turn it down altogether. Why didn't he suggest *that?* I thought Day was the more emotional of the two of us.

Day smiles bitterly when I don't respond right away. We sit with our hands separated, letting the world hang heavily between us, hearing the seconds tick soundlessly by. After a few minutes, he takes a deep breath and says, "I, ah . . . have something else I should tell you too."

I nod quietly, waiting for him to continue. Afraid of what he'll say. Afraid he'll explain *why.*

He hesitates for a long time, but when he does speak, he shakes his head and gives me a tragic little laugh. I can tell he's changed his mind, taking a secret and folding it back into his heart. "You know, sometimes I wonder what things would be like if I just . . . met you one day. Like normal people do. If I just walked by you on some street one sunny morning and thought you were cute, stopped, shook your hand, and said, 'Hi, I'm Daniel.' "

I close my eyes at such a sweet thought. How freeing that would be. How easy. "If only," I whisper.

Day picks at the gold chain on his glove. "Anden is the Elector Primo of the entire Republic. There might never be another chance like this."

I know what he's trying to say. "Don't worry, it's not like I can't influence the Republic if I turn this offer down, or find some middle ground. This is not the only way —"

"Hear me out, June," he says softly, holding up both hands to stop me. "I don't know if I'll have the guts to say all this again." I tremble at the way his lips form my name. He gives me a smile that shatters something inside me. I don't know why, but his expression is as if he were seeing me for the last time. "Come on, you and I both know what needs to happen. We've only known each other for a couple of months. But I've spent my *entire life* fighting the system that the Elector now wants to change. And you . . . well, your family suffered as much as mine did." He pauses, and his eyes take on a faraway appearance. "I might be okay at spewing speeches from the top of a building, and at working a crowd. I don't know anything about politics. I can only be a figurehead. But you . . . you've always been everything that the people need. You have the chance to *change* things." He takes my hand and touches the spot on my finger where his ring used to sit. I feel the calluses on his palms, the aching gentleness of his gesture. "It's your decision, of course, but you know what it has to be. Don't make up your mind just because you feel guilty or something. Don't worry about *me*. I know that's why you're holding back — I can see it on your face."

Still, I say nothing. What is he talking about? See *what* on my face? What do I look like right now?

Day sighs at my silence. His face is unbearable. "June," he says slowly. Behind his words, his voice sounds like it might break at any moment. "It will never, ever work out between us."

And here is the real reason why. I shake my head, unwilling to hear the rest. Not this. *Please don't say it, Day, please don't say it.* "We'll figure out a way," I begin to say. The details come pouring out. "I can work in the capital's patrols for a while. That would be a more feasible option, anyway. Shadow a Senator, if I really want to go into politics. Twelve of the Senators —"

Day can't even look at me. "We weren't meant to be. There are just . . . too many things that have happened." He grows quieter. "Too many things."

The weight of it hits me. This has nothing to do with the Princeps position, and everything to do with something else. Day would be saying all this even if Anden never offered anything. *Our argument in the underground tunnel.* I want to say how wrong he is, but I can't even argue his point. Because he's right. How could I *possibly* think that we'd never suffer the consequences of what I'd done to him? How could I be *so arrogant* to assume it would all work out for us in the end, that my doing a couple of good deeds could make up for all the pain I caused him? The truth will never change. No matter how hard he tries, every time he

475

looks at me, he'll see what happened to his family. He'll see what I did. It will always haunt him; it will forever stand between us.

I need to let him go.

I can feel the tears threatening to spill from my eyes, but I don't dare let them fall. "So," I whisper, my voice trembling from the effort. "Is that it? After everything?" Even as I say it, I know there's no point. The damage has already been done. There is no turning back.

Day hunches over and presses his hands against his eyes. "I'm so sorry," he whispers.

Long seconds pass.

After an eternity, I swallow hard. I will *not* cry. Love is illogical, love has consequences — I did this to myself, and I should be able to take it. *So take it, June.* I am the one who should be sorry. Finally, instead of saying what I want to say, I manage to wrestle down the tremor in my voice and give a more appropriate answer. What I *should* say.

"I'll let Anden know."

Day runs a hand through his hair, opens his mouth to say something, and closes it again. I can tell there's another part of this whole scenario that he's not telling me, but I don't press it. It wouldn't make a difference, anyway — there are already enough reasons why we weren't meant to be. His eyes catch the moonlight spilling in from the windows. Another moment passes between us, filled with nothing but the whisper of breathing. "Well, I —" His voice cracks, and he clenches his hands into fists. He stays there for a second, steeling himself. "I should let you get some sleep. You must be tired." He rises and straightens his coat. We exchange a final, parting nod. Then he gives me a polite bow, turns around, and starts walking away. "Good night, June."

My heart is ripped open, shredded, leaking blood. I can't let him leave like this. We've been through too much to turn into strangers. *A farewell between us should be more than a polite bow.* Suddenly I find my feet and rush toward him right as he reaches the door. "Day, wait —"

He spins around. Before I can say anything else, he steps forward and takes my face in his hands. Then he's kissing me one last time, overwhelming me with his warmth, breathing life and love and aching sorrow into me. I throw my arms around his neck as he wraps his around my waist. My lips part for him and his mouth moves desperately against mine, devouring me, taking every breath that I have. *Don't go,* I plead wordlessly. But I can taste the good-bye on his lips, and now I can no longer hold back my tears. He's trembling. His face is wet. I hang on to him like he'll disappear if I let go, like I'll be left alone in this dark room, standing in the empty air. Day, the boy from the streets with nothing except the clothes on his back and the earnestness in his eyes, owns my heart.

He is beauty, inside and out.

He is the silver lining in a world of darkness.

He is my light.

ACKNOWLEDGMENTS

Writing *Prodigy* was a thoroughly different experience from writing *Legend,* one that involved many panic attacks and much desperate sobbing in front of my laptop, and one that involved digging much deeper into my characters' cores and unearthing their darkest thoughts and memories. Luckily for me, I have the support of an amazing group of people who helped me put this book together:

To my literary agent Kristin Nelson, for being the first set of eyes on this manuscript. I would die in a quicksand swamp without your advice and feedback. To the entire team at NLA, for always getting my back. To beta reader extraordinaire Ellen Oh, for seeing an early draft of *Prodigy* and knocking some sense into me on some very crucial scenes. To JJ, for being my freakishly sharp sounding board and beta reader as *Prodigy* gradually formed.

To my unbelievable pair of editors, Jen Besser and Ari Lewin, for taking the first draft of *Prodigy* and transforming it into something much greater than I could create on my own. Thanks for pushing me hard to strengthen my characters, world, and plot; anyone who thinks that books don't get edited anymore has clearly never worked with either of you. You are amazing. (Special shout-out to Little Primo!)

To the entire team at Putnam Children's and Penguin Young Readers for their never-ending support — Don Weisberg, Shauna Fay, Anna Jarzab, Jessica Schoffel, Elyse Marshall, Scottie Bowditch, Lori Thorn, Linda McCarthy, Erin Dempsey, Shanta Newlin, Emily Romero, Erin Gallagher, Mia Garcia, Lisa Kelly, Courtney Wood, Marie Kent, and everyone else who has helped give life to both *Legend* and *Prodigy*. No author could ask for a greater support group.

To the awesome teams at CBS Films, Temple Hill, and UTA for the continued dedication to *Legend:* Wolfgang Hammer, Grey Munford, Matt Gilhooley, Ally Mielnicki, Christine Batista, Isaac Klausner, Wyck Godfrey, Marty Bowen, Gina Martinez, Kassie Evashevski, and Wayne Alexander. I can't believe how much I lucked out.

To all of the bloggers, reviewers, and media who covered *Legend* and *Prodigy,* and to the booksellers around the nation who put both books into the hands of shoppers. Thank you so much — I am so grateful for all that you do in connecting the right books to the right readers.

To my amazing readers and fans, for the enthusiastic letters and kind encouragement. Every time I saw your messages about *Legend,* I became that much more motivated to make *Prodigy* as good as I possibly could. Thank you for taking the time to read my books.

And finally, to the fam bam, my mom, Andre, and all of my friends. Thank you so much for all of your support — you guys are irreplaceable.

ABOUT THE AUTHOR

Marie Lu writes dystopian stories for the young adult audience. *Legend* was her debut novel. Before she started writing full time, she was the art director at a video game company. Lu was born in China and graduated from the University of Southern California in 2006. She lives in Los Angeles, where she spends her time reading, writing, drawing, playing Assassin's Creed, and getting stuck on the freeways.